JO

"You're good at what you do. But sometimes a person with such a gift of persuasion can create monsters."

Jo's smile faltered, and she stared at him. She had the feeling she'd seen him before. "Wait a minute," she said, beginning to get angry. "Do I know you?"

He laughed mirthlessly, then, tipping his glasses down to look at her over the frames. "Think about it," he said under his breath. "It'll come to you."

Jo watched him amble back down the aisle and then he disappeared outside the auditorium. It was something about the eyes that disturbed her . . . blue, penetrating, sultry eyes . . .

Trying to shake off the nagging feeling, Jo reached for the next album cover. She glanced down at the rock star posing seductively for his fans, his eyes blue, penetrating, sultry . . .

Her breath caught in her lungs. The eyes on the album cover were the same ones she'd looked into moments ago.

Jo by Tracy Hughes

is the second of four stories about the Calloway sisters. Four authors collaborated closely on this project which is based on the song "They Called the Wind Mariah". The lyrics run "The rain was Tess, the fire was Jo, they called the wind Mariah". This formed three of the characters, but a fourth element was needed for the fourth author, so Eden was created.

The decision about who wrote about which character wasn't difficult to make. With all four authors' personalities being as different as the four sisters', each author chose the sister who most closely resembled their own character. Sandra Canfield related well to the free-spirited Mariah, while Tracy Hughes felt drawn to the fiery-tempered Jo. Katherine Burton, who is emotional and sensitive, found an immediate affinity with the introverted Tess, and Penny Richards couldn't have been closer to the earth-mother, Eden.

Each book is independent of the others, but having read about one sister, you will be sure to want to follow the lives of the other Calloway women.

Tracy Hughes is also the author of ABOVE THE CLOUDS in *Worldwide*.

JO

BY
TRACY HUGHES

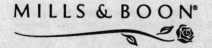

MILLS & BOON®

MILLS & BOON and MILLS & BOON with the Rose Device
are registered trademarks of the publisher.

First published in Great Britain 1989
by Harlequin Mills & Boon Limited,
Eton House, 18-24 Paradise Road, Richmond, Surrey, TW9 1SR

© Terri Herrington 1989

ISBN 0 263 80873 4

40-9711

Printed and bound in Great Britain
by Caledonian Book Manufacturing Ltd, Glasgow

This book is dedicated to
Sandra Canfield, Penny Richards
and Katherine Burton,
the other three authors in
the Calloway Corners Saga.
If not for the true sisterhood among us,
this collaborative effort
would never have been possible.

It is also dedicated
with much gratitude to
Nancy Roher, our editor,
who had the vision
to see the project
as we saw it
and allowed us the freedom
to express it in
our own individual ways.

CHAPTER ONE

THE ANGER IN Jo Calloway's voice was like a fire billowing across the crowded auditorium. Contagious fire, productive fire, unresolved fire. It blazed like the flaming color of her hair, which framed her ardent face and spiraled over her shoulders to her waist. It was as consuming as her impassioned, olive eyes, eyes that seemed to have some conviction all their own. He wondered where anger like that came from.

Inconspicuous among the captive audience, he watched her with an awe that was foreign to him. He marveled at how profoundly he had underestimated the woman who'd been creating new headaches for him...the woman he'd expected to be short and gnarly with a piercing witchlike voice and a brittle manner. The woman he saw now was definitely no witch, though he did feel a bit enchanted. That enchantment in itself was a deterrent that he hadn't expected. He had been warned she was dangerous. No one had told him she was beautiful.

She hadn't noticed him yet, sitting among the "enlightened" as if he embraced their cause. If she had, he doubted she would have recognized him. He'd grown skilled at looking like one of the crowd. Anonymity was important to his sanity, and as necessary for survival as food or water. It was usually simple to achieve, especially when he was out of his usual environment. All he had to do was hide behind the brown-framed, tinted glasses that gave him the status of boy next door, and comb back the pitch-black hair, which in photographs blew in sleepy disarray. His disguise was completed by a faded flannel shirt that had been in his wardrobe for eleven years, a fresh, new pair of Levi's and the ten-dollar sneakers that had worn out long before he'd been prepared to part with them. All he really had to do was be himself, and since no one knew him for who he truly was, he could go almost anywhere he wanted. Even if it meant facing the little spitfire who schemed to bring him to his knees.

Fresh concern that she could do just that arose as he watched the woman he'd begun to call the "Leader of the Pack" draw the three hundred people at the meeting under her spell. She was good; he'd give her that. Yes, the odds were against any group of citizens getting a law passed to censor rock lyrics in the United States…but she looked like just the one who could beat the odds. Forget the constitution, or the right to free speech, or democracy itself. This one could convince the president to declare the U.S. neutral territory, if she only had a forum. And she could certainly change the course of one man's career. That was what disturbed him. That was what frightened him. And that was why he was here.

"We're talking about the most destructive type of brainwashing in this country," she was saying as she set the turntable's needle onto the record disc spinning there. "This song is called 'Pumping,' and it's by E.Z. Ellis. As you listen, consider whether you want your children walking around chanting this." She paused while the chorus to the song, number one on the charts for five consecutive weeks, played across the awe-inspiring public address system she'd set up before the meeting.

"These lyrics are graphically suggestive and blatantly offensive," she said in a fire-and-brimstone voice to the accompaniment of the upbeat song. "If we're able to censor television shows in this country, why can't we censor music? Don't we care enough about our children to monitor what they hear as well as what they see?"

Applause erupted in a wave over the room, and she flicked her long, curling red hair back over her shoulder—a gesture he began to equate with her rising adrenaline—and went to an overhead projector set up at the side of the room. She stood in its light for a moment like a fiery spirit demanding respect and admiration. Fleetingly he wondered if she had practiced that visual effect in front of the mirror. She'd picked it up, no doubt, from one of the rock stars she maligned.

"But that isn't the worst of it," she went on. "There are other, more dangerous lyrics, lyrics that can undermine everything a parent has labored to teach a child, and cause irreparable damage." She stepped to the side of the overhead projector, and the lyrics to another song graced the screen. The fact that she'd lifted the words out of the context of the music and displayed them like Exhibit A in a murder trial galled him.

"These are the lyrics to another E.Z. Ellis song," she said. "I use his songs so often because last year *People* magazine labeled him the 'Most Admired Rock Super Star' of this decade. Because of that fame, his songs are heard more often than those by other musicians. He has the capacity to do much more harm." She slid her hands into her pockets and seemed to consider the floor. After a long, meaningful pause—what he was certain was predetermined right down to the last second—she looked up at the crowd. Her face was total vulnerability, and for a moment he wondered if she'd rehearsed that, too.

"A few months ago, I watched a fourteen-year-old neighbor of mine in Baton Rouge turn from a happy, healthy teenager to a troubled, rebellious, drug addict in just a few weeks. It seems she had gotten involved in a cult that encouraged things that would break your heart. And their anthem—their theme song, if you will—was this song. 'Shadow Child.'" She tapped the page lying flat on the overhead projector, making her pointing finger an ominous shadow on the screen.

"After several arrests and dropping out of school, she finally attempted suicide."

He heard Jo's voice crack with the last words, and her eyes seemed to mist over. Had she arranged the auditorium's lighting in such a way that it would catch the glossy tears, he wondered, or did the subject really move her that much? He doubted it. No one was that sincere.

"She left a note that quoted a line from the song—'Getting out while the blade's still sharp...freedom's wild...Shadow Child.'"

Anger welled in his throat, much like the anger he'd felt the first time he'd read about what the woman was saying. He compressed his lips to keep from standing up and shouting out who he was and squelched the urge to run to the front and yank the song off the projector. He wanted to tell the whole roomful of jerks that if they'd open their minds, they'd see past the obvious and find the real meaning behind "Shadow Child"...that maybe it could teach them a thing or two. Instead, he sat quietly, holding his anger inside, storing it up for the right time. He would have his chance to speak—on May 25th, as a matter of fact, only five weeks from now, when the Senate Commerce Committee would hear both sides of the issue. Now he could only measure her strengths against his and hope that he would be prepared when the time came.

He listened like one of the brainwashed crowd as she read from other offensive songs, told more condemning stories, and used special equipment to pick up subliminal messages hidden beneath the audible phrases on the records of other artists. Though he had to admit he found it distasteful that musicians would stoop so low to sell records, he felt her persuasive techniques of emotional control were just as harmful.

She ended the presentation by directing the crowd to the back of the room, where they could register as members of AFCRL, of Americans for Censorship of Rock Lyrics. They would be committing themselves to the cause, agreeing to rally and demonstrate and, in his opinion, make general jackasses of themselves until the country gave up its right to free choice.

The people sitting next to him and around him stood and applauded, then streamed into the aisles. But he sat still, his ankle thrown over his knee, his elbow propped on the chair next to him, his finger stroking long lines across his full lips...and watched her.

She was proud of herself, almost glowing in the admiration of those around her. He could feel the sense of accomplishment emanating from her as she spoke to those who waited to shake her hand, and when she smiled it made him angrier. He watched until the front of the room was cleared of well-wishers and kindred spirits and kept his eyes on her while she turned off her equipment, ordered her hired hands to break it down, slipped albums back into their covers. She was all order and purpose...all fever and spirit...all power and drive.

And he thought it was too bad that she wasted it all on this.

JO CALLOWAY'S EYES SHONE at the sight of the three hundred people cramming toward the back of the room, waiting to take up her banner and join in her cause. It felt good to make an impact. It always had.

She took the record off the turntable and slipped it back into its cover, while her eyes scanned the empty seats where all those potential new members had sat transfixed moments before. One man remained there—a man she had noticed earlier for his lack of enthusiasm, his intensity, his familiarity. The way he watched her now gave her an uncomfortable feeling. Even though he wore dark glasses, she could see contempt in his expression. Maybe even a little disgust.

She turned away and went for the box that held the albums she used in her demonstration. Straining as she carried it back to the table, Jo glanced up again and noted he'd left his seat. She breathed a sigh of relief. He had looked ready to let her have it, as one or two often did during or after each speech she gave. There were always a few who disagreed...always those bent on changing her views of the world's injustices in five minutes or less. Thankful that he wasn't one of them, she busied herself stacking the albums in the box.

"You're good at what you do." The gravelly, oddly familiar voice over her shoulder commanded her attention, and she swung around and saw that he'd come to confront her, after all. Something about him intimidated her—his broad, well-defined shoulders, his confident stance, his above-average height . . . and something else, something she couldn't quite pinpoint.

"Excuse me?" she asked, not certain she'd heard him correctly.

"I said, you're good at what you do. But sometimes a person with such a gift of persuasion can create monsters . . . and monsters are hard to handle."

As she always did when she was intimidated—which wasn't very often—Jo smiled and lifted her chin. "I don't create monsters," she said in her most professional voice. "I create enthusiasm. I inform. I organize."

"Yeah," he said. "But then, so did Hitler."

Jo's smile faded a degree, but remained, nonetheless. "Don't you think that's a little dramatic? Hitler?"

"You tell me," he said, his eyes—hauntingly familiar eyes—not letting her off the hook. "You're the one with all the answers."

Her smile faltered, and she stared at him, flabbergasted, struggling for a comeback. But it was hard to fight such evasive barbs, and being flustered was one of her least favorite experiences. She had the feeling she'd seen him before. He was probably one of Mariah's friends, sent here by her sister to shake her up. It was one of Mariah's favorite pastimes. "Wait a minute," she said, beginning to get angry. "Do I know you?"

He laughed mirthlessly, then, tipping his glasses down to look at her over the frames. "Think about it," he said under his breath. "It'll come to you."

Jo watched him amble back down the aisle, through the crowd waiting to sign up for her group, and then he disappeared outside the auditorium. Well, so much for the Mariah theory, she mused. Mariah would have gotten a lot more mileage out of such a confrontation. The man never would have left after such a vague statement. And he wouldn't have made her quite so uncomfortable.

It was something about the eyes that disturbed her...blue, penetrating, sultry eyes....

Trying to shake off the nagging feeling, Jo reached for the next album cover. She glanced down at the rock star posing seductively for his fans, his eyes blue, penetrating, sultry...

Her breath caught in her lungs, and she lifted her head, staring in the direction the man had gone. The eyes on the album cover were the same ones she'd looked into moments ago.

E.Z. Ellis's eyes.

THE CALLOWAY HOUSE was full of light when Jo pulled into the drive, and from her car she could see a vague image on a television screen. Ford and Mariah's car sat parked halfway down the drive, and she mused that her younger sister must have been driving. It had always been Mariah's way to simply stop the car wherever she pleased and get out. Never mind the people who parked behind her.

Jo allowed them room to get out when the time came, though she didn't know why the newlyweds didn't just move in, since they were here almost every night anyway. Mariah maintained that the old homestead at Calloway Corners was more comfortable than their trailer, where Ford's desk filled half the living room and his stacks of work-to-be-done filled the other half. When Eden had asked why she didn't just rearrange things, Mariah had dismissed the idea by saying that redecorating wasn't her strong suit, since she'd never stayed in one place long enough to even hang curtains, until now.

Jo got out of the car, thinking how Mariah would never change, despite her marriage to Ford Dunning, the feet-on-the-ground preacher who'd anchored her and *almost* tamed her. It was nice to know that her youngest sister, always as free as the wind and just as unpredictable, finally had a solid foundation on which to rest on the rare occasions when she came down from the clouds.

Grabbing whatever she could manage to carry inside, Jo headed for the front door and, unable to free a hand for the doorknob, kicked on it with her knee. Eden, the oldest of the four Calloway sisters at thirty-three, the childless matriarch of the family, opened it in an instant, holding a sewing needle between her teeth and a pair of Mariah's torn jeans under her arm. "You're late," Eden said around the needle. "Where've you been?"

Jo dropped the box of albums just inside the door and kicked it shut behind her. She glanced at Mariah and Ford cuddled on the sofa, noted Mariah's feet propped on the just-polished coffee table, and her half-empty Coke can sitting beside them in just such a way that she would knock it over as soon as she pulled her feet down.

"It took longer than usual to sign them all up. Three hundred people," Jo told her older sister, then went to the table and rescued Mariah's cola.

"So, the Save the Whales meeting was a success, huh?" Mariah asked.

Jo didn't bristle. It was a game that Mariah always played with her, with Eden and Tess, their absent sister, acting as referees. "It's not Save the Whales." She brought Mariah's drink to her lips and grimaced at its lukewarm taste.

"Oh, yeah," Mariah said, tossing some popcorn into her mouth. "That was last month. Let's see, this month it's Save the Furry Little Animals from Which Coats Are Made."

Ford grinned at the bantering he had grown used to. "Mariah..."

"That's all right, Ford," Jo said, unwilling to be daunted by a woman whose most serious recent cause had been raising money for choir robes by gambling. "Mariah knows full well what I'm about."

Mariah laughed her full-spirited laugh, which usually disarmed even those who wanted to be angry with her. Jo was no exception. "Of course," she said. "Now I remember. It's Save Little Innocent Minds from the Horrors of Rock and Roll. The bumper stickers are all over town."

"Poke fun all you want to," Jo said, grabbing the bowl of popcorn out of Mariah's hands to banish the taste of warm Coke. "But I'm getting a lot of support. In fact, the publicity's been so good, you'll never guess who showed up at my meeting tonight."

"Edwin Meese?" Eden asked, referring to the attorney general who'd done more than anyone in the decade to aid the cause of censorship.

"Nope. Someone a lot less sympathetic to my cause. In fact, he compared me to Hitler."

Ford tore his eyes from the television screen and looked up at her, all attention focused on her now. "Hitler?"

"Yes," Jo said, her eyebrows arched to increase the suspense. "Said I was good at what I did, but that I was creating a monster. And I guess he knows all about creating monsters. He's produced enough of his own."

"He didn't..." Ford said slowly. "He wouldn't come to your meeting..."

Jo glared at her brother-in-law, trying to glean whether they were talking about the same thing. There was nothing she hated worse than for someone to know her punch line before she could get it out.

"Who wouldn't?" Eden demanded, setting Mariah's jeans down and focusing completely on Ford.

Ford sat stiffer on the sofa, a dreadful wince on his face. "E.Z. Ellis?"

"E.Z. Ellis!" Mariah shouted. "Jo!"

"How did *you* know?" Jo's question was as near to an accusation as she could get without knowing the crime. "Did you know he was in town and not tell me, when you knew what I've been saying about him?"

Ford raised his hands innocently. "I didn't think he'd show—"

"Wait a minute!" Eden shouted. Because she shouted so seldom, all eyes turned to her. She stood up and set her hands on her trim hips. "Are we talking about E.Z. Ellis, the guy with that...that chest...and that white silk scarf trailing the ground...and those eyes...? *That* E.Z. Ellis?"

"The same," Jo said matter-of-factly. "Only he didn't have the chest or the scarf...well, the chest was covered, and of course the eyes were...Ford, how did you know!"

Mariah gave her husband a playful leer. "Yeah, Ford. How?"

Ford rose to his feet and pushed his fingers through his dark hair, thinking over his answer before he spoke. "It's supposed to be a secret," he said finally. "He asked me not to tell anybody he was in town. He's supposed to be hiding out, resting since his last tour and writing the songs for his next album. Who knew he'd show up at your meeting?"

"He asked *you* not to tell?" Jo asked, astounded. "Since when are you E.Z. Ellis's confidant?"

"Never mind that," Ford said, impatient with the third degree. "What was he doing at your meeting? He could have been recognized."

Frustrated, Jo slumped into the chair across from the couch and propped her feet on the coffee table. "Gathering ammunition, I suppose, for the Senate Commerce Committee Hearing. He's testifying, too, you know." She shook her head in amazement. "It's funny. I didn't even recognize him until he was gone. He had on tinted glasses, and his hair was combed differently. He was dressed just like anybody in the audience. No one else recognized him, either, and I didn't tell anyone after he left because they would have thought I was nuts."

"You mean those hypnotic eyes didn't give him away?" Mariah asked, grabbing another handful of popcorn. "Come on, Jo. Those eyes are insured. They're listed on the Pentagon's list of lethal weapons. Women just drop in his path when he looks at them."

Jo smiled sardonically at her sister. "Not everyone is the groupie type, Mariah. He's just a man. There's nothing supernatural about him."

"I don't know," Mariah said. She stood up and leaned over Jo, chanting "Doo-doo, doo-doo, doo-doo, doo-doo." Her voice dropping, she said, "Welcome to the Twilight Zone, where nothing is certain. You haven't been tested yet. You might just wake up in the middle of the night and find yourself wandering, mesmerized, to him. You know, all that

research you've been doing on those sensuous lyrics might
be subliminally drawing you in at this very moment. Drawing you all the way in . . . to the Twilight Zone of E.Z. Ellis's mind.''

"Well, Mariah,'' Jo volleyed, amused at her sister's an-
tics. "I'm sure you have the experience to back up that theory, but fortunately you and I aren't cut from the same
cloth. I like to think I have integrity.''

"You can have integrity and still lose your head over a
man,'' Mariah warned, the ticklish lilt returning to her
voice. "Stranger things have happened.'' She nudged her
husband and gave him a sexy wink.

"Not to me,'' Jo said, gazing pensively at the couple.
Ford and Mariah had a kind of chemistry Jo had never quite
experienced. Then, in her best attempt to change the subject before she started believing Mariah's warnings, asked,
"Now what is there to eat?''

"Cold cuts, beef jerky, and some leftover liver,'' Mariah
said. Next to Jo's causes, Mariah's favorite barbs had to do
with Jo's being a vegetarian.

Jo grinned, completely undaunted, and disappeared into
the kitchen.

AS MUCH AS JO hated to admit it, E.Z. Ellis's eyes did have
a haunting quality that kept her from sleeping that night.
She got out of bed, her white cotton gown trailing the floor,
and went to the window that looked out on the back of the
house. The moon shone down on the massive pine trees,
their limbs stretched in proud possession of the full lawn.
The lattice arbor that her father had built for her mother so
many years ago provided a romantic lure in the mottled
moonlight, inspiring thoughts that unsettled her. She sat
down on the wide window sill and rested her head against
the glass.

Now why was she losing sleep over some lascivious rock star who'd called her Hitler? It wasn't as if he'd had any effect on her. She wasn't an adoring fan. She was immune to those eyes.

Hitler. How could he have compared her to Hitler? Jo grinned slightly, realizing that the label sounded like one she might have given to someone else. But wasn't his comparison a little extreme for her situation? All she wanted to do was make the world a more pleasant place, a safer atmosphere for America's youth. It wasn't surprising that E.Z. Ellis would have trouble understanding, since her cause threatened his profession, his talent, possibly even his manhood. Wasn't a rock singer's music an extension of his masculinity? That would, at least, explain all the writhing and shaking that went on when he was on stage.

Her eyes strayed to the album cover on her dresser, the one she'd brought up to her room tonight, hoping to get some sort of handle on him. She'd seen the cover of "Easy Does It" in poster form all over the record stores. E.Z. Ellis in all his bare-chested glory, leaning against a wall, his frayed denim vest only highlighting the definition in his biceps, a white silk scarf wrapped around his neck and trailing the floor, tight jeans and fringed suede boots. And the eyes . . . good Lord, those eyes . . .

She wondered if he wore colored contacts or mascara on those dark lashes. . . .

Jo steered her thoughts back on course and tossed the record cover to the dresser. It wasn't as if those eyes had gotten to her. She simply couldn't sleep because she was trying to figure him out, trying to understand why he'd sat through her meeting, never identifying himself, never arguing, listening to all the condemning things she'd said about him. It was not at all what she would have expected from the irreverent star whose fans literally flung their underwear onto the stage.

She heard footsteps in the hall, and looked up to see Eden leaning against the doorway. She looked tousled and sleepy, her strawberry blonde hair full and teasing her shoulders in bold rebellion. If Eden would only wear it that way intentionally, Jo mused, men would be lined up at the door. But Eden's style was more subdued, almost calculatedly forbidding. "Couldn't sleep?" Eden asked.

Jo sighed and shook her head. "You?"

Eden turned on the lamp, casting her pale face in a yellow glow, and climbed onto the double bed. "It's been hard sleeping around here since Dad died. I was used to getting up a lot at night, helping him.... Now my body clock just doesn't want to readjust itself." She glanced at the album cover on the dresser and shot Jo a knowing look. "What's your excuse? E.Z. Ellis?"

"No," Jo said, though she did little to convince her sister otherwise. Eden wasn't like Mariah. Her perceptiveness manifested itself in maternal ways, unlike Mariah's relentless teasing. "I was thinking," Jo said. "I wonder what it would accomplish for me to meet him again . . . sort of appeal to his conscience."

Eden lay back on the bed, fluffed a pillow and stretched. "You've got to be kidding."

"No. It's only fair that I try before I zap him in front of a Senate committee. I mean, I'd want somebody to give me the chance."

"To what?" Eden asked, stifling a yawn. "You don't really think he'll change his mind because Jo Calloway told him to? I mean, let's face it, not everyone agrees with what you're fighting for."

"Not even you?"

"Sorry," Eden said. "How does that saying go, about not agreeing with what you say but fighting to the death for your right to say it? But of course, that in itself goes against your fight. If you believe what you say, you don't even believe E.Z. Ellis has the right to say what he wants."

Eden's logic always drove Jo up the wall. Especially when it made sense. "No, that's not it," she said. "You don't understand."

"Typical Jo Calloway answer," Eden pointed out, a soft smile taking the edge off the truth. "If someone disagrees with you, it's because they don't understand."

Jo looked out the window again. A breeze whispered through the leaves, shuffling the shadows over the arbor. "Come on, Eden. Don't start on me."

"Who's starting?" Eden asked. She pulled the covers up over her shoulders and yawned again. "If you have to go see him, you'll go see him."

The relaxed tone of Eden's voice made Jo glance back at her sister. "Hey, don't fall asleep in my bed!"

"It isn't yours, really," Eden muttered, not opening her eyes. "You don't even live here anymore."

"But you moved into Dad's room."

"Yeah," Eden whispered, her voice taking on a note of sadness. "Took me thirty-three years to get a room of my own, and now I'd rather sleep right back here with you. Isn't life a hoot?"

"Yeah," Jo whispered, no joy in her voice. "A real hoot."

She watched as Eden snuggled deeper into the pillow and drifted off to sleep. It had always been that way. Eden had always been the one to drop off to sleep first, while Jo lay awake planning, scheming, organizing...forever fighting the injustices of the world. Even the decor of the bedroom, untouched since high school—though Jo hadn't lived here in years—demonstrated their contrasting personalities. On Jo's side of the room were framed headlines from the junior high school newspaper, headlines of her leading a demonstration in the school corridors because girls weren't allowed to wear pants to school...headlines of her fighting to get high school dances thrown every Saturday night in the school gym...headlines of her staging a sit-in to protest the lack of senior privileges. Jo still managed to make the headlines. They grew bigger and more volatile every year, but somehow they never satiated her hunger for...for what? Some sort of justice that would bring sense to a nonsensical world?

Since she'd graduated from college with her master's degree in political science, Jo had searched for that elusive justice as she embraced tough causes and challenging ones. She liked to think she'd made a difference where she'd fought.

As much as Mariah liked to tease her sister about her causes, Jo knew that if Mariah ever needed someone to stand up for her, Jo would be the one she'd turn to. Jo was the angry one, the strong one, the one who believed. She never backed down from a fight, and she always fought until she won... E.Z. Ellis's famous blue eyes weren't going to change that now.

Jo raised the window and leaned out, letting the humid April wind fondle her hair and cool her face. The little creek that ran alongside their lawn seemed to whisper to her, reminding her why she'd started this particular fight. People had been hurt, changed, destroyed by something that was out of their control. And she knew, from deep inside her, how debilitating it was not to be able to hold out a hand to stem the pain...to have to endure it and forge on in spite of it.

What could a millionaire rock singer know about injustice? she asked herself. What could he know about pain? Not one thing, but maybe it was time he found out. He'd confronted her for a reason tonight. Maybe he *wanted* a debate. And she had to admit that going straight to the source of the lyrics she railed against would be more effective than fighting them indirectly. Maybe she could, at the very least, make him think.

She closed the window, shutting out the damp air, and crawled into the bed next to Eden. It had been a long time since she'd slept next to anyone...somehow it felt familiar...warm. Things had started moving too far away from the familiar lately...with her father's death and Mariah's marriage and Tess's divorce. All the things she'd taken for granted once had been rearranged. It was good to have one thing return to the way it was...it was good to be home. Even if she was only here long enough to launch her citizens' group, so that they could fight independently to bring about change.

Jo closed her eyes and made a decision. She was going to see E.Z. Ellis tomorrow, as soon as she could coax his address out of Ford.

FORD AND MARIAH'S trailer was nestled in a cove of pine trees set back from the noise of the street, and just a few miles from the nondenominational church where Ford preached. Jo left her car and went up the porch steps, knocking lightly on the door. An almost incoherent mumble was her only answer.

"Enter at your own risk."

Jo smiled as she opened the door, peeked inside and saw Mariah hunched over a cup of herbal tea at the tiny breakfast table. Her sister's blonde hair hung like silken strings in her eyes, and she wore a bright red satin gown that she'd found at some "little out-of-the-way boutique in San Francisco's China Town." Her eyes looked as if she had yet to recover from a three day drunk, but Jo knew better. Mariah always looked like that in the mornings.

At the sight of Jo, Mariah shoved back her bangs and rested her chin on her hand. "How dare you look so perky in the morning?" she asked. She checked out her sister's

cotton skirt that trailed to just below mid-thigh, and her soft
angora sweater, then regarded the French braid trailing
down Jo's back. "It isn't natural, Jo. No one can actually
manage a French braid this early in the morning."

Jo spotted a coffeepot on the counter, and went into the
kitchen for a cup. "Why do you bother to get up if it's so
'unnatural'?" she asked. "You never did before."

"Because," Mariah said, lifting her chin with a new kind
of pride Jo hadn't seen in her sister many times in her life.
"I'm a married woman now. And if I don't get up early, I
won't see Ford before he goes to work. And if I don't see
him, I'll miss him."

Jo smiled and poured some coffee. "So, where is this human miracle who can actually make my little sister crawl out
of bed before noon? I need to talk to him."

"He just left," Mariah said over the rim of her teacup.
"What do you want to talk to him about?"

Jo picked up the paper, shook it out and began to scan the
headlines. "Never mind. Just . . . something."

A slow smile crept across Mariah's sleepy face, and her
eyes stirred to life. "E.Z. Ellis? I knew you'd be over here
trying to get more out of Ford." Delighted, she laughed and
set down her cup. "Ole Jo has eyes for a rock star. I love it!"

Jo regarded her sister over the newspaper, and noted that
Mariah's vivid imagination was more potent than caffeine.
She didn't find such speculation amusing. "I do not have
eyes for a rock star. That's more your speed. The truth is,
if Mr. Ellis is in town, I'd like to air my complaints about his
lyrics to him directly. It's better than cowering around town
talking behind his back."

"Yeah, yeah," Mariah said, giggling again.

Realizing the conversation was going nowhere, Jo
dropped the paper to the table and started for the door. "I'll
see if I can find Ford at the church."

"Tell him I said to help you," Mariah said. "I want to see if my tough sister can really resist this guy."

Jo swung around. "Mariah, it's business. I am a professional doing the job I was hired to do. If that's beyond your comprehension, I'm sorry."

"Just be gentle with him," Mariah said, and her giggle rang through the little trailer once again.

WHEN JO ARRIVED at the church, she found Ford hard at work in the little cubicle he called an office. Since his secretary didn't seem to be around, Jo stuck her head in and knocked lightly on the open door. "Ford? Do you have a minute?"

Ford looked up from his papers and saw his sister-in-law. "Uh-oh."

Jo knitted her brows together and stepped inside. "'Uh-oh'? Is that any way to greet family?"

"No," Ford said, quickly shuffling the papers on his desk as if to keep Jo from seeing them. "It's just that . . . I'm expecting someone this morning . . ."

"Don't worry," Jo said, closing the door behind her and taking the chair in front of his desk. "It won't take long. I just came by to ask you about E.Z. Ellis. Where is he staying, Ford? Where can I reach him?"

"E.Z. Ellis?" He uttered a loud laugh. "You must be kidding. You really think I'm going to give you that information? You're the enemy."

"The enemy?" Jo repeated.

Ford checked his watch. "In *his* mind that's what you are. He wants to keep a low profile. That's the only reason I met him in the first place. He wanted anonymity, and I helped him get it."

"What do you think I'll do?" she asked, indignant. "Call a press conference?"

"I don't know," Ford said. "All I know is that he's here trying to work and relax, and if you let anyone know he's here, his cover would be blown. The guy deserves a little peace and quiet. He's a nice guy. He really is."

"Yeah," Jo said, cocking her head to one side and looking doubtful. "I'm sure he's just a real prince." She stood up and leaned her hands on Ford's desk. "Come on, Ford. Why are you helping this guy? Your sense of moral decency should make you want to help me."

"Now, wait a minute," Ford said. "I don't agree with censorship in any form, and my sense of moral decency has nothing to do with it."

"How can you say that? You're a preacher!"

"A preacher with values dictated by the Bible, Jo. Not by you."

Jo clamped her teeth together. "Never mind," she bit out. "I'll either find E.Z. Ellis myself or just wait for him to crawl out of the woodwork again. I wouldn't dream of asking your help."

Ford stood up, rolling his eyes. "Jo, come on. You're as dramatic as Mariah is sometimes."

Jo held her breath to contain her temper. She started for the door, glaring back at him over her shoulder. "I'll just pretend you didn't say that."

She reached for the doorknob, but found that the door moved before she pulled it. She stepped back and allowed the person on the other side to open it.

"Uh-oh," Ford muttered again.

Suddenly, that "uh-oh" took on vivid clarity when Jo found herself standing face to face, once again, with E.Z. Ellis.

CHAPTER TWO

JO GASPED AT THE SIGHT of the rock star filling up the doorway in a place where he was least expected. E.Z. Ellis stood like a compromise between the bare-chested blitz on the covers of his albums, and the boy next door who had escaped recognition last night. He wore a pair of worn-out jeans with ragged holes in both knees, and a white tank top that drew the eye to his massive chest and biceps. The subtle seduction of his appearance, in a *church*, no less, made Jo angry, but she reminded herself that she couldn't get indignant about the way the man looked. She could fight to get his lyrics censored, but no one could censor his physical appeal.

"Mr. Ellis," she said, trying to recover and wondering frantically how much he might have overhead. "So you were Ford's appointment. No wonder my brother-in-law was so anxious to get rid of me."

E.Z. didn't respond at first. For a moment he simply lingered in the doorway, subtle suspicion in those azure eyes. He took off his glasses and looked curiously at Ford, then regarded Jo with an expression near amusement. "Brother-in-law? Is this why you wanted to see me, Ford?"

Ford stood up, rubbing his face with rough fingers. "I left a message for you at Sullivan's, E.Z., because I wanted to tell you that Jo's my wife's sister. I didn't want you to find out and think it was a conflict of interest."

"Conflict of interest?" Jo cut in, looking at Ford. "What are you talking about?"

"Never mind that," E.Z. said. "It has nothing to do with my music." He regarded her again, his look intimate, and fleetingly, Jo wondered if he'd been that tall last night. Did the tank top he wore, defining the hard muscles that were a vital part of his appeal, really do that much for his charm? Or was it simply knowing who he was that explained the attraction? How much of his charisma was due to expectation, she mused. And how much was because of the man himself?

E.Z. leaned against the casing of the door, gazing down at her, a glimmer of satisfaction brightening his eyes. One side of his mouth lifted in that famous smile he'd probably had insured. "Well, well," he said. "You work faster than I thought. I'm impressed."

Jo lifted her chin and pushed her hands deeper into her skirt pockets. Though it wasn't the greeting she'd expected, it certainly got things off on the right track. "What do you mean, I work fast?"

E.Z. lifted a shoulder, the indolent gesture unconsciously sensuous. "Well, last night you didn't know me from any of the other poor idiots in your audience. And now you've not only figured out who I am, but here you are, delivered personally, like a pretty package with a booby trap inside."

Jo wasn't certain which analogy to attack first. The package or the booby trap. Whichever it was, she decided, she wouldn't surrender the offensive. She reached into the compartment of her purse that contained her business cards. She handed one to him. "This isn't a game to me, Mr. Ellis. The AFCRL pays me to do what I do. I'm sorry if I threaten you in some way."

E.Z. took the card, looking at it with further amusement. "'Jo Calloway, Lobbyist, Organizational and Strategic Consultant,'" he read. He brought his eyes back to her. "Is that why you wanted Ford to tell you where I'm staying? Part of your strategy?"

"So you listen at doors, too?"

"Only when I'm being discussed behind them," he said.

Ford stepped out from behind his desk, obviously chagrined. "Look, why don't I just step out and let you two talk here? Maybe you can come to some sort of understanding . . . or something."

Jo and E.Z. stood silently until Ford had left the room, and finally, E.Z. laughed, as if the situation struck him as hilariously funny. Then he stepped back from the doorway, motioning to a chair.

Jo took the seat Ford had just abandoned, hoping it might lend her an air of authority. Somehow, she felt it wouldn't, where E.Z. was concerned.

"So, what gave me away?" he asked, settling on the arm of the other chair. "I thought I looked pretty anonymous last night."

"You did," she said, unwilling to tell him his eyes had been the culprits. "But like you said, it came to me. I might have recognized you earlier, but I wasn't exactly expecting you to be in town, let alone at a censorship meeting. How long will you be here?"

E.Z. picked up the picture of Mariah on Ford's desk, idly looked at it, then set it back down. "I guess until you spread the word and my hiding place isn't a hiding place anymore."

"I don't intend to tell anyone you're here, Mr. Ellis. It isn't my style to gossip."

Those intense blue eyes bored into Jo, again making her feel uneasy. He stared at her for a long moment, evaluating, measuring, and finally the shutters of defensiveness over his eyes fell away. E.Z. released a heavy sigh and raked his hand through his hair. "I'd appreciate that, because I need a break. I need to be here to rest ... for recreation, in the purest sense of the word. I'm tired."

For a moment—the most fleeting of moments—Jo could see that he was indeed tired. The fire she'd seen in the pictures of him on stage was gone. Now there was only a cool, distant quality, a quality that warned one to stand far back. "I understand you just came off a long tour," she said. "I imagine that takes a lot out of you."

"It bleeds you dry. You can't do the kind of physical performance that I do, night after night for seven months, and not feel mentally and physically exhausted at the end. It makes you not want to see anybody or do anything for a very long time."

"I wouldn't know," she admitted. "I've never seen you perform."

He regarded her with amusement, as if the honest admission delighted him. "Why doesn't that surprise me? I guess you wouldn't want to know much about your prey before you attack, though, would you?"

Jo set her lips in a rigid line. "I don't consider you my prey, Mr. Ellis. We're simply rivals ... two people on different sides of an important issue."

E.Z. uttered a humorless laugh and went across the room, to where Ford had hung a photo of an old army buddy in fatigues. "Well, isn't that nice?" he asked, turning around. "You make it sound nice and equal, like the fight's a fair one."

"It is."

"The hell it is," he said. "What have you got to lose? From what I know about you—and believe me, I do my homework, too—you go wherever a fight is. As soon as this one's over, you'll move on to something else. On the other hand, I have my whole career. And since I don't happen to think I've done anything wrong, I don't like the idea that someone might be able to dictate which of my past records can stay in the stores, and how I'm going to write my future ones."

Jo stood up, facing him squarely. "The change might be for the better, Mr. Ellis. If you cleaned up your music, you might reach a whole new audience. *I* might even like it."

E.Z. smirked at that. "Thanks a lot, but I like my old audience. And frankly I couldn't care less what you think of my music. In fact the album I'm working on now is exactly in the tradition of all my others. I wouldn't dream of letting you down."

"Oh?" she asked. "What will you be calling this album? 'Sleazy E.Z.'?"

He grinned in a way that almost disarmed her. "Hey, that's pretty good. But no, I'm calling the next album, 'E.Z. To Be Hard.'"

Jo picked a piece of lint off her sweater. "Well, that's almost as bad."

His laugh was unexpected, disparaging. "I might have known you'd interpret that in a way that never even entered my mind."

"Give me a break," she said. "You know exactly what you're doing. You people are experts with plays on words."

The smile left his face. For a moment he inclined his head and stared at her, a weary flicker of defeat in his eyes. "See, I could mean just about anything with that title, and no matter how deep or profound I might get, people like you will always see what they want to. It's a shame that you have such tunnel vision. You miss an awful lot that way."

"If unceasing determination is tunnel vision, I guess that's what I have."

E.Z. shook his head dolefully, as if he couldn't believe her arrogance. "It must be nice being so sure of yourself. But the fact is, I write what moves me, without much judgment as to what some prudish group on a morality kick is going to think about it."

"I am not prudish, and I'm not on a morality kick! Your music is offensive to a lot of people."

He went to the small window in the cubicle and peered out. "Tell me. Do you consider all love songs junk, or just mine?"

Jo followed him to the tiny window. "Junk is your word for it, not mine," she said. "And let's face it, it doesn't have one iota of social value."

"No social value?" he repeated, astounded. "I don't know where you've been hiding, Red, but even a contemporary woman like you must need a good love song now and then."

Jo felt her shoulders square, and she flicked her hair back. "I have no objection at all to a good love song," she said. "It's your graphic, suggestive lyrics I object to."

E.Z. pushed past her and sat down in Ford's chair, leaving her standing. "All right. Why don't you sit down and tell me about my graphic, suggestive lyrics? I always get a kick out of hearing how people interpret my songs. They're like Rorschach Tests sometimes. But don't forget we're in a church." He threw his arm across the back of his chair, and gazed up at her a little too suggestively. "I should warn you, though. Your interpretation will say a lot about your own secret fantasies. I'd be careful if I were you. You look like a woman who has a lot of those."

The game was one Jo was familiar with, and her experience put her at ease. The congressmen she often lobbied played this game all the time. She managed a smile and sat down across the desk from him. "Let's not change the subject, Mr. Ellis. This isn't about me, it's about you."

"That's where you're wrong," he argued. "My songs are about everyone who listens to them. How you interpret them is your problem, not mine."

Jo stiffened and leaned over the desk, like a lawyer about to rest her case. "You see, that's what just kills me about you self-centered musicians. You honestly think that once your music is recorded, your responsibility to your fans is over. You don't consider how it affects real people. How it hurts them!"

"Hurts them?" E.Z. leaned forward as well, suddenly more animated than he'd been since she'd met him. "What about how it *helps* them? Have you even once considered that?"

Jo laughed dryly. "Oh, please. If your bawdy rock lyrics have ever helped anyone, I wish you'd tell me how. I'd just love to know."

E.Z. came to his feet then, lightning flashing in those sky-blazed eyes. She waited for him to light into her, but instead he only rubbed his stubbled chin and began to pace. Was he trying to contain his anger, she wondered, or groping for an answer to her challenge? "I don't know why I'm standing here talking to you," he said finally. "I don't even know what possessed me to get into this with you today. Your mind is closed up tighter than a virgin's knees."

"What an interesting image," Jo said. "Add an 'ooh baby baby' to that and it'll probably be a hit."

E.Z. spun around, clearly incensed by Jo's sarcasm. "I'm just curious," he said. "What exactly did you hope to accomplish by talking to me today? That is, if Ford had told you where to find me."

Jo's resolve weakened for a moment and she looked down at her hands. "I had hoped that I could talk some sense into you. Maybe appeal to your sense of decency. Change your mind, maybe."

His laugh was almost brutal. "Change *my* mind? Talk about secret fantasies! You must live in a dream world!"

"You're right," she said, standing up and moving toward the door. "I made a stupid assumption. I assumed you *had* a sense of decency. My mistake."

"That's right," he retorted. "We rock stars, we're all a bunch of indecent rabble-rousers with no morals and no values."

She opened the door, and turned back to him. "I might have known a man who calls himself 'Easy' wouldn't take responsibility for the damage he does."

"Who's gonna take responsibility for the damage *you* do?" he shouted behind her.

Ignoring the question, Jo marched past Ford, who leaned miserably against his secretary's desk. She turned back and looked at E.Z. just before leaving the church. "I'll see you in Washington, Mr. Ellis. We'll see what the Commerce Committee thinks about your sense of decency then!"

"Hey, my conscience is clear! I sleep fine at night. How about you?"

Again not gracing the question with an answer, Jo rushed out to her car. Gunning the engine, she tore out of the church parking lot, leaving a cloud of dust and the irate rock star in her wake.

E.Z. WATCHED UNTIL Jo was out of sight, then turned back to Ford, who stood at the doorway.

"I take it you two didn't hit it off," Ford ventured.

E.Z. didn't find the remark amusing. "I hope your wife has a better disposition." He started out to his car. "I'll talk to you later, Ford," he mumbled.

He went out to the vintage Volkswagen he drove, covered with rust and dents to prove its age, and cranked the loud engine. For this kind of infuriation, he could have stayed in New Orleans, E.Z. mused. But he had naively believed that hiding out in a small, out-in-the-middle-of-nowhere place like this one in North Louisiana would buffer him from the world and keep all those ulcer-provoking problems at bay. He couldn't have been more wrong. Before, he'd only had to deal with record company executives, nosy reporters, nagging accountants and promoters worrying about his image and his refusal to do interviews. That had been easy. He'd never before encountered a headache like Jo Calloway.

The day was shot now, as far as he was concerned. The lady had snuffed out any creativity he'd had going, so there was no use going home and trying to work. So much for peace and quiet and that inspirational flow he'd sought when he came here.

He reached into the back seat, retrieved his favorite faded maroon baseball cap and his tinted glasses, and instantly transformed his appearance. Shrugging on the wrinkled chambray shirt he'd tossed onto the passenger seat that morning, E.Z. pulled out of the parking lot.

The loud, broken sound of the muffler of his Volkswagen gave him a sense of perspective. It was imperfect...it was reality...it was something far removed from his fame or his talent. He drove the car out over the gravel drive, and told himself that one of these days he'd invest in a new set of tires. But these served him well for now.

The car didn't go much over forty without the front end trembling, and the engine sounded like a freight train running up his back, but E.Z. couldn't have loved it more. Driving it, he could be just anybody off the street. Women didn't swoon for the guy in the rusty VW. Teenagers didn't tear at his clothes. No one asked for his autograph. And irate cause-chasers didn't throw darts at him.

He parked the car at a little diner on the outskirts of Bossier City, a diner that had become one of his favorites over the past few weeks. It was always full of blue-collar workers—plumbers, carpenters, electricians. Men not afraid to get their hands dirty, men not afraid to sweat. Sometimes, on days like today, he wished he'd chosen one of those vocations.

He took a seat at the counter and ordered a hamburger. When it was served, it was bigger and greasier than ever...just the way he liked it. He took a bite, set it down and let his eyes stray past the people lined up at the cash register, to the busy street just beyond the window. A car slowed to a stop, and a kid, no more than sixteen, got out. He flung a duffel bag over his shoulder, said something to the driver, then closed the door. The car left him standing there.

Something about the boy reminded E.Z. of himself at that age. Maybe it was the way the sole of one shoe flopped against the teenager's foot when he walked, or the fact that his shirt looked as if he'd lived in it for days, or the hems of his jeans, which had been let out to accommodate new height, or the hitch-hiking thumb held up for another ride. He saw the boy drop his thumb when a hopeful prospect passed him by. He turned toward the diner, looking in the window with hungry eyes. A Help Wanted sign on the glass snagged his attention, and straightening his shirt and his raggedy, unkempt blond hair, the boy started inside.

E.Z. took another bite of his hamburger, making an effort not to stare. Like a customer anxious to be seated, the boy stood awkwardly at the front of the diner, waiting for someone to notice him. Finally a waitress approached him.

"I need to see someone about the job," he said.

The waitress eyed the duffel bag thrown over his shoulder, the wrinkled clothes, the worn-out shoes. It was the same kind of condescending look E.Z. had gotten for years before his "ship" had come in...the kind that made success more a matter of revenge than ambition. "What's your name, son?" the waitress asked.

"Chris," he said. "Chris...Smith."

A runaway, E.Z. thought without hesitation. Someone should tell the kid that Smith was a dead giveaway. He'd used the last name himself his first month on his own, wandering around in search of his pot at the end of the rainbow . . . the pot he now knew wasn't there. He glanced over his shoulder at the boy and wondered if he'd learned the hardest lessons yet . . .

The waitress reached behind the cash register and pulled out an application. "Here, fill this out. Then you can talk to the manager."

"Um . . . can I borrow a pen?" the kid asked.

Huffing as if he'd asked for a thousand-dollar loan rather than something to write with, the waitress handed him a pen.

The barstool next to E.Z. was vacant, and the boy took it and got right to work on the application. E.Z. kept eating, pretending not to be interested in what Chris was doing. From the corner of his eye, he saw him write his name. But then the boy stopped and stared at the next question, as if he hadn't expected it to appear on the form.

"Whatsa matter, kid?" the waitress asked. "Can't you read?"

Chris's face reddened. "'Course I can read . . . it's just . . . well, I've been traveling, you know. I haven't moved into my new apartment yet, so . . . my address . . ."

The waitress grabbed up the application and jerked the pen from the boy's hand. "Sorry, kid. If you ain't got an address, you probably ain't got references, either. Lou don't hire nobody that pops up outa nowhere."

Chris nodded dolefully. "Okay. Thanks, anyway." He glanced over at E.Z.'s hamburger, then up at the price list on the wall. E.Z. knew the look. The kid probably hadn't had a meal all day and didn't have the money to pay for one.

"So, you gonna just sit there or order?" the waitress asked.

Chris dug into his pocket, pulled out some loose change and eyed the price list again. When he saw that he didn't have enough, he crammed the money back into his pocket and shrugged. "No thanks. I have another appointment."

He got up to leave, holding the battered duffel bag like his bruised dignity, and started for the door. Quickly, E.Z. reached into his pocket, pulled out a twenty and dropped it on the floor. He half stood and crushed it with his foot. "Hey, kid. You dropped something."

The boy turned around, saw the dirty twenty on the floor, and eyed E.Z. suspiciously. "That ain't mine."

So much honesty and pride, E.Z. thought. Pride like he'd had when he had gone from bar to bar looking for a gig, just to get enough money to pay for a ride to the next town and the next gig. The boy turned back for the door, as if he knew E.Z. had planted the twenty, and didn't trust him because of it.

E.Z. leaned over and picked up the money. "Guess it's my lucky day," he said, straightening it out with two fingers. He looked at Chris again. "But I have this rule about found money. I figure when you find it, you should share part of it, you know? It's kind of like saying thanks to whoever dropped it."

Chris studied E.Z. as if he wanted a sign that the guy wasn't setting him up for some evil purpose. E.Z. realized the teenager probably hadn't come this far without learning something. "Well, maybe just a couple dollars," Chris said. "Since you found it."

E.Z. ordered Chris a hamburger, then stayed with him while he devoured it, careful not to let the conversation frighten the boy away. "So, you just passing through?"

"Yeah," Chris said. "On my way to New Orleans. I have friends there."

"I hope so," E.Z. said. "It can be a rough place to be by yourself."

Chris shrugged. "I can handle it."

E.Z. pulled a napkin out of the dispenser, and picked up the pen the waitress had left on the counter. "Look, if you need a place to stay tonight, there's this place I know about. It's safe...you can count on it. Not like some of the big city shelters. It's warm, and they'll give you a meal if you need it. You know, just until you're ready to go down to New Orleans." He wrote down the address and handed it to Chris.

"I don't need a place to stay," Chris said, his suspicions making him erect his barriers again. "I have friends I'll be staying with tonight."

"I know," E.Z. said. "But just in case they aren't home or something... It's a good place. No hassles, I promise."

Chris took the napkin, read the address, then wadded it in his hand. "Well, I gotta go. Thanks for the hamburger."

E.Z. pushed the change from the twenty down the counter to Chris. "Don't thank me," he said. "I found the money, remember? Next time you find a twenty, you'll do the same thing, right?"

"Yeah, sure." Chris left the money lying there. He stuck the napkin in his pocket and started out the door. "See ya."

"Yeah," E.Z. said, knowing better than to force the issue. "Take care."

E.Z. watched Chris leave the diner and walk down the sidewalk as if the boy had a clue where he was going and what he was going to do when he got there. E.Z. hoped to God Chris would wind up at the address he'd given him.

He took the last bite of his hamburger, washed it down, then rubbed his eyes under his glasses until he left them red. Chris hadn't trusted him. In his hat, with his dingy, wrinkled clothes and his dark glasses, he probably resembled some sinister lowlife who preyed on young runaways with nowhere left to turn. He hated being misunderstood, but he was glad Chris had enough street smarts to keep his distance. He didn't doubt for a moment that experience had given him reason to be suspicious.

Damn! He hated being famous when there was so much he could do anonymously. The thought that he had an adversary in town made his stomach twist with foreboding. He only hoped that Jo Calloway didn't plan to blow his cover and ruin everything he was about. Tackling his career was bad enough, but there were things he counted more important.

The dread of exposure nagged at him—dread of groupies showing up in his bed and camping out on his lawn; dread of not being able to walk out the door without security to keep them from mauling him; dread of reporters and hangers-on following him all over town. He couldn't take it right now. That's why he'd come here in the first place.

Deciding not to just sit by and wait for it to happen, E.Z. dug into his pocket for a quarter and went to the pay phone at the front of the diner. He thumbed through the white pages of the phone book for Ford Dunning's number at the church. He dialed, hoping Ford wasn't too shaken by the scene in his office to help E.Z. out. Ford seemed like someone he could trust. Maybe he'd have some pull with Jo.

The church secretary answered the phone and put Ford on. E.Z. turned toward the wall, keeping his voice low so that no one could overhear. "Hey, Ford. It's me...E.Z. Listen, I owe you an apology. I lost my temper before...things kind of got out of hand."

"No problem," Ford said. "I'm just sorry you two showed up at the same time."

E.Z. grinned and glanced around the diner. "I have to tell you, man, I'm a little worried. I need my privacy, and if your sister-in-law gets mad enough to let the word get out that I'm here—"

"Don't worry," Ford cut in quickly. "When Jo gives her word, she keeps it, no matter how mad she gets. That woman wears her honor like a coat of armor. That's why she's such a force to be reckoned with.''

"Yeah, that's what worries me," E.Z. said. "You don't think she'll turn on me, do you?''

Ford didn't sound worried. "She has a fiery temper, but she's relatively harmless. I'll talk to her if it makes you feel any better. And just for the record, E.Z., I'm not with her on this censorship fight.''

"Yeah, well, I appreciate that," E.Z. said, "but a lot of people are. It seems like the country is getting ripe for the idea. And she's a good spokesperson. To tell you the truth, I'd rather have her on my side.''

Ford laughed lightly at the unlikely prospect, but didn't leave E.Z. completely without hope. "Opinions have been changed. Maybe you should go see her. Give it another try. What have you got to lose?''

E.Z. considered the idea for a moment. Maybe Ford was right. Maybe he should go to her, apologize for yelling. And if he managed to convince Jo that she'd interpreted his lyrics incorrectly and explained what they really meant, maybe she'd get off his back. "All right," he said finally. "Tell me where she lives. It's worth a shot.''

When he'd hung up, E.Z. paid for his meal and walked outside, letting the April sun warm him. It was pleasant weather; spring was always his favorite time of year. But it still got cold at night, and cold could be a bitter enemy sometimes. For that reason he never took the mild seasons for granted. He walked out to the edge of the street, straining to look in the direction Chris had gone. No more than two blocks away, he saw the boy hitchhiking again.

It occurred to him that he could get into his car and pick the boy up himself, but E.Z. knew from experience that Chris would never accept his ride. E.Z. was someone who'd been nice to him, and therefore he was suspect.

He looked up at the sky, saw blustering clouds in the west.
It might rain tonight. He hoped not, for rain complicated so
many things. Sullivan's was always too crowded when it
rained. And when it was crowded, there was always trouble.

Maybe he'd go by there later and check things out, after
he'd paid his little visit to Jo Calloway. It was amazing the
different causes a man could be involved in, he thought.
From humanity to politics; from caring to defending; from
entertaining to protecting. But life was easier for him than
it was for most people, he supposed. At least, as easy as it
would probably ever get.

CHAPTER THREE

Jo PULLED INTO the old homestead at Calloway Corners, and saw her sister Mariah on her hands and knees, precariously balanced on the apex of the roof, hammering on a shingle to the chagrin of Seth Taylor, who'd been hired to do the job. The scene brought back the memory of the day they had searched everywhere for the twelve-year-old Mariah, only to find her sunbathing on the roof in the scandalous bikini she had borrowed from a friend with liberal parents. Their father had almost had a stroke when he'd seen Mariah scrambling down, concerned more with the towel she held around herself as protection from her father's wrath, than with her own safety.

"Mariah, what are you doing?" Jo asked now.

Mariah shaded her eyes from the sun and peered down at her sister. "I'm just auditioning Seth. He might build Ford and me a house."

Jo looked at Seth, saw that he'd thrown up his hands and laid down his tools, and was watching the blonde with amusement. "Mariah, hammering a few nails into a leaky roof isn't exactly a test of skills. Besides, Seth's houses are all over town."

Seth shoved back his pale hair. "That's okay, Jo," he said. "Mariah's doing a good job. I was thinking of hiring her."

Mariah lifted her brows as the two laughed at her. "I'll have you know I once dated a bridge builder in Paris. So it isn't like construction work is new to me.'' She tossed Seth the hammer, however, and scooted to the edge of the roof.

"Go ahead, Seth. I guess you know what you're doing." She found the ladder against the house and scurried down. "So, tell me everything. Did you get anything out of Ford? Did you see E.Z.?"

Jo's mirth vanished. "I don't want to talk about it," she said. She pushed open the front door, and Mariah followed her in.

"You saw him, didn't you?" Mariah prodded.

"Oh, I saw him, all right," Jo said. "We almost got into a knock-down-drag-out over his music."

"Joline Calloway, you would argue with a stump."

Jo stepped over the toys on the floor, left there by the children Eden kept during the day, and went into the kitchen, knowing Mariah would follow her. "I'd hardly call E.Z. Ellis a stump."

"No wonder you don't have a love life," Mariah observed wryly. "You have the uncanny ability to look all gift horses in the mouth!"

"Who says I don't have a love life?"

Mariah plopped down in a chair. "If you had one, dear sister, you'd be back home in Baton Rouge . . . not finding every excuse to be in Calloway Corners."

"Every excuse!" Jo repeated, indignant. "I came here to organize a censorship group in Shreveport, and I'm only staying until they're on their feet. That's my job. It is not an excuse!"

"I'm just saying that meeting a guy like E.Z. Ellis is a once in a lifetime opportunity. I went to one of his concerts once when I was in Jersey. Women threw their underwear on the stage. They beat their way past the security guards to get up there and kiss him. It was the most massive case of temporary insanity I've ever seen." She picked up a banana out of a fruit basket on the table, began to peel it. "But my sister takes one look at him and decides he's the enemy. I don't understand it."

"I don't expect you to understand," Jo said. "The strain might put your brain into overload."

Eden came in just as the remark was delivered, and in her best referee voice called them down. "Can't you two be left together in a room for five minutes? Honestly."

Mariah got out of her chair. "Go ahead, Jo. Tell Eden how you insulted E.Z. Ellis today."

Eden turned an accusing eye to Jo. "Oh, Jo, you didn't."

"I never told her that," Jo protested, her face reddening with rising anger. No one could provoke it like Mariah. "Her imagination is getting carried away, as usual. Now, if you'll both excuse me, I have work to do. As much as I'd love to sit around and spar with both of you, duty calls."

Mariah and Eden exchanged knowing looks as Jo left the room.

> *"Naughty, naughty, naughty, naughty pristine girl*
> *Standing on the corner at the edge of your world*
> *Show me how it used to be, take me for a whirl*
> *Naughty, naughty, naughty, naughty pristine girl..."*

The lyrics of E.Z. Ellis's most recent hit filled the living room, bringing Jo's temper all the way to the boiling point. She made a note on her clipboard to try to get some statistics for her report to the Commerce Committee, statistics on the number of juke boxes across the country that offered that song, the number of radio stations who played it and how many times per day.

She scratched a bold line beneath the title of the song, "Pristine Girl." Then, beneath that, she wrote, "BRAIN-WASHING." She wondered if the Bossier City Library had anything new on brainwashing techniques. Maybe they could be used in her arguments. Repetition was a form of brainwashing, wasn't it? Didn't a song like that eventually brainwash the children who heard it over and over and over? She'd start with this one then move on to some of the more suggestive songs he'd written. Songs about sadism, songs about rebellion, songs about suicide. By the time she got through with him, E.Z. Ellis would wish he'd never gotten into the music business.

The hammering on the roof disrupted her concentration, and she turned the music up a level and listened again. The song was about a fourteen-year-old prostitute, old beyond her years, selling her body for a bottle of booze. The very image made Jo ill, and she wondered how many girls he had drawn into the mind-set that there was any kind of glamour in that life, any kind of mystique. He had to be stopped.

The hammering again shattered her thoughts, and in the kitchen she heard the children of Eden's day-care giggling at the top of their lungs. Frustrated, she dropped her feet from where she had them propped on the table and stood up. How much longer would Seth be working up there, she wondered. And when were the parents going to come to get their children? It was all enough to drive a person nuts. Abandoning the song, still blaring on the stereo, Jo went into the kitchen to find her sister. The sight there almost knocked her off her feet.

Eden and Mariah were dancing around the kitchen like seasoned rockers in concert with the children cheering them on, mouthing the words of the chorus: *Naughty, naughty, naughty, naughty pristine girl....* Mariah strummed on a broom as if it were a guitar, and Eden held a wooden spoon to her mouth and belted out the words.

Jo was torn between laughter and downright disgust. Didn't they know what the song meant? Didn't they get the chauvinist implications of the man on the prowl, ready to take advantage of a child? And here they were, putting on this ridiculous display for all these innocent children. "Are you two enjoying yourselves?"

Eden instantly stopped her shenanigans and turned back to Jo, pushing her strawberry-blond hair out of her eyes. The children guffawed with glee as Mariah continued, undaunted. "Come on, Jo," Eden said breathlessly. "You've got to admit it's kind of catchy."

"That's exactly the problem," Jo said. "It's so catchy, that you don't even realize it's sucking you under."

Mariah threw her hands around her neck and pretended to choke. "Oh no! It's got me! It's sucking me under! Help me! *Help me!*" She started after the children, hands clutching her neck, and they scrambled, squealing with delight.

Eden fell against the counter laughing, and Jo suddenly decided that she'd trade in both of these sisters for Tess, who always took Jo seriously. Like Jo, Tess was able to see much deeper than the surface...much deeper than Jo felt Mariah or Eden could see.

Giving up on her sisters, Jo went back to the living room, pulled the tape out of the tape deck, gathered up all her papers and went back to the kitchen. She unplugged the big portable tape player Eden kept on the counter, snapped out the "Sesame Street" tape, checked the box for batteries, and started out the door.

"Where are you going?" Eden asked.

"Out back to the arbor," Jo said. "I can see I'm not going to get any work done here."

She slammed the door as she left the house and trekked through the pine trees to the little lattice arbor far in the back of the yard, the arbor that her father had built for her mother so long ago. She sat down on the swing, and sucked in the fresh scent of the wisteria vines weaving up through the criss-crossed planks. There should be peace here, she thought, distressed. Maybe she expected it because it had been her mother's special place. Absently, she tugged at the clip holding her French braid together. She allowed the strings of her hair to fall around her shoulders in wavy rebellion, let the wind whip it behind her the way her mother had always done. Jo would always remember the lovely sight of her on the squeaky swing, a look of deep serenity on her mother's face as the wind, and her father, toyed with her hair...

The memory left a deep ache in the depths of Jo's heart...an ache that never seemed to go away, especially now that she had her own life in another town. Maybe Mariah was right about her needing an excuse to come home to Calloway Corners every chance she got. As much as her sisters drove her crazy, the familiarity of everything here eased her loneliness. She'd never intended to reach the age of thirty all alone. But things always got so out of hand. She was always fighting for something, putting off real life until the battle was won. She was just beginning to realize there would always be another battle. And the war was getting lonely.

She slipped one of E.Z.'s tapes into the small tape deck, turned the machine on and leaned her head against the back of the swing. She set the notebook down on the swing beside her, and pulled her feet up. Hugging her knees, she closed her eyes and listened as E.Z.'s voice attempted to weave its magic. Magic was something Jo had never believed in.

She listened to the words of a less familiar song, something about feeling old before he'd ever been young, something about growing up before he'd finished growing. And for the life of her, she couldn't find one fault with the lyrics. Ironically, she felt she could have written those lines herself, if she'd only known the right words.

E.Z. PULLED INTO the gravel driveway, saw Jo's car and decided he'd found the right house. Dropping his baseball cap on the torn vinyl seat, but keeping his glasses on, he got out of the car. A man was on the roof, hammering like there was no tomorrow, and E.Z. had the brief, uneasy feeling that perhaps he was Jo Calloway's lover...or maybe even her husband. It had never occurred to him to ask about her marital status.

Seth stopped his work and gave E.Z. a friendly wave. "How's it goin'?" he asked.

"Pretty good," E.Z. called up. "I'm looking for Jo Calloway. This is the right place, isn't it?"

"Yeah," Seth said. "I just saw her walk out back to the arbor."

"Thanks."

Not her husband, E.Z. ascertained. And probably not her lover. Otherwise he wouldn't have been so quick to send him after her. Dismissing the carpenter, he walked around to the back of the house.

He saw her immediately, huddled up on the swing, hugging her knees under her big cotton skirt. Her eyes were closed, and her hair flowed down over the back of the swing, blowing with a freedom that he hadn't expected for someone so intense...so angry. She was like a beauty in a watercolor, her image about to blur as soon as an unskilled hand added the wrong hue. He heard music, muffled in the wind, playing softly as she swung, and he knew then that the pretty, untainted mood had been set by his song...

A gentle, hesitant smile touched his lips, and he stepped closer, heard the soft trills of the hit from his "Easy Street" Album. *I'll be damned,* he thought. *The lady's tainting herself by listening to an E.Z. Ellis song.*

Her face was virtually unguarded for the first time since he'd met her, and he studied it quietly, surprised at the look of yearning he saw there. The song was one of his saddest . . . it spoke of lost youth and too much drive. Of emptiness too deep to fill. Did she hear something in the words about herself?

The possibility linked them for a fleeting moment, making him feel a kinship between them that he didn't much want to feel. If she had at least some appreciation for his music . . . or his words . . . then it changed things between them. And he was much more comfortable keeping things the way they were. Rivals were easier to dislike.

He reached out and touched the swing, stopping its swaying motion, and Jo's eyes flew open. Fire and rage found their places on her face, as if they were more at home there than the peace he had witnessed.

"What are you doing here!" she demanded, springing off the swing.

E.Z. held onto the chain and wondered if she could be as ferocious as her eyes suggested. He doubted it. "I didn't mean to scare you," he said, pleased that he had knocked her off guard for the moment. "Your brother-in-law gave me your address."

Jo reached for the tape player and shut it off, as if the song playing was an indictment. "I . . . I was studying some more of your offensive lyrics. . . ."

He grinned, knowing he shouldn't, thinking it might push her too far. "You didn't seem to find anything too terribly offensive in that one, did you, Red? As a matter of fact you looked like you were really getting into it."

Jo hoped the heat in her cheeks wasn't visible through her pale skin. "My name is Jo. Not Red. And don't mistake boredom for appreciation, Mr. Ellis," she said. "I had just dozed off."

"Well, that at least answers my question about your sleeping nights," he said. "Conscience keeping you awake?"

She crossed her arms with a smugness that didn't quite seem genuine. "I assure you that isn't the case."

The wind whipped around them, blowing her hair into her face. She shoved it away, and he wondered if anyone had ever photographed her, all windblown and ruffled. He would have paid for a print.

"Do you always work in an arbor?" E.Z. asked, grabbing the beam on top of the structure with one hand and leaning into it.

Jo heaved a great sigh and gestured toward the house. "Two of my sisters are inside with five children, and there's a man banging on my roof. Not exactly the best environment for concentration, Mr. Ellis."

E.Z. laughed lightly. "Something about the way you say that. I like it."

"The way I say what?"

"Mr. Ellis," E.Z. said.

His approval didn't seem to be something she wanted. "I just find it hard to call a grown man 'Easy' with a straight face."

"It's getting hard to imagine any other kind of face on you," he observed.

She ignored the comment and groped for the offensive again. "How *did* you wind up with a name like that? Initials or not, most parents wouldn't give such a loaded nickname to a child."

His grin was pure seduction. "Given, nothing. Honey, I had to earn it."

Though the answer was no more than Jo would have expected, the idea that he'd admit it amazed her. She exhaled wearily. "Why doesn't that surprise me?"

He laughed and propped a foot on the swing, leaning into this knee. "So what does Jo stand for?" he asked, a flirty tilt to his head. "Josephine, Jo Ann...?"

"Joline," she provided grudgingly. "But no one's ever called me anything but Jo."

His eyes danced. "Are you sure about that?"

A tiny smile softened the lines of her lips. "No, actually, I'm not," she conceded. "Come to think of it, people have probably called me all sorts of things. And I probably earned those, too."

They both smiled, and E.Z. relaxed. *The lady has a sense of humor,* he mused. Somehow, it endeared her to him a bit.

But her smile blew away as if the breeze had taken it, and she tossed her hair back over her shoulder and leveled those direct eyes on him. "You didn't come here to talk about our names," she said.

He dropped his foot and stood straighter, his all-business expression mirroring hers. "I came to make peace . . . or try to," he said. "I thought I might talk you into coming back to my cabin, so we could go over some of the lyrics you find most offensive, and let me explain them to you. I lost my temper before. We both did."

She shook her head, not budging. "It won't do any good," she promised him. "I'm about as stubborn as they come. When I have convictions, I don't back down for anything."

"Not even when you're wrong?" he asked.

"I'm seldom wrong," Jo ventured. "Not when I've come this far."

The smile faded from his eyes, and he dropped his hand from the lattice over his head and slipped his hands into his pockets. "I don't think I've ever met anyone who's *never* wrong. I wonder if the Guinness people know about this."

"I didn't say *never*. I said *seldom*."

He let it go, not willing to start another word game. His eyes strayed to the white irises in the garden, their petals opening like layers about to peel away. He wished it were as easy with Jo. "Look, Jo, I know that there's a problem with some of the things going on in my industry today. I'm not even denying that some of the songs can have a bad influence on kids. Just like movies can and books and games.... But I think you've got me all wrong. If I thought I was hurting anybody, I'd change in a minute. I happen to really believe that occasionally, my music touches something in people that creates a positive reaction. Give me a chance to show you."

Her olive eyes seemed to soften for a moment as she regarded him. But as if she felt her convictions softening as well, she rallied and looked away. "No, I don't think so. Earlier today it seemed like a good idea. But now I don't think it would benefit either of us. You pull out all your arguments for the Senate Commerce Committee. I'm afraid they won't sway me at all."

E.Z.'s patience began to thin as he saw her erecting her roadblocks again. "You're a hard lady, you know that, Red? I wonder just *how* hard. I'd like to find out."

"You will, Mr. Ellis," she said, lifting her chin with determination. "I promise you that."

They stood facing each other for a long moment, like fighters listening for the next round's bell. The standoff was broken only when the back screen door slammed, and both Jo and E.Z. looked toward the house. Eden and Mariah came ambling out, as if both were merely taking an afternoon stroll. Jo crossed her arms and rolled her eyes in dread.

"Jo, you didn't tell us you had company." Eden's eyes brightened at the sight of E.Z. as she approached them. Mariah's eyes were beyond bright. They could have lit Hirsch Coliseum.

"You could have invited him in, instead of making him stand outside," Eden admonished.

Damn, E.Z. thought. *The more people who recognize me here, the less likely it is that I can stay hidden.* He straightened his glasses, wishing for the impossibility that they wouldn't know who he was. "That's okay," he said. "I was just leaving."

Eden looked crushed, and she extended a hand. "Don't go, Mr. Ellis. We have coffee inside, and we've been listening to your music all afternoon...."

"Eden!" Jo bit out.

E.Z. shook both their hands and looked down at the ground, torn between flattery and despair that they did, indeed, know him.

Mariah laughed and took his hand, forcing his eyes back to hers, and gave Jo a conspiratorial wink. Jo could have throttled her sister. "I'm Mariah, the one whose purpose in life is to drive my sister crazy," she said. "You know my husband. Don't worry, your secret is safe with us. Jo has the constitution of a Green Beret when it comes to keeping secrets, I don't want to get Ford mad at me and Eden thinks being a gossip is the next worse thing to being a hooker."

Eden gasped. "Mariah!"

E.Z. couldn't help laughing. Suddenly his fears seemed groundless. "No wonder Ford gave up his bachelorhood," he said.

Mariah gave Jo a sidelong glance. "Hey, he's good." Grinning, she turned back to E.Z. "Eden and I are big fans of yours, E.Z. I saw you last year in New Jersey. I've always wondered how you manage to perform with screaming teenyboppers ripping your clothes off."

The suggestion of a dimple cut into E.Z.'s stubbled jaw as he grinned at Mariah, those killer eyes doing as much damage as they could on a happily married woman. "You get used to it after a while," he said.

Jo bristled at her sister's blatant question, and wondered if the word *propriety* held any meaning for her. "My sister isn't always tactful," she said.

Mariah took the bait. "And *my* sister isn't always very tolerant of things she doesn't understand." Then, leaning closer to E.Z., she added, "My theory is that her love life is in shambles. She needs a distraction from this cause of hers, if you know what I mean."

Jo's teeth came together. "Mariah, don't you have some church function you need to attend?"

Eden stepped forward to intervene. "Come on, Mr. Ellis. Let me fix you a cup of coffee. It's all made and everything. The kids are all napping, and—"

"He was just leaving," Jo cut in, shooting Eden a searing look. She turned back to E.Z. "Weren't you?"

"Yes," he said pointedly, without accepting her lead. "I mistakenly thought I could talk some sense into Jo. I only came out to invite her back to my cabin. I thought we might get together, try a little harder to find some common ground. But she seems to have her mind made up. Is she always this stubborn?"

"Always," Mariah said without missing a beat.

Jo's daggerous eyes warned Mariah to keep quiet. "I appreciate your coming by," Jo bit out.

E.Z. shrugged. "Yeah. If you change your mind and decide that sometimes there might be more than one way to see things, just come on out. If your mind's so dead set, it certainly won't hurt anything to just listen. If we wind up in another fight, what the hell? I can use a good adrenaline workout now that I'm not performing."

Again Eden and Mariah shot her looks that warned her that they'd never forgive her if she turned him down. Consequently, she felt it her duty to do just that. "I'm sorry."

The three exchanged goodbyes and, quiet at last, the sisters watched E.Z. amble back to his rusty car. Jo busied herself gathering her things off the swing.

But no sooner had E.Z. cranked his horrendous engine, than Eden turned on her. "I can't believe you did that, Jo. What's happened to your sense of fairness? What's happened to your sense of justice?"

"Never mind that," Mariah piped up. "What's happened to your sense of sight? Did you *see* that man? He's even more gorgeous up close than he was in concert!"

Jo flung her hair over her shoulder and started for the door. "I don't want to talk about this."

Eden wouldn't be snuffed. "I never thought I'd see the day when Jo Calloway let herself be intimidated by a man!"

Jo swung around. "Intimidated! What are you talking about?"

"You know darn well that you'd go out there and give the man a chance if he weren't so darn good-looking and so nice!"

"What would it accomplish?" Jo demanded. "It would just give you two something more to ride me about."

"Leave her alone, Eden," Mariah said, suddenly, suspiciously, on Jo's side. "If he were to convince her she's wrong, she'd be horrible to live with. It would be too embarrassing for her. Let's just leave well enough alone."

"I am not wrong!"

"Of course you're not," Mariah said with a wry grin. She put her arm around Jo, and began ushering her inside. "Don't give it another thought."

Jo stopped cold and closed her eyes. "All right. If I promise to *consider* going to his cabin, will you two leave me alone? Will you be satisfied?"

Subdued delight danced in both their eyes. "I will," Mariah said with deliberate coyness. "How about you, Eden?"

"Not another word," Eden said, holding up her right hand in a mock vow.

With that Jo went into the house as her sisters collapsed into victorious laughter. "Honestly," Jo mumbled. "I'm glad my visit is giving you two so much entertainment. I don't know what you do when I'm not around."

Later that day, as she sat in the Chamber of Commerce meeting for which she'd been guest speaker, attempting to convince the town to ban concerts by the more offensive performers, Jo kept true to her word to her sisters. She considered taking E.Z. up on his offer to go over his lyrics with her... and considered... and considered.

Finally, resolving that she was not about to become a wimp at this stage in her life, she decided that she'd give him the chance. After all, what could it hurt? It might even give her more credibility in the hearing. She could say she'd had the meeting with him in hopes of gaining a better understanding of his lyrics, and that she still maintained that his music was harmful to teenagers.

It would also help her to quieten her sisters, and show them that E.Z. Ellis wasn't going to turn her to mush. Maybe he had been nice—even a bit charming—but he had an ulterior motive. He had much more to lose than she had, after all.

CHAPTER FOUR

"Pumpin' my life into you, babe
Pumpin', pumpin', right till the break of day..."

The E.Z. Ellis lyrics blared from Jo's car stereo on KTUX, and grumbling under her breath that the man's voice seemed to be everywhere, she turned the radio off.

Silence hit her suddenly, like an old friend who'd turned on her. Her thoughts seemed too loud...too vivid. What would he say when he saw her at his door tonight? Would he say he had known she'd come? Would he be surprised? Would his eyes look different in the twilight?

Hating the direction of her own thoughts, Jo turned the music back on and tried not to listen to the song. It was the noise she needed, she told herself. That was all. Just empty noise to keep out the empty thoughts.

She turned onto the small street that led to his portion of Lake Bisteneau and made her way through the trees skirting his plot of land, until a tiny log cabin set inconspicuously in a grove of pine trees came into sight, just yards away from the bank at the top of the lake. Jo pulled up to the front of the house and let her engine idle there for a moment. It was the wrong house, she decided quickly. Rock stars lived in gaudy mansions with bean-bag furniture and scores of superficial, drug-dazed yes-men surrounding them. Not matchbox log cabins out in the middle of the woods.

Turning off her engine, she looked down at the directions Ford had finally given her. Three streets past the fork in the road, a right, then left, then right....

This was the house with the little porch on front and a green barrel off to the side, just as Ford had described. This was where E.Z. lived. She looked around, saw that there were no lights inside the little house. And the VW was gone.

Since she'd come all that way, Jo left her car and went to the door anyway, on the off chance that he was home. Maybe the junkyard had come to tow away his car, she thought, and he was inside in the dark meditating... or whatever it was that rock musicians did in their spare time. She knocked, and after a moment accepted the fact that he wasn't home.

The breeze off the lake was growing cool, so she hugged her arms and pushed back the long curls blowing into her face. *Where could he be?* she wondered. If no one was supposed to know he was in town, he couldn't be seen just anywhere.

She walked back to her car and heard the wind's symphony across the lake, saw the early rays of the moon glistening on the water. It drew her, the way nature always did. She'd always been one to prefer the outdoors to the confinement of walls.

Idly she strolled around E.Z.'s house, and down to the lake. The smell of dawning spring had an intoxicating quality, and the scent lifted her spirits and softened them at the same time. It was difficult to be hostile when the night sky mated so poignantly with the lake, and moss-draped cypress trees grew up out of the water like offspring.

Was this how E.Z. spent his evenings here? she wondered. Did he sit out on the lake, inspired by nature's symphony? It wasn't difficult to picture him lounging on the bank with the cool wind whispering through his hair, his eyes soft and pensive as they gazed out over the water....

And some bawdy offensive lyrics in his mind.

The sudden thought sent Jo's spirits plummeting. Something about E.Z. Ellis disturbed her. It wasn't right. It wasn't natural.

Chafing her arms, she turned back to the house and saw the old rocking chair on the tiny patio, facing out toward the water, as if it was used often. A small hibachi sat on the floor against the house, its grill just barely large enough for one person. The sudden feeling of cold loneliness assaulted her, for the mood here was too similar to that of her own duplex in Baton Rouge. Instead of the rocking chair, she had a rickety old swing hanging from rafters on a rusty chain. And while she didn't use a hibachi, steamed vegetables for one were just as sad as barbecue for one.

Was E.Z. lonely, too? A man who could walk out his door and snap his fingers and have almost any girl he wanted? A man who'd had sellout concerts every night for seven months? A man who had to hide from the press like a fugitive hid from the police? Could a man like that be lonely?

Of course not, she told herself sternly. As usual she was romanticizing, trying to see some connection between herself and him, the way she often did with attractive men. But most of the time romanticizing only brought her disappointment. Men were a different breed, she'd decided long ago. They were never lonely, for they always found the kind of superficial gratification they wanted, if only they looked hard enough. She was certain that E.Z. Ellis was the rule, rather than the exception. He was a model by which other men measured their lives.

Tonight was the perfect example. He was probably out with some groupie, soaking up crude inspiration, rather than the quiet kind that the lake offered her. He was probably at some wild party...some...some orgy.

As if she knew her speculations to be true, Jo's anger renewed itself. Suddenly, as if she wouldn't grant him another thought when he was so busy being hedonistic, she marched back to her car and started the motor.

Why was she wasting her time, she asked herself, on a man interested only in "easy" bucks and "easy" women? It wasn't the kind of life-style that interested her. Hers was a life with a direction, with purposeful fulfillment. E.Z. Ellis could learn a great deal from her devotion to her causes, she thought. And she was just the one to teach him those lessons.

THERE WERE MORE PEOPLE here than there had been last week, E.Z. thought as he pulled the old Volkswagen onto the mud-slick stretch of land surrounding Sullivan's Furniture Manufacturing building. He looked around the grounds, saw children he hadn't seen before, new men with despair etching scars on their leathery faces, women with no hope in their lusterless eyes. It would be too crowded inside, and they'd have to rearrange things yet again. They'd need more pup tents and blankets. Thank God it wasn't raining.

He got out of his car, slung his twenty-year-old acoustic guitar over his back and sauntered up toward the building. The roaring, reverberating noise inside assaulted him at once, but he was growing used to it. It wasn't ideal, but it was better than nothing, he told himself. And nothing was what most of these people had had before.

"Hey, Ellis," a woman with a three-year-old on her hip called from a cot just inside the door. "Where you been?"

E.Z. stopped and stooped down beside her blankets, reached out his hands for the boy. The child came readily. "You know. Around," he said. "Job huntin'. No luck."

The woman—Hope was her name, as ironic as that seemed—took advantage of her free hands and bent to straighten her blankets. A small baby slept in the center of one. "Paul says if he doesn't find anything today, we're leaving tomorrow. East, he says. There's work over there."

E.Z. pressed a kiss on the little boy's nose and set him down on the blanket beside his mother. "What about bus money? Food? Where will you stay when you get there?"

Hope shrugged and nodded to the card table set up in the corner of the huge, hollowed-out room, where two men sat with forms and a checkbook for attending to specific, immediate needs of the homeless. "The Church said they'd give us the money for food and bus fare. We'll find a place to stay. If we go far enough east, we can sleep on the beach."

E.Z. looked toward the table, saw the line of helpless people waiting to talk to the representatives of what was known only as "The Church." No one knew *which* church, and no one even cared what denomination it was. He wanted it that way. "You know, I think they'd probably give you money for a few nights in a hotel if you wanted. It's not summer yet. The beaches are cold this time of year. And the shelters in the big cities…well, you don't want to take your kids there."

"We'll manage," Hope said. "We'll be fine."

E.Z. got to his feet, his face pale as he looked down at the three-month-old lying stomach down on the blanket, and thought about the baby sleeping in the damp April air. It made him want to blow his cover, offer them whatever he had. But they were proud people, their values nurtured with as much patience as they had nurtured their farm for years . . . until they'd lost it.

The smell of beef stew came from the break room that had once served the needs of the two thousand people who'd worked in this factory before it closed down. He headed toward it, stepping over sleeping children on mats and listless parents guarding the only territory they had in the world. A mother in a corner tried to change clothes under a blanket, since the privacy of the bathroom took over twenty minutes standing in line to obtain. The lack of privacy robbed the dignity of these people more than anything, E.Z. thought. Maybe he should see about some standing room partitions to separate families. But that privacy could prove to be a danger in itself. Evil people often preyed on those down in their luck, but that wasn't likely to happen when there were no hiding places.

He made his way to the food room, answering occasional lukewarm greetings as he went. They knew him as Ellis, those who knew him at all, and none recognized him as the rock star whose net worth was somewhere in the eight-figure range. To them he was just as poor, just as broken, just as homeless as they were. And when he was here among them, he wasn't so sure that wasn't the case.

The break room was packed with wall-to-wall people standing in line to get their bowls of stew. E.Z. knew it wouldn't be the best stew they'd ever had. The food had all been donated in cans by local civic groups and served by volunteers. But it filled empty stomachs for a time. He stepped into the hot room, glanced around at the mothers trying to keep their children corralled, the men with trembling hands waiting patiently for their sustenance. The sound of anxious voices held fast at a fever level, adding to the anxiety and stress of those sentenced by circumstances to stay here.

Above the din, E.Z. heard the sound of a small child screaming loudly enough to break his heart. He looked around and saw a baby no more than two years old, clutched in the arms of a girl of around ten. The older girl was thin and pale, and wore the ghostlike pallor of someone who'd learned to accept that life wouldn't get any better. The child struggled to hold the baby, who flailed and thrashed as if she felt her misery straight through to her tiny bones. E.Z. slid his guitar around to hang from his back and stooped down, at eye level with the girl on the floor.

"Hi," he said over the child's sobs. "I haven't seen you before. Are you new here?"

The girl, sweating as a result of her fight, wrapped her arms tighter around the thrashing, angry baby. "We came in today. My dad, he's in line getting food."

E.Z. touched the baby's head gently, noted the dirt on her cheeks, broken by wet streaks of tears. "Is she your little sister?"

"Cousin," the girl said. "Her mom died. My dad had to bring her with us."

Despite the horror stories he heard every time he came here, E.Z. was never prepared for the fresh fissures that opened his heart each time he heard of another injustice to an innocent child. He glanced to the line she indicated and saw a thin man with six other children behind him. He had just reached the food table, and was trying to explain over the noise that there were two more not in line. But the policy was that each person was entitled only to one bowl at a time, and each person had to be there to claim it. Otherwise, they reasoned, anyone could eat as much as he wanted, and there wouldn't be enough for everyone.

Seeing the distress on the man's face, E.Z. turned to the older girl. "Let me hold her so you can go up and get your bowl," he offered.

"She'll scream," the girl warned him. "All she does is scream."

E.Z. grinned. "I'm used to screaming girls," he said, though he knew she'd never understand the subtlety. "I can handle her. Go get your food."

He reached out for the baby, and the girl thrust her eagerly into his arms. "Her name's Carmen," she said, then scrambled away to where her father argued with the volunteers.

In the fashion E.Z. had seen so many of the mothers here quiet their children, he crushed Carmen against his chest as tightly as he could. In moments her sobbing hushed, and she laid her head against his shoulder. He felt the tension ease out of her small body.

The girl's father turned his head around, looking suddenly fearful when he saw his daughter beside him. He cast suspicious eyes on E.Z. and almost abandoned the long-awaited place at the table.

"It's okay," E.Z. mouthed to him, knowing the man couldn't hear him through the noise. "I'll wait here."

Reluctantly the man nodded, then turned back to the table to make sure that each of the children with him was fed.

The feel of the child in his arms gave E.Z. a greater sensation of warmth than all the lights they used to illuminate the stage at his concerts. Carmen's surrender to him made his heart hurt, and he felt his eyes burning with a mist he hadn't experienced many times in his life. He wanted to get her out of this place, put her down in a soft bed with a warm comforter and lull her to sleep with one of his slow songs, one that even Jo Calloway couldn't balk at. But sometimes, as he'd learned long ago, a man couldn't do what he wanted. Sometimes he couldn't even do what was right. He could only make strides toward that end, never seeing a real impact, and wondering all the while if he was helping at all.

Tonight he felt he was.

He followed the family out of the break room and back into the warehouse, to their little patch in the center of the room where they'd been assigned blankets and cots to sleep on. When the children were settled with their food bowls, the man turned to E.Z.

"I appreciate your help with Carmen. She's been upset ever since we came here."

Without really lifting his right arm from Carmen's back, E.Z. awkwardly extended his hand. "My name's Ellis," he said.

The man shook. His hand was rough, callused, work seasoned, a testament to the hard work he was accustomed to. "Call me Juarez," he said. "Do you want me to take her?"

"No," E.Z. said, unwilling to give the child up yet. "Go ahead and eat. I'll just sit down here and hold her."

Juarez straightened him a patch of blanket to sit on and helped E.Z. with his guitar as he sat down. "Carmen ate earlier," he said. "A woman gave her half a bowlful. Her child had had some left over, and Carmen was too hungry to wait."

The little girl hiccuped against E.Z.'s shirt, an aftershock of the sobs. "Are you here alone with these kids?" he asked.

Juarez nodded glumly. "I lost my wife last year and then the farm I worked on in Texas closed down, so I lost my job. I heard there might be work here, so I came." He glanced around at the quiet children, eating their stew as if it was the first meal they'd had all day. "These are all my children. Carmen was my sister's."

Again, E.Z.'s heart broke at the thought of the child losing her mother and being thrust into a family with so many members that she was lost in the shuffle. "How long has her mother been dead?"

Juarez reached across the blanket to wipe his son's nose. "She died last month. Pneumonia. She made me promise not to let the state take the baby."

E.Z. wondered if the child wouldn't have been better off. He shifted her to his other shoulder, saw that her face was still wet and dirt streaked, and her nose was running. He looked around for a napkin, found one wadded on the floor beside one of the bowls, and wiped her nose. She looked up at him and hiccuped a ghost of a sob again. Her eyes were round and as black as onyx, as trusting as those of a cherub fallen from heaven. His heart melted like lava.

"Hi," he whispered.

The child didn't answer, so he tried again.

"Sleepy? You want to lie down?"

In answer she buried her little face in his shoulder and tightened her hold around his neck.

E.Z. swallowed the emotion obstructing his throat and closed his eyes. He tilted his head so that his rough-stubbled jaw was against her hair. It was funny, he thought, that in all his life he'd somehow missed feeling quite like this.

It hadn't occurred to him before that the place needed rocking chairs...it would be such a little thing, but would go so far toward comforting these poor misplaced, often uprooted children. He'd have to remember to see about it. Swaying in a slow, gentle rhythm, he pressed a soft kiss against Carmen's hair and began humming one of his favorite old blues songs, slow and soft, until her head rolled against his neck. He sang each verse for her ears only, slowly, patiently, and even after he realized he'd lulled her to sleep, he was reluctant to let her go.

If only they could turn out these damn lights, he thought, suddenly angry with his surroundings, when before he'd always seen the place as a godsend to desperate people. A child shouldn't have to sleep in a place lit up like a parking lot, he thought. And she should be able to rely on quiet. But the noise continued, too many voices in too small a place. And the lights had to stay on for security reasons.

When the children had finished eating and the bowls were returned to the break room, E.Z. finally laid the baby down. She squirmed restlessly, on the verge of waking up, and he looked over at Juarez, busy putting the others to bed with an efficiency that left him cold. There was no time for comforting one child when there were seven others. There was no time for fairy tales when the man had so little to believe in.

E.Z. got his guitar, began to strum a few soft chords and saw that Carmen instantly relaxed again. One of the new songs that he'd been working on took shape, and he could feel the noise level decreasing slightly, as others began to listen. He sang along with the melody...the sad, slow lyrics reflecting what everyone here harbored in his heart but hadn't the strength to articulate. And although no one was impressed by the musical skill in the simple strumming, or the voice that came out almost whispered and undressed, they listened with a hunger for peace that E.Z. understood.

And for a while he was able to fill that hunger

JO SAT UP LATE that night, watching television in a dark living room, the sound turned down to a barely audible level to keep from waking Eden. "Late Night Videos" was on, complete with lewd rock stars dancing and singing across the screen in a montage of images intended to pull out the meanings of the songs they sang. Jo thought some of them should be banned from the air.

E.Z. Ellis's video didn't seem to be one of them, however. His "Pristine Girl" was quite different than Jo would have expected. He didn't even appear in it, except as a ghostlike figure wandering through rough slums, where drug dealers hung out on street corners among the young girls who sold themselves for a place to sleep. The "pristine girl" in the video was no more than a miserable young waif who seemed to have no choices left. Funny that Jo had thought the song portrayed prostitution as a glamorous occupation, and suicide as something honorable. The video gave the song a whole new meaning, and the realization disturbed her. It was so much easier to document mere words.

She had no choice but to get more familiar with what E.Z. thought the songs meant, Jo told herself. Otherwise she just might wind up looking foolish in front of the Commerce Committee. Maybe tomorrow she'd pay him another visit,

if he wasn't too hung over from whatever he was doing tonight, or too tired from whomever he was with.

The idea of some adoring groupie ripping his clothes off
made her angry all over again, though she didn't know why.
What did she care who he spent his time with? It had nothing to do with her. A man like E.Z. Ellis lived by his own
rules. She was just thankful that she didn't have to live by
them, too.

LATER THAT NIGHT, when the noise level at Sullivan's had
quieted sufficiently to enable many of the people there to
sleep, E.Z. slung his guitar on his back again and went outside, where rows of old, patched pup tents were set up as
sleeping quarters for the men without families and couples
without children. Since there were few empty ones and still
too many people wandering around the grounds, E.Z. decided not to take one. Instead, he went to the bashed-in
trunk of his Volkswagen, pulled out a tattered sleeping bag
and spread it out on the ground.

The air smelled of smoke, for some of the men had started
a fire in a garbage drum a few yards away. Still, the cold
wind blew across their skin like age.

Headlights illuminated the front gates of Sullivan's, and
E.Z. looked up. No doubt it was some new family, desperate for a place to sleep, he thought. He peered through the
fence and saw a small silhouette against the headlights. The
car started to pull away.

Chris! he thought, a jolt of hope rising inside him. The
kid he'd met in the diner. E.Z. left his sleeping bag and
stepped forward, watching the shadow anxiously.

The darkness swallowed the boy's form once again, but
as he came closer, E.Z. saw that he'd been right. He watched
the teenager walk through the stragglers near the gate, saw
him stiffen his shoulders in a defensive gesture and set his

chin in a way that said he knew exactly where he was headed.

"Hey, Chris," he called as the boy passed, and Chris swung around as if he'd been ambushed. "Glad you came."

Chris kept his distance, assessing E.Z. with suspicious eyes. "Yeah . . . my friends weren't home . . . they—"

"No problem," E.Z. cut in, sparing him the prideful lie. "There's stew inside if you're hungry."

Chris's hand went into his pocket, as if by touch he could assess his wealth. "Naw, I'm not hungry."

"It's free," E.Z. coaxed. "Only requirement is an empty stomach."

Chris glanced uneasily toward the building, then back at E.Z., still maintaining his distance. "You comin'?"

E.Z. recognized the question as a request. The boy was nervous about going in alone. He couldn't blame him.

"Yeah," E.Z. said. "I haven't eaten yet, either."

Then, rolling up his bag and grabbing his guitar, he led Chris in. They brought their bowls outside and ate on wooden crates without speaking. Finally, when Chris's bowl was polished, he looked up at E.Z. "You sleep here?" he asked.

E.Z. nodded. "We have pup tents, but sometimes I just sleep out under the stars. The men have to sleep outside to make room for the children, unless they're solely responsible for them."

Chris glanced around. Suddenly he looked much younger than E.Z. had first imagined. He looked like a little boy, lost in a world he barely understood. E.Z. wondered what had driven him from his home.

"That tent over there looks empty," E.Z. said, pointing to one strung up nearby. "If you don't mind, I'll just stretch my bag out beside it."

Chris feigned disinterest. "I don't mind."

"They'll have breakfast at seven. Most of the men start job hunting after that."

Chris nodded. "Yeah, me, too."

He followed the pride-filled boy to the tent and watched him settle in as if he hadn't had a place to lay his head in days. E.Z. rolled out his sleeping bag in front of the tent, sat on it and began strumming his guitar.

Chris left the tent flap open and listened, his eyes full of a thousand haunted thoughts. The boy's expression and the doleful sounds of the guitar brought back memories of a youth too soon discarded. In those days—when E.Z. had been wandering like Chris—his guitar had been his best friend. It had been there for him at night and again in the mornings, the only constant in his life. It had earned him money and a place to stay when he needed one. It had kept him from being bitter. Eventually it had even brought him fame.

It wasn't long before Chris, much more alone than E.Z. had ever been because he *didn't* have a friend, fell into a deep sleep, much like Carmen had done earlier. Finally E.Z. set down his guitar and lay down, exhausted by the intimate knowledge of the misery around him.

He zipped up the sleeping bag and crossed his arms behind his head. It was cold, but the stars were clear and bright. One would never know from looking at the uncluttered beauty of the heavens that so much hell existed on earth. But these people around him knew, he thought, and little Carmen knew. And Chris knew.

But there were too many people out there who didn't know—people more concerned about animals and politics and...censorship. His thoughts suddenly turned to Jo Calloway, swinging gently in that swing yesterday, her face full of peace, her hair floating in the breeze. When he'd disturbed her, she'd puffed up with defiance and self-righteousness. But hell, he couldn't really hold it against her much. She was like a sheltered child, one who'd never had the chance to learn such things as this existed. If she knew the same things he did, she'd probably be just as angry as he was. She just didn't understand that there were things more important than picking on a bunch of rock musicians because she didn't like what they sang.

He hadn't helped matters much, E.Z. thought with a smile. That bull he'd given her about earning his name had only reinforced her image of him. He chuckled lightly and thought how disappointed she would be to learn that the nickname "Easy" and the initials E.Z. were no studio gimmick, that they had evolved from the initials of his real name, Ezekiel Zechariah. If her mother had named *her* that, he was quite sure she'd have opted for the initials, as well. The nickname "Easy" had more to do with his being from New Orleans—the Big Easy—than with his being a pushover with women.

But Jo Calloway would never have believed that.

He closed his eyes and thought that maybe it was his duty to teach her that there was more than one side to things. Maybe she needed a little less sheltering and a little more exposure to the different facets of life. Maybe she needed a little help getting her priorities straight.

It would be worth the effort, he thought, because he needed someone like Jo Calloway on his side.

CHAPTER FIVE

JO HAD JUST PULLED into E.Z.'s driveway the next morning when his old VW sputtered in behind her, bucking and coughing and generally looking as worn-out as its driver.

She got out of her car, crossed her arms and waited like a sentinel guarding her own frailties. She watched him pull his car to a stop and get out, the door creaking as if it pained it to move on its hinges. He closed it carefully and looked at her over the roof. He looked as though he'd been on a weekend drunk, but somehow, even with his jaw covered in thick stubble and his hair disheveled and unbrushed, he still wore his charisma like a comfortable old jacket.

He took off his glasses, chewed on one arm of the frames.

"You're the last person I expected to see here this morning," he said in a lazy, gravelly voice.

"Sometimes I surprise even myself," she said, sliding her hands into the pockets of her khaki skirt. "My sisters convinced me I should come."

E.Z. unlocked the front door and gestured for her to go inside.

Jo stepped into the cabin, built of bare, varnished wood, and glanced around at the simple decor. Again, she was surprised. Except for the musical equipment, there were only a few chairs, a straw love seat and a table. Through two doors she saw other rooms—a tiny kitchen, and a bedroom furnished with nothing more than a bed and table in the center of the floor. The room was cluttered, unkempt, as if he'd had better things to do than keep it picked up for company.

"I was here last night," she said, feeling awkward. "But you weren't."

E.Z. nodded and tousled his hair even more. "I went out."

A tiny smile played on her lips. "I gathered that," she said, amused at the wrinkled condition of his clothes and the way he moved toward the door as if his muscles rebelled. "You know, you don't look so good."

He smiled weakly at her bluntness. "Nothing a cup of coffee and a shower won't fix."

Jo fingered the pearls at her throat. "I don't know. Those all-nighters can catch up with you after a while."

He grinned and gave her a visual up-and-down sweep as if considering her innocence. Suddenly, Jo felt that her blouse was cut too low and that her legs beneath her skirt were too bare. "And what do you know about all-nighters?" he asked.

Her smile was meant to be disarming. "Only what I've read, Mr. Ellis."

"Well, then," he drawled, "you've led a sheltered life. You know, there's something to be said for decadent living."

His comment sounded too much like an invitation into E.Z.'s School of Decadence, and Jo wasn't in the mood for a crash course. "There's also something to be said for ordered living. I like to know where I'm going to wake up from day to day."

"Now, there's an original idea," he said sardonically. He went into the kitchen, and she watched through the door while he filled the coffee maker. "But you know us reckless rock stars. Always living on the edge."

Something about his tone told her he was still being sarcastic, but she couldn't imagine that his remarks didn't bear some truth. He reached for a box of cereal he kept in the cabinet over his head—not exactly the breakfast she would have expected. "Have you eaten?" he asked.

"Yes," she said. "But you go ahead."

"I will." He grabbed a carton of milk from the refrigerator. "I don't like to miss breakfast. It's where I get my daily recommended allowance of moral fiber."

Jo smiled down at the floor. "I guess you'd need it after the night, huh?"

"You bet."

His easy agreement made something inside Jo tighten. Somewhere deep down she wanted him to refute her ideas about how he'd spent his evening. She wanted him to say he was off somewhere with his car broken down and couldn't get home, or that he'd been nursing a sick friend... something endearing that would justify her liking him. But she knew that wasn't the case. "What was her name?" she ventured, maintaining her amused smile, though she didn't find it all that funny. "Or did you ask?"

His smirk was downright audacious. He hiked an eyebrow and winked. "Oh, I asked. Her name was Carmen, and she's the sweetest little thing it's been my pleasure to know in a long time."

Struggling to hold on to her smile, Jo went to the coffeepot. *Damn him*, she thought. He could have at least had the grace to deny her accusation, or to pretend that he was embarrassed by it. Instead, it was almost as if he enjoyed goading her!

She poured the coffee into both cups he'd gotten out and handed him one. The close quarters of the tiny kitchen suddenly struck her, and she realized that this was as near to him as she'd been. She looked up at him as they sipped from the steaming brew, saw that his eyes were still dancing with amusement. Was he laughing at her? She honestly wasn't sure.

Deciding she wasn't doing a very good job of arming herself against him, Jo backed out of the kitchen in favor of the more spacious living room. He followed her, carrying his bowl of cereal in one hand and his coffee cup in the other. He set them down on the small round table in the corner and started to eat. She watched as he did, berating herself for noting the drop of milk on his bottom lip and the way his tongue skimmed over it. Was his sensuality intentional, she wondered. Did he know how much power it held? "So, what brings you here?" he asked. "Last night you said coming over would be a waste of time."

Jo picked up a cushion off his love seat, fluffed it absently to keep her hands busy. "I reconsidered," she said. "I do that sometimes."

The possibility seemed to delight him. "Then you *are* human?"

She laughed lightly. "Only when I have no choice. My sisters have gotten pretty good at reminding me when that is."

Jo sat down on the love seat near the table, and watched him as he ate. Something about the way he chewed seemed as provocative as the beat of his music. She forced her eyes back to the pillow in her lap.

"Truth is," she went on, "I saw one of your videos on television last night. The one for 'Pristine Girl.' It made me think that maybe there *was* more than one way of looking at your songs. I like to think I'm a fair person, Mr. Ellis. And since you asked me to come and give you a shot at explaining your music, here I am." She dropped the pillow and set her eyes fully on him, offering him a teasing smile. "But, if you aren't feeling up to it after being out all night, maybe we could get together another time."

"And miss hearing your secret fantasies?" he asked, setting down his spoon and leaning toward her, those fascinatingly pastel eyes cutting through her defenses. "You've got to be kidding. I wouldn't miss this for the world. It isn't every day that I get to hear what goes through the minds of women like you when they hear my music. It might be downright entertaining."

Jo refused to let his barbs intimidate her this time. "I think I can assure you that what goes through my mind isn't nearly as entertaining as what goes through the minds of the frenzied teenagers you manipulate in your concerts. I've heard that you have quite an interesting collection of lingerie."

"Bras, mostly," he clarified without batting an eye. "Occasionally a pair of panties."

"Well, now. There's something to be proud of. And you accuse *me* of having secret fantasies."

He laughed aloud and wiped his mouth with a napkin. "There's nothing secret about mine. According to you I've laid my soul out on a piece of wax to corrupt and brainwash adolescent minds. I have no secrets."

He left the bowl and empty coffee cup on the table and came to sit next to her on the love seat. Her instinct was to move away, but Jo would have walked barefoot across hot coals to keep him from knowing she was unnerved by his nearness.

"So," he said, propping his arm behind her. "Why don't you pick the song that offends you the most, and we'll talk about the lyrics?"

"All right," she said quickly. "Let's start with the one that has little to do with sex, which you seem to think this is all about. It's 'Shadow Child.'"

As if she'd found just the right weapon to change his mood from flip to serious, he straightened in his seat. His face suddenly grew tense.

"Fine," he said. "I'd just as soon start with the one that gets misinterpreted the most."

"Misinterpreted?" she asked, astounded. "There is a cult in south Louisiana that considers this their anthem! How can you say it's just a mistake?"

"Because of the way I wrote it!" He sprang off the couch, as if suddenly the closeness was uncomfortable to him, and glared at her from across the room. "I know what it means!"

"But don't you understand, that it doesn't matter what it means to you? All that matters is how your fans interpret it. When it winds up being a catalyst for all the things that give parents nightmares, it's time to admit that maybe you've gone too far."

Under the stubble shadowing his jaw, she could see the heat of anger reddening his skin. "That song is about a kid who's left home and is trying to be a man. It's about what's going on in *his* head. If you listen to it, really listen to it, you'll hear the desperation, the anger, the fear in the words."

"But when *they* listen to it, they hear glamour and freedom and rebellion," she replied. "It says, 'Don't have to take it anymore, not when there's somewhere to go, night lights, concrete heights, no ties, freedom flies . . .' And then in the chorus, it repeats over and over, 'Getting out while the blade's still sharp . . .' It's glamorizing suicide!"

"Suicide! Where in hell did you come up with that?" he shouted.

"The blade. What else could it mean?"

E.Z. rubbed a rough hand over his face and cast his amazed eyes on the ceiling. When he brought his focus back to her, he held his hands up as if they could help to illustrate his point. "The way I write . . . I pick a character, someone I've met . . . and I tell a story about them. The kid in that song is running from an abusive home. The blade isn't something he's running *to*, but what he's running *from*.'

Jo refused to be made to feel stupid. "That's an interesting rationale, Mr. Ellis, but it doesn't work. If I've interpreted it the way I have, so have thousands of others. And you must see how these kids are using it."

"Look, some people could interpret 'Rock-A-Bye Baby' as a violent song about a baby falling out of a tree! But censoring the song isn't going to end the madness. Kids don't need a song to tell them what to do. They make their own choices." He went to his synthesizer, stared at the keys as if they were his accomplices in a crime he didn't even commit. Then he turned back to her. "And by the way, if you listen to the last verse of that song, you'll hear that everything else is qualified. The kid learns that being a man isn't wandering the streets alone, and being free isn't having no one to answer to. The song has a moral, and you'd see it if you opened your mind."

Jo shook her head, unwilling to let his argument sway her. "It doesn't matter whether or not you think you have a moral in the song. The teenaged girl who lived next door to me didn't hear one, and neither did her friends...."

"You know what I've noticed about you?" he cut in, stopping her speech mid-sentence. "You're always talking about your next door neighbor or the kid up the street or your sisters. Don't you have a life of your own?"

Jo stood up, all fire and fury. "They're *examples!* This has nothing to do with my life, which is quite full, thank you very much. We're talking about the kids affected by your music."

"Well, you're going to have to find something stronger than that song if you want to nail me," he shouted.

Jo took a deep breath to reign in her temper, and forced her voice back to a reasonable volume, directly contrasting his. It always behooved her, she'd found, to appear as the only rational one in the room. "All right," she said, sitting back down. "Let's talk about the song, 'Shut the Door.' Are you telling me that it has a moral, too? That it's more dimensional than a man telling a woman to 'strip down to bare skin' and suggesting the most lewd and disgusting things I've ever heard?''

E.Z. gaped at her for a moment, a disbelieving sparkle in his eyes, and finally he threw his head back and belted out a laugh that would have shaken the cabin had it not been firmly planted on the ground. "You're kidding, right? You don't really think that song is about sex!''

"*Of course* it's about sex," she cried. "What else could it be?''

"Politics," he returned. "That song is about the Iran-Contra scheme. It didn't have one thing to do with sex.''

Jo felt exasperated. She didn't like being played with. "I'm not crazy. That song is about two lovers having some sort of forbidden affair!''

"Or two countries involved in a covert operation!'' He began laughing again and came toward her, delighting in her ire. He braced his arms on the love seat and leaned over her, his face inches from hers. His breath tickled her lips, and she fought the urge to look away. "Oh, man," he said with an infuriating grin. "I'm gonna have to get to know you better if that's the way you think.''

She ducked out from under him and came to her feet. Clamping her teeth together, she tossed her hair back over her shoulder and planted her hands on her hips. No one had ever had the power to make her feel so... foolish.

"All right," she shouted, desperate to get off the subject of the song she'd grossly misinterpreted. "Explain the song 'Pumpin'.... And please don't insult my intelligence by telling me you wrote it about the heat pump in your mansion.''

E.Z. crossed his arms and offered the most irreverent grin she'd ever seen. "Nope. That song means exactly what you think it does. But I'd be fascinated to hear your exact impressions. Maybe you've seen something there that even I didn't mean to put in. You seem to have a gift for that.''

Jo seethed with indignation and suddenly realized that the trip out here had been futile. There was no talking to him. "I must be crazy," she said. "I thought we could discuss this like two adults."

"Two consenting adults," he said, on the verge of laughter. "That's what we're doing, isn't it?"

"No, that isn't what we're doing," she said. "And since I can see that we're wasting time, I think I'll just leave."

She went to the door and pulled it open. "It's been interesting."

The remark sent him over the edge and into full-fledged laughter. "Where are you going?" he asked. "I didn't mean to scare you off."

The wind whipped her hair into her face, and she swatted it away. Jo was almost to her car when he reached her, and he grabbed her arm. "Come on," he said, still chuckling. "Don't go away mad."

She felt the heat of her wrath mottling her cheeks. "I'm not mad. I'm frustrated."

"You're telling me," he said.

Jerking herself out of his grasp, Jo opened her car door, but E.Z. pushed it closed before she could slip inside. "Come on, I'm sorry. I just can't resist. You set yourself up for it, you know."

Realizing he wasn't going to let her leave, she stalked toward the lake, determined to put some distance between them. E.Z. followed on her heels.

"*You're* the one setting yourself up!" she railed. "I can't wait to see how you turn all the questions of the Commerce Committee around the way you've done with me. Insult *them* and see where it gets you!"

She reached the edge of the lake and picked up a rock, then launched it across the water. It landed with a mild, anticlimactic splash.

"Hey, I wasn't insulting you. I was just trying to lighten you up a little. You're so tense." His amused apology was almost endearing . . . almost, but not quite.

"I am not tense!" Jo gathered a palmful of rocks and threw another one into the water.

He took her shoulders from behind and squeezed lightly with strong, confident hands. "Yes you are. Your muscles are as hard as those rocks that you'd like to be throwing at me."

He began a slow, deep massage, one that felt a little better than she dared acknowledge, even to herself. "I don't need a massage," she said.

"Just be still," he told her. "I'm good at this."

"I'll just bet you are." She stared over the water, trying to resist the underpull of his deep massage, trying to hold on to the anger slipping away from her like the tension in her shoulders. "But I'm not really interested in finding out how good."

She moved away, and E.Z. dropped his hands to his sides. "You might have noticed that I'm not one of those groupies who swoon at your feet," she said.

His lascivious grin grew broader. "Yeah, I had noticed that you're still wearing your panties and bra."

As much as she wanted to be enraged by the comment, Jo's sober expression began to change. She turned away when she realized she couldn't stop the laughter welling up inside her throat, ready to spill out. But he didn't miss it. He turned her around and watched with pleasure as she covered her face and giggled. "You're incorrigible," she said when she could speak again.

"And you're a real tough guy," he said, a softer smile on his face now. "Face it, Red. Your cover's blown. I've seen you laugh."

She looked up at him, her eyes glossy with mirth, and wondered how she'd get her indignation back now. He was right. Her cover was blown. And without her anger, she didn't know how to relate to him at all. "I have to go," she said.

E.Z. caught her hand and stopped her. "Don't." She turned back to him, saw that the laughter in his eyes had faded. He was all sincerity now. "I like the company," he said. "It gets too quiet out here sometimes."

Her face burned again, this time with awareness rather than anger or embarrassment. Her heartbeat accelerated. "I thought that was what you wanted. Quiet."

He lifted a strand of her hair, wrapping it around his finger. "I wanted peace," he said. "Not necessarily quiet."

She offered a flip laugh, but her words were dead serious. "Peace isn't one of my strong points."

"And anger isn't one of mine," he said. "Maybe we should get together, swap traits now and then. I'm really not such a bad guy. The press hardly ever has anything too condemning to say about me, unless they're repeating something *you* said."

"The press rarely has anything to say about you at all," she said, pulling the silken strand of hair away from his fingers. Undaunted, he touched the strand of pearls at her throat. She swallowed then, trying not to let him know his touch moved her, and kept talking. "Apparently the star refuses to be interviewed."

"You got that right," he said, distracted by the luster of her pearls and the pale column of her neck. "My life is private. It's none of the public's business."

"Or mine?" she asked, feeling that the comment had been directed at her.

He touched the hollow of her throat beneath the necklace. Again her throat convulsed.

E.Z. gazed down at her, his eyes smoky with intention. He was much too close. He smelled of wind and morning, and his breath was a seduction against her mouth. "I'll let you know," he whispered.

His smile caught fire in her heart, smoldered up into her head, making her a little dizzy. She was falling under his spell, falling just as Mariah had warned her. But even when his face began its descent to hers...even when he wet his lips with sultry purpose...when his eyes softened to the effervescence of ocean waves...she couldn't turn away.

Their lips came together with the power of two separate flames that grow and flourish when united. The union was tentative, and yet it had the strength to singe her heart in a way that was foreign to her. His tongue slipped through her lips, swirled against hers, gently, sweetly. And she wondered if all the star-struck groupies he'd kissed had been affected just as profoundly. The thought brought her to her senses, and she broke the kiss and backed quickly away. E.Z. dropped his hands and watched her passively, a glint in his eyes.

"This isn't right." Her voice broke. "I'm not interested in you. Not at all."

His smile was too perceptive. "Coulda fooled me."

Jo folded her arms over her stomach and started backing toward her car. "Look, I know what you're up to, and it won't work. No amount of E.Z. Ellis charm is going to make me back down from my fight. You're not even my type."

He moved toward her, the calmness in his eyes flustering her even more. "What type am I?"

"You're more my sister Mariah's type."

"The one married to the *preacher*?" he asked, laughing. "You've got to be kidding. I'm *her* type?"

Jo kept backing toward the car. "Well, a few months ago you would have been. But she came to her senses and stopped hanging around with motorcycle bums and disreputable hooligans."

"Like me," he suggested, trying to make the picture more clear. He laughed again, restoring her rage.

"Yes, like you. I, on the other hand, am not the least bit interested in a man whose every vulgar thought is recorded for posterity, heaven help them."

"Posterity?"

"Yes," she said. She tripped over a tree root, caught herself and continued to back away. "So, I'm going home now. And I won't be back. I think we've about covered everything we need to cover."

E.Z. seemed genuinely amused by her stammering. As if to fluster her further, he added, "All that's left now is the *un*covering. Sure you have to rush off?"

At that Jo spun around, turning her back to him, and marched to her car. With one last look over her shoulder and a final flick of her hair, she slammed the car door and skidded out of the drive.

As she drove out of sight, her last view from her rear-view mirror was of E.Z. Ellis waving goodbye and smiling so smugly that, for a moment, she considered doing a power spin and running him down.

FOR THE REST of the day Jo felt as if she were balanced on a log about to roll and send her reeling into the water at any moment. It was all she could do to hang on.

The only saving grace of the day was the fact that Tess, Jo's sister who lived in Dallas, made a surprise appearance. They spent the afternoon making cookies and *not* talking about Tess's divorce. It was silently understood among the four sisters that Tess would bare her soul when she was ready and not a moment before.

Jo avoided the subject of E.Z. Ellis as much as she could, and since Mariah was only in and out for short stretches of time, it proved easier than she expected. But that night, when Eden had gone to bed and Tess was in the room she had once shared with Mariah, Jo wandered out to the hammock in the backyard near the arbor, climbed inside it and lay back looking at the stars.

He kissed me. For the first time since that morning, Jo allowed herself to acknowledge it. E.Z. Ellis had kissed her, and she couldn't remember when a kiss had affected her so deeply. In spite of the fact that she hadn't mentioned his name today, or that she'd kept her mind cluttered with other things, there had been many times when her heart had jolted as if the kiss were happening all over again at that very moment.

What was the matter with her? She'd been kissed before. It wasn't even her first brush with celebrity. She had once dated a U.S. senator who many said would some day be president. *He* had been her type...not like E.Z. Ellis, disreputable rock and roller. Trouble was, the senator had bored her to death.

The wind was cool as it swept off the creek and through the woven pattern of the hammock. The sky was clear, without a cloud, and every star shone vividly. She counted a group, assigned it to a constellation and wondered if heaven were as beautiful. Could her mother see those stars tonight? Could her father?

Her mind strayed back to E.Z. Ellis, and an uncomfortable question presented itself. What would her mother have thought of him? Would she have shaken her head and clicked her tongue, as Jo had seen other mothers do in her life when their daughters got involved with the wrong men? Or would Grace Calloway have taken the liberal view, and told Jo to follow her heart? The tragedy was that Jo hadn't a clue how her mother would have reacted, because she'd never gotten the chance to really know her. The injustice of that fact was sometimes more than she could bear.

Tears came to Jo's eyes and she wiped them away before they could touch her face. Tears were for weaklings, and she was strong, Jo told herself. She didn't need anyone's approval to think about E.Z. Ellis. She had always been hard enough on herself.

Jo heard the back screen door close and, in the moonlight, she could make out Tess, heading for her in the darkness, a glass of iced tea in her hand. Her brown hair blew back from her shoulders, and she squinted her eyes slightly against the wind. Jo smiled and thought how beautiful her younger sister had become. One would never know by looking at her that her life had been less than perfect.

"Hi," Jo said.

Tess pulled up a lawn chair and sat down beside the hammock. "Hi. Watcha thinking about?"

Jo sighed and regarded the sky again. "Nothing. Everything." She propped herself on her elbow and looked down at her sister. The darkness had an intimate quality, a quality that made her feel close to Tess...close enough to broach the subject she'd tap-danced around all day. "How's it going with you, Tess? You haven't mentioned your divorce."

She could sense Tess tensing up. "There's nothing to mention. My marriage is history, and life goes on."

"But how are you?" Jo asked. "How are you handling it?"

"Just fine," Tess said, her voice lacking conviction. "I'm great."

Jo wasn't fooled by Tess's dead-end answers, but she knew that when Tess clammed up, there was no getting through to her. Pushing only made Tess back away. For that reason Jo let the subject go and regarded her sister quietly, wishing there was some sign of Tess's state of mind. Was she really fine? Did she cope as well as she seemed to?

Inevitably, Tess changed the subject.

"How about you? I hear you're really gung ho on this censorship fight. Eden says it's all you think about."

The reminder brought back heart-racing thoughts of E.Z. Ellis. "Yeah," Jo whispered, looking toward the babbling creek a few feet away. The moonlight danced from the water's surface in white slivers of light, but Jo had never been satisfied with mere reflections. She rolled on her back and looked toward the heavens again, wishing she could wipe the rock star out of her mind. A deep emptiness yawned inside her, surrounded by regrets and fading memories. "Tess, do you think Mama would have been proud of us?"

Tess's momentary silence spoke of her surprise at the question. As always, Tess considered her words carefully before she spoke. "Is that why you do the things you do, Jo? To make Mama proud?"

Jo shook her head, uncertain. "I don't know. Maybe I do it more for revenge."

"Revenge?"

Jo propped herself up again and gazed down at her sister as the thought took form. "Maybe. Like deep inside I'm saying, 'Look what you missed, Mama. I'm a good person. You should have stuck around.'"

The silence between them for the next several moments was eloquent. Jo's tears dropped over her lashes, and spread across her cheeks. The moonlight shining over them cast a white reflection on Tess's own pale eyes. When she spoke, it seemed to be with great effort.

"Mama died, Jo. She didn't run away."

"I know that," Jo whispered on an expelled breath. "But I didn't know that when I was five...." The injustice of never understanding twisted inside her like a knife wound that had never healed. She wondered why she was feeling it now.

Tess's eyes grew haunted, grief filled. "At least you remember her."

"Yeah, at least..." Jo's words faded on a breeze, as did Tess's sad comment. Jo's heart felt crushed, heavy. Why, why was she thinking of all this now? Had E.Z.'s kiss opened a Pandora's box of feelings she hadn't dealt with before? Was it because the feelings he had evoked were so difficult to deal with? On some level beyond intellect, Jo wondered if she'd ever really dealt with any of her feelings, or did she just keep running...thinking she was running toward something, when she was really just running away? A deep frown cleft her forehead, and as if her words had some connection to the subject at hand, Jo whispered, "He kissed me."

"Who?" Tess asked. "E.Z. Ellis?"

Jo looked at her sister, wondering how she'd known.

"Mariah told me about him," Tess confessed. "And I could see where your mind was all day. It was him, wasn't it?"

Jo swallowed and wet her lips, wondering if she should go on. If she could talk to anyone, it would be Tess. Tess never judged, never criticized. Jo knew she could have confessed a murder, and Tess wouldn't have condemned her. "Yes. He just kissed me. And heaven help me, I melted just like Mariah said I would." The confession had a purging effect, but it seemed to create a plethora of deeper emotions. "Are you shocked?"

Tess's smile told her she wasn't. "Are you?"

Jo considered the question and realized she was. "Yes. I never thought a man could move me that way. I thought I was—"

"Invincible?" Tess suggested. "Jo, take it from me. No one is invincible."

"But he's all wrong for me. We're practically enemies, Tess. And he stands for things that I hate."

Tess's sigh was from deep down inside. "That chemistry doesn't happen very often. If it happens to you, go for it."

Jo couldn't help smiling, and she shook her head in amazement. "I never thought you'd tell me to go after a rake like E.Z. Ellis. Not Tess, who makes all the right decisions, and does all the right things."

Tess stared down at her drink, as if she needed something to hide the sadness in her eyes. "Surprise," she whispered. "Sometimes doing the right thing is all wrong."

Jo pulled her feet over the side of the hammock and rested her elbows on her knees. "But Tess, what if he's using me, just trying to get me to change my mind about testifying before the Commerce Committee? What if it's just manipulation?"

Tess brought her eyes back to her sister, and Jo saw the affectionate smile nestled somewhere in the sadness. "Jo, you've never been able to believe it when someone other than your sisters cares about you. It isn't like he's the first man to be attracted to you. You've been breaking hearts since you were thirteen years old. If someone's finally gotten a hold on yours, I'd say he's pretty special."

Jo rubbed her eyes, feeling a headache beginning.

"Oh, Lord. Life is so complicated."

Tess's laugh was soft on the wind. "If it were easy, you'd just lose interest."

Jo couldn't deny it. "You're right. I probably would."

Later that night, Jo lay awake in bed with her headphones on, listening to E.Z. Ellis's voice weaving its magic. Tonight, to her chagrin, she heard more than offensive words…tonight she heard a weeping spirit in the licks of his guitar…a lonely heart against the screams of a million fans…a poet in an electric jungle.

She wondered if he got some thrill at having women strip for his attention during his show. She wondered if he was like the rockers she'd read about, who chose a groupie or two after every concert to take back to his room . . . and she wondered what the latest Jezebel named Carmen looked like. What kind of woman attracted a man who could have his pick?

The thought that she might be one of those to choose from riled her just enough to restore her fighting spirit and bring her back to her senses. Sometime during the night, Jo swore that she wouldn't let herself see him again. She believed in her fight, and there wasn't a man in existence who could sway her from her path.

Not even E.Z. Ellis. Especially not E.Z. Ellis.

CHAPTER SIX

JO WAS THANKFUL, the next few days, that she was able to keep busy. A debate at the Shreveport branch of Louisiana State University, a lecture before the Baptist Women, an interview on cable television. Staying booked helped her to keep her mind off the man who had gotten under her skin. Moving full speed ahead, she vowed to put him out of her mind.

Wednesday evening, as her second Shreveport meeting of AFCRL met to elect officers and set an agenda for taking action, she found herself the focus of several television cameras and reporters. After the meeting, which was filmed carefully, she agreed to field their questions.

"Miss Calloway," one reporter asked, "don't you think you're overreacting to this music? Do you think that children really pay attention to the lyrics of songs?"

"Somebody *has* to overreact," she said. "And yes, of course children pay attention! They walk around chanting these songs like they were prayers to some god they're worshiping. I have documented proof that subliminal techniques are used in recording studios, and I even have studio musicians who have agreed to testify on our behalf before the committee. They're feeding our kids Satanic messages ... and unless we do something, innocent children are defenseless against them."

"But haven't rock musicians done equal amounts of good in the past few years?" someone else asked. "Look at Live

Aid, Farm Aid, Band Aid...there were huge amounts of money raised at those concerts.''

"That's fine," Jo acknowledged, unimpressed. "But let's face it. Most rock stars appeared in those concerts for the publicity, not out of generosity or concern for the poor. Let's not let a few strategic gestures blind us to what's really going on.''

"Jo," a reporter shouted from the back of the room. "Give us some examples of the musicians you're trying to get censored.''

"I'll be glad to," Jo said, lifting her head high as cameras flashed all over the room. "E.Z. Ellis, Alan Byzantine, Sob Sister, the John Michael Band.... The list goes on and on, but those are some of the offenders I like to use as examples.''

As the questions continued in the same vein, Jo reveled in the excitement, even in the controversy, that this new publicity would incite.

ALTHOUGH PARTS of Jo's impromptu press conference appeared on the evening news, E.Z. didn't hear about it until the next afternoon when he bought a newspaper. He brought it home and sat down on the back patio overlooking the lake, propped his feet on an old crate and flipped through the pages. Like a gust of icy wind on a hot day, the headline knocked the breath out of him. It said, "Satanic messages in Ellis LP's.''

E.Z.'s feet hit the ground and he stood up, glaring down at the article that said that Jo Calloway had named him as one of those who used subliminal techniques to hide satanic messages in his songs.

"Oh, hell," he said through his teeth, and as his color drained to a pale gray beneath the stubble he'd let grow that day, he wondered what he should do first. Call his lawyer?

Or throttle the little firebrand who was making his life so miserable?

"OH, NO!" JO SHOUTED after Mariah dropped the paper down in front of her. "That's not what I said! They misquoted me!"

"Did they ever. You know, if I were him, I'd sue you," Mariah said matter-of-factly.

"I didn't *do* anything. What could he sue me for?"

Ford shrugged and shook his head as if he couldn't believe Jo had gotten herself into such a mess. "Well, there's always slander, defamation of character, loss of income if he could prove a drop in sales, punitive damages, mental anguish."

"He won't sue me," she said. "He'll know I didn't say that."

Mariah tossed her fine hair out of her eyes and sat down at the dinner table. "I don't know, Jo. I'd sue you. Wouldn't you, Eden?"

"In a minute," Eden agreed. "You can't go around saying anything you want to about people, Jo. It isn't right."

Jo banged her fist on the table, rattling the silverware. "I'm telling you people, I was misquoted! I said that he was one of the ones I was particularly offended by. The stuff about the satanic messages was in a whole different context."

Mariah, Eden and Ford began to serve their plates as if the issue didn't concern them one way or another. "Well," Eden said finally. "I guess if they misquoted you, you could demand a retraction."

Jo dropped her face into her hands. "Oh, Lord. Why is this happening to me?"

As if her moan was an opening to an invocation, the others bowed their heads, and Ford took up where she'd left off. "Lord, please help Jo to learn from this mistake, and to operate with more caution and more attention to the people she'll hurt in the future..."

Jo raised her head and glared at her brother-in-law, who was still bowed in humble prayer.

"And bestow on her the gift of more patience and less defensiveness, so that she might reach her full potential."

Jo's face turned a livid red, and she started to attack those snickering around her. But how did one attack someone who had just prayed that she wouldn't lose her temper! Picking up a fork, she stabbed a piece of roast, put it in her mouth and chewed with all the wrath she felt in her heart. Ford ended the prayer and with a wicked grin, winked at her across the table.

No wonder he fell in love with Mariah, Jo thought, stewing. They were perfect for each other. Absolutely perfect!

E.Z. SEETHED ALL THE WAY to Jo's house, his little Volkswagen coughing and putting as if it shared his outrage. He warned himself not to give his temper full rein, for fear he'd hurt her. He'd simply put her in her place. But how did one do that with someone who thought she had the world figured out and had enough confidence to single-handedly right all its wrongs?

That's just it, he thought. *She really believes that she has all the answers. Some kid attempts suicide, blame the music he listens to. Someone runs away, blame the last musician he saw in concert. And fight like hell to get that musician censored, as if that would change anything. So simple... and so obtuse.*

Satanic messages! The thought sent spiral waves of fury through him, and he tried to speed his little car up, but it only bucked and shivered in protest. *Damn her!* She knew he didn't use dirty tricks like that in his music. Why would she say a thing like that? Now he'd have more than just the censorship people breathing down his neck. Now he'd have churches, education systems, parent groups.... The dread of it all boggled his mind.

Her and her cause! The emptiness, the futility of it all, the waste...it all made him sick. It was time someone showed Jo Calloway a cause worth fighting for. It was time to show her some real injustices. Some that she couldn't stand back and supervise without getting her hands dirty. Some that weren't sterile and organized and nice.

E.Z. pulled off the interstate at the exit to Calloway Corners and stretched the limits of his car's abilities, struggling to speed down the street leading to her house. When it was in view, he cursed under his breath at the peacefulness of it all. Dusk was setting in, and against the twilight he could see warm lights inside the house. He wondered if there had been one day in her life when she hadn't felt secure and warm...when she hadn't had someone to turn to...when she hadn't had a place to lay her head. He doubted it, but he intended to change all that. Tonight he would show Jo Calloway what a real cause was.

JO PICKED AT HER FOOD, scarcely able to swallow a bite. The others at the table chatted idly about the weather, about the blueprints Seth was having drawn up for Ford and Mariah's house, about the family plywood mill that wasn't faring very well. But all Jo could think about was what E.Z. must be thinking, how angry he must be and whether or not she should break her rule to stay away and go out to his place to explain.

But before the thought took firm root in her mind, she heard the doorbell, followed by a firm, angry knock. As if it were second nature—since it was her house—Eden sprang up and hurried to the door.

Jo looked up just in time to see E.Z. bolting inside as if he'd been invited—which he would have been had he given it a chance—and crossing to the dining room where they all sat.

"E.Z.!" Jo said, alarm coloring her cheeks. "You read the article...but I didn't say those things...I was misquoted...."

Embarrassed by the situation, Eden said, "Mr. Ellis, can I get you a plate? We have plenty—"

"No thanks," E.Z. said, going straight for Jo. He grabbed her hand, and pulled her to her feet. "Jo and I have a little date."

"What?" Jo asked, too flabbergasted to fight back.

Ford stood up and took a cautious step toward him. "Come on, E.Z. She didn't mean any harm..."

"Don't worry," E.Z. said. "I'm not a violent man. I just want to teach her a couple of lessons about how important her cause really is. We're going to Sullivan's."

"Sullivan's?" Jo asked. "What's Sullivan's?"

She turned to Ford, beseeching him to rescue her, but a slow grin crept across Ford's face. "I see," he said, suddenly calmer. "Not a bad idea."

Mariah turned to her husband, saw the twinkle of conspiracy in his eyes and caught his smile, though she didn't know the reason behind it.

Jo grasped for her bearings and tried to wrench her hand out of E.Z.'s. "I'm not going anywhere with you in this mood!"

"The hell you aren't," E.Z. muttered and dragged her to the door. With one final, angry look over his shoulder, he told Eden, "I wouldn't wait up if I were you."

The last thing Jo saw before he pulled her out the door was Mariah's face, beaming with delight, as if her prayer for Jo had finally been answered. Eden, on the other hand, looked torn between grabbing a lamp to crash over his head and giving him her blessing.

With short, rough movements, E.Z. put Jo into his car and slammed the door. He got in beside her, cranked the sick engine and screeched out of the driveway.

"Who do you think you are?" Jo shouted. "You can't storm into someone's house and grab them up from the table. It's kidnapping!"

"Yeah, well," he muttered. "When they lock me up, it'll only reinforce my satanic image."

"If you'll just listen, you'll see that I did not say that! They got it all wrong!"

"You said enough, lady," he shouted, pulling back onto the interstate. "You gave them just enough to work with."

"You can't blame me for a mistake the reporters made!"

"I *can* blame you, and I do. You're responsible for everything that comes out of that 'citizen's' group of yours. The good, the bad and the ugly."

Jo tried to calm down and sat back in her seat. It occurred to her that she needed her seat belt on, since the reliability of the Volkswagen was questionable. There was, indeed, a seat belt, but it was shredded and lacked a buckle. "Look, you can't fault me for this. You asked me not to tell them you were here and I didn't."

"Right," he said. "I forgot to ask you not to tell blatant lies about me. My mistake."

"I told you, I did not—"

"Let it rest!" E.Z. shouted over her protest. "I don't want to talk about it anymore. If I do, my temper is liable to get the best of me!"

"Then *why* did you abduct me?" she demanded.

"I did not abduct you," he said through his teeth. "I told you, I'm taking you on a date."

"I'm not exactly in the mood for a movie, E.Z.," she said, knowing he had no intention of taking her to one. She gestured toward her clothes—an old pair of jeans and an oversized button-down sweater. "And I'm not dressed for one, either."

He pushed his hair back from his face, leaving it as ruffled as his mood. "Oh, this is no movie, babe. This is real life. Real people. Real problems. And where we're going, those clothes'll fit right in."

Jo looked at him in the dimness of the growing night, and frowned at the suppressed fury, the anger welling in his eyes. Where on earth was he taking her? The only thought that kept her from being afraid was the fact that Ford hadn't seemed too concerned when he'd mentioned Sullivan's . . . whatever that was.

E.Z.'s nostrils flared and his jaw clenched. Was this the same man who had laughed with her the other day and kissed her, melting her heart?

"E.Z., please," she said, her tone less explosive now. "Where are we going?"

"We're going to meet some of my friends," he said.

Jo felt her muscles stiffening. Was he making her confront all the other rock stars she'd condemned last night, she wondered. Was that his idea of revenge? Before she could protest, he went on.

"Here are the ground rules. Number one, these people don't know who I am. They know me only as Ellis. While we're there, that's what you'll call me. Number two, these people don't know that I have a cabin on the lake or any other place to live. Don't enlighten them. Number three, they think that I'm down on my luck and unemployed—which may be accurate by the time you get through with me—You won't tell them otherwise . . ."

As he laid down the rules, Jo stared at him, amazed. *Ellis? Unemployed? Down on his luck?* "This is a joke, right?" she asked.

"No joke," he said. "You want a cause? I'll give you a cause. You want to get mad? I'll give you something that'll make your blood boil."

Fear of the unknown took hold of her, and Jo felt her hands shaking. She clamped them together in her lap, and watched out the window, hoping for a glimpse of his morbid surprise before they reached it. "Please," she whispered again. "E.Z., just tell me where we're going. You're scaring me."

The waver in her voice caught his attention, and as he pulled off the interstate into Bossier City, he glanced over at her. When he spoke again, his tone was grudgingly gentle. "You don't have to be afraid..."

DESPITE E.Z.'S ATTEMPTS to hold fast to his anger, the fear on Jo's face robbed him of the better part of it. Did she honestly think he'd take her someplace dangerous? He had to admit, his words had been delivered with a measured harshness, and the whole point of taking her to Sullivan's was to shock her into realizing that there were better causes to fight for. He didn't know what kind of reaction he wanted from her, but fear wasn't one of them.

After a moment, the little car coughed and sputtered past a peeling sign that read "Sullivan's Furniture Manufacturing", and he reached into the doorless glove compartment and withdrew his glasses. Putting them on, E.Z. pulled his car into a muddy drive behind other ailing cars that looked as if they belonged in a junkyard. He'd found some of these families living in vehicles before they'd known they could come here. For that reason he saw the cars as last resorts rather than throwaways. He looked over at Jo as he parked. Her face was markedly confused. He could almost see the wheels of her mind turning as she struggled to figure out where they were.

"A furniture plant?" Jo asked. "E.Z., why are we coming here?"

E.Z. reached to the back seat for his acoustic guitar. "It isn't a furniture plant anymore," he said. "It closed down a year ago."

Jo looked at the guitar, then back at the building to the people standing outside. Bedraggled people, their leathered faces lined in despair; people who looked as if they hadn't bathed in days, wearing torn and wrinkled clothes marred with stains; people with an unspoken kinship that only made them look more distraught. E.Z. wondered if Jo was repulsed by them, if she cringed inside and yearned to pretend they didn't exist, like most people did.

"Is it a bar now?" she asked. "Do you play here?"

"Nope," he said. "It's not a bar." He got out of the car, came around to her side and opened the door. She looked up at him, again with that fear in her eyes.

"Just relax," he said. "You're about to get the education of your life."

"Relax?" she asked, her lips trembling with the word. "You look like you're about to throw me to the dogs, and you want me to relax?"

"This isn't about you," E.Z. said. "You'll see in a minute. Come on." He took her hand, and reluctantly she got out of the small car. The vulnerability in her eyes reminded him that she wasn't the tough guy she pretended to be. Sometimes she looked small and frail, like someone who needed protecting, too. Somehow he wished she'd start spitting fire or lashing out at him instead of looking so fragile and lost. That way he could remember how mad she'd made him.

Holding her hand, E.Z. pulled Jo toward the door of the warehouse, through the people loitering outside, smoking cigarettes, trading hard-luck stories. He knew she hadn't yet noticed the lines of pup tents near the back of the building . . . she was too busy trying to categorize the people, the building, the extent of E.Z.'s anger.

They reached a group of men he was acquainted with, men who probably looked like the types little girls' mothers warned them to run from, and he felt her hand tightening its hold on his. The nervous gesture made his heart jolt, and he pulled her closer to him. She was shaking like a child on her first day at school, he mused. He reached the men, who called out various tepid greetings.

"How's it goin'?" he asked.

"Been better, Ellis," the man E.Z. knew as Amos responded. "You had any luck with those leads you were followin'?"

"Not yet," E.Z. said.

Another man who had been leaning against the wall smoking a cigarette, dropped it to the ground and mashed it out with his foot. "I'm leavin' tomorrow," he said. "Dallas is bigger. There might be more jobs."

"Yeah, and more people tryin' to get 'em," Amos said.

"Still," the downcast man went on, "it's time to move on. We've been here too long. My kids'll think I'm not even tryin'."

"You gonna introduce us to your lady?" Amos asked, dismissing the man's words as if the despair in them was mundane.

E.Z. glanced over at Jo and smiled. *His lady.* He could just see her biting her tongue, and the thought amused him. "Amos, meet Jo. Jo, this is Amos and Roy."

E.Z. suspected that for the first time in her life, Jo didn't know what to say. Her usual facade of assertiveness was out of place here. Quietly she said, "Hello," and extended her hand to the two men. They both shook it.

"Where you been hidin' her?" Amos asked goodnaturedly.

E.Z. shrugged. "Around. What's for supper?"

Roy pulled another cigarette out of a pack in his shirt pocket. "Ham, beans, potato salad. Not too bad."

E.Z. gazed down at Jo, astutely reading her for signs of her response. Those olive eyes were as round as quarters, and against her pale skin her hair blew softly like flames fanned by a man's breath. "Come on," he said quietly, hating to breach the innocence of a woman who'd led a sheltered life, but had the naïveté to think she was streetwise. It was time to show her real life. "Let's go in."

They stepped into the brightly lit warehouse, and he saw the horror in Jo's eyes. The room had an odd odor; a combination of food, sawdust, diapers and too many people in too small a place. The noise level as voices resounded and echoed off the aluminum roof was too much for an adult to bear, and yet for every adult there was an average of three children, sitting on cots trying to eat the sparse meal.

Jo swung around to E.Z. at the door, and looked up into his eyes with a searing accusation. "What's going on here?"

"These people are homeless," E.Z. explained, his anger reasserting itself. "This is a shelter."

She turned around again, scanned the accommodations, the hopelessness on the faces, the lack of joy in any of the people's expressions. "But...the children..."

"Did you think only adults could be homeless?" he asked.

"No, of course not. But the government provides for these people...there are services to protect children..."

"And what do they do while they're waiting to be processed?" he asked softly, so that no one would overhear. "What do they do when they're making an earnest attempt to find work, and they move from town to town, never in one place long enough to get government aid? And what about those who've lost their farms, their land, their jobs, and have too much pride to ask for help until it's way too late?"

"Are you telling me these people have no place else to go?" she whispered. "That they *sleep* here?"

"That's exactly what I'm telling you," he said. "Come on, I'll introduce you to some of them."

She pulled back, stopping him. "E.Z., how do you know these people?"

"I told you," he said. "They're my friends. And please, call me Ellis here."

She gazed up at him, understanding dawning on her face. "They think you're homeless, too, don't they? They think you're one of them."

"That's right," he said. "Now come on."

Instead of backing down, as he would have expected her to do, Jo seemed to anticipate meeting the people with great relish. He saw the Juarez children in a corner. Their father sat on a fold-out chair with a newspaper, marking off the want ads. One of the older children sat reading a book to some of the others, while the rest did mock battle with some toy trucks the church had provided. Lying on a mat on the floor was Carmen, thumb in her mouth, watching the people around her with a listless expression that said she didn't expect anyone to notice her.

Slipping his guitar strap over his shoulder to free his hands, E.Z. led Jo through the cots and mattresses covering the floor. They reached the Juarezes, and he stooped down next to the baby. Carmen looked up at him with eyes as black as coal, and her thumb came out of her mouth. She reached for E.Z. That unnamable something in his heart burst, and without hesitation, he picked her up.

He turned to Jo, his eyes suddenly softer, and he bounced Carmen lightly. Jo tried to smile, but he could see the despair in her eyes. "Jo, I want you to meet Carmen."

"*Carmen?*" Jo's jaw dropped, and she gaped at the baby. Self-conscious guilt added to the amazement on her features. "*This* is Carmen? The one you said you spent the night with the other night?"

He grinned like a devil. "Another case of Jo Calloway's mind being in the gutter."

She covered her mouth with her hand, mortified that he'd played with her again…and won. Jo expelled a heavy breath and nodded her head glumly. "I deserve that," she said.

She reached out to take the little girl's hand, and her eyes looked haunted. "Where's her mother?" Jo asked softly.

The timbre of E.Z.'s voice changed to almost a whisper. "She lost her a month ago," E.Z. said. "Her uncle is raising her and his seven children."

Jo looked past them at the thin, broken man and the children at his feet. E.Z. saw incipient tears spring to her eyes and admired her valiant effort to blink them back. "Can I hold her?" she asked.

E.Z. hesitated, reluctant to let the baby go, but finally, he surrendered her. Carmen went readily, as if she'd grown accustomed to being passed around. That, in itself, struck him as tragic. As Jo held her, she smiled through misty eyes and pushed the baby's pitch-black hair back from her face. "Can you say Jo?" she whispered. "Jo?"

Carmen's thumb went instantly to her mouth, but her other hand found Jo's long red locks. With fascination, she stroked Jo's hair as if it was some rare, expensive fabric she'd never been allowed to touch.

Easy watched, moved anew, as Jo whispered to the girl, making her smile for the first time since he'd seen her. After a moment Jo looked up at him, and her face was distorted. "This is a disgrace," she whispered from her heart. "No child should have to live like this."

And for the first time since he'd known her, E.Z. was glad to see her angry. Anger was what got things changed. Anger vented in the right direction.

CHAPTER SEVEN

IN JO'S MIND, hell had always been some obscure fiery pit in another dimension, smoking and smoldering, set there to punish the wicked. But that night, she learned that hell was as vivid and clear as home was, that the only thing smoking and smoldering was the garbage the men outside burned to keep warm, and that none of those who suffered here had done anything to be punished for.

That night, as she followed E.Z. around like another one of the homeless, carrying Carmen as if the baby were her own child, Jo learned some things about herself that she wasn't happy to acknowledge. It took seeing the decadent rock star she'd all but slandered publicly, interacting with the poverty-stricken as if he were no better, no different, than they, to see that she held humanity at arm's length.

She watched E.Z. offer kind words of hope to those who confided in him, saw him working with his hands along with the other men to mend some cots that had broken, saw him fall from the pedestal of superstar to an anything-but-ordinary man. She wondered why she couldn't walk up to some of these women, start conversations, help them with their children while they rested. And finally she knew that she avoided talking to them, not out of cowardice or superiority, but because she had grown good at avoiding people on a personal level. That is, most people, except for her family. Perhaps it had to do with feeling abandoned as a child by a mother who'd had no choice but to die. Perhaps it had to do with the heartbreak of a father who'd grieved so hard over his young wife's death that he'd lost his capacity to express love. Perhaps it had to do with a part of her that had never been nurtured, so had never been allowed to mature.

Whatever the cause, it pained Jo now, for she very much wanted to do something, to reach out, to correct these injustices as they became clear to her. E.Z. had been right. The sight of this place did make her blood boil. It did make her want to take action. But there was so much wrong, and she didn't begin to know how to right it.

Carmen squirmed in her arms, reminding her that she didn't have to solve it all right now, that there was one little girl who could use whatever she had to give. She sat down on Carmen's cot, smiled down at the precious child, and Carmen wrinkled her nose and smiled back at her. Jo's eyes misted over, and she swallowed hard. She looked over the baby's head to E.Z. across the room, saw him watching her with a gentle pensiveness that made her want to surrender to her tears. But she didn't.

Slowly he approached her, stooped in front of her and stroked Carmen's hair. The little girl turned around and smiled. He looked up at Jo, his eyes as serious as she'd seen them, and his hand slid from Carmen's hair to Jo's, long and trailing down her arm. "Don't look so sad, Red," he whispered.

Tears beaded in her eyes, and she held them wide to keep the tears from falling. "Somebody's got to do something about this," she whispered.

"Somebody's trying," he said.

After a moment, he reached his hands out to take Carmen, but Jo held her tight. "Don't take her yet," she said, her voice too high, too close to breaking. "Let me hold her. She's so sweet...."

E.Z. didn't answer for a moment. Instead he only watched her lower her face to Carmen's hair, as though she had found something too precious to part with, and he didn't want to force her to do it. He knew how difficult it could be. "Can I get you a plate?" he asked finally. "I'm starting to feel a little guilty about taking you from your dinner."

She shook her head. "I'm not hungry."

"Well, we could step outside. Get some air," he suggested carefully. "I'll tell Juarez so he won't worry."

Jo nodded and stood up, hiking Carmen on her small hip. The little girl stared up at her, wide-eyed, as she started for the door.

When E.Z. came back from speaking to Juarez, he set his hand on the back of Jo's neck. His touch was warm and reassuring, a soft declaration that what she felt was okay. Gently, he ushered her to the door.

Jo looked up at him thoughtfully, wondering how this new picture of E.Z. Ellis fit into the scheme of things. He opened the door for her, and she walked through.

The night air was growing cool, and she cuddled Carmen closer to her. The little girl's head rolled back until she was looking up at the sky, at the stars beginning to peer out.

"Stars," Jo said softly, hoping Carmen would try to repeat the word. "Sky."

Carmen pointed up, smiled at Jo, and slid her arms around her neck.

"Looks like I have competition," E.Z. said, grinning. "Until you came along, Carmen only had eyes for me."

From somewhere past the sadness, Jo found laughter. "I'd say she has eyes for anybody who has time for her." She looked around, trying to decide how much privacy they had. Lowering her voice, she asked, "E.Z., how do you—"

"Ellis," he whispered. "I told you—"

"Ellis," she corrected, glancing at the strangers who hadn't heard. "How do you know about this place? Why do you come here?"

E.Z. looked around at the shadowed faces in the night. "Later," he said. "We'll talk later. Right now it's more important for you to know why *you're* here."

"That was my next question," Jo said.

"Because," he whispered, stepping close enough that she smelled the minty scent of his breath. "You're so busy with those empty causes of yours, I thought it was time you learned firsthand what a real cause is—that sometimes it's better to embrace people than causes."

"I don't embrace causes," Jo replied, as adamant about her convictions as he was about his. "I fight for things I believe in. I try to make things right."

"Then you haven't had the chance to see enough that's wrong." E.Z. opened his arms, encompassing the entire structure and all the grounds. "Here it is. Put some of your energy where it counts. Make a real impact."

"I *do* make an impact," she whispered, her anger returning to her tone. "What I do *does* count."

"You're playing at changing the world, Jo," he whispered back. "It's a game."

"If it were just a game," she challenged, "then you wouldn't be so worried about dissuading me."

Carmen's lip began to pout, and she turned her umbrous eyes up to them, fearful at their tones. Jo noticed it instantly, and began to bounce her. Keeping her harsh eyes on E.Z., she whispered, "It's okay, honey. We were just talking. Nobody's mad."

E.Z. bit back his own retort and concentrated on Carmen, as well. "She's sleepy," he said, soberness still clinging to his features. "We need to take her back in."

Jo didn't wait for him to lead her. She pushed the door open herself and launched into the warehouse. E.Z. followed behind her.

As it grew later and Carmen fell asleep in her arms, Jo wondered when the lights would be turned off, when the families here would settle down for the night, when the babies would stop crying. It wasn't until E.Z. began playing his guitar, quietly, with a kind of solitude that seemed to reflect the feelings of everyone in the room, that peace seemed to settle over the place at all. She watched, baffled, as mothers and their children lay down on the cots fully clothed, for a night's sleep. She heard the sound of sniffing as tears rolled into stained mattresses, and she wanted to cry herself. And she felt the warmth and melancholy of the music as it seeped into weary bones and empty hearts.

She laid Carmen down on her bed, covering her gently. A tear dropped to her cheek, and she smeared it across her face. It wasn't fair that the child had no mother. She knew that injustice far more than she knew any other. But suddenly the injustice she had suffered in her childhood seemed to pale in comparison. She had had a home and three sisters who loved her. And her father had loved her, too, in his way. Carmen had nothing.

Juarez came to Carmen's cot, stooping beside it. "Thank you for being so kind to her," he said softly over the music.

Jo smiled with grief as deep as any she'd ever felt. "She's so special. How could anyone not be kind to her?"

Juarez rubbed his weary, leathery face and looked around at the other children sleeping on the cots around him. "Sometimes it's easy to overlook one when there are so many others."

Ruefully, Jo brought her eyes back to E.Z., reminding herself not to blame Juarez, who was as much a victim as the child they spoke of.

"Her mother...my sister...was a very gentle woman," Juarez went on. "She was good to Carmen. It's been hard for her to understand..."

Jo felt her tears begin, and she stared down at Carmen. "Frankly, Juarez, it's hard for *me* to understand. It isn't fair."

Juarez looked down at the gray concrete beneath his feet, as if it held some answers rather than more questions. "The game of life doesn't operate on the principle of fairness. The sooner we learn that, the better off we are."

Jo regarded him with less judgment, wondering at the doleful acceptance in his tone. Was defeat the result of poverty, she wondered, or the result of being knocked down so many times that it was something he had come to expect? Juarez gave her a slight smile that told her not to worry, that he would always find a way to get back up again. He looked at E.Z., who sat on the floor leaning back against a concrete column, strumming his guitar. "He's good with the guitar," he observed quietly. "As good as he is with people."

Jo frowned and looked across to E.Z., trying to see him through the eyes of those around him.

"He has a way of making people feel a little better about themselves," Juarez whispered. "If there were such a thing as fairness, a man like that wouldn't be here. He'd have a job, and a family, and a nice house with central heat and air, carpet..." The image played out on Juarez's voice like a dying dream, and he sighed. "If anyone is worthy of that, Ellis is."

"Worthy?" Jo asked, turning back to Juarez. "You don't think people have those things just because they're worthy of them, do you? If you believe that, you'd have to believe that you're only here because you're *not* worthy. You don't believe that, do you?"

"Sometimes I wonder," Juarez said, his eyes set, unseeing, on some distant thought. "Sometimes I just don't know."

"Well, what about your children?" Jo asked, adamantly making her point. "Are *they* unworthy? What about little Carmen?"

Juarez looked affectionately, worriedly, at each of his children one by one, then brought his tired eyes back to Jo. "You see, in my head I know that's not how it is. But in my heart, I feel different. Sometimes I feel like there's a cycle in this family—generations of being poor. I got it from my father. They'll get it from me. There's no way around it."

Juarez's despairing words lay heavy on Jo's heart as the night wore on, and she realized the lights weren't going off, and the stop-gap home wasn't getting any quieter. And when E.Z. stopped strumming, all that was left was the blundering sound of acceptance, fallen over the place like a death knell.

E.Z. pushed the guitar strap over his head and slid the instrument to his back. He looked at Chris, sitting nearby on the cold concrete, saw the distant thoughts in his eyes and wondered if he was thinking of home. "I thought you were headed to New Orleans," E.Z. said softly.

"Yeah, I might," Chris said. "Haven't decided yet."

"Just rambling around, huh? Seeing a little of the world?"

Chris looked around him with the same waiflike innocence E.Z. had seen in so many of the kids here. "Too much of the world."

"I know what you mean," E.Z. said. He scanned the warehouse, the families attempting to settle down in the harsh glare of light. "Most of these people would do anything for four walls of their own...just something to call home. You must have one somewhere."

Chris didn't answer. Instead he looked past E.Z. to a family nearby where a mother was tucking her son into bed.

"Where are you from?" E.Z. asked, knowing Chris wouldn't answer.

Chris brought his dull gray eyes back to E.Z. "Why?"

E.Z. raised his hands in protest. "Just making conversation," he said. "I figured you weren't from around here."

"It's not where I came from that matters," Chris said coldly. "It's where I'm going."

"And you haven't decided where that is, yet."

Chris shrugged. "I'll know when I get there."

E.Z. recognized the false bravado in the boy's words, but decided not to press the issue further. He looked over at Jo and wondered what she and Juarez had been talking about, and why a wistful look lingered in her eyes. It occurred to him that he might have made a mistake in bringing her here. Maybe she just wasn't ready to see the real world so suddenly. But then he reminded himself of the misleading newspaper headlines and decided that her shattered innocence wouldn't weigh all that heavily on his conscience, after all.

"She your wife?" Chris asked.

In spite of himself, E.Z. had to laugh. "Wife? No, she's not my wife."

"She's real pretty."

E.Z.'s eyes grew serious again as he regarded her. "Yeah. Yeah, she is."

"My mom has hair that color," Chris said.

E.Z. looked back at the boy, saw the melancholy in his eyes. "You miss her?"

Chris gave an I-don't-care shrug that revealed just how much he did care. "She don't need me," he said, his eyes hardening once again. "She has enough problems."

Enough problems. The words suggested a barrage of possibilities to E.Z.—drugs, prostitution, child abuse—

possibilities that reinforced his decision not to turn the run-away in. He looked back at Jo, trying not to seem too concerned to Chris. Jo was watching the boy as if she, too, knew he was a runaway, and wondered why no one had sent him home. As if to voice those thoughts, Jo got up.

E.Z. met Jo's eyes as she started toward him and gave her a look of warning not to frighten Chris away. The boy didn't trust easily. E.Z. didn't want him to feel he couldn't come back here when he had no place else to go. Worried at the convicted look in her eyes when she was beside him, he turned back to Chris. "You'd better go out and claim a tent, Chris, or there won't be any left."

Chris hesitated and looked toward the door as if dreading what lay beyond it. "Where are you sleeping?"

He was still afraid, E.Z. thought, even after all the nights he'd spent here. And E.Z. didn't blame him. "We're getting a tent, too," he said. "We'll see if we can find one near yours."

Jo gasped so hard she almost choked, and leveled stunned eyes on him. "Ellis," she said through her teeth. "May I speak to you privately for a moment?"

E.Z. turned back to Chris. "You go on out and find two tents. We'll be along in a minute."

Chris gathered up his duffel bag and left them alone, but before Jo could start her tirade, E.Z. took her hand and pulled her rapidly out the door. The darkness encompassed them like a shroud of privacy, and he pulled her back into the shadows by the cars, where no one else loitered.

He let her go when he was satisfied that they were alone, and she turned on him instantly. "I have no intentions of sleeping here with you! This is going too far."

E.Z. leaned back against the fender of a car, crossing his arms over his chest. "What's the matter?" he asked. "It's one thing to feel sorry for these people, pat them on the heads, and say how somebody has to do something to change things. But it's another thing entirely to actually live among them the way they live, isn't it?''

"It's hypocritical!" Jo said. "I don't know what your motives are for pretending to be one of these people, but I don't happen to share them. Now, take me home." Jo started to go to the car, but E.Z. grabbed her arm and stopped her.

"I'm not taking you anywhere," he said. "I brought you here to teach you something, and the lesson's not over yet."

"You're out of your mind!" Her voice was as loud as she could manage without shouting. "Absolutely, positively, out of your mind!"

"Maybe so," he said. "But the fact is that you are going to sleep in a pup tent with me tonight, just the way the other people here have to sleep. I'm not taking you back until morning."

Her eyes went wild with rage. "Then I'll walk! I swear, either you take me home, or I'll walk. I'm not spending the night with you here or anywhere!"

His presence was so strong that even when he let her go Jo felt as if he still held her in his grip. E.Z. gestured toward the gates and the dark, eery road beyond. "Take off," he said. "It's a pretty rough part of town for a good-looking woman to be in alone. I wouldn't recommend it, but go right ahead."

She looked through the gates, furiously considering his words, and realized that she probably wouldn't make it a mile. Seething, she spun back to him. "You've got a lot of nerve. I don't have to sleep here to know that there's a problem. You've fulfilled your purpose. If I'm not home soon Eden will call the police."

E.Z. wasn't daunted by the flimsy threat. "No, she won't. Ford knows where we are, and he knows I'll take care of you. No one's coming after you, and you aren't going anywhere. Now, let's go find our tent before we wind up sleeping without one."

Still desperate to prove that he couldn't bully her, Jo eyed the road and the darkness and measured her courage against her anger. Flustered, she turned around, looked at the tents and wondered if E.Z. would call her a coward if she burst into tears. "I've never slept in a tent in my life and I don't want to start now...especially not with some man that I can barely tolerate."

"Don't worry about it," E.Z. drawled. "My ego can take the rejection."

"It's kidnapping," she went on. "That's against the law."

E.Z. parried her threat with a smile. "So is slander," he pointed out. "I won't press charges, if you won't."

"I did *not* slander you."

"And I didn't kidnap you. You're going home in the morning, so you might as well make the best of it. You're in no danger. I'll take care of you."

"You? You're the one I need to be protected from!"

E.Z.'s grin told her he considered that a compliment. "Somehow I think you can hold your own with me." He pushed away from the car and started walking away. "Come on now. We have to go find Chris. He's just a scared kid, and I don't want to leave him alone for too long."

Jo hung back for a moment, refusing to follow him like a scared little girl. But as E.Z. left her and strolled on ahead, she understood Chris's fears. And the protection E.Z. offered was looking better all the time.

The tent Chris had found them was a couple of rows away from the boy, a fact that didn't add to the teenager's sense of security. But all the others had been claimed by men who were tattered and tired, men whose children were inside with their wives, men who had been hopelessly penalized for being poor.

Jo gritted her teeth and stewed while E.Z. opened the sleeping bag inside their tent and laid it out like a pallet. Then he gestured for her to crawl in and take one side, while he took the other.

Only because she didn't want to be left alone outside the tent, Jo climbed in, cursing him in her mind as she had never cursed anyone before. Instead of lying down next to him, she sat up hugging her knees, and stared furiously out the open door.

E.Z. found her attitude amusing. "You won't get much sleep like that," he said. "You might as well lie down."

"If I have to spend the entire night in this with you, I intend to sit up all night."

His grin nettled her further. "You know, I'm not so bad," he said. "There are one or two women who wouldn't mind being in your place at all."

Jo knew it was more like one or two million…minus one. He was perfectly at ease, lying with his hands clasped behind his head, and Jo glared at him. "Tell me, do you usually take your enemies hostage? Is that always how you handle your problems?"

"Nope," he said with downright glee. "This is the first time."

Jo decided not to honor the flip remark with a reply. Instead she sat stiffly, biting her lip and staring at the tent door as if the canvas flap had offended her.

"I don't expect you to be star struck," he goaded her in an indolent tone, "but you could at least pretend to be cordial. I mean, I wouldn't have brought just anyone here."

Jo ventured to look at him again, wishing he'd put his glasses back on and wipe the snicker off his face. "Am I supposed to be *grateful* for that?"

He laughed aloud, then, and tugged on a strand of her hair. "Heaven help me, that's probably why I like you, even though you make me crazy. You're the first woman I've met in years who doesn't give a dog's damn whether I'm E.Z. Ellis or John Doe."

A long tense silence stretched between them as she tried not to respond to his admitting he liked her. The fact that he did, however, forced her to make a self-confession as well. As incensed as she was about being forced to stay here, she had found him to be...different from what she'd expected. Different, and almost...likable.

Finally, like a melody in the night, his voice broke the quiet again. "You're sitting there so stiff and so self-righteous. And I can't help wondering what it takes to get through to you."

Tears blurred Jo's vision, and she turned to him, looking at him fully. "You *have* gotten through to me, E.Z. I saw the way those people are living. I held Carmen and felt how terrible life is for her. I heard those women crying in their beds. I'm not some statue without a heart." A tear fell over her bottom lashes, and she batted it away.

At the sight of her crying, E.Z. propped himself up on his elbow, his face just inches from hers. "Come on," he whispered. "I didn't mean to make you cry."

"Didn't you?" she asked. Another tear escaped and then another, and she gave up trying to stop them. "Isn't that exactly what you wanted?"

He couldn't answer honestly, for he wasn't sure. "I just wanted you to see that there are better things to do with your energy."

Jo wiped her tears on her jeans. "There's always a greater need, no matter what you're fighting for. Don't you think I know that? But just because there are other injustices, it doesn't mean that the one I've chosen is insignificant. Laws get changed because of people like me."

"But if you can change laws, then why not change the ones that will help these people? Why not fight where it counts?"

"These people do have government aid," she said. "They just need someone to show them how to get it."

He sat up, facing her. "You see, there you go with your naïveté again. You're just like all the other idiots out there who think the homeless don't exist, have unlimited government aid, or are just sick vagrants. But they're farmers and factory workers and women whose sorry husbands have abandoned them and their children. They're people who could find a job and a place to live, if they didn't have the problem of deposits and first and last month rents, or if they had somebody to keep their kids. There's a cycle that's been created here, and the government isn't acknowledging it. It's too complicated for them, and they like things cut and dried."

"Then why don't *you* change it?" she asked. "Instead of parading around here like one of the underprivileged, you could be spending your own money, using your own clout. But no. You'd rather pretend to be one of them so that you can get new material for your songs."

The only other time she'd seen E.Z.'s face turn crimson was when he said she'd misinterpreted "Shadow Child." "You don't know a damned thing about it!" he said. "Yeah, maybe I've written a couple of songs about this life, but as far as what else I'm doing, it's none of your business. And for your information these people need a hell of a lot more than money."

Jo realized she'd pushed too far, and the last thing she wanted now, in this small space they would have to share for the night, was to make E.Z. angry. Besides, she admitted, he was right. She exhaled deeply and when she spoke, her tone was gentle. "Look, I'm not condemning you. You obviously help these people by being here. You make them feel good. But don't condemn me for fighting for a cause that I think is worthwhile. Sure, I want to help the homeless. But that won't make me give up my censorship fight."

"That's all you see, here, isn't it? You think I only brought you here to emotionally manipulate you into trading in one fight for another."

"Of course that's why."

"Wrong, lady," he said, the rage in his voice sending a chill down her spine. "I brought you here because I think you spend too much time thinking of clever persuasive tactics about the wrong things. *This* is the real world."

He shoved his glasses back on, grabbed his guitar and pushed through the tent flap, leaving her alone in the canvas structure, wishing she'd never opened her mouth. Jo sat alone there for a while, determined not to let him know his leaving had frightened her, until she heard muffled voices outside. Sheer trepidation forced her to look outside to see just how far away E.Z. was.

To her relief the voices she heard were his and Chris's, and they sat only yards away from her tent. Her eyes collided with E.Z.'s as she peered out the door, and she knew then that he had been carefully guarding her since he'd left.

Knowing he'd spotted her looking out, Jo decided to swallow her pride and go all the way. She got to her feet as she left the tent and sat down on a crate across from E.Z. He was letting Chris play his guitar and coaching the boy on some chords.

"Press a little harder with your finger," he told Chris softly, his eyes still on Jo.

Even though he had his glasses on again, E.Z.'s eyes indicted her. Jo felt his hurt at what she'd said about his motives and regretted the accusation.

Chris did as he was told, smiling at the smooth sound he made. "That's a C?" he asked.

"C minor," E.Z. corrected. "Now change to G."

Carefully placing his fingers and holding his tongue poised between his teeth, Chris changed chords. The look of accomplishment on his face warmed Jo's heart. "Hey, that sounds okay."

"You'll be ready for Carnegie Hall in no time," E.Z. said with a smile.

Jo sat quietly for the next hour as E.Z. showed Chris more, further shattering the image she'd had of the self-centered star on a search for new material. He had nothing to gain by patiently teaching Chris, she realized, any more than he had by interacting with the others in the shelter.

When Chris's fingers got too sore to continue, E.Z. took back his guitar and began to play himself. Again Jo found herself transported to a more peaceful place, nestled in the melody of his tune. Finally Chris went to bed, and Jo found herself sitting alone with E.Z. in the night, a solitary listener to his special brand of magic. He began to sing softly to her, a song that she knew he had never recorded, a song that spoke of illusions and delusions, visions and revisions. A song too sad to condemn. Finally the song came to an end, and he sat looking at her over the guitar, gazing at her in the darkness. She gazed back, wondering who on earth this man was who could rock an entire stadium one night and sleep like a hobo the next; who could make an album that went platinum one week and teach a boy to trust the next; who could appall someone like her one minute and melt her heart the next.

The wind swept through her hair, rustling it over her breasts, and she shivered in the chill. E.Z. saw that she was cold and stopped strumming. He set his guitar down and stood up, shrugged out of his shirt, leaving only a blue tank top for his own warmth. Then he quietly closed the distance between them and set the shirt over her shoulders.

His own warmth still clung to it, and his clean, natural scent hung around her like a borrowed aura. There was something intimate, bonding, about wearing his clothes. Jo accepted the shirt, fearing her voice would give her away if she refused.

He moved his crate next to her, set the guitar back in his lap and propped his elbow on it. Beneath the sparse moonlight, his eyes were luminous as he gazed at her.

E.Z. reached out to lift a strand of her hair and wove it through his fingers. "You have the most phantasmic hair," he whispered. "It's like the hair on those spirits you see in movies, long and flowing and magical..."

"Theirs is always white," she whispered, struggling to make light of the moment.

"It's the fire in yours that's so enchanting," he said. "One minute it burns you, the next it draws you into its warmth."

For the first time in a long time, Jo couldn't speak. She only sat looking at him, watching him fondle the silken strand of her hair as if it were something precious.

"I'm sorry for what I said," she whispered, "about your just wanting new material. It was stupid, and I know it wasn't true."

He took off his glasses, revealing eyes that shone in the moonlight. "Let's go in," he whispered, "before someone overhears."

The emotion obstructing her throat grew larger as Jo crawled into the tent beside him, and when he closed the flap and lay on his back, she felt her heart leap and flutter. She sat up, but this time she faced him, looking down at him, trying to decipher the complex enigma named E.Z. Ellis. His eyes were sober, soft, seductive as he watched her.

"I mean it," she said. "I'm sorry. It's just that you surprise me over and over, and I keep trying to peg you, so I can figure out who you really are."

"I am what you see. That's all. I don't hide that much."

"No," she whispered. "There's much more than what I see."

He took her hand, fondled each finger, watching captivated as they bent and moved against his. The sensuous
stroking made her heart jolt in a strange kind of rhythm.
"And what do you see?" he asked.

She swallowed hard. "I see compassion. I see humility. I
see sensitivity...you *care* about that boy. You aren't just
acting."

He ran a finger down the center of her palm, circled it
with his thumb. "I'm not an actor."

"No," she said, beginning to tremble at the touch. "But
you're a star. And most stars wouldn't lower themselves to
this. I look at you, and I see a nice man. And that really
bothers me."

E.Z. rose up on his elbow, and laced her hair in his fingers. For the life of her, Jo wished his eyes weren't so blue.
"Why?" he asked, his lips only inches from hers. She wondered what they tasted like...how they would feel, this time,
against hers.

She wet her lips and saw that his were already moist. "I
don't know...I guess it's easier to fight someone I don't
like."

"We don't *always* have to fight," he whispered. "We
don't always have to dislike each other. As crazy as you've
made me, I haven't always disliked you."

His lips moved infinitesimally closer to hers, and she
found herself too enchanted to pull away. "I'm not always
that easy to like," she whispered.

"Sometimes it's a breeze," he said. "Like when you were
holding Carmen—" his face moved a degree closer "—and
when you cry—" his lips were only a breath away. "And
when I kissed you the other day..."

He took her hand from where she had it tucked under her
arm and pressed it to his chest. She felt his heart racing

against her hand, felt his breath tickling her lips, felt his eyes caressing her soul.

And when he kissed her, the empty corridors of her spirit and all the injustices in her life seemed to fade away. There was no more truth except for what he gave her.

CHAPTER EIGHT

HIS KISS WAS A GENTLE SIGH, a whisper across her lips, a breath of seduction. It became an offering rather than a demand, a question rather than a statement.

Their lips parted, withdrew ever so slightly, and his forehead pressed against hers. "Let's not be enemies tonight," he whispered.

Jo opened her lips and gazed into his eyes, smoky and smoldering in the black of the tent.

"You're beautiful," E.Z. whispered as his hand came up to thread through the roots of her hair. "So beautiful."

His lips brushed hers again, exacting more of a claim as her heart responded with triple-time flutters. Her breath came in shaky suspirations. She moved her hand up his strong chest to his neck, pulsating against her fingers, to his jaw, thick with stubble. His face was rough against her hand, but the mere texture of it excited her. She slid her hand into his hair, felt the satiny smoothness of it igniting nerve endings that had lain dormant for a lifetime.

He deepened the kiss and moved so that he was sitting opposite her. His arms closed around her, cradling her in their strength, and Jo wondered why a man's arms had never felt so protective before. Tears came to her eyes at the poignancy of his touch, and she felt her tongue swirl against his, dancing in anticipation, hope, intention.... She closed her eyes and inhaled the scent of night and earth on his skin.

Despite the coolness outside the tent, E.Z.'s skin felt feverishly warm. Their lips broke away, and he kissed her neck. Jo arched back and tried to catch her breath, but the sensation of drowning in a paradise sea pulled her under. His rough jaw brushed along her neck as he nipped her ear, his breath teasing and exciting, inciting a madness that left little room for control.

E.Z. buried his face in a handful of hair, inhaling deeply. "I knew your hair would smell this way," he said. "I knew it would feel this way against my face."

He touched her throat, then let his hand slide down to trace the curve of one breast, stirring her nipple to budded life. She held her breath.

His mouth captured hers again, and his touch grew less subtle. Magic hands molded and massaged, making her believe—for the first time in her life—that such power could exist. Suddenly she felt him releasing a button of her sweater, peeling it away inch by patient inch, until it opened enough for his callused hand to slip inside.

The kiss became deeper as he cupped her breasts in hungry fascination, letting them fill his hands. Yearning ate inside her, a hunger too fierce to fill.

Shivering in torment, Jo slid her hand down his chest, to the waistband of his jeans, and slipped his tank top out. Her hand crept under his shirt. Suddenly it seemed of utmost important to feel the texture of the bare, hair-sprinkled chest that had tantalized her in his photographs...to feel it against her breasts. Her hand rose higher beneath his shirt, up the flat, hard stomach that responded subtly to her touch, and further to the hard muscles heaving with each escalating breath. Her fingertips teased his brown, flat nipples. E.Z. groaned with sweet anguish, and quickly stripped the shirt off over his head.

Her mouth followed her hands, and she tasted his chest with her tongue, painting it in short, maddening strokes. She felt him shuddering against her, fighting the rush that summoned them both. And suddenly his hands were on her, pulling his own shirt off her shoulders, peeling her sweater down her arms to completely expose the breasts that invoked more, much more, than mere touch.

Her breath came in short gasps, and his lips found hers again as his callused hands worked their magic over her, but now the kiss couldn't satisfy, for there was no depth deep enough. Her sweater fell to the ground, and he pulled her flush against his chest, bare skin against bare skin. Her nipples hardened to rosy pebbles, swelling and straining. Teasing, she rose up slightly on her knees and moved them over his chest.

E.Z. issued a shaky breath and slid his hands down her hips, crushing her tightly against him, and he arched her back until her hair swept the ground. Quickly he dipped his head and caught one nipple in his mouth, bit and suckled, his hot breath coming in rapid suspirations. Jo raked her fingers through his satiny hair, feeling his ministrations straight to her core, where he swelled against her, warning that there was no turning back. His eyes, as he moved his mouth over her, were as smoky and hazed as a man seeing a woman bare for the first time. Jo felt a moment of panic. What if she disappointed him, a man who'd seen so many other women this way? But the pleasured way he held her, tasted her, teased her, put those fears to rest.

"You're perfect," he whispered. "So perfect."

As they kissed, E.Z. pulled her down to the sleeping bag. Jo looked up at him, her olive eyes pale in the darkness of the tent. He lowered himself over her, cradling his body against hers. His mouth trailed down to her throat, lingered to taste the indentation at the base of her neck, traveled again to the swelling breasts wet with his kiss, then further down, to the small stomach below, where he circled her navel with his tongue.

His mouth came back to hers, sweet and sultry, addictive, and as their tongues performed a mating dance, she felt him lift up slightly to let his hand slip between them. The kiss grew harder, more urgent, and in a slow, sensuous gesture, he released the zipper of her pants. Her last thread of control snapped as he eased her jeans over her hips, and suddenly, she felt the fiery sting of exigency throbbing through her. He moved too slowly, stopping to explore her womanhood, stirring her to distraction. Jo's eyes closed, and he performed a fantasy that made her shiver and gasp for breath, a fantasy of a star frenzying a stadium full of lust-crazed fans...a star who was hers alone for the night. But as she burst and quivered with his touch, she knew the fantasy was real. E.Z. Ellis was no mirage.

Muffling her moan in his kiss, she tore at his tight jeans, battled them off him, but felt no relief, only ferocious need when they were both bare against each other.

"I want to...love you...slowly," he breathed against her mouth, his words a study in restraint. "I want to love you thoroughly."

"No, E.Z.," she beseeched, a thin sheen of perspiration glowing over her in the darkness. She trembled for completion. "Now."

Their union was immediate and she gasped at its fullness. Their breaths mingled and their heartbeats raced, and the fires that raged within them both joined forces in a raging conflagration.

Gone were the causes for which Jo fought. Gone were the fans for whom E.Z. performed. Gone were the disguises and all the armor. All that was left was a raging fire, swallowing the tattered fragments of their sanity, consuming rational thought. All that was left was a primitive percussive beat, pounding to a crescendo, exploding in scorching waves again and again and again...leaving in its wake a complex woman, and an enigmatic man...both addicted to the searing feeling of completion that neither had known or imagined before, like a drug that one would kill or die for.

And that addiction wasn't one that either would kick
easily.

IN THE AFTERMATH of their passion, Jo and E.Z. lay en-
twined on the sleeping bag in the tiny pup tent. He held her
as if she were a treasure he didn't intend to part with, and
she held him as if he were the protector she had sought all
her life. He pulled the blanket over them, and they slept
more deeply than either of them had since they'd met.

And it didn't matter that they were at opposing sides of
forces neither could agree on. Tonight they had a common
bond....

It wasn't yet dawn when the cold awoke her. Fleetingly Jo
remembered that the temperature had been expected to drop
to forty that night. Now, as she lay on the sleeping bag beneath one skimpy blanket, she knew the weather had done
as expected.

She shivered against him and looked around for her
clothes. They lay scattered over the blanket. She eased out
of his embrace and sat up, reaching for her sweater.

What have I done? she thought.

She had gone and proven Mariah right... *that* was what
she had done. She had gone and fallen under his spell. So
why didn't it feel wrong?

Jo found the rest of her clothes, pulled them on, then
snuggled back under the blanket. For a while she lay on her
side, watching him sleep. In repose, E.Z.'s features looked
more gentle than ever, almost boyish.

A strand of hair hung over his forehead, and Jo brushed
it back with her fingertips. There was so much inside him,
so much more than she would have guessed... than anyone
could guess. She wondered now what she had yet to see.

He stirred and reached out for her, and she let him hold
her in his sleep as she gazed at him in the twilight. What had

he been like as a boy? What did his mother look like? Did
he have sisters and brothers? Cousins? Were they close?

Fragments of his songs that she hadn't understood before played in her mind, and now she wondered if the lyrics
weren't glimpses of his past. There were images of a boy
much like Chris, trying to be a man before his time, thrust
into the world with no one to turn to.

His words of the other day echoed in her head, like the
beginning of an answer she needed. *The kid learns that
being a man isn't wandering the streets alone, and being free
isn't having no one to answer to.* He'd been talking about
the kid in "Shadow Child," but now Jo realized that he
could have been talking about himself. The man alone in a
log cabin, the man in disguise, the man no one really knew.

She moved slightly, pressed a kiss to his chin. He needed
a shave, she thought, and a shower and a change of clothes.
But even so, lying with the blanket halfway up his torso, he
was the most beautiful sight she had ever awakened to. She
knew it wouldn't be hard to get used to this.

The thought sent a chill down her spine, and she sat up
carefully. *You've fallen in love with him,* she thought,
stricken. *You've gone and done it.* And what now? Did she
expect him to be in love with her, as well? Of course not.
Men like E.Z. ran from commitment, from attachment. Intimacy was a prelude to affection, she thought miserably.
Not the result of it. Why should he care about her? She was
hotheaded, and said what she thought, and she was
generally hard to live with. And he hated the things that
meant a lot to her.

Jo got out from under the blanket and slipped out of the
tent. The sun hinted of its coming in the east, and she
breathed in the brisk morning air and chafed her arms. How
would she face him this morning? Should she be coy? Act
as if it was a common occurrence to wake up with a man?
Or be honest, and let him see that she adored him?

Jo brushed her hair back with her fingers and realized she must look awful. What would he think when he saw her looking like a witch with her hair all tangled? Would it disgust him to see the mascara smudged beneath her eyes?

She started out for the warehouse, hoping to find a bathroom somewhere inside, one with mirrors, where she could freshen up before he woke.

Quietly, she opened the door and slipped inside.

The lights, once again, were a shock against the darkness outside. Though the place was quieter, since most everyone was still asleep, the sound of babies fussing and early waking children resounded too loudly for this hour of morning. She glanced around, saw a mother breast-feeding a baby, another at the water fountain mixing formula while bouncing her crying baby on her hip. And all over the room were people draped across the cots, lifeless, hopeless. . . .

Like cold water thrown into a sleepy face, reality hit her again. These people lived here, slept here, ate here. And though Jo had spent the night here herself, it had been a mockery, for something wonderful had come of it. Nothing wonderful had happened to these destitute souls.

She looked toward the corner where the Juarez family slept, and tiptoed toward them. Although there was a warm bed for each of them she couldn't help being touched by the fact that they doubled up. Juarez was with his youngest son of about six, sleeping in what Eden used to call "spoon position." His oldest daughter was with one of her sisters, arms tangled together. And the four other boys were in two pairs, sleeping in sloppy arrangements, but together, all together, as if home and family could be achieved by simple touching and basic human warmth.

But no one slept with Carmen.

Jo tilted her head and frowned down at the baby, who slept dressed in only a dirty T-shirt and panties. She had kicked off her blanket and it had fallen on the concrete floor. Jo bent over, touched the child's leg, and felt that she was cold.

A tear fell on her cheek, ran down to her lip, and she licked it away. *It isn't fair,* she thought. *It's so unfair.* She picked the blanket up and covered the baby, then carefully sat beside her on the bed. The sight of Carmen with her thumb in her mouth, all forgotten and alone, broke Jo's heart. Instinctively Jo took off her shoes, pulled up her feet, and slipped under the covers with her. She slid her arms around the child and snuggled her close. As if Carmen knew in her sleep that she was being loved, her hand came out of her mouth and went across Jo's stomach. Her little fist closed over her shirt, as if to hold that love in her grasp, to keep it from getting away again.

Wrapped in that warmth, in the second type of unique love she had felt that night, Jo fell asleep again. And though she lay in a warehouse that scorned the homelessness of the people here and portrayed despair like she had never seen it, Jo felt strangely complete. Two voids had been filled in her soul that night. And though she had little hope of either of them lasting, she knew her life had been changed irrevocably.

THE EARLIEST RAYS of sunlight were just seeping through the tent flap when E.Z. awoke. The emptiness of the sleeping bag startled him, and he jolted upright. *Where the hell was she?*

Quickly, he pulled on his clothes and glasses and went outside, looked around the grounds for her. A few early risers leaned against the building smoking cigarettes, but there was no sign of Jo.

She'd left him. The abysmal thought sank deep in his soul, restoring the darkness she had temporarily brightened. She'd regretted the night and had gotten up early. Maybe she'd used the pay phone to call a cab, and gone home. At this very moment she was probably cursing herself for sinking so low as to make love to E.Z. Ellis.

He picked up a rock, tossed it in his hand, then gritted his teeth and sent it flying without destination . . . just like him. *Damn her,* he thought. He'd begun to believe she was special. He'd thought he could share with her.

Suddenly he felt tired and old . . . and more alone than he had in some time. It was all right, though, he told himself. He'd been a loner for a long time. He didn't need anyone else. Least of all Jo Calloway.

Still, the scent of her, fresh and breezy, lingered on him. She was on his skin, he thought. *Under* his skin, and he didn't want her there. He started toward the warehouse, intent on going into the men's room before it got too crowded, and washing her scent from him.

It was still too early for most of those housed inside to be up yet, since it was such a late hour before most of them could fall asleep. Despite that, there was already a short line outside the men's room. He took his place at the end of the line, leaned back against the wall and waited.

Absently his eyes drifted to the Juarez family. For a moment, he almost envied their warmth, their closeness. He counted five beds in which two people each slept. Juarez and the boy, the other four sons, the two girls, and . . .

In Carmen's bed, a long mane of red hair draped over the pillow and tickled the floor. E.Z. straightened instantly, and the anger and guardedness on his face vanished. She was here, holding Carmen like a mother held a sick child, sound asleep next to her.

She didn't leave me, he thought as a slow smile tugged at his lips and spread to his eyes. *She's still here.* He left the line in front of the men's room, and went to her bed. Stooping next to it, he lifted her hair from the floor and pushed it back over her face. Jo was more beautiful than he had ever imagined, lying there without pretense, with Carmen's little head on her breast. And her skin was warm, so warm. For a moment he wanted to climb onto the bed beside them, hold them both in his embrace....

Jo stirred, and her eyes opened, squinting against the light. She saw him standing over her and groaned as her hand came up to hide her face. "Oh, Lord, I didn't want you to see me this way."

E.Z.'s heart swelled, and he smiled. "What way?"

"This way. Looking like a hag."

His laughter came from deep inside him. "I swear, you've never looked better."

Spirit danced in her eyes. "Gee, thanks. That says a lot for my daily appearance."

He looked down at Carmen, still cradled against Jo and sleeping soundly. "What in the world are you doing here?"

The humor in Jo's eyes faded, and she laid her hand over Carmen's back. "I came in to try and repair myself before you woke up," she confessed, "and when I saw her lying here all alone..." Her voice broke, and she cleared her throat and started over. "They're all sleeping together, E.Z.," she whispered. "And she's left out. She was cold. I didn't want her to be cold."

E.Z. stroked Carmen's hair with a hand Jo knew to be the most sensitive on the planet. Then, gently, he set that hand over Jo's. "She isn't cold now."

"No," Jo whispered. "She isn't."

Their fingers laced together as they gazed at each other, quietly acknowledging that what they felt was good.

"You'd make a wonderful mom," E.Z. said after a moment.

"No," she said. "I'm too selfish. Eden's the mother type. And Tess would be a good mother, but she's divorced now. Mariah and I, we'd just make good aunts."

"You sell yourself short," he said, his eyes sparkling. "Just look at you lying there with her." He smiled. "I could watch you with her all day."

Jo frowned, and her eyes grew troubled again. "I wish I *were* her mother, E.Z. I'd take her away from all this, and give her a frilly little bed of her own, with a warm comforter to pull over her at night, and ruffled curtains and a teddy bear."

He moved his hand to cup Jo's chin, and made her look at him. "But you aren't her mother," he whispered. "And no matter how much attention you show her now, when you leave, things will go back to being the way they were for her."

"Still," she said. "That's no reason not to do something. We can do what we can."

"Yeah," E.Z. said. "We can do what we can. That's why I'm here."

His hand went to her cheek, stroking it with the back of a knuckle. Jo's heart had never felt more full, and she wanted to bottle the feeling.

"I guess the night backfired on me," E.Z. said.

"What do you mean?"

"I brought you here to teach you a lesson. And you taught me something instead."

Jo smiled. "What did I teach you?"

"That there was more to you than fire and anger. That, while you do tend to stand back and fight, you are capable of reaching out, too."

"Well," Jo whispered solemnly. "If it makes you feel any better, I learned a few things, too."

He brushed his fingers through her silky hair, bringing a strand to his lips. Jo watched the sensuous way he kissed it, making her mouth ache for attention of its own. "I'll take you home now, whenever you're ready."

"Not yet," she whispered. "Not until Carmen wakes up."

E.Z. shook his head and leaned over to kiss Jo's forehead. "Amazing. Last night you were fighting to go home, and this morning I can't pry you away."

"A lot of things became clearer last night," she said.

"Yeah, they did," he agreed.

And as the morning grew older and the others woke and rose, E.Z. sat beside Carmen's bed, watching Jo become more and more human to him.

IT WASN'T EASY for Jo to leave Carmen when it was time for E.Z. to take her home, but digging deeply into her reservoirs of strength, she forced herself to do what she had to. The ride home was quiet, pensive, as both were lost in their private thoughts...thoughts so similar that they required no discussion. When he finally reached her driveway at Calloway Corners, E.Z. silenced the thunderous VW, but made no attempt to get out.

He took off his glasses, tossed them onto the dashboard, and brought his eyes to hers. They were vulnerable eyes, she thought as she gazed at him. The eyes of a man who gave more then he expected to get in return. Gently caressing her cheek with his knuckle, he smiled. "Well, that was some night."

"Yeah," she whispered. "Some night." The reminder of their intimacy seemed awkward in the daylight, and she suddenly felt the need to let him know that she didn't expect anything more from him. She looked down at her hands, growing clammy in her lap. "You know, what happened last night...well, it just happened. I mean, we were both caught up in some emotional wave...I don't think—"

E.Z. stiffened, and a frown altered his peaceful expression. He hooked a finger under her chin and turned her face up to his. "Wait a minute. You aren't about to give me a polite kiss-off, are you?"

Jo recognized the alarm in his eyes, and marveled at the fact that he saw himself at the disadvantage. For the umpteenth time since she'd met him, Jo found herself without an answer.

"Because I don't believe in one-night stands," he went on. "It isn't my style."

"Oh." The word expressed both pleasant surprise and profound relief. She couldn't stop the smile sparkling in her eyes. "I don't, either. I just thought—"

"That the big rock star likes shuffling his women like a card hand," he finished.

She smiled, feeling foolish that he had read her thoughts so clearly. "Something like that. If I'd been right, though, I'd have been mad as heck."

He picked up her hair, wound it around a finger and drew her closer to him. "You have so much fire, Jo," he whispered against her lips. "Such drive. You don't even know your own power, do you?"

Her answer was lost when he kissed her so gently that she felt her heart melting. When he pulled back, he didn't release his hold on her hair . . . or her heart. "You know, I'm not going to be easy to get rid of."

"I'm not sure I want to get rid of you," she said.

"Despite our cross purposes," he went on. "I think I can separate my professional and personal life. Can you?"

"I'll give it a try," she promised. "We'll just see."

After another long, lingering, until-later kiss, he left her. And as she watched him drive away in the little car that threatened to drop its engine before it ever got him home, Jo wondered if it could really be possible to reconcile her fight with her feelings.

IT DIDN'T OCCUR to Jo that she'd have some serious explaining to do to Mariah until later that morning, when she was already at her sister's door, facing her, hoping to drill

Ford for some more insight into E.Z. Ellis. Mariah was bound to have a field day with what had happened last night.

"All right," Jo said, stretching her arms out defenselessly. "Here I am. Give me your best shot."

The spirit that usually brightened Mariah's face was absent today, but Jo simply wrote it off to the early hour. "What are you talking about?" Mariah grumped.

Jo stepped inside the trailer and closed the door behind her. The room was a mess, and the curtains were still drawn. No lights were on, and Jo wondered if Mariah had been sitting alone in the dark. "I'm talking about last night," Jo said. "Don't tell me you haven't been sitting around chuckling all night, since E.Z. jerked me up from the dinner table."

Mariah sat down and pulled a pillow to her stomach. "Oh that. Maybe I had a chuckle or two last night. I haven't given it much thought this morning, though."

Jo opened a curtain, allowing some light to chase away the oppressive darkness. Mariah only shaded her eyes and dropped her head back against the sofa cushion. "Are you all right?"

"Sure." Mariah's voice cracked. Her lips began to twitch, and tears sprang to her eyes. "I'm fine. Why?"

Jo felt suddenly alarmed, for Mariah rarely cried. What could be so wrong that it could hinder her sister's spirit so? Jo sank to the couch next to Mariah and pressed her hand to her forehead. It felt normal, if anything about her sister ever could be. "Riah, What's the matter? You're sick aren't you?"

Mariah swatted Jo's hand away. "Just a little headache. I don't have a fever. I'm fine."

"I'll take you to the doctor," Jo offered.

"No." Mariah's refusal was adamant and quick... suspiciously so. "I don't need to go to the doctor, Jo. It's probably the flu. I just need to lie down or something. I'm fine. Really.''

Jo only stared at her, unconvinced. Mariah hadn't brushed her hair, and the dark circles beneath her eyes hinted that she hadn't slept well, either.

She released a huge sigh, and glanced around the trailer, wondering if Ford could enlighten her on Mariah's mood. Had they had a fight? Was she worried about her marriage? "Where's Ford?" she asked. "I need to see him."

"He's at work."

"Does he know about your condition?"

Mariah's eyes snapped to Jo. "What condition?"

"Does he know that you're sick?" Jo asked. "Does he know that your body was snatched last night and inhabited by some alien?"

Mariah got up slowly and went into the tiny kitchen for a glass of water. "I wasn't sick when he left. It came on all of a sudden." She drank from the glass, touched her stomach again, and turned back to Jo. "And, Jo, if you see him, don't tell him. Do you hear me?"

"Good grief, Riah. It isn't like it's some deep dark secret, is it?" Jo asked, and went into the kitchen to feel Mariah's head again, as though something might have changed in the last few minutes. When her forehead was still cool, she dropped her hands helplessly. "Besides, I don't think I'll be seeing him before you do. I'll just wait for him to get home tonight."

"He won't be home until late," Mariah said, gripping her head again. "He has a gig."

"A gig? He's a preacher, not a musician."

Mariah waved her hand impatiently. "A *wedding!* He has to do a wedding."

"Oh." Jo sighed with frustration and started for the door. "Okay, well, I'll just go see him at his office, then." She turned back and regarded Mariah with worried eyes. "Are you sure you'll be all right here alone?"

"I'll be great here alone," Mariah said. "And don't say a word to him about this. I mean it."

"I wouldn't dream of it," Jo said. "It could ruin your marriage, after all, if he found out you were vulnerable enough to catch the flu. Heaven forbid. As a matter of fact, I think that's legitimate grounds for divorce."

Mariah didn't find that amusing. "I'm warning you," she said with utmost conviction in her pale eyes. "This is not a joke."

Jo knew then that there was more to Mariah's problem than physical illness. There was something terribly wrong. "Okay, Riah," she said quietly. "But I'm coming back later to check on you. And if you need me or Eden, call, okay? I'll be right over."

Mariah didn't answer. Instead, she started back to her bedroom, leaving Jo confused and feeling like the big sister being shunned and shut out of Mariah's life.

CHAPTER NINE

ALTHOUGH IT WAS AGAINST her better judgment to keep quiet about Mariah's illness, Jo kept her word. Almost a dozen times while she was with Ford, she started to tell him to go home and check on his wife. But if there was anything worse than Mariah's teasing, it was her wrath. And Jo didn't want it turned on her. So instead of making small talk about Mariah or the church or the Calloway mill, she got right to the point.

"I want you to tell me how E.Z. knows about Sullivan's, and how he's connected to you," she said, as if the answers were simple.

Ford fidgeted and put the top on the pen he held. "I don't think it's my place to tell you that. E.Z.'s not the type to want a lot of credit. He operates quietly."

Jo tried to read what Ford *wasn't* saying. "Then he's connected with Sullivan's in some way?"

"You could say that," Ford said.

"How? Is he contributing money to it?"

"Something like that," Ford said.

Jo leaned forward in her chair and zeroed in on Ford's face. She had always been good at reading between the lines. "Is he financing it?"

Ford stroked his lip with his finger, and looked off to the side, considering the question.

"He is! He's financing it," Jo said. Ford brought his eyes back to hers and didn't answer. Instead he sat there as stone-faced as a statue, and she mused that he would have made a fortune as a professional poker player. "Blink twice if I'm right."

Ford couldn't help grinning, and he dropped his pen on his desk and steepled his fingers in front of his mouth. "I just don't feel right about telling you this. You're still his enemy."

"His enemy!" Jo leaned back against the cushion, shaking her head helplessly. Should she tell him how she felt about E.Z.? Would he believe her if she said that her night with him just may have affected the rest of her life, how she viewed things, how she acted upon them? "Ford, you have no idea. I'm anything but his enemy."

Ford studied her expression carefully. "Then what are you? Why do you want to know all this?"

Jo propped her elbow on the chair's arm, and set her chin on her palm. Something about her brother-in-law inspired trust, but she had to know that her secrets wouldn't become the family joke. "Can I tell you this in absolute confidence? Will you promise to keep it from my sisters? Especially Mariah?"

Ford raised his hand in a mock vow. "If you can't trust a preacher, who can you trust?"

"I think I'm falling in love with him," Jo said suddenly, before she lost her courage.

Ford came close to flinching, but he didn't say a word. He was good, Jo thought. His psychology training had served him well.

Unable to meet his eyes, she looked down at her hands, traced the lines on one damp palm. "I've never felt like this before, Ford. And I didn't want it to happen. But now it has, and I want to know more about him. He goes so deep, and I only know what I can see. I want to know what else is inside of him." She raised her eyes to his across the desk, beseeching him to help her. "I need to know, Ford. What if he's just playing with me to divert me from the censorship fight?''

Ford breathed a deep sigh, and shook his head with a soft smile. "I never would have counted on Mariah being right."

Jo offered a self-conscious grin. "If you let her know she was, I'll deny it. And then I'll have to hire someone to crush your kneecaps. I can be a pretty violent person, you know."

He chuckled at the mock threat and leaned his elbows on his desk. "All right," he said finally. "I'll tell you what you want to know, because I don't want you to start imagining something's going on with him that isn't. He isn't the type to play with you, Jo. He's for real."

"Then he did finance Sullivan's, right?"

Ford tapped a finger on his pencil sharpener, considering his words. When his eyes met hers again, Jo saw openness, and knew he would tell her everything. "He did more than finance it. He searched out the building, asked me to take care of buying it for him so his name would be left out, and stocked it with beds, blankets, tents—everything you saw there last night. I got together some volunteers to help out, but as far as the money that 'The Church' is loaning those people, well, that's E.Z.'s money. He's spending it hand over fist to help them. Even the volunteers don't know who's behind it."

Jo sat speechless for a moment, letting the information sink in. Then he wasn't just using the people as a test audience or a source of material. And he wasn't just paying lip service to his cause. He was giving, not getting.

"The unique thing about E.Z.," Ford went on, his voice as reverent as if they spoke of someone sanctified, "is that he's willing to do more than just donate his money. To him, that's no big deal. He's gone in there and lived with them, slept with them, eaten with them, played with their kids.... In a few cases, he's found a job for some of them. He knows their needs intimately. And I get the feeling he's just begin-

ning. He seems to have a real passion for the work he's
started."

Jo's heart sank. Why hadn't he told her just how far he'd
gone in this struggle? It would have made a difference in the
things she'd said last night.

Jo stood up, went to the window looking out on the
church grounds. Spring had taken firm hold, and the dog-
woods near the building were beginning to bloom, lending
an elegance to such a simple place . . . the way E.Z. lent his
own beauty to Sullivan's. How could she have doubted him,
even for a moment? "All morning, I've been kicking myself for falling for him. But maybe my instincts were wiser
than I was," she whispered. "It's just so hard for me to understand why someone like him would be attracted to me."

Ford flashed the grin that had charmed Mariah's heart
months ago. "There's just something about those Calloway women," he said.

When Jo left the church to go back home, she couldn't
help wishing from some deep chamber of her heart that it
was in her stars to be half as lucky as Mariah had been upon
finding Ford.

But the reality of things never quite escaped her. E.Z. was
still the rock star she was trying to get censored, and for that
reason alone their relationship was as volatile as her fight
itself.

Later that day, Jo stood under the hot spraying water of
the shower, aware of how complicated she had made his life.
It would be difficult to represent E.Z. to the committee as
someone who didn't care how his lyrics affected people,
when she knew that he cared for others more than the average person. It would be impossible to malign him as some
bawdy trickster when she was in love with him.

She tried to shake off the thoughts, tried to consider her
responsibilities instead. Mentally she made a list of all the
things she should be doing . . . phone calls that needed re-

turning, letters that had to be answered, speeches she needed to write. But all she could think of was going out to see E.Z., to find out if last night hadn't been a dream, if his eyes really did light up when he looked at her, if his smile was genuine.

All she could think of was clinging to the moment while she had it, before reality intruded and made their relationship just another injustice in Jo's life.

When she'd dried her hair and donned a fresh white blouse and a denim skirt, Jo decided the hours she'd spent away from E.Z. so far were long enough. Why hadn't he called? Had he already forgotten about her? Had he remembered what a bear she could be?

And then it dawned on her that he didn't have a phone in his house. So, in her mind, there was only one thing to do.

It was mid-afternoon when Jo reached Lake Bisteneau and saw the VW sitting in his yard. The car was becoming like a dear old friend. Nervously, almost shyly, she knocked on the door.

E.Z. came to the door wearing only a pair of jeans and a smile, and looking like the fantasy of every female from thirteen to eighty-two. Propping his elbow on the casing, he grinned down at her. "You must have ESP." His words were delivered in an intimate rumble that made her shiver.

She smiled. "Why?"

"Because I was just wishing you were here."

She dropped her gaze and saw the most sensuous bare feet she'd ever seen, then swept her eyes up his legs, to his hard, flat stomach, to the well-defined chest that spoke of a man with strength both inside and out. The memory of the taste of his neck made her heart flutter, and she forced herself to swallow. "I hope you don't mind. I was just in the neighborhood..."

Her words faded, as though the explanation was secondary and as flimsy as the cool facade she hid behind. E.Z.

grinned with satisfaction, the delight in his eyes making something in her chest dance. Dipping down, he kissed her with the flirtatious gentleness of a raindrop. Her heart did a tailspin.

"Were you working?" she managed to ask. "I didn't want to interrupt—"

He took her hand and pulled her inside the door, his no-doubt actions making her feel like putty. It was the first time in her life that she wanted to be molded. "I'm always working. There's a song in everything. Even you. 'Course, you might not approve of the lyrics that have been going through my mind today." His seductive eyes softened to the smoky color of the sky before a storm.

"That's all I need," Jo said, a teasing grin softening her words. "To be the inspiration of an example of what I want banned. The way things are going lately, the irony wouldn't surprise me."

"That's the hazard of fooling around with a song-writer," he said. "Sometimes we forget to live life, we're so busy writing about it."

"Oh, you live your life," she said, nodding with an insight that she hadn't had yesterday. "You live your life just fine. In fact, that's what I wanted to talk to you about. The way you live it."

The joy in his eyes faded a degree, and his heavy brows drew together just slightly. "Is this going to be a Jo Callo-way lecture?"

She laughed with a lightness that carried more soberness than mirth. "No, it isn't a lecture."

She went to his synthesizer, which he'd left on, and pressed a few keys, listening to it ring beneath her fingers. The sound gave her a feeling of power, and she wondered why she'd never learned to play. It was a shame, having something there that could satisfy in such a unique way, and never to have known it. "I talked to Ford today," she said, still fingering the keys. "About you."

E.Z. hiked a hip against the keyboard, and tipped his head down to see her face. His eyes sparkled with humor. "Don't tell me he told you about my gruesome past as an axe murderer."

Jo smiled up at him. "Worse. He told me what a good person you are."

The sardonic teasing expression he wore suddenly vanished, and he stood straighter. "Oh."

Jo abandoned the keyboard and faced him. "E.Z., why didn't you tell me about your part in setting up Sullivan's? I accused you of using those people."

"For all you knew I was," he said. He went across the room and gathered up papers he'd left scattered out with music and lyrics tentatively jotted down, started to throw them away, then stopped and stacked them instead. "What difference would it have made?"

The manner in which he tried to seem distracted, undaunted, made her all the more sure of his discomfort. "A big difference," she said. "I had been making you out to be some awful person.... It would have changed my opinion of you...."

"But it wouldn't have changed your mind," he said, turning back to her. "You still wouldn't have liked my lyrics any better."

"Maybe not. But I would have liked *you* better."

His eyes grew smoky and the timbre of his voice dropped. "You seemed to like me okay last night. You didn't need any inside knowledge then."

Jo hedged again and found a knot on the wood floor to focus on. "I followed my instincts last night. I didn't think..."

E.Z. noted the trouble she had with meeting his eyes when she spoke of it. Smiling sadly, he reached out and pushed a

strand of hair out of her eyes, then cupped her chin and
tipped her face up. "That's why it was special. You didn't
need a printout of all my past sins and good deeds to feel the
chemistry between us. It went deeper than what was in your
head."

Jo wondered if he could read in her eyes just how confused she was. "You've changed the subject," she pointed
out. "Why can't you talk about Sullivan's?"

"Why can't you talk about what happened between us?"
he asked.

"Because," she said, turning away and putting some distance between them in the small living room.

"Because why?"

"Just because," she said. Jo turned back around, her
skirt swaying against her bare legs. "It's none of my business. That's it, isn't it? You don't want to talk about your
personal life with me because it's none of my business."

The pain in her eyes was too defined, she thought, and she
tried to harden them, to look less bereft. But she'd never
been good at disguising her feelings. E.Z. smiled and sat
down on the keyboard stool. Reaching out and taking her
hips, he pulled her into the V of his legs. Just when Jo would
have protested, he pressed his forehead against hers and
whispered, "Wrong. What do you want to know that you
don't already know? Just ask me."

Jo looked into his eyes, so blue that they made her heart
mourn that another color even existed. Was he really going
to open up to her? Share with her? Or was it just a way of
appeasing her for the moment?

She felt herself trembling at the feel of his arms around
her and the warm aura that enveloped her. Trying to control her voice, she lifted her hand between their faces and
trailed her fingertip along his bottom lip. "I want to know
why you got involved with the homeless," she said.

"You have the longest eyelashes," he marveled, nipping at one with lips that drove her wild.

She let her cheek press against his. "Why you bought Sullivan's."

"You smell so good," he said. He wadded her hair in his fingers.

"Whether there are more places like it," Jo went on as dispassionately as was possible when her passion was escalating.

His lips grazed hers with a tentativeness that made her ache. "You taste like strawberries," he said.

She closed her eyes and tried to hold on to the questions that seemed to be growing dimmer and dimmer. "Where you came from."

"Damn, you talk a lot." His hot breath tickled her ear. She shivered.

"E.Z., you're evading again," she whispered. "If you don't want me to know, just say so."

His hands slid down to her hips, and he pressed her against him with more sensual pressure. "I want you to know everything," he said, his breath getting shallow. "Just . . . can't we wait a little while . . . my mind's not exactly on it right now."

His lips captured hers before Jo could protest, and she felt herself growing weak and spineless. For the first time in her life, she didn't mind the feeling. His kiss was a reminder of the heights he'd shown her last night, of the joy of surrender, of the ecstasy of no control. She slid her arms around his neck, felt her breasts crushing against him, and his own response as she moved subtly, following those instincts again.

When the kiss was finished, she caught her breath and tried to speak. "But there's so much I want to know," she whispered.

E.Z.'s tongue made a journey down her neck, stopped at the first button of her blouse. "Go ahead," he breathed. "I'm listening."

He released one button of her blouse and nipped at her chest.

The words came quicker as her breath expelled more rapidly. "What your mother's maiden name was. How many sisters and brothers you have."

He opened another button, then another. His lips found the swelling mound of one bare breast.

"If your father's proud of you. If you go back to your class reunions... If you eat meat...if you like cheesecake."

His hand slid inside her blouse, found one straining nipple, massaged it lightly with his thumb. She gasped. She felt her blouse falling off one shoulder, and her mind went cloudy.

"E.Z...." she moaned.

His mouth came back to hers, urgently, ardently, and when Jo surrendered, he lifted her in his arms. The kiss grew deeper, more demanding, more commanding, as he carried her to his unmade bed. He let her legs slide down his body, but he kept his hand on her bare thigh, letting the skirt slide upward until his fingers trailed the elastic of her panties, making her suddenly impatient and frustrated with desire.

Trembling, she pressed hard against him, feeling the swell of his own need. Her mouth went to his neck, then his chest. She groped for his jeans, pulled the snap and released the zipper. Before she could do more, he had her out of her blouse and bra and had opened her skirt. It fell in a puddle at her feet, leaving her only in the skimpy bikini panties that she'd chosen just for him.

In the daze of passion, they made the disrobing complete, and suddenly she was on the bed, the goose-down mattress surrendering to her shape, then surrendering again when his weight anchored her more deeply. Their kiss was hot and melding, breathless and desperate. The contact of emblazoned flesh maddened them both.

Jo gasped as they finished the union and wondered if there would ever be a moment in her life again when she would feel as complete. The joy escalated as they moved together, and she felt herself losing all control, all thought, all consciousness, but it was good. For the flight she took with E.Z. was to a higher level than she had flown before. The sights seemed clearer there, the sounds more vivid, the colors sharper. And then she fell back to earth again, her skin damp with passion, and savored the ecstasy in his arms.

The release gave her such a feeling of peace, so much contentment, so much sleepy joy, that she fell into a deep slumber in just a few moments. And E.Z. never let her go.

IT WAS HOURS LATER when Jo awoke, and she saw that darkness was invading the room. She was still in E.Z.'s arms, warm and secure, and it occurred to her that she could spend a lifetime in just this position. With sleepy eyes she turned her face up to his and saw that he wasn't asleep. Instead he was watching her with a poignant smile on the most heart-stopping face she'd ever seen. "I could get used to this," he whispered.

She smiled and stretched like a kitten and turned to see him more clearly. "You're dangerous," she said. "You know that, don't you?"

"Me?" he asked. "I was just sitting here minding my own business. You were the one who showed up out here looking like one of my favorite fantasies."

She pulled the sheet over her bare breasts and sat up. "You had ulterior motives," she accused him, gently. "You didn't want to answer my questions, so you seduced me."

He pulled the sheet back down, traced the pad of his thumb over one warm breast. Its tip hardened to life. "I really will answer all your questions," he said. "I just got a little sidetracked."

Seeing they were headed in that direction again, Jo pushed his hand away and reached for her blouse on the floor.

E.Z. sat up in bed and watched her getting dressed. With the sheet rumpled around and over him, he was the perfect centerfold image. What the world wouldn't pay for a poster of him this way, Jo mused. And she'd be the highest bidder.

"What is it?" he asked. "Not regrets..."

"No, not regrets," she said with a sad sigh. "It's just that I don't know what happens to me. I've never been like this before...just getting off track and distracted.... It isn't like me."

"It isn't really like me, either," E.Z. said. "Does that make you feel any better?"

She buttoned her skirt and looked at him, seeing the seriousness, the intensity in his eyes. "That's just it," she said. "I don't really know what *is* like you. I don't really know you at all. We've been intimate...but we don't know each other. There's something wrong with that."

Jo found her shoes, slipped them on, and started for the bedroom door.

E.Z. got out of bed and reached her before she left the room. When she turned around she saw that he wasn't going to let her down. "Those questions you wanted to ask. They meant a lot, didn't they?"

"Yes," she said. "I don't make love to just anybody, you know. It bothers me a lot that I don't know anything more about you than *People* magazine does."

E.Z. gazed down at her, and she felt her soul stripped and exposed for his eyes only. And she realized she didn't mind the feeling all that much. "Let's talk now," he said. "I'll tell you whatever you want to know. Right down to the cheesecake."

Feeling as if she'd won something too special to name, she sat back on the bed. Her eyes were bright with anticipation as he came to sit beside her. "Start with Sullivan's," she said.

He looked down at the rumpled sheets, as if it wasn't easy disclosing secrets that he'd held locked inside so long. The dusk grew thicker in the room, but Jo didn't reach for the lamp. E.Z. wouldn't be as open with her in the light, she feared. He got his brush off the table beside the bed, sat behind her, and began to brush her hair as he spoke. The gesture made her feel closer to him. No one other than her sisters had ever brushed her hair before. "I like to be with people," he began, sneaking up on the subject as though he could tackle it better that way. "Ordinary people. People who don't know who I am. When I'm in a new town, I like to walk at night alone, just talking to them, meeting them, finding out about them. Sometimes I don't like what I see."

"Meaning, people without places to live?" she prodded.

"Yeah," he said. His brushing had a hypnotic effect, like his quiet voice. "I ran across a family living in their car. They had been driving across the country to find work, and their money was stolen. They'd had to stop here to find work enough to get them where they were going, but they didn't have enough for a hotel. It seemed wrong."

She glanced back at him over her shoulder. "But the bad luck of one family couldn't have been the only catalyst."

"It wasn't," he admitted. He set down the brush and separated her hair into three sections. It took a moment for her to realize that he was braiding the long tendrils, as he went on with his confession. "I started looking and found more and more people who had no place to go. Some of them slept under the overpasses on the highways, in old, abandoned buildings infested with rats, in cardboard boxes to keep out the wind. So I started looking for a place where they could stay. And I found Sullivan's. The plant had gone out of business, and it was sitting there empty, all boarded up. And one day I ran into Ford and some of his church members, doling out food to some of the homeless. So I approached him and told him who I was and asked him to buy the building for me. I didn't want anyone to know I was involved, because I didn't want to turn it into some media event. It was a private matter, and I wanted it kept that way. And I wanted to be able to go there whenever I wanted, to keep an eye on things."

Jo's eyebrows knit together, and she tried to picture the people...the children...sleeping the way E.Z. had described, before they'd had Sullivan's. "Are there other places like Sullivan's? Places that you've financed?"

"Not yet," he said, his fingers weaving her hair with a deftness that amazed her. "But I'd like to find more. I keep discovering new needs. New ways to make things a little better for them. But one empty warehouse with a bunch of beds isn't going to solve the problem. It's a national problem. It won't go away."

She marveled at the way he hid behind his famous facade—the way he hid behind her as he revealed himself—never comfortable with anyone knowing the man who had such a capacity for love. "It would go away if there were more people like you," she said.

He finished the braid and pressed his lips against her neck. "Or you," he whispered. "People who can get mad. People who aren't afraid to cause a little trouble." His fingers began to unweave the braid, as if he couldn't bear to leave it bound.

Jo's eyes filled with tears and she got up to look out the window over the lake, glistening in the early moonlight. "I don't know. What you said last night, about my embracing empty causes. I don't agree with you, and I'm still passionate about censorship, but sometimes..."

"Sometimes you wonder if you really have an effect, and what the hell the difference will be if you do," he finished for her. "I know the feeling."

She leaned back against the window. "What I don't understand, though, is why it's such a secret. Why don't you tackle it on a national basis? You're famous. You could do so much, just lobbying senators, getting some press attention, arranging charity concerts..."

E.Z. smiled sadly, as if she'd missed the point entirely. "See, Jo, that's the difference between you and me. You like to help people en masse. I like to do it one on one. It's better to touch people, to talk to them. As soon as you start organizing, you get into the bureaucracy that's already failed them. You just wind up with new problems."

"But I organize," Jo pointed out. "It works, E.Z. I've helped a lot of people. Changed a lot of laws. That doesn't create new problems."

"How do you know?" he asked. "Do you ever stay with one fight long enough to know if you've created new problems? For instance, you have no idea how many problems censorship will create. Who's going to decide what's good and what's bad?"

"It won't be a person. It'll be a committee. A government appointed committee."

"Please," E.Z. said, dismissing the idea as absurd. "Get realistic here. Government appointed committees have a way of getting lost in paperwork. We're talking about *opinions*. *Impressions*. It'll never work." He saw the defensive look on her face, and sensed her readiness to pounce on the argument. He got off the bed and came to her, taking both her hands in his. "Look, I don't want to argue with you about this," he said softly. "I'm just saying that there are more important things you could be doing with your energy. There are people who need help...one on one."

"But how?" Jo asked, frustrated that she didn't have the answers. "How can one person help one on one? It's physically impossible."

"If you want immediate, broad-reaching results, maybe. But if you're just willing to start somewhere and do a little at a time, it isn't impossible. It's a slow way to change the world, I admit. But sometimes it's the best way."

Downcast, Jo gazed at him for a moment. She didn't like the image he seemed to have of her. "You think I'm full of a lot of hot air, don't you? You think I just spin my wheels."

E.Z. lifted her hand to his lips and kissed her fingertips tenderly. "I think you're a woman packed so full of power that you don't know what to do with it. That's why I wish I had you on my side, instead of fighting against me."

Jo dropped her eyes to her fingers, lingering at his mouth. At the moment, she couldn't conceive of ever fighting him, and yet she knew that this moment had no bearing on the other facets of her life.

As though he sensed her thoughts, E.Z. pulled her back to the bed, sat her down and reached for the acoustic guitar leaning against the wall.

He turned on the lamp, bathing the room in a sparse yellow light, and their shadows merged. E.Z. set one foot on the corner of her bed, rested the guitar on his knee and began to play a melody that was soft and slow and as smooth as honey dripping from its comb. She pulled her feet up, hugged her knees under the loose skirt and rested her chin on her knees. Was it true, his picture of her? Did she hide behind the organizations she fought for? Jo asked herself. Was she so caught up in the broad picture of things that she couldn't reach people?

E.Z. began to sing, and her eyes drifted to him. The song formed out of nowhere, the lyrics about a woman whose fire consumed one moment and ignited the next. A woman whose light made the darkest night bright. A woman who was both devil and angel. And before he'd gotten far into the verse, Jo realized he was singing about her, the sweetest, most poignant song she'd ever heard, painting her as an angel with a tipped halo, rather than as a spitfire who steamrollered anyone in her way. He spoke of her vitality and her vulnerability, her honor and her passion, her courage and her beauty. And he sang the song in such a way that had she not known better, she would have interpreted it as a declaration of love for her, an understated commitment.

But she did know better.

Still her eyes welled with tears, and before she could stop them they were rolling down her face, wetting her lips, clinging to her chin.

E.Z. brought the song to an end and regarded her carefully. "You like it?" he asked.

Jo couldn't find her voice. She only nodded.

He set the guitar down and went to her on the bed, pulled her into his arms and held her against him. Her crying came harder, as if the song had loosened chunks of misery from her soul, making her waver between devastation and delirium.

"What is it?" he asked, wiping away her tears. "Why are you crying? I wrote it for you."

"Because," she said. "I've never had anything like that ... of my own ... really my own ... before."

He kissed her wet cheek and tasted her tears. "You have it now," he whispered.

And this time when they made love it was slower and even more profound than the time before.

CHAPTER TEN

TIME PASSED, and Jo still lay with her head on his chest, savoring the feel of E.Z. stroking her hair as if his rough, hardened hands couldn't get enough of the satiny texture. Beneath her head, she heard his heart still pounding, in slower but more precise rhythm, testifying to the fact that even the aftermath of their lovemaking wasn't anticlimactic.

Jo raised herself to see the clock on his bed table. It was after eight. *Mariah,* she thought suddenly. *I have to check on Mariah.* She looked at E.Z. and propped her head with her hand. "I have to go," she whispered.

His arms closed around her more possessively. "Don't," he said. "Stay with me tonight."

She smiled at the temptation in the offer. "I can't. My sister needs me. I told her I'd come by tonight to check on her."

"Eden?" he asked.

The fact that he remembered her sister's name gave Jo a small feeling of pleasure. "No. Mariah."

His eyebrows rose perceptibly. "Mariah? The one who drives you crazy?"

Jo got up wearily and reached for her clothes. "That's the one. She wasn't feeling very well when I saw her this morning. I'm a little worried about her."

E.Z.'s eyes swept the length of her as she dressed, his gaze a sleepy seduction that made it difficult to keep her distance. "I thought you didn't like her," he said.

Jo stopped what she was doing and looked at him as if he'd said something inconceivable. "Not like her? She's my *sister*."

The seduction in E.Z.'s eyes faded, and a distant sadness filled them. "No law says you have to like your sister," he said. "I've seen sisters and brothers tear each other apart. Almost made me glad I don't have a family."

Jo was horrified. "You don't have a family?"

A guarded look suddenly came to E.Z.'s eyes, and he sat up. "Don't look so sad," he said. "Not everybody is like the Calloways. There are a lot of people out there who get by just fine on their own."

Jo finished buttoning her blouse without taking her stricken eyes from him, and when she was done, she climbed back on the bed and pulled up her feet beneath her. "On your own? What about your parents? You weren't—"

E.Z. suddenly found the need to get dressed, himself. He got out of bed and began to dress, turning his face away from her. "On my own," he said. He glanced back at her, offered a spurious smile. "And I didn't turn out so bad, did I?"

Jo didn't know what to say, but suddenly the room seemed too dark, and E.Z. seemed too distant. Even the lamplight didn't brighten things enough. "E.Z., please," she whispered. "What happened to your parents? How young were you when you were on your own?"

Wearing only his jeans and looking much too much as he did on the covers of his albums, E.Z. turned back to her and met her eyes. His guarded look melted away. "It's no big deal," he said. "Really. My mom died when I was about ten."

Jo's heart contorted, for she knew how harsh that reality could be. "And your father?" she asked.

"I never knew him," E.Z. said.

Jo stood up and took his hands as if she could pull him into herself and soothe his injustices. "What happened to you?"

E.Z. shrugged. "Foster homes. I took off when I was sixteen and took care of myself." A slow, sad smile came to his lips. "Come on," he told her, touching her cheek. "I'm not bitter. That's why I don't like to tell people. They always look at me like I've suffered some kind of unbearable torture. I'm not the victim type, Jo. It wasn't all that terrible."

Jo stared up at him, fathomless sadness in her eyes at the thought of a sixteen-year-old E.Z. wandering the country on his own. The thought was too unsettling to bear. "No wonder you relate so to people who don't have homes. You didn't have one, either."

E.Z. stepped away from her and busied himself straightening up. It was obviously something he wasn't comfortable doing. "Don't make more of this than there is," he said. "The only reason I brought up the whole thing is that I was a little surprised...maybe even a little jealous...that you would leave me to rush off and help the sister you're usually butting heads with."

Jo knew it must present a confusing picture. "Mariah is...Mariah. She drives me absolutely nuts. Sometimes I could strangle her. But she's my sister, and I love her. And when something's wrong, I want to be there for her. Even when I'd rather be here with you."

E.Z. leaned back against his window, crossed his arms and looked down at the floor. He began to laugh lightly, mirthlessly.

She caught the smile and shared it. "What's so funny?"

"You," he said. "When I'm on tour, I have a couple of hundred groupies stand outside my dressing room after each gig, screaming when I come out, begging me to take them back to my room. I've got to admit, it does go to a guy's head after a while. And now here I am with you...and you're going off to be with your sister. It sort of puts things in perspective.''

Jo didn't find the comparison amusing. That angry fire reignited in her eyes. "Good. I hope it puts it in real good perspective, E.Z., because I'm not a groupie, and I never will be. If that's what you want—"

"Hell, no, that's not what I want," E.Z. cut in, suddenly serious again. "If it were, do you think I'd be hiding out here like a criminal? I got tired of the pick-of-the-litter mentality about eight years ago. It gets old, Jo. Real old."

Jo got his brush off of the table and began jerking it through her hair. She turned away from him and faced his mirror on the wall. "You expect me to believe that you let all those groupies down? When they're all just *begging* for the star to take them to bed?"

"I hope you do believe it," he said. "I can't say that my band members don't take advantage of the situation. Even some of the ones who are married. But I found out a long time ago that I can't fill my voids with momentary pleasures. Those only make the voids bigger."

Jo turned back to him and flicked her hair over her shoulder. "Then what was this?" she asked, not really wanting to know the answer.

As if to catch her from falling off the edge of a cliff—or the edge of her imagination—E.Z. left the window and pulled her into his arms. "I told you this morning," he said. "I don't believe in one-night stands. And if you thought I did, you never would have come back here today."

His kiss was growing familiar, excitingly so, but that familiarity left a dull ache in Jo's heart. For as much as she wanted to believe this thing between them was something special, something unusual, Jo couldn't help feeling that it was destined for an early death. If the relationship survived the Senate Commerce hearing, which was doubtful, what would happen when E.Z. went back to his life and his mansion in New Orleans and the women lined up at his doors? What would happen when they realized this relationship wasn't invincible?

He broke the kiss and framed her face with his hands. "Are you sure you can't stay?" he pleaded. "Couldn't you go to her and then come back here later? Or I could come with you?"

The soft plea moved Jo to tears, but she couldn't compromise. Besides she needed some distance to sort out her feelings. "Not tonight," she whispered. "Mariah's upset and sick. It wouldn't be right."

Frustration hardened his face, and he released her from his embrace. "I hope she appreciates it," he said.

"She won't," Jo assured him, going to the door. "But that doesn't change one thing."

She kissed him again, a profound, heart-melding kiss, before she left. And as she pulled away from his house, Jo saw him leaning in the doorway, looking after her like one of the disassociated, one of the forlorn, as alone and lonely as any of the homeless she had met last night.

And she knew that she had left her heart there with him. The thing was, he didn't seem to know it.

IT WAS ALMOST NINE before Jo reached Mariah's trailer. Ford's car wasn't parked in its usual place, but Jo knew Mariah was home, for light flooded the house. She knocked, but when there was no answer, Jo tested the doorknob.

It was unlocked, so she opened it tentatively and stuck her head inside. "Mariah?" she called. "It's me. Are you here?"

She heard the toilet flush, and went into the trailer. The breakfast dishes still cluttered the table where they'd been that morning, and the place had a musty, oppressive feel, as though the doors and windows had been closed tightly all day. Pulling the door shut behind her, she called out again. "Mariah?"

"I'm in here." The voice she heard was hoarse and weak, but it was unmistakably Mariah's.

Jo set her bag down and started back through the trailer to the small bathroom. The door was open, so she reluctantly proceeded. There sat Mariah, on the floor in front of the toilet, looking like an escapee from intensive care. Jo gasped and fell to her knees in front of her sister. "Riah, what's wrong?"

Mariah covered her mouth and waved her sister away. "I'm just a little nauseous," she said. "I'm okay."

"A little nauseous?" Jo asked. "You look like death. Have you been like this all day?"

"No," Mariah whispered, shaking her head. "Mostly I've just had this headache that won't quit. The nausea kind of comes and goes. I think I'm over it now."

She wobbled a little as she got to her feet, and Jo tried to steady her. Mariah grew more ashen as Jo helped her out of the bathroom.

"You didn't have to come, Jo," she said. "I'm fine. Really. I hate it when I'm sick. And this stupid headache..."

"Mariah, have you eaten today?"

Mariah made her way to the kitchen, filled a glass with water. "A little. Didn't do any good."

"What do you mean?"

Mariah gulped down the water. "I mean that none of it stayed down."

Jo gaped at her sister in horror. "Nothing? All day? Mariah, why didn't you call me? Eden knew where I was. Either one of us could have—"

Mariah grabbed her stomach, wavered a bit, then dashed toward the bathroom again. Jo ran behind her and watched her sister lean over the toilet, retching what was left in her stomach. Then Mariah groped for the sink and splashed cold water in her face. "Damn, this is awful."

Jo flushed the commode, grabbed a washcloth from the linen closet and handed it to Mariah. Her sister held it under the running water, then pressed it against her face. "Where's Ford?" Jo demanded. "I'm calling him."

"No!" Mariah said. "And you've got to help me get over this before he gets home. I don't want him to see me this way."

Jo couldn't believe Mariah's attitude. "Don't be ridiculous. You think he'll stop loving you because you're sick? I'm not going to lie to him."

"You'll have to!" Mariah shouted. "He's not going to find out! I'm not ready for him to know yet!"

Jo grabbed Mariah's shoulders and turned her around to look at her. Her eyes were red and tainted with dark shadows. "You must have a fever," she said. "You're talking crazy and you look awful. Come on, I'm taking you to the emergency room."

"No!" Mariah shook out of Jo's hands and backed away from her. "I'm not going."

"Yes, you are!" Jo took her arm, tried to pull her out of the bathroom, but again Mariah moved away.

"Why are you fighting this?" Jo demanded. "You could be dehydrated. You're sick, and you need medical attention."

"You don't go to the emergency room just because your period's two weeks late!" Mariah yelled. "It's asinine!"

Jo stared at her, too stunned, at first, to understand. "What did you say?"

"Oh, Jo." Mariah's forehead broke out in sweat beads, and she leaned over the commode again.

Even though she knew that Mariah was nauseous, a slow smile dawned in Jo's eyes. "Are you pregnant, Riah? Is that what all this is?"

"No...maybe...I don't know." Mariah's eyes filled with tears, and she covered them with a trembling hand. "We've been trying to have a baby...it's possible...."

Jo threw her arms around Mariah's shoulders and laughed out loud. "Riah, that's wonderful! That's... that's..."

Her voice faded as Mariah straightened and looked at her with absolute terror in her eyes. Tears spilled over her lashes and streamed down her cheeks. "Please don't tell Ford, Jo," she whispered, her voice high and cracked. "Not until I'm happy about it. Not until he can look me in the eye and see nothing but pure joy."

Jo cupped Mariah's chin, wiped the hair away from her clammy forehead and gazed into her eyes. "You're not happy? You don't want the baby?"

"Of *course* I want it," Mariah said, breathing in a sharp sob. "I'm just...scared...I don't know if I'm ready...for this...."

Mariah leaned over again, as if to retch into the toilet, but when she didn't, she stood up and fell into Jo's embrace. "I'm so scared, Jo."

Jo held her the way her mother would have, had she been there...had she *ever* been there for Mariah. But the truth was that their mother had never held her youngest daughter. Mariah had never in her life known a mother's love, for Grace Calloway had died during Mariah's own birth. The terror in Mariah's heart now was not new, or surprising, to Jo. Mariah had always lived with the guilt of being the one whose life had caused their mother's death, and she'd always expected to be punished for it, with an early death of her own. Childbirth was her biggest fear of all, and while Ford had helped her to overcome much of her guilt and misery, Jo knew now that Mariah hadn't conquered all of it.

She tightened her hold on Mariah and closed her eyes. "It's okay, Riah," she whispered as her sister wept on her shoulder. "It's going to be fine. Come on. I still want to take you to the emergency room. If you are pregnant, you need to know. This constant vomiting wouldn't be good for you or the baby. And if you aren't, then you're sick and you need help, anyway."

Weak and too weary to fight any longer, Mariah finally nodded. "Just let me leave him a note," she said. She wiped her eyes, her nose, then wobbled into the kitchen and found a pen. "I'll tell him I'm with you. I won't say where, or he'll panic." She scrawled out the note, left it on the refrigerator and grabbed her stomach again. "We might have to pull over a few times on the way."

"That's fine," Jo said. "Just tell me when."

An hour later, Jo sat in the Bossier Medical Center waiting room with Mariah, anticipating the results of the pregnancy test. The nausea had subsided, and now her sister sat numb, pale, clinging to Jo's hand as if it were her final grip on life.

Jo brushed the baby-fine hair out of Mariah's eyes. Something about the fear in her face told her how much Mariah had changed. There was a time when she would have gone to any lengths to keep from letting anyone know she was afraid. The mask Mariah had worn for years had grown to be a vital part of her, and while her sisters were sometimes able to see past it, it was difficult at other times to know the facade from the person it shielded. There was no question now. Mariah was the one who sat like a lonely, misplaced spirit who *believed* she hovered somewhere between life and death...that this possible pregnancy somehow thrust her there.

A deep protective feeling rooted in their childhood came back to Jo as she sat watching the nurses come and go. Unbeckoned came the almost forgotten memory of Mariah at six years old, playing recklessly in the backyard, attempting things that were destined to harm her. Jo had assigned herself as Mariah's protector then, although she, at age ten, had pretended that she didn't want to hear her sister whine when she hurt herself. But Mariah had never whined in her life, and everyone had know that Jo's motives went much deeper.

As if it were yesterday, Jo remembered the day she had found Mariah perched on the green, swaying twigs at the very top of the pecan tree in the backyard. She had screamed for Mariah to get down, but the stubborn child wouldn't move.

"You're going to break your neck!" Jo had shouted.

"No, I'm not," Mariah called down. "I'm trying to see the Empire State Building."

"The Empire State Building is in New York, you little twerp."

"But if I climb high enough," Mariah had said with absolute certainty, "I'll be able to see it, anyway."

Jo had coaxed Mariah for an hour to come down, when Tess, only eight at the time, had nonchalantly informed Jo what the problem was. "She's scared," Tess whispered. "She always climbs too high and can't get down. The limbs are too thin, and she panics. Last time, Mr. Henderson had to go up and get her."

Jo had looked up to the top of the tree, saw Mariah's foot slip, and watched her arms tighten around the limb she held. "Mariah, be still. Don't move. I'm coming up after you!" Jo had called.

Jo would never forget the meticulous way she had negotiated the limbs, testing her weight on each one before she reached her sister. She would also never forget the way

Mariah's hands had trembled when she reached her. With Mariah's arms around her neck, Jo had carefully brought her sister down. But when they got to the bottom, Mariah had lifted her chin high and strutted off as if nothing had happened.

"Don't you ever do that again!" Jo had ordered.

"I will if I want to," Mariah had replied.

"You're crazy, you know that? You could have killed yourself!" Jo remembered having what she thought was the final word. Then Mariah had turned back to Jo, hands on her straight little hips. "I knew you'd come get me if I got stuck," she'd said with all the haughtiness she could muster. "I wasn't even scared."

Now, Jo smiled softly and wondered if this were another of Mariah's death-defying acts. She had tried to get pregnant, even though she felt in her heart that it would be the end of her. Had she known that Jo would be there for her this time, now that she was stuck again?

Trying to get Mariah's mind off her terror, Jo changed the subject. "I was with E.Z. this afternoon," she said. "As much as I hate to admit it, you were right."

Mariah met Jo's eyes, the sadness in her own breaking her sister's heart. "About what?"

"About him mesmerizing me. I'm mesmerized. I admit it."

A tentative smile came to Mariah's lips. "I think I see a pattern developing here. Eden said you spent the night with him, and now the entire afternoon? Sounds serious."

"Hmm," Jo said, looking off into the distance. "It does, doesn't it?" She heaved a heavy sigh.

"My sister with E.Z. Ellis," Mariah said wistfully. "It's about time this family got a little fame. I've done my share for its notoriety, but something tells me E.Z. will do a lot more." She squeezed Jo's hand and managed to smile. "You did catch the bouquet at my wedding."

Jo rolled her eyes. "Mariah, the only reason I caught it was to keep it from hitting me in the face. You practically slam-dunked it into my hands."

A small laugh rose up in Mariah's throat. "It was fate. I had nothing to do with it."

"Nevertheless," Jo said, "this thing between E.Z. and me is not that serious. I'm not the wife type any more than I'm the groupie type." She paused for a moment, and when she spoke, her voice had dropped. "Before we know it, it'll be over. We'll go our separate ways, and he'll forget he ever knew me."

"And during the day the moon is hanging from a pothole in Cincinnati," Mariah said. "Give me a break."

Both sisters smiled, and for a moment it was as if Mariah had forgotten her fears. But Mariah's anxiety returned when she saw the lab technician approach the nurse behind the desk.

"I'm gonna be sick again," Mariah whispered, staring white-faced at the woman smiling at her. "She knows. It's on that piece of paper she's holding."

Jo realized that she held her breath, as well. "She's smiling. It must be good news."

"That I'm pregnant?" Mariah asked. "Or that I'm not?"

Jo looked at Mariah again, not certain herself. "Which would be good news to you, Riah?"

Mariah's hand came up to wad her hair the way she had done as a child. "I don't know," she whispered. "I honestly don't know."

The nurse rounded her desk, smiling as if she were coming to tell Mariah she'd won the Irish Sweepstakes. Mariah's hand tightened on Jo's, trembling like a young leaf blowing in a brisk winter wind. Rarely in her life had Mariah struck Jo as fragile, but now, sitting there with tears in her eyes, looking so young and afraid, Jo realized that Mariah was as brittle as a dry twig.

"Congratulations," the nurse said with a delightful lilt to her voice. "You're pregnant."

Jo caught her breath, but for a moment or so Mariah only gaped up at the woman, expressionless, as though she hadn't heard. And just when Jo was ready to scream for the nurse to do CPR, a soft, feeble smile tugged at Mariah's lips. "I am?"

"Yes," the nurse said, waiting patiently for the slow-arriving joy. "We'll give you a shot and a prescription to help with the nausea. You may have a little virus, too, but you're definitely going to have a baby."

Mariah's hand came up to cover her mouth, and that special Mariah smile spread to her eyes. "Jo? Did you hear her? I'm going to have a baby!"

"Oh, Mariah..." Jo's voice rose to a reverent pitch, just above a whisper. "You're going to have a baby..." Carefully Jo set her hand on Mariah's stomach. Mariah looked down at it, her eyes full of wonder, as if for the first time, she'd acknowledged the miracle inside her.

"Let's go get that shot," Jo said, pulling the shocked Mariah to her feet. "Then we've got to go tell Ford."

Mariah's smile faded a degree, but she reinforced it as best she could. "Yeah. We have to do that, don't we?"

Once they were in the car after the shot, on the way home on the interstate, Mariah laid her head back on the seat and stared out at the passing lights. Was the melancholy returning, Jo wondered. Was it something that wasn't going to go away?

"It was a wedding present, you know," Mariah whispered.

"What was?" Jo asked.

"My having his baby. Ford was willing to wait until I'd overcome this ... whatever it is. But on our wedding night, I told him that I was ready. That I wanted to give him a baby." Mariah's eyes were glossy with tears when she brought them back to Jo. "I really did, Jo."

"And you are," Jo said. "It's wonderful. You should be thrilled."

"I am," Mariah said in a less-than-thrilled voice. "I . . . really I am. . . ."

Jo glanced at her sister in the darkness. A passing pair of headlights illuminated the tears beginning to tumble down her face again. "Mariah, I know you're scared," she said softly. "Your life is about to change. But you'll be great."

The words designed to comfort only seemed to upset Mariah more. When she dropped her head down into her hand, her platinum hair fell around her face. It was their mother, Jo thought without hesitation. Mariah expected to be punished for causing her mother's death, and what more fitting way than in childbirth?

"What happened to Mama," Jo said, her voice too loud in the darkness, "it doesn't happen very often. You know that, don't you?"

Mariah nodded and stifled a sob.

"It won't happen to you, no matter what you might think."

Mariah lifted her head and leaned her face against the glass. "How do you know what I might think?"

The question was almost bitter, almost challenging, but Jo didn't back off. "As great an actress as you are, Mariah, I know you. I know the way you think."

Mariah didn't answer. Instead, she wiped her face, and continued to stare out the window.

"I think each of us was profoundly affected by Mama's death," Jo continued, that same old sense of injustice welling inside her heart. "For the rest of our lives, everything we think and do will be influenced by it. But, Riah, we have to go on."

Mariah didn't answer, but after a moment she grabbed a tissue off the floorboard and dried her face. She dug into her huge purse for a compact, flipped down Jo's visor and found the mirror beneath it. "I look like a nauseous pregnant woman," Mariah said, patting powder under her eyes. "Ford will take one look and run for his life."

The attempt at levity didn't fool Jo, but she let the subject die, realizing that Mariah was handling things the best way she could. "When you tell him you're pregnant, he'll be your slave for the next eight months. You'll never have this kind of leverage again," she said.

Mariah worked on the red circles under her eyes, but it was impossible to cosmetically hide the pain. Still, she tried. "I wonder if my ankles will swell. If there's anything I hate it's big ankles."

"You have to take vitamins, you know," Jo said. "Lots of vitamins."

"Nick will have a stroke when he hears," Mariah mumbled. "He never thought I could pull off a marriage, much less a family."

"Nick?" Jo asked. "That motorcycle buff you rode into town with?"

"Yeah," Mariah said. "My best traveling buddy. He keeps saying he's coming back to Calloway Corners to see if marriage has ruined me. Wait'll he sees me barefoot and pregnant." She leaned back in her seat, rested her head and closed her eyes. "I wonder if it's a boy or a girl," she whispered.

Jo looked at Mariah, who was still staring at herself in the mirror. The pain seemed to have drained out of her with the question, and a tentative joy—an uncertain joy—reigned in her eyes again. "What if it's one of each?" Jo teased.

Mariah started to laugh, and her eyes danced. "Oh, no. Can you imagine? Me with two kids? Just one stretches the outer limits of fantasy." She laid her head back on the seat, smiling at her reflection in the mirror. "I hope it looks like Ford."

Jo smiled, glanced down at Mariah's stomach, and felt a lonely longing in her heart. Automatically she thought of E.Z., and wondered if he had ever wanted children of his own. He was so good with Carmen, she thought. A man that sensitive to a child must have paternal longings. Just as she had maternal ones.

"Do you feel any different, Mariah?" she asked. "Having a little life inside you?"

Mariah looked down at her stomach and covered it with a protective hand. "I think so," she said. "I feel... somewhere between giddy and devastated." Her smile faded, and that fear filled her eyes again. "Will you stay with me while I tell him?"

Jo shook her head adamantly. "No. You've got to be alone with him to tell him this. I don't belong there."

"Please, Jo," Mariah pleaded. "If you don't stay, I'll break down, and I want him to see just the joy... just the ecstasy. There's plenty of that...he shouldn't have to see all this other stuff. I'll deal with it. But I need you to help me tell him."

Jo saw the gravel road that led to the trailer coming into view, and she breathed a heavy sigh. "All right. But if it gets intense, I'm leaving. I mean it, Mariah."

Mariah ran a brush quickly through her hair and snapped the visor up as they parked behind Ford's sports car. Jo sat still, waiting for Mariah to get out first. She didn't.

"Did I ever tell you about the time I jumped from an airplane?" Mariah asked, looking with feverish eyes toward the trailer door.

"Only a hundred times," Jo said.

"Well, it felt a lot like this," Mariah went on. "Like jumping with the feeling that your parachute won't open...the absolute *conviction* that your parachute won't open, even though you did everything beforehand to make sure it would.''

''Your parachute will open,'' Jo said quietly. ''I know it will.''

Mariah nodded blandly and got out of the car. Feeling miserable, as if she was intruding on one of the most intimate moments between a man and woman, Jo got out and followed Mariah inside.

Ford met them at the door, as if he'd been waiting right beside it, like a worried husband trying desperately not to panic. ''Where have you two been?'' he demanded. He pulled Mariah into his arms, and she planted a cheery kiss on his lips. ''I called Eden, and she didn't know—''

''Girl talk,'' Mariah said, her smile a little too broad and her eyes a bit too bright. Ford looked down at her and frowned suspiciously.

Tell him, Jo coaxed Mariah with her eyes. *Just do it.*

''Jo's falling in love with E.Z. Ellis,'' Mariah announced.

''What!'' Jo snapped. ''Mariah—!''

Mariah went to the kitchen and began pulling out coffee cups. ''She actually spent the night with him last night,'' she told Ford. ''And all afternoon.''

''Mariah!'' The word whiplashed across the room, but her sister wouldn't be stopped.

Ford was neither amused nor interested. Something in his eyes told Jo that he wasn't fooled, either. ''Mariah, are you all right?''

''No,'' Mariah said, her voice too upbeat to be believed at the late hour. ''I happen to be dying for a cup of tea. Want some coffee?''

Jo looked down at the floor, wishing beyond hope that she could just back away toward the door and let Ford handle her sister. ''Mariah, I really should go. It's been a long—''

"Don't go yet," Mariah said, filling the tea kettle. "We have to celebrate."

Jo slid her hands into her pockets and found that she couldn't look Ford in the eye.

"Celebrate what?" Ford asked cautiously.

"Our new images," Mariah said.

"What new images?"

"Well," Mariah said, bustling around for the sugar, "mine might be a little dumpy for a while. Yours will just be more upright."

Impatience sharpened the edge of Ford's voice. "Mariah, what are you talking about?"

Relieved, Jo couldn't help but smile. Mariah was going to tell him, after all.

"Will you still love me when I look like Shamu the Whale?" Mariah teased. "When Omar the tentmaker has to do my wardrobe?"

Ford squinted and shook his head, trying to decode Mariah's message. A deep frown cut between his brows. "Mariah, what in the world are you talking about?"

The water began to boil, but Mariah didn't seem to notice. Instead she came out of the kitchen, kicked off her shoes, and did a mock waltz to her husband. "Whatsa matter, Rev? Can't you understand plain English? We're talking bambino, papoose, l'enfant..."

Ford's eyes doubled in size, and he stared down at his wife, flabbergasted. "A baby?" he asked in a stunned whisper. He turned to Jo, as if Mariah was too vague to be believed. "A *baby*?"

Jo's smile provided the answer he needed.

"A baby!" He framed Mariah's pale face with his hands, pressed a kiss on her mouth, then lifted her in his arms. Suddenly he set her down, touched her stomach as if he could feel the life, himself. "Are you sure? It isn't just a false alarm? It's really—"

"A baby," Mariah said. She struck a ballerina pose and spun around in a circle. "Get a good look, because I'll start billowing any day now."

Ford lifted her up again and spun her around himself, gales of ecstatic laughter rolling out of him. "Billow all you want! You'll be beautiful."

Mariah's face seemed to drain of whatever color was left. "I wouldn't shake me up too much," she managed to say. "I'm not feeling too steady...."

Ford set her down carefully and gazed into her face. "Are you all right?"

"I'm fine," Mariah almost sang.

Jo wouldn't stand by and listen to that particular deception. "She isn't all right, Ford. She's been nauseous all day. We've been at the emergency room, and she had to get a shot. It could be a virus, or she might have to put up with this for a few months."

Mariah turned on her sister. "Oh, Jo, you're such an alarmist. I'm great. Never felt better. I thought I might start knitting some booties tonight." She slipped out of Ford's arms and went to the closet in the hall.

Jo and Ford watched her as she pulled a bag out of it and began digging. Ford's expression revealed poignant excitement with the shaded beginnings of apprehension.

"Voilà," Mariah said, pulling out a ball of yarn. "What do you think? Pink or blue? Maybe I should go with green. Do you think going along with that pink-blue stuff reinforces gender stereotypes? I used to know this psychologist who thought it did. He said that—"

"Mariah." Ford's gentle utterance of her name forced her to stop mid-sentence, but not for long.

"All right," Mariah said, tossing the yarn back into the bag. "I'll go to the craft store tomorrow and get some red. Primary colors are probably best, anyway."

"Mariah, what is it?" Ford asked, cutting right to the heart of her babbling.

Jo backed toward the door, suddenly feeling like an intruder. "I really have to go. Eden will wonder where I am, and—"

"No!" Mariah said too quickly. "Stay. You haven't had your tea, yet."

Jo looked at the stove, where the pot sat on the burner. The water had almost boiled dry.

"Good grief," Mariah said, darting back to the kitchen. "I must have traded in a few brain cells for the extra hormones." She grabbed the pot without a pot holder, burned her hand, and dropped the kettle on the floor. "Damn!" she cried.

Ford rushed forward to grab her hand and thrust it under a stream of cold running water. "Is it all right? Are *you* all right?"

Mariah jerked her hand away and put a smile back on her face. "Of course I'm all right. How many times are you going to ask that? It's just a little burn . . . no big deal."

"Look at me, Mariah," Ford ordered.

Mariah lifted her brows with a spirit it was obvious she didn't feel. "What?"

"Tell me what's wrong," he said.

"Wrong?" Mariah asked, slipping away from his grasp again. "What could be wrong? Everything's right. Everything. I couldn't be more ecstatic." She bopped across the room to Ford's desk and began stacking papers.

"This is me, Mariah," Ford said. "I know what a fraud you are, remember? Don't hide from me."

Jo saw fresh tears in Mariah's eyes, but her smile didn't waiver. Her brave front broke Jo's heart, forcing her to interfere where she knew she shouldn't. "Mariah . . ." she began, but somehow she couldn't think of the right thing to say to get through to her sister.

"You're scared, aren't you?" Ford asked.

Mariah pivoted on her heel. Her lips were quivering now, and the tears gave her eyes a soft effervescence. "Of course not. I told you I was ready to give you a baby. It was a wedding present, remember? I didn't just make that up."

"I know you didn't," Ford said, obviously hurt that she was shutting him out. "But something's wrong. I can see it. I love you, Mariah. Tell me what's bothering you."

Mariah's smile lost its luster, and hot tears fell onto her cheeks. "Ford, let me be happy. Let me think of the good things. Please, don't analyze. Don't let me spoil it."

Ford pulled his wife into his arms, crushed her face against his shirt. "You crazy little con artist," he said into her hair. "You think I'm gonna think badly of you if you have mixed feelings? You think I'll stop loving you? You think my joy will be any less?"

"Yes," she whispered on a sob. "Because it's crazy, what I'm feeling. One minute I'm flying, the next I'm dragging. It doesn't make sense, and I don't want it to be this way. It isn't supposed to be this way!"

"There isn't a rule book, babe," he whispered. "No one's published a list of permissible feelings."

"But I've spoiled it!" Mariah cried. "I've ruined it. I wanted to wait and tell you when I'd gotten over this. I wanted to tell you while I was floating."

"Thank God you didn't wait," Ford said, holding his wife so tightly that even Mariah couldn't flit away. "Thank God you gave me the chance to help you through this. It's our baby, Mariah. It isn't just your gift to me. It's my gift to you. God's gift to us. A gift isn't supposed to hurt anybody."

"Tell that to my mother," Mariah wept.

Ford closed his eyes and held her tighter, and pulled her down with him onto the couch. She curled up in his lap, crying like a lost child as he held her in his arms.

Mariah is in good hands, Jo thought. And there was nothing more that she could say. Ford could take care of her sister, rescue her, bring her to safety, for he understood Mariah as well, or better, than Jo did herself. From now on he would be the one to "go up and get her if she got stuck." It wasn't Jo's place anymore.

Slowly, sadly, Jo slipped out the front door, feeling the weight of the world on her shoulders as she got back into her car. And for all that her complex younger sister frustrated her, Jo wasn't sure she was ready to stop protecting Mariah just yet.

CHAPTER ELEVEN

JO WOKE BEFORE DAWN the next morning after a restless night filled with hopeless dreams of E.Z. Ellis and all the unjust circumstances that were out of her control—Mariah's, Carmen's, E.Z.'s. She got out of bed, feverishly fighting her depression. She worked on her agenda for the group meeting that evening. The organization would be electing officers, and after tonight she wouldn't be the group's leader. Jo made a list of other civic organizations she needed to contact that day.

When the hour was reasonable, she went to Mariah's to see if Ford had worked her sister out of her misery. Ford answered the door.

"How is she?" Jo asked, peeking around him to the dark, quiet interior of the trailer.

"She's fine," Ford said. "Still sleeping. Don't worry. Before she fell asleep last night, she was laughing and making up names for the baby. We'll get through this. We just need to keep her focusing on the baby itself, rather than the birth. She has trouble seeing past that right now. And Jo, until she feels better about it, let's not tell Eden and Tess, okay? She feels like they won't understand these roller-coaster emotions."

Again, Jo felt as if Mariah's plight was out of her control, and there was little she could do to help. She got back in her car and drove around for an hour, thinking how she felt lonelier and more detached than she ever had in her life.

Why now, when she was back home, albeit temporarily, and when she was in love for the first time since . . . since ever?

The baby Mariah was carrying kept passing through her mind like a lonesome spirit, and suddenly Jo knew the origin of her sadness. It was the order, she thought. Everything was out of order. They were supposed to give birth in order of their ages. Eden would be first, and then Jo, and then Tess and finally Mariah. But nothing had worked out right, she told herself. And life rarely followed any obvious order.

That was why she was sad. She was sad because fate hadn't made *her* a mother. She was sad that her life hadn't made her the mother type. She was sad that there was nothing to indicate that anything was likely to change soon. She was sad that she couldn't see past today with E.Z.

It wasn't fair, and Jo cried as she drove aimlessly toward Bossier City. So many children were out there without mothers . . . so many potential mothers without children. . . .

She thought of Carmen, of the way she had lain alone on the shelter's cot, cold, with no one to cover her. As if it was a logical association, she recalled Mariah as a child, running around Calloway Corners in hand-me-downs from three sisters, barefoot and wild. And she thought of E.Z. at sixteen, roaming the country alone like Chris, because there was no one who knew or cared where he came from or where he was going.

E.Z. had survived, she thought. And Mariah would, too. But Carmen was still young enough to be molded into someone secure and happy, someone who didn't have to chase down the world's injustices the rest of her life, or run from them the way Mariah had once done.

Before Jo realized where she was going, she found herself outside the gates of Sullivan's. She parked her car a block up the road out of sight and walked back to the warehouse.

She wasn't certain why she'd come. All she knew was that she wanted to be there when Carmen woke that morning. She wanted to coax her to eat. She wanted to persuade Juarez to spend more time and energy with his niece. She wanted to see the child smile.

And when Jo entered the warehouse and saw the baby lying sprawled on top of her covers, unbathed and ungroomed, and without a soul around her who really cared, she knew her heart had been right in leading her here.

E.Z.'S FIRST THOUGHT when he awoke that morning in the pup tent at Sullivan's was of Jo Calloway. He thought of her hair trailing over his chest like falling flames, of her skin as white and soft as ivory, of her taste as sweet as the sweetest thing he'd ever known. And he wondered if she slept late on Saturdays.

He got up, picked up his guitar—because he never left it anywhere—shoved on his glasses and pushed through the flap. He stretched under the misty morning sun. Chris, who had taken the tent next to him the night before, was already outside, sitting in solitary pensiveness, staring at the street beyond the gates.

"Mornin'," E.Z. said.

Chris didn't look up. "Mornin'."

"Didn't sleep very well, huh?" E.Z. asked.

"I slept okay." He glanced at E.Z. with empty eyes, and made a poor attempt to sound more upbeat. "That woman you had here the other night. She didn't leave you already, did she?"

E.Z. sat down on the dirt next to Chris and grinned. "She said she'd be back."

Chris raised his brows like he'd heard that before. "Yeah, sure."

E.Z. regarded Chris with amusement. "You don't have a lot of faith, do you?"

"I don't have much luck with girls," Chris muttered. "The ones who like me aren't my type. And girls like yours, well, they're pretty much out of my league."

E.Z. nudged the boy playfully. "Come on, Chris. You've got to give yourself more credit."

Chris shook his head bitterly and pulled a lone weed from the ground in front of him, tore it into tiny bits. "It's true. Don't you ever feel like life just dealt you a certain hand, and no matter what you do or where you go, you'll never really get away from it?"

E.Z.'s smiled faded, and the despair of Chris's worldview began to penetrate like cold metal. Chris was too young to be defeated. "We can change our fate, Chris," he said. "I believe we can become whatever we want to."

"Oh yeah?" Chris's metallic voice was as cold as his words. "Then how come you're sleeping here nights? How come you ain't nursing a cigar with your feet propped up on some fancy desk in an office?"

The hypocrisy of what he was doing struck E.Z. full force, and he wasn't able to answer. He only stared at Chris, at his angry expression, at the hurt in his eyes.

The boy rubbed his face, took a deep, ragged breath, and brought remorseful eyes back to E.Z. "I'm sorry," he said. "You've been nothing but nice to me. I didn't mean it."

"Yes, you did." E.Z. sighed from his soul, looked over the tents and tried to find the words to help the boy without telling him who he was, and that he hadn't let life keep him down . . . that he had made something of himself. But what meaning would hopeful words have coming from a man Chris saw as destitute? "Look, I know things aren't too clear right now," he said quietly. "Nothing makes sense. But sometimes things aren't the way they seem. Sometimes there's a lot more than what we can see."

Chris wasn't buying. He looked at E.Z., vivid doubt in his eyes. "And sometimes things are just what they look like. Hopeless."

E.Z. considered the boy's attitude for a stretch of time. Was Chris homesick? Regretting that he had left whatever he was running from, only to wind up here? E.Z. remembered that same homesickness as a boy, but *his* mother had died. There had been no way to find his way back home. No choices, like Chris seemed to still have.

Finally he felt the time was right for directness. "Why did you run away, Chris?" he asked.

Chris looked up at him, startled. "I didn't run away. I'm of age. I just felt like it was time to move on."

E.Z. leveled his eyes on the boy, not backing down. "You're fifteen if you're a day."

"Sixteen!" Chris corrected indignantly, then sank a little at the realization that he'd given his age away. He mumbled a curse. "Okay, so I ran away. It wasn't like I hurt anybody. I was one less mouth to feed. My mother won't have to break her back to get by, anymore, and when I find a job, I can send money home to help her."

So that was it. The boy was trying to be a man, because he thought that was what his mother needed. "Does she know where you are?" E.Z. asked.

Chris stood up, his face red. "What are *you* gonna do about it? Turn me in? I thought I could trust you!"

"Of course you can trust me," E.Z. said. "If I were going to turn you in, I'd have done it by now. I know what you're going through . . . I've been there."

Chris took a few steps back and leaned against the building. He was a portrait of misery and despair, and E.Z. knew both profoundly. It hadn't been all that many years since he'd lived the way Chris did himself.

You need a singer, mister? I'll play cheap.

The memory came back to him of an awkward teenaged kid with a guitar strapped to his back—the only friend he'd had in the world—standing in the door of a bar he wasn't old enough to walk into.

The bartenders usually snickered at E.Z.'s gumption, and the managers inevitably scoffed...until they heard him play. Then they always got serious, with visions of packed houses, adding up to dollar signs.

Fifty dollars a week and a room in the back, kid. But no booze or I could lose my license.

E.Z. had learned early that his guitar was more than his best friend. It was his ticket to a better life. It was the guitar that got him noticed. It was the guitar that earned him respect. It was the guitar that made him somebody.

Now, he looked down at it sitting on his lap, poised for his fingers to strum. Pensively, he stroked the old, scratched wood, the dull, worn neck, and thought how none of the expensive guitars he'd bought since sounded half as good. There would never be another one like it. He played a gentle chord, and looked up at the boy who was leaning forlornly against the side of the building, unaware of one reason in the world why anyone would notice or respect him...because he truly believed he was nobody. E.Z. wanted Chris to have a shot at changing his life; he wanted to give him a friend that he could take with him and depend on no matter where he wound up. He picked the guitar up by the neck, and handed it to him. "Here," he said softly. "It's yours."

Confusion distorted Chris's face, and he shook his head. "No, I can't take that. I can't even pl—"

"I'll teach you," E.Z. cut in, still extending the guitar for the boy. "It's about the only thing I'm good at."

Chris took a step toward him. E.Z. saw by the way Chris looked at the guitar that he wanted it, but didn't know what it would cost him. "Then why are you giving it away?" he asked. "You won't have one."

E.Z. shrugged as if the overture was insignificant. The more he made of it, the less likely Chris would be to accept it. "I have another one in hock. I'll be able to get it out in a week or two. I want you to have this one."

Tentatively, Chris reached out and took the guitar, staring, astounded, at E.Z. "Why?" he asked, the question a profound whisper.

The words didn't come readily, for E.Z. felt he was handing over the only surviving member of his family. "Because," E.Z. said. "It might bring you luck." He forced a smile. "And just between you and me, if you learn to play it real good, your luck with women just might change, too."

The first real smile he'd ever seen on Chris's face blossomed to life. The expression looked awkward, unfamiliar. The boy sat down on a crate and strummed the instrument reverently. "Man," he whispered. "It's really mine?"

E.Z. knew then that he'd made the right choice, and that he'd put his guitar in the hands of someone who needed it much more than he did. "Take good care of it," he said.

Chris looked as if fate just might be flexible, after all. "You bet I will," he said.

When Chris got caught up in practicing chords, E.Z. left him alone. He scuffed inside the warehouse for a cup of coffee, feeling like a kid who'd just surrendered his security blanket to the town bonfire. Most of the mothers there were up, and the younger children scurried around in high spirits, as if they didn't know there was a better place to be.

Automatically he glanced toward the Juarez family, and to little Carmen's bed. It was empty. He counted the others, realized that she wasn't among them. A deep, startled frown cut into his forehead, and he started toward them.

And that was when he saw her.

Carmen was happily embraced in Jo Calloway's arms, eating a piece of bacon from the plate Jo held on the floor next to them. As if it were the most natural thing in the world for her to be here, in a shelter for the homeless, feeding an orphan child before eight in the morning, she laughed and talked to Carmen.

It was at that moment E.Z. realized he had never cared for a woman before. For the feeling in his heart was so wonderful, so painful, that it had to be something rare. It had to be something binding. It had to be something he could hold on to and depend on, even more than his guitar.

It had to be love.

In the face of such a feeling, he felt awkward, uncertain. He stepped forward, a poignant smile on his face and in his eyes, and gazed down at her.

Jo looked up. "E—" She caught herself, looked around, and started again. "Ellis," she said. "I wondered if you'd stayed here last night."

Laughter tickled up in his throat at the sight of her, at home among the homeless. "What in the world are you doing here?"

Jo's green eyes danced under the bright warehouse lights. "I came to see Carmen. We're buddies now, aren't we, Carmen?"

Carmen touched her face and giggled aloud. Then she turned to E.Z., and held her hands up for him to take her. Deftly he swept her into his arms.

"She does grow on you, doesn't she?" he asked.

"Yeah. It's hard to sleep nights knowing she's here."

E.Z.'s eyes met hers and locked. "You could sleep here, too, Red. I'm perfectly willing to share a tent with you."

Jo's smile was pensive, soft . . . but not accepting.

"Or," he said, lowering his voice to a whisper, "we could stay at my place, like I wanted to do last night . . ." He glanced at Carmen, who seemed to be intently listening to their conversation, and laughed as though he'd been caught mid-fantasy.

"How *was* Mariah?" he asked, changing the subject. "Did she realize the sacrifice I'd made in the name of her health?"

Jo picked up the plate and offered Carmen another piece of bacon. Carmen took it, and began to chew on it. "Mariah's pregnant," Jo said. "She was nauseous and a little upset."

"Mariah?" E.Z. asked. "I haven't seen her that much, but she strikes me as someone who has to work at getting depressed."

"That's just a facade," Jo said. "Mariah runs a lot deeper than that. She carries around a lot of baggage from when she was a kid."

"Don't we all?" E.Z. said.

Jo set down the plate and looked at him, memories of what he'd told her about his life flowing back. "Yeah. I guess we do."

Her gaze fell back to Carmen, who had grown impatient and was reaching for the plate. E.Z. set her down and she scooped up a spoonful of scrambled eggs, jabbed them into her mouth and smiled in satisfaction. Neither Jo nor E.Z. could resist laughing.

"Good?" Jo asked.

"Good," Carmen replied.

The door to the warehouse opened, and Chris came inside, clutching the guitar with the possessiveness of a child with a new and cherished toy. He spotted E.Z. across the warehouse, and ran to him. "Hey, Ellis," he said. "You gotta hear. I've got it now."

Jo looked at the guitar, saw that it was E.Z.'s, and leveled questioning eyes on him. His nod told her that yes, he had given the guitar away.

Chris noticed Jo sitting there and smiled tentatively, though he was too shy to address her directly. "Oh. She's back, huh?"

E.Z. put his arm around her shoulders. "Yeah. I told you she would be."

Chris sat down and strummed the guitar. "Shows what I know about women."

Jo lifted Carmen and gave E.Z. a suspicious look. "What are you two talking about?"

E.Z. slid both arms around her waist. His mouth was against her ear, making her shiver. "Chris thought you'd dumped me. Figured he'd prepare me for it."

"And you told him I'd be back?" Jo asked with a grin.

E.Z.'s voice deepened to a whisper, and he spoke into her ear. "I knew I might have to go get you, but I wasn't ready to give up yet."

Jo's heart burst into a million tiny pieces, each aching for a moment alone with him. He smelled of springtime and morning mist, the way he had when she'd awakened with him here the other morning. The thought sent her pulse careering.

"Listen," Chris said, shattering the moment and forcing their attention to the guitar.

He stuck his tongue between his lips in fierce concentration and strummed the three chords E.Z. had taught him. The crude sounds began to come together, creating a reluctant melody.

When he was finished, Jo and E.Z. made a big deal over his natural "talent," and E.Z. spent some time teaching him a little more while Jo cleaned Carmen up in the bathroom.

Later, when Jo knew she had to get home and dress for the appointments she'd scheduled for that afternoon, E.Z. walked with her to the car. When they reached it, he stood beside her door, reluctant to let her get in.

Jo, too, was in no hurry to go. "It kills me leaving Carmen like that," she said. "I honestly don't know how long I can stay away. We've got to talk to Juarez. Make him spend more time with her."

"The man does the best he can," E.Z. said. "He's trying to find work that can support eight children. Farm work, at that. It's virtually impossible. He's doing everything he can right now just to keep the state from taking any of his kids. A man can only be divided so many ways."

Jo studied the ground, her face sober as she contemplated the horrors of the world in which homeless children had to suffer. E.Z. lifted her chin and feathered his fingers to her cheek.

"You really shouldn't get so involved with her," he whispered. "It only makes it hurt worse when they move on. Besides, it won't be good for her to get attached to you if you won't always be there."

Jo had told herself the same thing a thousand times. Still, she couldn't make herself believe it. "You're just as involved with her as I am," she said. "And you're involved with Chris, too. You gave him your guitar, E.Z. The one you drag around wherever you go. It doesn't take a psychiatrist to know what it means to you."

E.Z. turned back to the warehouse a block up the road, squinting into the breeze. "He needed it more than I did," he said. "It was no big deal."

Jo slid her hand up his back, rested her face between his shoulder blades. His special, unique scent made her want to run away with him to some private place. "Yes it was. It was a real big deal. You know it, and I know it. And someday, when he realizes who you really are, he'll know it, too."

E.Z. turned around and pulled her against him. She looked up at him, adoration in her eyes.

"You're a nice man, E.Z. Ellis," she whispered.

"Nice?" he asked, his head tilting in amused wonder. "Me? The obscene rock star? The one who's corrupting America's youth?"

Jo expelled a weary breath. "I know it doesn't make sense, E.Z. I'm as confused as anyone. Everything is changing color."

"It isn't changing color, Jo," he said. "It's just that you're only now beginning to see those colors. Not black and white. Grays."

"And blues," she said, melting in his eyes.

"And greens," he said, gazing into hers. "And reds." He buried his fingers in her hair. "Beautiful reds."

Their lips came together. Every color blended in a brilliant kaleidoscope of feeling, their embrace drawing them into a pure, hot white light, the product of wholes and halves and fractions of their lives.

When the kiss broke, E.Z. didn't let her go. "I have to go home to New Orleans tomorrow," he said. "To make a video for my next release. Come with me, Jo."

Jo felt the temptation rising inside her as both denial and desire battled in her heart. "You've got to be kidding," she said. "I can't do that."

"Why?"

"Because," she said. She slipped out of his arms, backed away so that she could think. "If I were seen with you, everything I've worked for would be ruined. Nothing I did would have meaning anymore. My work is important to me."

"You're with me now. Why is that different?" he asked.

"You know perfectly well why," she said. "Here, you're Ellis. In New Orleans everyone would know you're E.Z. You're like two different people."

"One person," he said. "I'm only one person. I've told you that."

She went to her car, trying to make sense of her feelings. "I can't go with you, E.Z." The words came without hesitation, but she turned back to him and punctured her inflated resolve with one last question. "When will you be back?"

He shrugged. "I'll only be gone a couple of days, as long as things go okay."

"Good," she said, opening her car door, more shaken than she had been moments before. "Good. Then call me when you get back."

"When I'm just Ellis again?" he asked quietly.

"Something like that," she said. Then, wrenching her eyes away from his sad, knowing ones, she got in her car and drove away.

AS WEARY AS SHE FELT with the fight she had embarked upon, Jo went through her schedule of appointments, earnestly rebuilding her enthusiasm with those she met. But all that day her mind wandered. *It's happening,* she thought. *The end has already begun.* Already they were facing the reality of two worlds too different to unite.

She felt herself growing more divided than ever, zigzagging from poverty to power, from groupie to gang leader, from melting-in-her-shoes fascination to the most frustration she'd ever known.

That's love, a voice in her heart kept chanting. But she did her best to deny it.

She really did believe in her censorship fight, Jo told herself, and she couldn't compromise it for a temporary affair. It was important that children's minds weren't corrupted by satanists and perverts. If she didn't fight, who would?

By the time Jo got to the meeting that night, she felt her old fighting self again, ready to rally the citizens into action, ready to urge them to write letters, make their voices heard, come to Washington with her if they could. What she found that night, however, was that none of the citizens needed her enthusiasm anymore. They had enough of their own.

Half the group was conspicuously absent when she arrived, while the other half hunched over tables and squatted on the floor painting picket signs. "Where have you been?" one of them asked her when she rushed in.

"I had meetings all afternoon," she said. She looked at her watch, noting that she was still ten minutes early for the meeting. "What's going on? I'm not late."

"We tried to call you all afternoon," someone said. "Alan Byzantine's band is giving a concert in town tonight."

"I know that," Jo said. "The ads are all over the radio."

"Well, we're going to picket the concert. Make sure that our voices are heard."

Jo hesitated, looked around and felt a surge of guilt that the idea hadn't been hers. It was a good one, and it would generate a lot of publicity. A peaceful demonstration often was the turning point in such a fight. "I see. Where is everyone else?"

"Already at Hirsch Coliseum," someone said. "We're going over as soon as we get these signs done. We've all been here about an hour and a half. We tried to reach you...."

Jo looked around her, saw the activity in the room, the exuberance in the members' faces, and realized that this was already a bona fide, active organization, without her. She really had no more reason to stay in town. There were other people that needed organizing, other censorship groups that needed leaders. Trying not to be disheartened by the whole situation, she pushed up her sleeves and grabbed a paintbrush. "Where do I start?" she asked.

THE DOORS OF THE COLISEUM were just opening when the rest of the group arrived in a convoy of cars and trucks. It was only a matter of moments before they had piled out and joined the others already picketing the doors. Thousands of young people waited in a thick pack to get in, but the picketers created new confusion.

As she approached, Jo saw that a fight had broken out near one of the signs. A man with a television camera was pushing through the throng trying to get footage of the action. As the crowd parted, Jo gasped. One of her members was engaged in a push-shove joust with a ticket holder.

"Oh no!" she cried, turning to some of the other protesters. "Stop him! That isn't what we came here for!"

Some of them rushed forward and parted the two, but another demonstrator hurled herself in front of the door, barricading it. The crowd began shouting and throwing things at the censorship supporter. They pushed forward, knocking the woman off her feet.

"End the brainwashing," some of the picketers shouted. "Stop Byzantine from corrupting our youth!"

Jo wasn't certain who moved first: her group's members, or the teenaged ticket holders. But suddenly chaos reigned as the picketers were knocked to the side, young teenagers were grabbed and prevented from reaching the doors, demonstrators were cursed and screamed at, fans were jostled and bumped.

"Stop it!" Jo screamed in vain, both to her own people and the ones they fought with. "This was supposed to be peaceful. This isn't getting us anywhere!"

But despite her earnest efforts to control the fray, the television cameras rolled throughout it all.

JO DROVE HOME in a haze that night, shaken to the point of breaking down, but mercifully in too much shock to feel the full impact of what had happened. How had things gotten out of hand, she asked herself. How could she have stopped it?

Jo's forehead grew damp, and she wiped at it with her sleeve as she remembered the way the police with night-

sticks had broken up the crowd. Her group had looked like
violent maniacs rather than peaceful demonstrators trying
to make a point. Hadn't they understood *anything* she'd
taught them? Did they honestly think that scene had helped
their cause?

I'm sunk, she thought dismally. If the Commerce Committee members got wind of the violence, they wouldn't even
listen to her.

Thoughts of Alan Byzantine's lyrics raged through her
mind. They were satanic. Some, the musician had admitted, were even pornographic. His videos portrayed blood-
streaked children with mohawks slashing switchblades at
each other and scantily clad women performing suggestive
acts.

It was her fault. She had called people's attention to the
lyrics. She had gotten them mad. If they'd been able to get
their hands on Alan Byzantine tonight, there was no telling
where it would have stopped. And it would have been her
fault.

They can't know about E.Z., she told herself. If they
knew, they'd be after him. Her, too, probably. If they found
out he was living here among them, they'd expose him and
ruin all his anonymous efforts at Sullivan's. She could never
get them to understand what kind of man he was. Not after
she'd convinced them he was base and obscene.

Jo pulled off the interstate and followed the long, dark
road down to Calloway Corners. The house was lit up, as it
usually was, but it wasn't the lights that caught her eye. It
was the sight of E.Z.'s car in the drive.

He must have seen the news, she thought, her heart
plummeting.

Jo held her breath and got out of her car, waiting for him
to lash out at her the way he had done when she'd been
misquoted in the newspaper. What was going to be her excuse this time? Would he believe that she hadn't been in

control of the crowd? Or would that admission just be damning?

He was leaning against the bashed-in trunk of his car, the darkness hovering over him like a faithful friend. His expression was difficult to read in the night.

"I know what you're thinking," she said.

He didn't move. "What am I thinking?"

"That you told me so," she said.

E.Z. stepped toward her, allowing the moonlight to reveal his face. His eyes were neither harsh nor condemning. "I told you so," he said.

"I tried to stop them," she began, but her voice broke and tears sprang to her eyes. "Oh, E.Z., they were shouting and throwing things and pushing and shoving.... It wasn't what I wanted."

He pulled Jo against him, enclosed her in his strong embrace. "It got out of hand," he said. "It always does."

"Not always," she said. "I've been part of peaceful demonstrations. This was ... just—"

"Asinine," he provided.

Though she didn't like it, the word seemed more than accurate. "Oh, hell. They'll never listen to me in Washington if they hear about this. It makes us look like a bunch of crazy idiots..." She stopped suddenly, wiped her eyes and stepped back from E.Z.'s arms.

"And they'd be right," she added. "At least one of us is a crazy idiot. I'm standing here in the arms of one of the men I'm going to publicly condemn, feeling as if I've found comfort after a day at war, showing him my Achilles heel and telling him how I've screwed up my fight!"

E.Z.'s soft, deep laughter wasn't what she had expected. "I won't use it against you," he said. "I swear. As far as I'm concerned, I plan to zap you in Washington, too. But for now I don't want to think about that, and I don't think you do, either."

She fell back into his arms, tears filling her eyes again. His crushing embrace was the nicest thing she'd experienced since she left him that morning. "No, E.Z., no."

"Then come with me to New Orleans to shoot my video," he entreated again. "You can wear a hat, so no one will recognize that sexy hair. And dark glasses. And a mysterious trench coat if you want. Just come with me. See how I work. See the other side of E.Z. Ellis, rock monster. The side that you think needs taming. It's only fair, you know. You can't really go into that hearing not knowing what goes on behind the scenes."

He pressed his forehead against hers, and her hand strayed to his heart. "Besides," he added. "I don't want to be without you for that long."

Jo looked up into his eyes and saw peace and the promise of escape and the most vivid sense of security she'd ever felt. All that from someone who probably wouldn't be there for her two weeks from now. But like the demonstration at the concert, the choice was out of her control. "Okay," she whispered huskily. "I'll come with you."

CHAPTER TWELVE

THEY SNEAKED AWAY like thieves at the wee morning hour of four, and met the plane at an unmarked gate at the airport. The morning smelled of a unique kind of excitement Jo hadn't encountered before. There was a sense of mystery in the air, a charged alacrity. Jo was excited, for she was rushing off into a world she'd never seen—a world that was E.Z.'s home. There was so much to him, she thought, and she wanted to know it all. She'd seen the good; now it was time to see the bad.

But something told her that her mind wasn't going to change. And neither was her heart. She stood back, quietly watching him as he spoke with the pilot of his plane in a private corridor of the airport where no one would recognize him. He looked so unpretentious, so human, so...so E.Z. He wore a pair of faded jeans that had taken years to break in, and a clean white T-shirt that said "Ski Louisiana," depicting a gator in the swamp on a pair of snow skis. As usual when there was a chance of being recognized, he hid his eyes behind his tinted glasses.

E.Z. reached for her, bringing her into his warm aura, and placed his arm over her shoulders in a gesture that felt very possessive. But the fact that she enjoyed the feeling made her feel guilty. She shouldn't enjoy being his lady on this trip. She should keep her distance, stand back, take notes...something. But it was clear that her heart had other intentions, and this was anything but business.

The pilot opened the door, letting the sound of thunderous engines intrude on the silence.

"Come on," E.Z. said. "That's our plane over there."

Jo saw the plane he pointed to and turned back to him. She hadn't been naive enough to think they'd fly to New Orleans commercially, but she hadn't expected a Lear jet, either.

He pulled her out the door, and holding her hand, began running toward the plane.

"Did you rent this just for this trip?" she asked, holding her beige fedora on with her free hand as they ran. Her hair streamed loosely behind her, though she intended to bind it and tuck it into the hat before they landed.

"No," he said. "It's mine."

"Yours? You *own* this?"

E.Z. reached the steps of the plane and pushed her ahead of him. "It's a minor convenience," he said over the rumbling engine. "The band has a bus, too, but sometimes our concerts are too far apart to go by bus, so we have to fly."

He gestured for her to precede him inside the open door, and she took a tentative step into the cabin.

"Welcome to the sinfully indulgent world of the rock musician," E.Z. whispered in her ear.

Jo caught her breath at the sight of the extravagance that confronted her. The interior of the plane resembled a hotel lobby, complete with wet bar. There was a private bedroom in the back. The furniture was rich leather and velvet, especially designed for comfort.

A man stepped out of the cockpit, his baggy jeans and sweatshirt testimony that he was anything but a pilot. "Where the hell 'ave you been?" he asked in a decidedly Australian accent.

Jo looked at E.Z., wondering if he was about to get reprimanded for something she wasn't aware of. Did rock stars have bosses? But E.Z. only smiled, undaunted. "Jo, meet my manager, Max Cole. Max, Jo."

"Yeah, hi," Max said, grabbing one of the half dozen pens out of his shirt pocket, and a writing tablet from his pants. "E.Z.," he said—pronouncing it "Ayzee"—"I've called every friggin' 'otel in this area trying to reach you. Where the 'ell 'ave you been staying?"

E.Z. went to the bar, got a glass, and made a silent offer to Jo, gesturing toward the chilled orange juice waiting for them. She nodded. "I've just been around, Max," he said. "No big deal. I called when I said I would."

"No big deal?" Max cried. He spun around to the cockpit. "Shut the door and get this plane in the air, will ya?" Then, without missing a beat, he pivoted back to E.Z., his voice escalating in pitch. "I've a stack of contracts a foot 'igh for you to sign. Offers for an entire year that need to be accepted or denied. You won another godforsaken award, E.Z., and the record company wants to know if you'll go to accept it. And your last album just went platinum!"

All the while Max ranted, E.Z. kept smiling. He poured the two glasses of juice, offered one to Jo, then gestured for her to sit down and buckle up. He sat beside her, took off his glasses and stuffed them into his shirt pocket. Sliding down, he slung an ankle over his knee and leaned over to Jo's ear. "He's a little hyper, but he's harmless, really."

Jo managed to keep a straight face.

"The band's gettin' jumpy, E.Z.," Max went on. "They don't know what you're writing. If you could just send a couple of tapes down to them, they could start working on them."

That seemed to catch E.Z.'s attention. "No way, Max. I told you. No one hears them until I'm finished. There's no rush."

"No rush!" Max punched the air. "Damn you, man. You have a contract to record another album next month. What do you intend to do about that?"

"I don't know," E.Z. said, unruffled, but on the edge of impatience. "I thought I might record an album."

"With what? And 'ow can I plan for sessions, producers, anything if I can't get in touch with you to clear it?" He turned to Jo, finally acknowledging her.

"I'll bet *you* know where he lays his head at night," he said, accusingly.

Jo looked at E.Z., trying not to smile.

"Don't you?" Max drilled.

Jo couldn't keep silent any longer. "Yes, as a matter of fact, I do, Mr. Cole, not that you'll believe it if I tell you."

Max's eyes widened to the size of quarters. "Try me," he said. "The man is the closest thing to a nut I know. Tell me where."

Jo met E.Z.'s amused eyes and saw that they were offering her free rein. "He's been sleeping in a pup tent outside an abandoned warehouse," she said.

Max muttered a curse and poured himself a glass of Scotch that he retrieved from beneath the bar. "I'm dying 'ere, and you people are crackin' jokes."

Jo and E.Z. began to laugh, provoking Max further.

"Look, Max," E.Z. said finally, "there's a reason why I don't want anyone to know where I am. I want a little peace."

"But I'm your *manager*!" Max shouted. "What 'n 'ell am I supposed to do while you're 'iding out?"

"Take a vacation," E.Z. suggested. "Relax. You'll still get paid."

Max threw up his hands and addressed Jo again. "Relax. The man says to relax." His eyes bored into E.Z. "What about the Congressional 'earing? Are you gonna be ready for that? They're after you, you know. They'll get you if you aren't ready."

Jo felt herself go rigid, but E.Z. slid his arm around her. His expression sobered noticeably, however. "I'll be ready," he assured Max. He gestured toward the stack of contracts piled in a box on the floor. "As for the offers, no live concerts until further notice, no personal appearances, no interviews, no tours, no acceptance speeches—"

"E.Z., you can't do this! You 'ave responsibilities. People want to see you!"

"Tell them I'm busy working on my album," he said with a businessman's calm that was oddly different from the fly-by-night E.Z. Jo knew. "It's true. I am."

Max threw back his Scotch and grimaced. "Seven o'clock in the morning and you've already driven me to drink. I give up. I'm managing the 'ottest property in the country, and I don't even know where 'n 'ell he lives! A pup tent..." He shook his head and rubbed his face. "And I don't s'pose I can talk you out of pledging all your money on the next album to a bunch of bums, either, can I?"

The plane began to move, but instead of looking out the window, Jo's eyes were fixed on the daggerous look transforming E.Z.'s expression. "I told you, Max. They're not bums. And I don't want to talk about it right now."

Jo felt the plane lifting off the ground, but she hardly noticed. Instinctively she knew that E.Z. didn't want her to hear more. It made her feel uncomfortable, left out. She let go of his hand and clasped hers in her lap.

"All right," Max said. "The godforsaken 'omeless, if that's what you prefer. Man, you can't just sign over everything you make on that album. You're talking about millions of dollars!"

E.Z. jerked his seat belt off and stalked to the stereo. He flipped through the tapes, every fiber of his being rejecting the conversation. "Let it go, Max."

Max went to Jo, beseeching her help. "Tell 'im. A man doesn't give away everything 'e makes for a bunch o' bums. He's got every penny tied up!"

"That's enough!" E.Z. shouted. "I've got plenty. How many mansions and Lear jets and cars can one man have? If I want to give my money to the Timbuktu School of Tap Dancing, then that's what I'll do. Don't worry, you'll still get your cut!"

The sun was just beginning to peek out of the eastern sky, lighting Max's weary face. "That ain't the point, and you know it. But you win. It's your money to throw away."

E.Z. turned on the awe-inspiring stereo in the wall, stared at it for a moment as a Bach concerto began. Jo sat transfixed, watching with awe as E.Z. tried to shake the subject of the homeless, as though his generosity was something to be ashamed of. Finally, he turned back to Max. "What's gonna be there when we land?" he asked, his voice still hard. "Anybody know we're coming?"

"'Ell, yes, they know," Max said. "One of the roadies leaked it to a DJ. You'll be mauled when you get off the plane. I've 'ired extra security."

A sick feeling rose up inside Jo, a feeling that she'd had no business coming here with him. She looked out the window, wishing they hadn't left the ground. E.Z. sensed her trepidation at once.

"You'd better stuff up your hair," he told her balefully. "And put on those shades. I don't think anybody'll recognize you, but there might be television crews."

Max picked up on the comment. "You mean she doesn't want anyone to know she's with you?" he asked E.Z. He began to laugh, the sound as anxious and hyper as his raving had been moments ago. "You've got to be kidding, 'oney. Do you know 'ow many movie stars 'ave tried to nail this guy? Do you know 'ow many models 'ave thrown themselves at 'im?"

Jo didn't want to hear about her competition at the moment. The very idea needled her. Straightening her spine, she began to twist her hair into a bun and muttered, "I'm not a movie star or a model."

"'Ell, E.Z.," Max said. "You can 'ave your pick and you pick someone who has to wear a disguise? What is she? A fugitive?"

Before E.Z. could defend her, Jo answered the question. "Yes, I'm a fugitive. I was convicted of murdering the last man who insulted me."

Max was quiet long enough to grin. He set down his glass and shook his head at E.Z. "So she's a secret, too?" he asked. "What are you? Married?"

Jo choked and began to cough. E.Z.'s angry expression cracked, and he smiled.

"Okay, right," Max said, continuing to guess. "You're not married. You just live together in a pup tent while she runs from the penitentiary."

E.Z. grinned and opened his hands. "Hey, what can I say? You caught us."

They both laughed in spite of the tension, and finally Max collapsed into a chair, giving up on getting any information out of either of them.

Despite his efforts to evade Max's attempt to make him work, E.Z. wound up reading contracts and signing papers for the next half hour. Jo watched and listened, amazed at the legalities involved in being a performer. He hadn't struck her as a businessman before, and this Max person didn't paint the picture of a man with power, a man who dotted every *I* and crossed every *T*. Her image of E.Z. was beginning to change, uncomfortably so, now that she saw him in the context of his real world.

When he at last put his foot down and refused to look at more paperwork, he came back to Jo, took her hand and pulled her into the bedroom at the back of the plane. "We'll be landing soon," he said.

"Where are we going?" she asked.

He left the bedroom door open and went to a weight bench set in the back center of the room. "I have to work out and change clothes before I get off the plane."

"Work out?" she asked. "At this hour of the morning?"

He cocked one side of his mouth in that E.Z. Ellis grin. "It's how I transform myself from human being to rock star." He pulled his shirt over his head, tossed it onto the bed. "The bare chest is part of my trademark," he added. "Wouldn't want to disappoint anyone."

Jo sat on the edge of the bed and smirked at his admitted vanity. She watched him lie back on the bench, hoist the free weights over his chest. "So you have to pump yourself up every time you make an appearance?"

His face reddened as he spoke, and the words came out in grunts. "Don't look so smug... I work out every day, anyway.... it's my job to look a certain way.... The farther I go... to look the way they expect... the less likely I am to be recognized when I... don't want to be...."

Jo looked around, saw the famous white silk scarf hung over a closet door, the tight jeans with a hole strategically placed in the right knee, the suede boots, the vest. Before her eyes, he was changing, she thought. The E.Z. she knew would be gone with hardly any effort at all, and this new person, this new rock beast would emerge in his place. The thought set an aching in her heart. Part of her wanted to cry out, *Don't change. Don't let me see who you really are. I'll miss who I thought you were...*

But still he pumped like a weightlifter in training. And still she watched, unable to take her eyes off him.

He set the free weights back in their holder, sat up and grabbed two barbells from the floor. Bending his arms to build his biceps, he cocked his head to one side and regarded her. "What's the matter? Having second thoughts?"

Jo pulled the fedora lower on her head and wished she could disappear herself. She felt awkward in the presence of the rock star as he came to life. The feeling filled her with self-deprecation. "I don't know," she said.

He kept pumping the weights, making the swelling veins strain against his tanned skin. "It'll be okay. When we get off, you go with Max. That way you won't get hurt."

"Hurt? Why on earth would I get hurt?"

E.Z. shrugged, as if she'd understand soon enough. "The fans get a little crazy sometimes."

"Well, I don't think it's *my* clothes they'll want to tear off," she said.

E.Z. grinned wickedly and set his barbells down. Leaning over her, he whispered, "No, but that isn't such a bad idea now that you mention it."

His lips met hers in a tentative, breathless kiss. But it seemed different now, sitting in the decked-out bedroom of a Lear jet. It seemed odd that she would be kissing the man hundreds of women would be waiting for at the airport. Suddenly she wished she were as ignorant of his identity as the people at Sullivan's. Then she wouldn't have to deal with this anxiety.

E.Z. pulled back and looked into her eyes, as if he sensed the change in her mood, the distance she had put between them. "What are you thinking?" he asked.

She sighed and stood up, then turned away. "That you're such a paradox."

"Why?"

She shook her head and waved off the question. "No, I don't want to get into an argument. It's your life. I don't have any business questioning it."

"Uh-oh." He walked up behind her, turning Jo around to face him. "Come on. Let's hear it."

She gestured toward the weights, as if to change the subject. "No. We'll be on the ground soon. You have to finish working out and change."

"I have all the time I need," he said. "I just won't get off the plane until I'm ready. Now, what's wrong?"

Jo hated herself for feeling the way she did. She averted her eyes. "It's just that I was getting used to seeing you as this humanitarian who selflessly helps the poor...now here we sit while you step into your other identity like it's a robe you wear when it's cold. It doesn't fit. Just when I think I know you, I don't."

"What did you expect?" he asked. "That I'd drive to New Orleans in my VW?"

"No, E.Z., but there's a world of difference between an old VW with the doors threatening to fall off, and a jet that cost in the seven figures, don't you think?"

"It's not just *my* jet," he said. "I bought it for the band. It's been our salvation when we've done world tours. From Japan to Bombay to Cairo to Greece...the tours are exhausting. We can relax up here, have a little privacy, sleep if we need to. I don't make any apologies for that. You get a dozen or so people in here, and it isn't quite as comfortable or luxurious as it looks."

Jo felt ridiculous for making him defend himself. "You don't owe me an explanation," she said, waving him off. "Just...just go back to your weights."

E.Z. set his mouth in a grim line, but finally he lifted the free weights over his head and began pumping his pectorals. "Look," he grunted as he held the weights in the air. "I happen to love what I do. I'm tired of touring...but I love being a musician. I like...that people buy my records...and that they want to meet me...because they like my songs. I *like* being E.Z. Ellis."

"*Which* E.Z. Ellis?" she asked.

He dropped the weights, set them in their holder and placed his hands on his hips. His shoulders heaved as he breathed deeply. "There's only one E.Z. Ellis," he said. "With one set of values and one set of priorities. Just one. If you don't learn anything else on this trip, I hope you'll learn that."

Angry, he turned to the clothes hanging in the closet and began to dress. "Your hair's slipping out of the hat," he said quietly.

Feeling as if she'd been reprimanded for something she hadn't meant to do, Jo got up and went to the mirror. She looked ludicrous, trying to disguise herself with a hat and shades. And yet, if anyone recognized her . . . well, her credibility in the fight for censorship would be ruined.

Miserably she tucked her hair back into the chignon, and felt tears sting her eyes. Why had she come? What had she been thinking?

Jo felt two warm hands on her shoulders, and E.Z. pulled her back against his bare chest. He took the fedora from her head, freed the pins and let her hair tumble around her shoulders. Burying his face in it, he slid his arms around her waist, and she closed her eyes and let her head roll back against his neck. "All dressed up in that hat and those glasses," he whispered, "you don't look like the same Jo Calloway, either. But you feel just the same. . . ."

He turned her to face him, and she felt all her resolve, all her doubts, melting away. For he felt the same, too. E.Z.'s lips found hers and the taste was warm, familiar, gentle as a soft summer breeze. Her hands went to his bare waist. Tentatively they slid up to his chest, felt the rigid, pumped muscles, the smooth, hair-sprinkled flesh, the hard, granuled nipples. For a moment it seemed that nothing had changed.

"You know," she whispered when their lips parted, "I could be really setting myself up for a fall here. You could be planning to get me out there in front of the television cameras, and expose me publicly as a Benedict Arnold."

"Is that what you feel like?" he asked. "A Benedict Arnold?"

She shrugged and turned back to the mirror and began restoring her hair. "Just being here with you makes me feel disloyal to the people I represent."

"Then I'm disloyal, too," he said. "I represent the rock industry. The thing is, I don't see the conflict. Neither of us has changed the other's mind. We haven't hurt anybody. We haven't even been malicious in any of our deceptions." He helped her bind her hair again and watched her turn from a swaying-haired beauty into a chic sophisticate. "What goes on in our personal lives is none of the public's business. The line has to be drawn somewhere."

He turned her away from the mirror, studying her new appearance. "A whole new Jo," he whispered. "I hardly recognize you."

She looked back in the mirror and put her sunglasses on to hide the pain in her eyes. "I hardly recognize myself," she said quietly. And that, she realized, was the most startling truth of all.

E.Z. KEPT THE CROWD WAITING for forty-five minutes after they'd landed while he finished working out and dressing...or undressing. Hundreds of girls were barricaded off from the runway, screaming and shouting as if they hoped that E.Z. was inside looking out, noticing each of them individually.

"Doesn't that noise drive you nuts?" Jo asked, peering out the window.

"I guess I've gotten used to it." E.Z. turned to Max and the six security guards he'd brought on board, all of whom carried walkie-talkies. "You ready, mates?"

They all nodded but Jo wanted to scream out that *she* wasn't ready, and that she'd just wait on the plane until he came back tomorrow, thank you very much. She straightened her sunglasses, her beige fedora and the oversized beige blazer she wore and took a deep breath.

"I'll go out first," E.Z. told her. "Then you come out with Max. I'll wait for you in the limo."

"Limo?" Jo asked, then realized that he couldn't very well push through a thousand screaming fans and be seen getting into a Buick. "Of course. The limo."

She felt dizzy as they opened the door to the plane, then gulped as two security guards preceded E.Z. out. Jo got nauseous as the fans screamed in fever pitch. She wanted to faint when E.Z. stepped out in all his bare-chested glory, and waved at the frenzied crowd.

He started down the steps, surrounded by security men, and Max took Jo's arm, escorting her through the door. The wind whipped up, threatening to blow her hat off, and Jo put her hand over her head to hold it on. E.Z. headed for the crowd, still waving like a conquering hero. Suddenly, part of the baricade fell down, and twenty or thirty fans burst through, bent on reaching the star.

"Oh, my Lord!" Jo whispered.

Max only chuckled and held his walkie-talkie to his ear so that he could hear if any problems developed. "It's okay. 'Appens everytime. They get a little wild, but the guards'll pretty much keep them off 'im. Just keep walking."

Jo watched, astounded, as one of the girls threw her arms around him. E.Z. laughed, as if it were the first time it had happened, and a guard pried her off him. The others held the rest of the women at bay, but he stopped long enough to make their bravado worthwhile. Reaching around the guards, he took four or five of their hands and dropped kisses on them. The girls' ecstatic faces collapsed instantly into tearful adoration. The others behind the barricades went crazy.

The car idled just on the other side of a narrow strip of fans. It had probably been the first to arrive there that morning before that part of the runway had been roped off, Jo reasoned. E.Z. picked up his pace. The guards parted the crowd, and he started through. A few who couldn't be restrained bolted forward. Arms flew around him again, and someone grabbed his scarf. Jo flinched when she saw that the force with which it was being pulled was making it tighten around his neck. Finally it slid off, but E.Z. still couldn't get to the car. He kissed the cheek of the girl who had him in a lock, and the guards pulled her away, freeing him just long enough to make a break for the car. Hands grabbed at him as he fell onto the seat, and he wrestled the door away from them, smiling all the while as if thoroughly enjoying the attention. Never once had he looked annoyed or bedraggled.

Instantly the fever pitch rose, and the barricade fell. A pack of frenzied girls ran to the windows and climbed onto the hood of the car, desperate for one last glimpse of the star.

"Get the 'ell out of 'ere," Max said into the walkie-talkie. "We'll take the other car. Just move before somebody gets hurt!"

To Jo's horror, she saw the car begin to move. Some of the girls hung on, refusing to let go until guards running beside the car pulled them off. And then the limo was speeding around the corner, leaving the crowd, the guards and Jo behind.

Quickly Max put her into another limo and climbed in beside her. The crowd hardly noticed as they pulled out after E.Z.'s car.

Jo fell back in her seat, clutching her chest as she tried to catch her breath. *He left me,* she thought with furious disbelief. Like one of the screaming fans, she'd been abandoned. But what choice had E.Z. had? She closed her eyes and tried to find her bearings, but she feared they'd been left back on the plane. *What a mistake,* she thought of her coming with him. *What a fool I am...*

They hadn't gone a mile before they saw E.Z.'s limo, waiting on the side of the road. "What 'n 'ell's going on?" Max asked the walkie-talkie.

"He wants the girl," E.Z.'s driver answered.

Jo bit her lip and felt her cheeks flushing. She doubted things could get much worse. *"The girl?"* she bit out in a rage.

"He means you," Max said. "Hurry up and get in his car before someone catches up to us."

Jo stayed put, grating her teeth together. "I am not *the girl.*"

Max breathed a curse and turned on the walkie-talkie again. "Could you put that another way, Bill?" Max asked the chauffeur in a patronizing tone. "She says she's not 'the girl.'"

A few seconds passed, and suddenly she heard E.Z.'s laughing, gravelly voice on the speaker. "Jo, this is E.Z. Would you please accept my cordial invitation to join me in my car? It would make me ever so happy."

A tiny smile tugged at Jo's lips, and she took the box from Max. "I'd be happy to," she said into it, then got out and strolled to E.Z.'s car.

He was chuckling when she slipped onto the back seat beside him. "Sorry 'bout that," he said. "Those were Bill's words, not mine."

Jo cast the driver a curt look, but he was too busy pulling back into traffic to notice. She looked over at E.Z., noting the chafed spots on his neck, where the woman who'd grabbed him had hung on. Despite his amusement, he looked a little less together than he had on the plane.

"Your scarf," she said, touching his neck gently. "They took your scarf."

E.Z. gave her a wink and opened a little door in the limo where she expected to see a wet bar. Instead there was a stack of white silk scarves, a bag of peanuts and a roll of throat lozenges. "I lose it every time," he said. Then giving her a teasing smile, added, "That's why I quit wearing shirts. I never got through the crowd still wearing one. Finally I figured if they wanted to see my chest so bad, then I'd just start out that way. That's also why I wear my hair short. When it was long, I lost a handful everytime I went out in public."

Jo had little doubt that the cockamamy stories were true. "How do you live like that?"

"I *don't* live like that," he said. "I work like that. You've seen the way I live."

"But they were tearing you apart. If it weren't for the security guards..."

"I don't even want to think about that," he said. "But, hey. I'm not complaining. Most guys would kill to have women tearing their clothes off."

Jo stared at him, at the genuine laughter in his eyes. She took off her sunglasses and studied him at length as her expression sobered. "Let me ask you something," she said.

His eyes were unguarded. "What?"

"When your life is a masculine fantasy come true, how do you top it? What kind of fantasy is left?"

His eyelids lowered in indolent seduction. "Believe me, I don't have any trouble coming up with new fantasies. Lately there's been an overabundance."

Heat scored her cheeks. "Oh? Like what?"

"Like—" E.Z. pushed the button to raise the middle window, shutting them off from the driver, and leaned closer to her "—making love to a red-haired spitfire in the back of a limousine."

Jo shook her head and tried to hold him off. "No, E.Z. Not here."

"You asked," he reminded her.

His mouth found hers with fever-hot ardor, wet passion that made her heart race out of control. His tongue swirled against hers in a Dionysian dance, making the pit of her stomach ache with wanting him. He moved his hand to her breasts, to the buttons on her blouse. Jo caught his hand as he released the first one.

"No, E.Z.," she repeated.

"Why not?" he whispered. "The windows are black, the driver can't see, we have a good forty-five minutes to kill before we're on the set...."

His mouth found hers again, and she felt herself melting like candle wax. But along with desire, despair escalated within her. Something wasn't right...she felt...cheap. Jo broke free.

"You're making me feel like a groupie," she whispered. "Don't make me feel like that, E.Z."

He sobered and pulled back to study her fully. "A groupie? Why?"

"Groupies satisfy stars in the back of limousines," she said.

The passion in his eyes faded, and something else—regret, self-reproach—replaced it. Suddenly he was buttoning her shirt again and straightening her skirt.

"It's okay," Jo said. "I'll do it."

E.Z. nodded and watched her, his eyes so soft and ocean blue that they made her want to throw her principles out the window. "I'm sorry, Red. I don't want you to feel like that."

"It's okay."

"No, really. I wasn't thinking. I didn't presume—"

"Don't worry about it," she whispered. "Just give me a rain check."

His devilish grin returned. "So...could we at least neck?"

Like two love-struck teenagers, they necked in the back of the limo until they both realized they had fogged the windows. Forcing themselves away from each other, they watched the sights.

Jo was no stranger to New Orleans, but as they made their way to wherever "the set" was, E.Z. passed the time pointing out little-known places that he seemed intimately familiar with. A bar named Jezzie's, where he swore he once worked as a bartender before he'd made it big; a little broken-down nondenominational church where he said his mother had taken him as a kid; a hole-in-the-wall restaurant that he said made the best crawfish known to man.

They wove through the slum section of town, where people wandered the streets with no place to go, where buildings were half-burned-out, where Condemned signs hung on the doors and windows were boarded up. The car slowed, and she saw a crowd forming outside one of those condemned buildings and a line of cars and vans parked up and down the street.

"This is it," E.Z. said, pointing to the most barren, forsaken building she had ever seen. "Isn't it great?"

"Yeah," Jo muttered in a monotone, wondering if she'd actually have to go inside. "Great."

He squeezed her hand and kissed her cheek. "Ready to go see what ole E.Z. Ellis really does for a living?"

She nodded and wondered if there were rats inside.

"We'll have to run through the crowd," he told her, then winking, added, "I'll come back out a little later and let them tear off a few scarves."

And before she could protest, he had opened the door and pulled her through the screaming fans, into the building that looked as if it would fall around them at any moment.

CHAPTER THIRTEEN

IF JO HAD NURTURED any hopes that the dilapidated building would look better on the inside, they were dashed when she stepped inside. The old structure had a dusty aura that lit up like a dry haze when the lights came on. There were few walls for several floors. Only rotting beams that led up and up and up. Technicians and cameramen filled the place, stringing wires and hanging mikes and lights. A multitude of cameras had been placed on dollies and cranes. Above her, on different levels of the old edifice, sat other cameras. Crew members set up microphones and tested lights. Jo couldn't imagine how a video could be filmed here, and yet everyone took the procedure extremely seriously, as if it were the most grave business in the world.

Inside the building the adoration that she had witnessed outside vanished. Now there was only camaraderie and respect. E.Z. stalked in with an authority that left no doubt that he was in command, though he had a director with whom he conferred instantly. After a moment he was back at Jo's side.

"You'll want to stay out of the way of any of the cameras," he said quietly, so that no one else could hear. "That is, if you want to remain anonymous. And I'd keep the hat and glasses on if I were you."

Jo looked around her, beginning to feel a bit paranoid. "Well, I will. But I doubt seriously that any of those cameras will be pointing at me. It's your video."

"It isn't those cameras I'm worried about," he said. "See, beside the video, they're filming a video of how the video was made. Max milks these things for all they're worth. Those cameras will be everywhere, and they'll pick up everything we say. You'll be a curiosity, since you're with me. Just be careful."

Jo saw a camera coming toward them as he spoke, and she stepped back and pulled the hat lower over her forehead. E.Z. was prepared.

"My manager wants to explain the setup of this video to you guys," he said, gesturing toward an unsuspecting Max. "He's over there."

The cameraman nodded and backed away, more interested in the information Max could give him than in Jo at the moment.

"You want to meet the band?" E.Z. asked her.

Feeling more uncomfortable and out of place than she liked to admit, Jo nodded. She tried to lift her chin and straighten her posture, almost daring any one of them to intimidate her, for she felt keenly that they would. She followed E.Z. over to where they lounged in a corner, reading newspapers, talking and drinking soft drinks. It was anything but the picture she had envisioned. With a grin that exposed that slight dimple on his face, E.Z. introduced her to Harris, the bass player, Ivy, the drummer, Sig, the lead guitar player, Master Jones, the saxophone player, and Mulligan, the keyboard player. And then she sat down quietly while they each tried to pry information from E.Z.: his retreat location; the state of their next album; the kind of songs that would be on it.

But even when E.Z. wouldn't budge an inch, she still sensed the camaraderie that had made them one of the world's most popular bands. She wondered how long the men had known each other, what they'd been through together, what they meant to one another. The comfortable feeling they seemed to share was much like that between brothers...she supposed they were the closest thing E.Z. had to a family.

He found Jo a chair in a discreet corner, and she sat there, inconspicuously watching the meticulous activity around her, the expert way E.Z. gave his input and made requests, the artistic direction he insisted upon in precise detail. Max wandered over to her when they were ready to start shooting. E.Z. stood on the set in a pool of light, practicing jumping up to one of the precariously hung beams over his head. Again she wondered what on earth would be the point of this video. So far it didn't make any sense.

"This song'll be a hit," Max said, watching the director organize the crew more efficiently for the scene. "It's my favorite on the album. What do you think of it?"

Jo hated to admit that she didn't know what song they were using. Instantly, she felt stupid. "Refresh my memory," she said.

"Refresh your memory?" Max repeated, astounded. He took a step back and gaped at her. "First you don't want to be seen with 'im, and now you don't even know what song all this 'ooplah is about?"

"So shoot me," Jo retorted. "It hasn't come up."

Max mumbled some unintelligible Australian curse under his breath, as if she had personally insulted him. "The song is called 'Black Walls,'" he said, his accent-heavy voice patronizing her. "Ring a bell?"

She straightened her posture a bit and racked her brain. It did ring a bell... "Off his 'E.Z. Does It' album," she said tentatively. "His latest, right?"

Max's mouth hung open. "Yes, his latest," he said. "So...what do you think o' the song?"

Jo considered the question for a moment and vaguely remembered the song being sandwiched on the album between two others she had been angry about. She fiddled with her hat and sat taller in her chair. "It's fine," she said non-committally, "if you like that sort of thing."

"That sort o' thing!" Max cried, then looked around him and lowered his voice again. "Lady, I don't know where 'e found you—"

Jo stood up and grabbed his shoulder condescendingly, before he called the probing cameras' attention to them. "Calm down. I like the song, if you want to know the truth. I just don't happen to like the ones it comes between on the album. He can do better than those. Much better."

"Oh really?" Max asked. "'Is fans seemed to like 'em all right. Do you know 'ow many millions 'e raked in on those two?"

Jo adjusted her jacket and sat back down. "Money doesn't impress me. Neither does fame." What did impress her, however, was the way E.Z. stood beneath the lights like some mythical god come to enchant the world...at least the female half of it. As much as she fought it, she wasn't exempt from that enchantment.

Before Max had time for a sardonic reply, the director shouted for music, and suddenly the building resounded with E.Z.'s recorded voice. And she realized they were shooting.

Jo sat, captivated, as E.Z. began the scene that seemed nonsensical at first. She watched take after take, piecing the fragmented imagery together. In each scene, as he mouthed the words to his recorded voice, he climbed the beams frantically, perspiring in his effort, until he reached the next floor. There, he would see his band members, leaning around in dark, indolent poses, singing to the chorus. Occasionally as the crew readjusted equipment, E.Z. wandered over to her until the "behind the scenes" camera began to follow him. Then he would move away from her and fraternize with the band.

It wasn't until late that afternoon, when they shot the final scene, that the whole video came together in Jo's mind. It was filmed in a cleared-out room on the very top level, its walls as marred and crumbling as those on previous floors. But there was a difference. In the middle of the concrete slab, near a broken window, lay an oriental rug on which the set designers had placed a deep recliner, a table and a lamp. The video was the story of a man's search for a home, Jo realized at last, and the best he could find was the one he'd built between four "black walls," on the top level of a building that literally crumbled as he climbed.

It was art, she thought suddenly, when they were perfecting the final take of the last scene. Not sleaze. Not seedy. Not even haphazard. And as she watched him perform the final chorus, rocking his hips as he swayed next to the beams, pushing his hair back from his forehead, perspiring down a chest so compelling that it made her palpitate, she realized why, outside, the crowd had swelled, and the roaring cry of "E.Z., E.Z., E.Z." had begun to penetrate the music.

He wasn't two people, she finally admitted to herself. He was one. He was a caring, generous, sweet man who put himself into his music. And this time he'd also told the story of all those homeless souls at Sullivan's, as well. The story was theirs. It was the story of a struggle, and of little hope once they found what they wanted. It was the story of feigned peace in a concrete desert. It was the story of home where no home could exist.

The crew was breaking down when E.Z. got away and came back to her, wiping his neck and face on a clean towel. "Hi," he said. "Bored?"

Jo was almost too moved to speak. "Hardly."

He flung the towel over his shoulder and pulled her against him, blocking her from the cameras with his body.

"Well, what do you think?" he asked quietly, genuine hope for her approval in his azure eyes.

Jo felt tears tighten her throat, and she tried to swallow them back before she spoke. She reached up and touched his face, felt the smooth, shaven skin along his angular jaw and wondered when she'd ever have him to herself. Her eyes glistened as she gazed up at him. "What I think," she whispered, "is that I'm falling in love with you. And heaven only knows what I'm going to do about it."

E.Z.'s eyes softened to the blue of a spring dawn. He opened his mouth to answer, but suddenly there were lights blaring on them, and he looked up to see that the camera was targeting them again. Standing so that his back blocked her from the lens, he whispered, "I can't wait to get my hands in your hair," and then he was off toward the band again, leading the cameras away from Jo.

THAT NIGHT, when the limo took them back to the home E.Z. kept in New Orleans, Jo learned still more about the man inside him.

His house was a huge version of a French castle, surrounded by gates and bars and guards.

"It's beautiful," she whispered, absolutely awestruck when he helped her out of the car.

He looked up at it as if he saw it for the first time, himself. "Yeah. I guess."

Curious at his detached manner, she took his hand and let him lead her up the steps, leaving the driver to take care of the car. They reached the double doors of the house, and he stopped and held her back, hesitating. "Look, I'm not here all that much.... It probably isn't what you expect."

"What do you think I expect?" she asked.

He lifted a shoulder, shook his head. "I don't know. Just . . . well, come on in. You'll see."

Jo frowned at his mysteriousness as he opened the large, creaky door. Tentatively, she stepped inside. There, in the huge, ornate house that should have been a showcase for all that money could buy, Jo saw...nothing. No furniture, no curtains, no warm carpets, no paintings...just...nothing.

"It's empty," she whispered.

E.Z.'s face was full of apology, and she could see the embarassment there, as if he'd let her down. "Pretty bad, huh?" he asked.

She tried to look less surprised. "No...it isn't bad. Just...why is it so empty?"

He took a few steps into the foyer, his boot heels clicking on the cold marble floor. "See, the truth is, I don't feel very comfortable here. I have my bedroom furnished upstairs and a music room, but..."

Jo gaped at him, unable to grasp just how rootless he really was. "Then, where do you live?"

"Here," he said, "when I'm not hiding from the world. Be it ever so humble...well, it's my home..."

Jo gazed up at him, stricken with the sudden realization that even after all these years, E.Z. still didn't really have a home. The video had been uniquely representative of his life, climbing broken beams, searching empty rooms, finally putting his mark on crumbling walls, where he could put a chair and a table and a bed...

But it would never really be home.

She couldn't tell him that, not when her throat was full of emotion and her eyes ached with tears she couldn't cry. This was the closest thing he knew to home. He had nothing to compare it to. That was the saddest thing of all.

She turned back to him, saw him regarding the room with the detachment of a man out of place. Funny, she thought, but he had looked infinitely more at home at Sullivan's. "Why did you buy it, if it doesn't make you comfortable?" she asked quietly.

E.Z. shrugged and considered the question for a moment. "It seemed like the right thing to do at the time. All these rooms...it could sleep so many people."

"But there's only one of you," she whispered.

He nodded as if the idea had hit him for the first time. "Yeah," he said. "Seems like a waste, doesn't it?"

Sober at the acknowledgment of a life as empty as these rooms, E.Z. took Jo's hand and led her up the stairs. His bedroom looked something like his cabin at the lake. It, too, was only half-lived-in. There were no pictures on the wall, no human touches, not even any semblance of luxury or comfort. The bed was draped in a plain blue spread, one he might have chosen from a mail-order catalogue. There was a faded print sofa on one side of the huge room, a small television, a massive stereo and a recliner. The only personal touch was a five-by-seven yellowed photograph of a woman, set in an antique frame and sitting beside his bed.

Jo went to the table and picked up the portrait. She ran her fingers along the frame. "Who is she?" Jo asked.

He didn't answer for a moment, and when she brought her eyes back to him, she saw the distant look there, the nostalgic melancholy in his eyes. Finally, he took the picture from her hand and studied it himself. "She's my mother," he whispered.

Jo heard the pain in his voice, the pain of a ten-year-old boy left to virtually fend for himself after his mother was gone. She knew that pain intimately.

Following the instincts that had ruled her the past few days, she slid her arms around E.Z.'s waist and laid her head against his chest, still bare from the day's shooting. "You know, my mom died when I was five," she whispered, as if speaking in normal tones would taint their memories. "I remember hating her for it. In my mind it was just as if she had abandoned me intentionally. Sometimes I still feel that rage I felt back then."

He wiped his hand over the dusty glass. Then, carefully, not taking his eyes from the image captured there, E.Z. set the picture back down. It wasn't the picture of his mother he saw there, Jo knew, but some hurt too far back in his past for her to see. "I came home one day after school," he said, "and our apartment was full of people. Neighbors waiting for me. They said she'd had an accident."

Jo buried her face in his chest, wishing she could take on his pain along with her own, and set him free of it.

"And I remember thinking that if I just hadn't made her late for work that morning, maybe she would have driven more carefully, and maybe she wouldn't have—"

"No!" Jo's denial was issued as firmly as she felt it. She would not let him accept blame, the way Mariah had spent her life taking the blame for their mothers' death. "It was her time, E.Z. It had nothing to do with you."

He didn't refute what she said, but she saw in his eyes that he didn't accept it, either. His voice was soft, hypnotic, as he went on. "All of a sudden I didn't live anywhere anymore, and I didn't know anyone very well, and everything changed." He frowned and pulled her back far enough to gaze into her eyes. Slowly his hand touched her face, and he looked at her, seeing that she understood. "Was it that way for you?"

Because the question was so important, Jo considered it seriously before she answered. All her life she had felt sorry for herself, angry at the world ... her mother ... her father. But in all honesty now, she couldn't say that she had ever been quite as alone as E.Z. "No," she whispered. "It wasn't that way for me. I still had my father, though he was never quite the same. And I had my sisters. And I had my home."

"You were one of the lucky ones." His fingers released the pins in her hair, as if the silky mane had some magic that could heal old wounds.

"Yes," she whispered. "I guess I was. I just never knew it." Her eyes filled with tears, and she framed his face with her hands, thinking how precious he was to finally make her see that, after a lifetime of feeling like a victim.

"Come on," he said, drying her tears. "I made it just fine. The kid rose above it."

Jo tried to smile, but her eyes still glistened. "Yes, he did," she said. But in her heart, she knew he was still that lonely little boy without a home. Until someone anchored him, gave him a place to belong, he would forever be that child.

"You know," he whispered, "I've never talked about this to anyone before."

"I'm glad you talked to me," she said.

His kiss was like a vow, a quiet promise that he would never disclose her secrets, if she would not disclose his. It was a proclamation that for as long as the kiss lasted—at least—they would be bound by what he had told her and what she had told him.

But the kiss was not enough, and soon there was an urgency between them, an urgency that said the length of the kiss was no time at all for such a pledge, that there had to be more time, more loving, more promises.

The promise blossomed as his hands moved over her, freeing her buttons and peeling the blouse and jacket off together, dropping them to the floor. She slid his vest off and swept her full, peaking breasts across his chest—the same chest that had taunted her all day with its nakedness, marking both his strength and vulnerability. For while it represented his power, it also hid his heart. She wanted to nestle that heart against hers, keeping it safe and whole. Even if she did so at the expense of her own.

"I love you, E.Z.," she whispered. "I love you."

He didn't answer, only crushed her against him, stricken by the profound declaration. But the tight way he held her against him was answer enough.

Their lips came together again, stirring the fire of passion to blazing life. She moved her hand between them, opening the button of his jeans. His stomach constricted with restraint, and he kissed her more deeply, making her throb against him. Slowly she lowered his zipper, and he groaned with the pressure of her hand.

And then he had opened her skirt, and was sliding it down her hips, his hands shaking with desire and the need to hurry, as if the pledge would die if they didn't seal it now.

Breath mingled and tongues mated, and before thoughts could be voiced, they were both unclothed, flesh pressed against flesh, man against woman, heart against heart.

As if it were the first time they'd loved, they merged with the exigency of those allotted only a short span of time before they'd be torn apart. His voice, his lyrics, echoed through her head as he loved her, showing her that he wasn't separate from the man who recorded his most sensual thoughts along with his most sensitive ones on a flat piece of wax.

They flew together into realms that exceeded fantasy, felt their hearts burst as their bodies seemed to, knew their heartbeats grew dangerously close to failing...and it still wasn't enough. They couldn't let each other go, couldn't release the feeling that the vows they'd made in their quiet ways were binding, that if they ever let each other go, a vital part of themselves would forever be lost.

So they lay in bed, tangled in the covers, feeling more in tune with one another than they had ever felt with anyone else. E.Z. pulled out the drawer next to his bed table and reached for a brush. Sitting Jo in front of him, he began to slide the bristles through the long tendrils. The feeling was gently sensual, and it made her shiver inside. It was the sec-

ond time he'd brushed her hair, sealing the fascination he
had with it, setting him apart—once again—from any of the
other men she'd known.

"I love your hair," he said. "That first day I saw you at
the meeting, it was hard to hate you with that hair falling
over your shoulders. It's downright enchanting."

She smiled and watched as he dropped a shimmering
strand over her shoulder, and began brushing the next section. "Your power's in your eyes," she told him. "Mariah
warned me about those hypnotic eyes. She was right."

E.Z. lifted her hair, pressing a kiss on the back of her
neck. "You smell intoxicating," he said.

She shivered. "You probably say that to all the girls."

"I've said it to some," he admitted. "But never here. I've
never brought anyone here before. Not until you."

Jo's heart jolted, and she turned around, met his eyes and
saw the honesty there. Was the subtle pronouncement meant
to tell her that she meant more to him than the other women
he'd known? That she was special?

"I want to take you out tonight," he whispered, as if the
simple intention bore some connection to the intimate
confession he'd just made. "And we'll pretend we're ordinary people. I'll show you the real New Orleans. The back
streets. The people who live there. I've never shown another woman that, either. No one but you would ever see it
the way I do."

Too full of emotion to deny him anything, Jo followed
him blindly. Holding hands, they slipped out to the motorcycle he kept in his garage, and rode it through the back
gates of his estate.

Wind whipped through the hair E.Z. had brushed for her,
cut through the clothes E.Z. had dressed her in, but it
couldn't cool the new kind of fire E.Z. had set in her. It was
a permanent fire, she feared, one that would never burn it-

self out. Strange, that fire like that didn't have to come from anger . . . there *was* an emotion deeper.

As inconspicuous as the night clouds, he took her through the poorest streets of New Orleans, where men slept on sidewalks and on the steps of storefronts; where cars full of families slept the night away; where teenagers slept in garbage bins because they were safer than the streets.

And then he showed her where those who perceived no choice stood on street corners, selling themselves for a warm meal or a drug that would make them forget.

Finally, they wound up at a café on the southern side of town, sitting across from each other over steaming cups of café au lait.

"Something has to be done," Jo said, haunted by the things she'd seen. "This can't go on."

"Don't make the mistake of getting all indignant over it, just because it looks so bad here," he warned her. "It's almost as bad in Baton Rouge, in Shreveport, in Bossier City. I'd dare say even Calloway Corners has a few homeless people swept under the rug."

Jo leaned across the table and spoke with deep conviction. "I want to help, E.Z.," she said, keeping her voice low so that none of the late-night diners would notice them.

"So do I," he said. "All you have to do is do it."

Jo sipped the strong brew and stared at him over the cup. "You're doing more than I know, aren't you?" she asked. "I heard what Max said on the plane, about donating the proceeds of the next album to a bunch of bums. You're giving it to the homeless, aren't you?"

He shrugged. "Those people need a hell of a lot more than money."

"Then, what?" she asked. "Tell me what they need."

E.Z. set down his cup and pointed to the table, as if it were a blueprint laid out that he could show her. "Jo, I plan to set up a foundation to help them. The money will go toward educating them, teaching them new skills, creating new jobs, setting up low-income, *decent* housing, providing child care while they work, temporary housing while they're job hunting—''

"That's a lot," Jo cut in. "Who's going to administrate? You can't do it, not with your own career. You have no idea how hard it is to organize something like that."

"No, but you do," he said, a glimmer of hope in his eye. "You have the best organizational abilities I know. You're probably even better than Max."

Jo smiled, not certain whether or not that was a compliment. "Are you offering me a job?"

He sipped his coffee, looking thoughtful. "I would," he said, "but you're overcommitted right now. I need someone who can devote all their time to this. Not someone who's busy fighting empty battles for empty causes."

Jo felt as if she'd been slapped. "That isn't fair, E.Z. Just because you don't believe what I believe, doesn't mean my cause is empty. I feel very deeply about censorship. I feel an obligation to the others who feel this way. I feel responsible, since I have the power, through my own convictions and talents, to persuade the country to change its laws."

"Already practicing your speech for the committee, I see," he said in a baleful monotone.

Jo blanched and stared at him, as if she didn't know him at all. Suddenly his harsh expression faded and the old E.Z. was back, reaching for her hand, nestling it tightly in his.

"All right," he said. "So we'll fight it out to the bitter end. As long as no one gets hurt, we'll weather it."

Jo couldn't match the certainty in his voice. Her heart sank with the inevitability of an ending. She only hoped it wasn't soon. She couldn't bear it if it was soon.

CHAPTER FOURTEEN

THE SKY BLAZED with crimson sun tones the next morning when they flew out of New Orleans just after dawn, before word could get out that the star would be at the airport again. In his nag-until-he-budges way of managing his client, Max flew with them, forcing E.Z. to finish whatever business couldn't be ignored.

When they landed, it was back to just the two of them again, alone in the bashed-in Volkswagen, on their way home. But home didn't seem like home anymore, and a sense of sadness prevailed in Jo's heart, as if instinctively, she knew that she had left an era of her life behind and faced a newer, less certain one.

She looked out the window at the familiar sights of Bossier City...the Pierre Bossier Mall, the sprinkle of hotels along the interstate, the Louisiana Downs Racetrack. "Strange," she whispered, thinking aloud. "We've only been gone a day, but things don't look quite the same."

E.Z. took her hand and set it on the stick shift, shifting while he held it. His warm touch was more familiar than the things that she'd known all her life, and that familiarity made her heart ache. Her gaze swept his face in a mental caress, and silently she adored the angles of his jaw, the straight nose, the crystalline blueness of his eyes. "I don't really want to go home," she said.

"Where do you want to go?" he asked. "Just name a place."

"Are you sure? Don't you have to work on your album?"

He shook his head. "It's really almost finished. I've got most of it on tape. I just need to polish a few things, and it'll be ready to start recording. The day is yours."

Jo considered for a moment, wondering what would fill the hunger inside her. The thought of staying with him, being alone in each others' arms, had a compelling appeal. And yet, there was more. There was a little girl who was lost in the shuffle . . . a little girl who preyed on her heart almost as strongly as E.Z. did. "I want to go check on Carmen," she said. "I want to make sure she's all right."

From his smile Jo knew he'd been thinking the same thing. "Okay. I need to check on my guitar, anyway. Make sure Chris hasn't sold it as scrap lumber."

The unaffected comment made Jo laugh. "Liar. You just want to check on Chris. One night away, and you act like a dad who hasn't seen his kids in a week."

One side of E.Z.'s mouth cocked upward. "We're a real pair, Red. Tough talkers, but nothing but mush inside."

Mush, Jo thought as E.Z. took the off ramp leading to Sullivan's. Was that what he called the miserable ache in her soul?

In record time the little VW putted through the gates of Sullivan's.

They found Carmen outside, sitting on packed dirt, screaming, with tears streaming down her face. Nearby, her cousins played with an old extension cord they used as a jump rope, and Jo suspected they were growing so used to the crying that they didn't hear it anymore. Jo's heart cracked in two and she knew it would take a miracle to repair it.

Abandoning E.Z., she ran forward, stooped in front of Carmen, and the child's arms instantly came up for Jo to hold her. And before Jo knew what was happening, she was comforting the baby the way a mother comforts a hurt child, and Carmen had hushed and thrust her thumb back into her mouth. Big tears still plopped and plummeted down the baby's cheeks.

"They were ignoring her," Jo whispered to E.Z., her voice raspy. "Just ignoring her."

E.Z. regarded the children, pity in his eyes for them as well as for Carmen. "They're just kids," he said. "They don't know any better."

Jo turned to the children, who hadn't even noticed that Carmen had been comforted. Trying to temper the hostility in her voice—for she knew their plight was no fault of their own—she asked, "Where's your father? I want to talk to him."

The oldest girl turned from the jump rope long enough to direct Jo inside, and told her that he was getting ready to go to work picking strawberries on a farm nearby. It was a one-day-only job, she said, and Carmen had been left in the care of the older children.

Jo felt indignant, and full of purpose, she stomped inside, holding Carmen like a wounded baby she didn't intend to release until all danger had passed. Juarez sat at a table which the church volunteers had set up, struggling to fill out a government form before he left for the day. With her outrage barely contained, Jo confronted him.

"I found her outside screaming," she said. "No one paid any attention."

Juarez looked up at the sad child, still hiccuping her sobs, then settled doleful eyes on E.Z. It was clear the man was soul weary, and the burden he carried was loading him down. "It's hard to make the children understand that she's only a baby," he said so quietly Jo almost couldn't hear. "They lose patience with her."

"And still you're going off to work and leaving her here with them?" Jo asked.

Juarez's meek expression faded as he stood up to face her, and a spark of anger colored his dull eyes, reminding Jo that he was a victim, as well. "I have no choice," he bit out.

The anger in Jo's heart faded at the pain in his eyes, and she dropped her blurring eyes, focusing on the ground. This was no time, no place, for anger. It wouldn't serve her this time. She felt E.Z.'s hand on her shoulder, recognized the subtle squeeze that warned her to calm down, and she regarded the baby, whose head nuzzled against her neck. She wiped the dirty tears from Carmen's dark little face, and wondered where in heaven's name solutions could be found. Judgment wasn't the answer, she told herself, but neither was letting the cycle of poverty continue.

Moved by instinct rather than rationality, she turned back to the broken man, her eyes intense, anxious. "Let me keep her," she entreated. "I'll take care of her today while you work."

The lines on Juarez's face deepened, and he set his weathered hand on Carmen's back, stroking her gently. It was clear he cared for her, though he had few resources with which to show it. It was also clear he was too proud to accept help easily. "We can manage. I'll talk to the kids."

"No...*please*." Tears sprang to her eyes, and her lips trembled. "I want to take her to show my sister," she said, grasping for some explanation that wouldn't intrude on his pride. "See, she's pregnant, and a little scared, and I want her to see how sweet Carmen is, so that she can think past the birth.... It would help her so much. Please, Juarez. She could even spend the night..."

Even as the words came out, Jo knew she had said too much. E.Z.'s grip on her shoulder tightened, a harsh warning that she was about to expose them both as frauds.

"Spend the night where?" Juarez asked. "You sleep here, don't you?"

Her throat went dry, but she tried to clear it. "My sister..." she began again. "She has a little trailer..." The lie caught in her throat, and Jo had the sudden fear that Juarez wouldn't let her take Carmen if he wasn't confident that she'd have a decent place to stay. She looked at E.Z., apology in her eyes before she spoke, and met Juarez's eyes again. "I can't lie to you, Juarez. I'm not homeless. I have two sisters here. I've been staying with one of them, in the house I grew up in. I've only been sleeping here sometimes so that I could be with—" E.Z. dropped his hand helplessly, and she saw the dread in his eyes. "—with Ellis."

"I see." Juarez cast suspicious eyes on both of them, but E.Z. rallied.

"Her sister doesn't approve of me," he lied. "So I can't stay there."

Juarez nodded, but the hint of mistrust still lingered in his eyes. "But you don't think she'd mind letting Carmen spend the night?"

"Not at all," Jo said quickly. "She could sleep in a warm bed and have a bath and a good meal.... Please, Juarez. I'll bring her back tomorrow. I promise."

Juarez touched Carmen's head and saw that she was falling asleep on Jo's shoulder. "I suppose it would be good for her to have someone's undivided attention for a change. She isn't used to being the center of things."

Jo held her breath, waiting for him to consent... praying he would. Finally, he gave in.

"Is there a phone number I can call if I need you? An address?"

Quickly, Jo called it out to him, watched him write it down.

Then he packed Carmen's meager belongings, unlaundered pajamas, underwear that was torn, hand-me-down socks, and folded them in a paper bag he kept under his cot. The size and substance of that bag revealed to Jo just how profoundly alone and uncared for Carmen was. All she owned in the world fit into that little paper bag. "She may not want to come back when you're finished with her," Juarez muttered.

Jo didn't know how to answer that. She wasn't sure anyone would want to come back, given the choice. She took the bag, handed it to E.Z. and started to the door with Carmen before Juarez could change his mind. Before she left she looked back over her shoulder. Already the man was hunched over the form, as if he truly believed that the hope he needed lay somewhere in one of the blank spaces.

"We've got to do something for them, E.Z.," she said.

E.Z. gave a dismal shrug, the hopelessness of it all illustrated in the dull gesture. "We're giving it a hell of a try."

MARIAH TRIED HER BEST to cling to her free-spirited façade when they took Carmen to see her, but Jo sensed that it was still a cover for fragile feelings. Carmen seemed to help Mariah become more genuine, however, and as the morning wore on, they became great pals, co-conspirators, and Mariah didn't want them to take her home. At Mariah's insistence, they packed a picnic lunch, picked up Ford and went to a park to let Carmen play on the swings and the slide. Then they carried her, exhausted, back to Calloway Corners.

It was mid-afternoon before they were back at the house, with Carmen tucked into Jo's bed for a nap. Mariah and Ford had gone home, and Eden had taken the children she kept out into the backyard to read them a story. E.Z. lounged on the couch, savoring the peaceful feeling of a family day and watching Jo at the table, buried in the newspaper.

It was funny, he thought, that all these years, he'd believed he knew what family was. Today he'd discovered he hadn't a clue. Family was more than burdensome relatives who avoided one another, the way he'd always imagined. Family was camaraderie. It was caring. It was sharing.

Family was home.

Home. Now there was another concept he'd never understood. That, too, was beginning to take on clearer meaning. Home wasn't just a place where you laid your head at night. It was people. It was love. And it was something he didn't have.

He looked across the room to Jo, and wondered with dread if she was growing tired of him. She had become distant since they'd gotten back, and he was beginning to feel alienated. He should probably leave, he told himself. But he wasn't ready to lose this feeling, and besides, Eden had invited him to stay for dinner. He propped his arm on the back of the sofa and peered at Jo across the room. "Must be a big news day," he said.

Jo looked up, realized she'd shut him out, and dropped the paper at once. Her eyes told him her adoration hadn't diminished at all. "Come help me," she said.

"Help you?" he asked. "You're reading the paper. How can I help?"

"No, I'm not reading the paper," she said. "I'm looking through the want ads. For jobs."

"Jobs?"

"Yes," she said. "For the people at Sullivan's."

E.Z. smiled his most poignant smile at her naïveté, then got up and ambled to the big table and leaned over her. "Babe, that's sweet of you, but don't you think everybody there reads the classifieds every day?"

Her head snapped up, and before his eyes the excitement in Jo's eyes vanished. "Well, then...I'll start calling around. Businesses where I know people, maybe even in other cities...."

E.Z. caught her hand as she reached for the phone and forced her to look at him. "Jo, there are too many. You can't find a job for each of them."

"Maybe not," she said. "But I can help them one at a time. Isn't that what you said I needed to do? Stop worrying about the broad picture, and concentrate on the individual? Didn't you say that?"

"Yes, but . . . it's a big job."

Jo's smile crept back over her face like a light that could not be extinguished, and she reached for the phone on the buffet behind her. "I can do it, E.Z. I've tackled bigger jobs. And while I'm at it, I'm going to call a few churches and get them to donate clothes and blankets and things. Most of those children are dressed in rags. Carmen's not the only one cold at night."

Seeing he couldn't dissuade her, E.Z. grabbed her pencil off the table and hunted for a piece of paper. "Okay," he said, deciding that—just maybe—he should trust her to dig up a miracle. Maybe Jo's innocent, optimistic approach was just what was needed. "While we're at it, we'll make some lists of more things that my money can go for," he said. "I was thinking of rocking chairs for Sullivan's, and a few microwaves for warming babies' bottles."

"And huts!" Jo said, her eyes growing brighter as ideas came to her. "We could get some volunteers, maybe some of the men who live there, to help build huts to replace the pup tents. It would give them a little more privacy, a little more dignity." She stood up, shaking her pen as the ideas occurred to her. "I could get some lumber from the seconds store we have at the mill. Heck, we own the place. It's about time I got something out of it. And maybe Seth Taylor could donate some of his surplus supplies from construction projects."

E.Z.'s eyes shone with admiration, and he knew from Jo's fiery determination that her strategy just might work. "Let's hit it,'' he said, handing her the phone. "There aren't that many hours left in the day."

They spent the afternoon like two kids scheming to change the world, and E.Z. marveled at the professional way Jo handled her contacts, stroking their egos and convincing them that aiding her cause would not only benefit the homeless, but themselves, as well. By the end of the day, she had put out feelers for jobs in six Louisiana towns, had asked seven pastors to get their churches involved in donations and volunteer child care for those seeking work. She had convinced Ford to order fifty rocking chairs to be delivered to Sullivan's—for which E.Z. would pay anonymously—and had designed the little huts that she planned to get the men at Sullivan's involved in building.

And all the while E.Z. watched and listened, wishing he could get her committed entirely to this cause, so that they could tackle the whole problem, rather than just part of it. And as the day wore on, he fell more and more deeply into the abyss of love, from which he feared it would be hell escaping when and if the time ever came.

LATE THAT NIGHT, they sat beneath the arbor outside, Jo leaning back with her head resting on E.Z.'s chest. Carmen, who had been fed and bathed, lay on Jo's lap, asleep once more. The distant sound of bullfrogs provided simple orchestration, along with the melody of the babbling, moonlit creek and the leaves whispering in the trees.

The soft, gentle motion of the swing had them all lulled into the most serene state Jo could remember. E.Z. bent his head and pressed a kiss on her silky hair. He let his mouth linger there a moment and tightened his arms around her. "You're a miracle," he whispered. "You know that, don't you?"

She shook her head. "I was just thinking that you were."

"Maybe we're two of a kind," he went on. "We both think we can change the world. We just don't know how to go about it."

"We made a start today," she said.

He nodded and stroked her hair back from her face. "Maybe we should join forces. Conquer the world together."

Jo's heart did a pirouette, but her head told her to think rationally. It wasn't a subtle marriage proposal, she told herself. Just a passing comment. Innocent. And she didn't want it to mean anything else...did she?

So why did her heart burn with hunger at the quiet comment? She groped for a reply, something that didn't sound so...so hopeful. "Which world would we conquer?" she asked finally. "Yours or mine?"

"Ours," he said.

A lump rose in Jo's throat. Tears came to her eyes, but she blinked them back. *I must be crazy,* she thought, actually wishing he meant that he wanted to share his life with her. But it was just one simple word, after all. *Ours.* It meant next to nothing. And there were so many reasons why she shouldn't hope.

"We don't always believe the same things," she whispered. "Sometimes, if you remember, we fight on opposite sides."

The reminder fell like a veil between them—not impenetrable, but a barrier nevertheless. Finally E.Z. touched Jo's shoulders. She sat up and turned to look at him.

"Come on," he said, his voice heavy. "Let's take her up to bed."

Jo got up and allowed E.Z. to take Carmen. Mutely she followed them inside, up the stairs and into the little room where Carmen and Jo would sleep. E.Z. put Carmen gently on the bed, pulled off her socks, and like a father in complete adoration of his child, pressed a kiss on her cheek.

He stood back and watched Jo work Carmen's shirt over her shoulders without waking her, then strip the child of her ragged pants. She slipped one of her own T-shirts over Carmen's head, pulled her arms through, and covered her up. Then she, too, kissed her.

"You're a natural," E.Z. whispered. Jo turned back to him, saw him leaning back against her dresser, his head inclined in quiet devotion. "Real mother material."

An awkward smile tugged at her lips? "Me?"

"Yes, you," he said, and she saw in his eyes that he believed every word. "As independent and detached as you pretend to be, Red, family is your element. You should have one of your own."

Her cheeks burned with self-consciousness, and averting her eyes, she looked down at the baby. Carmen's thumb had found her mouth, and she was sucking with contentment. "So should she."

E.Z. pushed away from the dresser and pulled Jo back against him, resting his chin on her shoulder.

Both of them watched the child, caught in a moment of awareness of the parental picture they represented. But they were not Carmen's parents, and they weren't a family. They were a patchwork of sadness and injustice, love and hope.

The realization, along with the impossibility of their situation, left an unbearable cold spot on Jo's soul. She shivered and slipped out of E.Z.'s embrace, taking his hand in hers. Sadly, she led him back downstairs. When they were in the living room, she sat at the table, staring at the paper as if there must be more she could do to fill the emptiness washing through her.

"I was serious when I said we should join forces," E.Z. said, the importance of his convictions on his face. "We could do so much together. For Carmen. For Juarez's whole family. For all the families at Sullivan's."

Disappointment fell over her like a mist that cooled her fire. He hadn't meant what he'd said personally, she thought. He was still only trying to recruit her to his cause. A new hostility chilled her heart, and she looked at him coldly. "E.Z., you can't lay the guilt of poverty on my shoulders just because I'm involved in something else. I don't quit things that I start! I made a commitment to the issue of censorship, and I intend to see it through. Then, and only then, I can concentrate exclusively on those people."

E.Z. wouldn't back down. He leaned over her chair, caging her with his arms. "They could fight that cause without you, Jo, and you know it. You want to devote yourself to the homeless, and you can. I have plenty of money and ideas. You have all the fire. We'd be so good together."

She shook her head in frustration, knowing that they could argue for years, and he'd never understand. Her words came out as a careworn sigh...a broken utterance of pain. "You just want me off your back about the lyrics," she said. "Keep it up, E.Z. and I might start to think all your attention is only to distract me."

A flicker of rage showed on his face, and he stepped back. "You don't believe that," he said. "If you did, you wouldn't have ever let me near you."

Jo stood up and turned her back to him, trying to hide what he already knew was there. He turned her around, tipping her angry face up to his. "I'm worried about you," he said, his tone more gentle. "You're going to get hurt one of these days. *Somebody* will eventually. Those people are getting out of hand."

"I can handle them," Jo maintained. She struggled not to allow his touch to weaken her resolve. "And instead of worrying about me, I wish you'd spend your time being a little more conscious of the children you influence."

"I am conscious of them," he said. "I don't want to hurt anybody. I just want to make music. But already your opinion has altered the lyrics I'm writing now. I weigh every line against how it'll sit with you.''

That old spark returned to her eyes. ''Then my work *has* been successful,'' she said. ''I have made a difference. You see? Maybe if I can influence you, I can influence some others!''

Instantly his eyes hardened, and he shook his head as if she'd never in a million years see the picture clearly. ''You go around trying to make your value system retroactive, and you won't influence a damn soul. Start banning any of the songs *I've* written, and I'll fight you tooth and nail.''

''But you said—''

''I *said* I've been thinking twice about what I write. Not because I think my past lyrics are bad, but because I'm not a monster. I don't want the reputation that's being hung on me, thanks to you.''

''Thanks to me!'' Jo half shouted. ''E.Z. you're responsible for your own reputation. If it isn't everything you want it to be, you can't blame me.''

His features distorted in disbelief, and he opened his mouth and gestured for the door, as though it represented the time they'd spent together. ''You just saw how I work. You know what my songs mean. How can you say that?''

''Because it's true,'' she said. ''Interpretation is the problem, E.Z. Not what you meant to say. It's time this country fought for its values.''

''You mean it's time they fought for *your* values,'' he stormed. ''To hell with everybody else's. If you don't agree with them, they're wrong. Is that it?''

''No! That's not it. But I could accuse you of the same thing. If someone isn't devoted to *your* cause, then they're wasting their time!''

''My *cause*?'' E.Z. shouted, his lips stretching taut over his teeth. His tone dripped with disgust. ''You think this is just a *cause*? I don't know why I ever thought you would be the right person to administrate my foundation. Just forget I ever asked, all right? Just forget everything!''

"Fine!" she almost screamed. "Because if you think you're going to change my mind, you're mistaken!"

"And if you think I care, then *you* are!" he threw back. He moved toward the door, but swung back at the threshold. "Just think about one thing when you're planning your attack, Jo. What's more important? Changing a few lyrics, or changing a few lives?" And before she could respond, he was outside and in his car, screeching the tires as he tore out of her driveway.

Jo yelled with frustration and slammed the door. She turned around and saw Eden leaning in the kitchen doorway, arms crossed and accusation in her eyes. "You did it again."

"I didn't do anything, Eden. He expects me to drop everything just because—"

"Just because he means something to you?" Eden asked, her voice so calm that it made Jo want to break something. "Just because you know he isn't the rake you thought he was? Just because he doesn't deserve what you've said about him?"

Jo threw up her hands. "Go ahead," she shouted. "Side with him. I don't expect you to understand. But if you don't mind, there's a little girl upstairs whom I don't want to wake up. So I'd like to end this right now."

"You're the one who's yelling," Eden said.

Jo grabbed her head with both hands, as if it would split right down the middle. "God, you're just like him!"

She left Eden standing in the living room, shaking her head. The older, wiser woman saw her sister making a grave mistake. But Eden wasn't that much older, and in Jo's opinion, she could save her wisdom for someone who needed it. She'd had about as much advice as she could take for one night.

THE ILLUSIVE FEELING of family shattered when E.Z. left Jo that night. His heart hammered with anger, but that hammering had a resounding effect, as if it pounded against a hollow chasm, a space that couldn't be filled. Of all the women in the world who could get under his skin, why did it have to be her? As stubborn as Jo was, as maddening as she could be, why did he already miss her? Why did he feel so empty inside? Why did he feel as if he'd just lost his one chance at a home, a family, a love of his own? It was silly, he told himself. Silly because Calloway Corners wasn't his home, and the Calloways weren't his family. Carmen wasn't his baby. And Jo wasn't his wife.

The emptiness inside him diminished the anger, and soon the feeling of loneliness encompassed him like a thick fog. He didn't want to make it thicker by going home and facing the solitude. He needed to be around people. Finally E.Z. opted to be with those who were the closest people he had to family, next to his band. He drove back to Sullivan's.

Juarez was too busy with his children, and too exhausted after the back-breaking job of farm labor all day to worry much about Carmen, but E.Z. gave him a report and saw that he was satisifed that she was in good hands.

Too restless and jumpy after his fight with Jo to be alone, E.Z. found Chris and spent the next two hours teaching him some more guitar chords. Already the boy had gotten comfortable with the ones he'd taught him, and had begun to put them together, picking out popular songs and playing with a gifted ear.

It was after midnight before Chris finally set the guitar down and regarded E.Z. with perceptiveness he was too young, by rights, to possess. "She left you again, huh?"

E.Z. didn't find the old conversation amusing this time. "How do you know I didn't leave her?"

Chris shoved his tawny hair back with his hand and looked at the massive stars in the cloudless sky. E.Z. followed his gaze, wishing life could be as clear. "Maybe you did leave her," he said. "But you're sorry you did."

E.Z. expelled a frustrated breath. "She's stubborn as they come, and has a temper that'll start a blaze in a rainstorm."

Chris smiled. "Well, you know what they say about redheads."

"It's all true," E.Z. assured him. He reflected on the argument with her tonight and laughed mirthlessly. "She said that if everybody didn't believe in the things I believe in, that I think they're wasting their time. That's not true." He looked at Chris, intent on seeing things from another viewpoint. "Do I come across that way to you?"

The boy shrugged noncommittally. "I don't know. What do you believe in?"

E.Z. let his shoulders drop, and he stared down at the dirt between his feet. Pensively he began to trace a square in it with his finger. What did he believe in, he wondered. Did he really know?

The answers came to him in images, rather than words. The tears in Jo's eyes when he'd sung her the song he'd written for her. The smile in her eyes when she played with Carmen. The anger in her eyes when she talked of the homeless. The fire in her eyes when she made love to him.

Those were the things he believed in, but he couldn't tell Chris. "I believe in her," he said, realizing the truth only as he spoke. "And I guess I want her to believe in me, so much that she doesn't care about anything else."

Chris whistled. "Uh-oh," he said. "You've got it bad."

The boy's nail-on-the-head observation brought a smile to E.Z.'s lips. "Yeah. I guess I do. I guess I've got it bad." He surveyed the stars and thought they didn't match the brilliance in Jo's eyes when they were ablaze with passion.

Maybe that was the problem. She was passionate about things other than him. And he didn't want to share that with anyone. Not even with the homeless. "I'm such a jerk," he muttered.

Chris grinned and held out the guitar to E.Z. "You want it back?" he asked. "You said it gave you luck with women."

E.Z. didn't take it. "Believe me," he said. "That kind of luck doesn't work on her. Keep the guitar."

Chris chuckled and took it back and began to strum. As the chords came together, E.Z. realized Chris was playing one of his own songs. It was true, he thought, that imitation was the sincerest form of flattery, even though Chris had no inkling that the song was at all familiar to him. But even that small surprise didn't soothe the craving in E.Z.'s heart, or make it any easier to bear.

E.Z. ELLIS WAS an exhausting all-night dream Jo couldn't shake until Carmen roused early the next morning and snuggled in Jo's arms like the teddy bear she'd slept with as a child. As Carmen laughed with delight, adjusting to her new surroundings, the misery Jo had embraced all night faded away.

Someone loved her. Even if it was temporary. Even if the love was borrowed.

She took Carmen downstairs, still wearing her robe, and padded barefoot into the kitchen. What did one feed a two-year-old for breakfast, she wondered, browsing through Eden's pantry.

Not quite sure, she opted for a little of everything, from waffles to hash browns, from an omelete to toast. But to her chagrin, Carmen was only interested in the colorful cereal shaped like shamrocks that Eden kept for the children she babysat.

Jo sat with Carmen at the table, nursing a cup of black coffee, watching the child devour the cereal after playing in it with her fingers. Unbidden, her melancholy returned. Why had she gotten so angry last night, she chided herself. What had it gotten her? A morning without the promise of E.Z. She dropped her forehead into her hand and contemplated going to him. Was he still angry? Would he even talk to her?

Before she could rationalize her thoughts, the doorbell rang. Her heart did a double flip. Telling herself to look calm, she ran to the door and opened it. As she hoped—as she prayed—E.Z. greeted her with a handful of wildflowers and tired, bloodshot eyes. "I didn't sleep at all last night," he whispered. "I missed you like crazy."

She threw open the screen door and fell into his embrace. "Me, too," she said.

He closed his eyes and held her so securely that for a moment she let herself believe that he would never let her go. "No more arguments, he promised. "Let's just concentrate on the good stuff."

He kissed her with the fever of a man who'd been deprived of his lover for much too long, and all thoughts of causes and convictions melted from her bones, along with her residual anger. When he let her go, they stood gazing at each other for a moment as though they hadn't seen each other in days. And then they remembered Carmen.

They turned around and saw her standing over the kitchen threshold, Jo's oversized shirt hanging comically from her tiny frame and dragging the floor. Spaniel eyes smiled up at them, and wiping her milk mustache with the back of her hand, she cried, "Els!"

The strange pronunciation didn't evade them, for it was clear she had said "Ellis." With an expression that pushed him near emotional overload, E.Z. picked Carmen up and kissed her. "How'd she do?" he asked Jo.

Jo smiled through misty eyes and decided she'd never seen a more beautiful sight than E.Z. and Carmen together. "She has a new love for hopelessly unnutritious cereals packed full of sugar and preservatives. Other than that, she's great."

"Sounds like a healthy kid to me," he said, going after Carmen's neck with his mouth. She scrunched up and squealed with delight.

"She's such an angel," Jo mumbled distantly.

He stepped toward Jo and kissed her again in spite of the child between them. "You're not so bad, yourself. I was hateful last night. I'm sorry."

Jo sighed, and touched his face, savoring the rough texture with her palm. "Lord, I'm glad you came back," she said. "I was miserable all night long."

"So was I." He laughed softly and sadly, then set Carmen down, watching her scurry off to the box of day-care toys in the corner. "I was so bad off I even found myself asking Chris for advice."

Jo tried to imagine it. "Did he give you any?"

E.Z. reflected on the attempt Chris had made and laughed again. "He offered to give me the guitar back. Reminded me that it was a good luck charm with women."

Jo shook her head slowly. "You don't need a good luck charm, E.Z. Not with me."

"No," he said, his fragile smile fading. "With you, I just need a few miracles."

Then, not giving Jo the chance to answer that challenge, he picked Carmen up and carried her over to the table. Jo stood back, watching them both, loving them both. And as dismal as things had looked last night, she realized that her life wasn't beyond miracles. E.Z. had come back, after all.

CHAPTER FIFTEEN

MIRACLES WERE RARE commodities, Jo realized later that morning when it came time to return Carmen to Sullivan's. As the VW sputtered through the gates, the child clung to Jo with vicelike strength and began crying, "No!"

The misery in the mournful plea tore like a dull switch-blade through Jo's heart, and she bit her lip and held Carmen tighter, desperately wishing she could comfort her, telling her things would be all right. But things weren't going to be all right, and all the wishes in the world wouldn't change that. She looked at E.Z. as he stopped the car, the despair in her eyes begging him to find a better answer than they'd come up with yet. But E.Z. was as lost as she.

"We have to take her back, babe," he said.

Jo took a breath that reached into the deepest recesses of her soul and forced herself to get out of the car. Carmen's arms clamped tighter around her neck. "No-o-o-o!"

Tears scurried down Jo's face, but she tried to harden herself, tried to believe this was for the best. But with each step she took, the child fought harder as though Jo was deliberately marching her into the confinement she feared most in her young life. Would she hate her for doing this, Jo wondered dismally. The screaming escalated, and Carmen clung to her with a death grip that turned Jo's heart inside out.

They reached the building and entered the loud place, where Carmen's cries seemed lost in the roar. Juarez came toward them at once, but Carmen only buried her head in

Jo's shoulder, sobbing tragically, as if she knew she was about to be abandoned. *It won't be the first time,* a hollow voice within Jo said. Carmen knew all the signs.

Before Juarez was close enough to hear, Jo swung around to E.Z., frantic liquid fire illuminating her eyes. "I can't leave her like this," she said. "I won't."

E.Z. looked grief-stricken. "We don't have a choice."

"Then I'll stay here all day if I have to," Jo bit out through trembling lips. "But I will *not* leave her here when she's screaming."

Juarez reached them, and with a weary, pain-ridden look on his bedraggled face, reached out to pry Carmen away. It seemed cruel to Jo, pushing Carmen away, fighting her cry for love, running out on her... Knowing she had no right, Jo backed away from Juarez, refusing to hand the child over. "Let me hold her a little while," Jo said trying to suppress the urgency in her voice. "Just until she's quiet."

"It will just start again when you leave," Juarez uttered over Carmen's wails, impatient at Jo's contribution to the tantrum. "It's best to go now."

"I won't do it!" Jo cried.

E.Z. looked at her, his own anguish evident on his face. The soft indictment there made Jo angry at herself for putting them all through this, but Carmen's state of mind was the priority now. After a moment, when he saw that Jo wouldn't back down without fighting them just as Carmen fought, E.Z. took Juarez aside. She heard him urging Juarez to let her hold Carmen a little while longer, and promised that he'd make her leave when the child was calm. But Jo wasn't sure she could keep that promise. Reluctantly, because the choice was out of his hands, Juarez consented.

As quickly as she could move, Jo took the child outside, hoping the change in the noise level would soothe her nerves. But the misery was equally great outdoors, and even at her young age, Carmen sensed it, and continued to wail with all the accumulated sorrow her young heart could hold.

"Do something," Jo told E.Z., her voice as broken as the child's. "Sing to her or something. You can make her stop crying."

E.Z. looked around helplessly for Chris and the guitar, and found him standing alone. He looked as forlorn as the child Jo held, leaning on the corner of the building with the guitar hanging from his hand like a vital part of himself. Not knowing what else to do, E.Z. led Jo and Carmen to him.

Chris looked up when they approached him, and he regarded the screaming baby with dull eyes. "Can I borrow the guitar, Chris?" E.Z. asked. "Just until she's quiet?"

"Sure." Chris handed it to him.

E.Z. went back in for one of the rockers that had been delivered the day before and brought it back out for Jo to sit on with Carmen. Sitting on a crate next to them, he began to play in a sultry, sad rhythm. After Carmen's weeping hushed to weary, silent tears, Jo recognized the song as "Shadow Child."

She had heard the song before, many times, but now, without the studio effects and the electric orchestrations, the song had a haunting quality that gave it new dimension.

E.Z. sang of getting out and being free, of searching for a better way. He sang of the hard core loneliness of the dark streets, and the realities of becoming a man. And in the final verse, Jo heard what she'd never listened to—*really* listened to—before. She heard the subtle message that solitude wasn't freedom, but just another prison, and that being a man has nothing to do with being on your own. She heard the heartrending truth that detachment leads to death, and that human warmth is the key to going on....

As he sang Carmen relaxed her hold and laid her damp little head, hot and perspiring with the fight, against Jo's shoulder. She didn't sleep...only stared with lusterless eyes out into a distance that was too closed-in, not knowing that her future was just as limited ... but knowing instinctively, Jo was sure, that the human warmth she needed wouldn't be there.

When the song came to an end, Chris slid down the wall and sat on the bare concrete, staring at the ground beneath his feet. The air seemed charged with emotion. Jo rocked Carmen gently and turned her concerned gaze on the boy.

For a moment they all sat in a quiet triangle, poignant eyes all leveled on the ground, for that was as high as hope got at Sullivan's. Finally, Chris stirred.

"I have to use the phone," he told E.Z., his voice wobbling. "Do you have a quarter? I don't have any change."

A flicker of surprise—and modest hope—passed across E.Z.'s face. He reached into his pocket, withdrew a quarter and tossed it to the boy. Quietly, with all the prayers they could still summon for the small miracle they sensed was taking place, Jo and E.Z. both watched him as he went to the pay phone a few feet away from them, and listened while he solicited the operator's help.

Then they saw Chris's eyes fill with tears that burned down his cheeks, and heard the catch in his voice as he said, "Hello ... Mom?"

THEY DROVE CHRIS to the bus station that morning and stayed with him while he waited to board. Jo still held Carmen, for Jo had convinced Juarez to let the child come along. They would bring her back as soon as Chris was gone, she promised. She just needed a little more time with her. Just the rest of the morning.

Jo watched E.Z. say goodbye to the boy just before he climbed the steps onto the bus. His eyes were misty, awkwardly so, and Chris extended his hand in goodbye. But there was more than that in the tight handshake. There was

"Thank you," and "I'll remember you," and all the other things he was not able to say.

"Don't guess I'll ever see you again," he said.

E.Z. held Chris's hand in both of his a bit too long. "I don't know about that," he said. "You just might be surprised one day."

Chris managed to smile. "I hope so." He nodded goodbye to Jo, whom he had never yet addressed directly, and gave E.Z. a conspiratorial nudge. "Good luck with your lady," he whispered.

E.Z. smiled and took a deep, cleansing breath as Chris got on the bus. He went back to Jo, picked up Carmen and held her close, like a shield from the emotions he needed to hide, and made her wave goodbye.

They stood still for a while after the bus had driven away, watching the empty street as if the bus would turn around and come back. But that wasn't really what he wanted. Jo slipped her arm through E.Z.'s and rested her face against his shoulder as she peered into the distance with him. "You did it," she whispered.

"I didn't do anything," E.Z. said.

"Yes, you did," she said. "You and your music." Jo reflected how she had once believed that "Shadow Child" should be banned. She'd grown a lot since then. So much had changed.

"It was hard saying goodbye to him, wasn't it?" Jo asked.

E.Z. shrugged, but she could see the dejection in his eyes. "He belongs at home," he said. "He's just a kid." He pressed an absent kiss on Carmen's head and pulled her to rest against his shoulder. Chris was gone . . . it was time to concentrate on the child now. "We've got to take Carmen back now, babe," he whispered, sadness in his eyes. "I know how hard it'll be for you, but we have to. For her sake. The more we cling to her, the more she'll cling to us."

Jo bit her lip again and told herself she wouldn't cry anymore, wouldn't fight it, wouldn't add to Carmen's pain. How could she expect the child to accept her plight, if a grown woman couldn't? E.Z. was right. It was best to leave her quickly, and let her get used to Sullivan's again . . . but it seemed so wrong. . . .

Carmen fell asleep on the way back to Sullivan's, and a deep aching emptiness welled up inside Jo. Maybe it was best to leave her sleeping, she thought. Maybe then the ordeal wouldn't linger on. Carmen would never even know they'd left.

Until she woke up.

Still, the thought of running out with her kicking and screaming was an impossible alternative, so when they were back at the warehouse, Jo tucked Carmen into her little cot, pulled the blanket over her and slipped an old, donated teddy bear under her arm. And then, battling the tears prickling her eyes, she ran out and got in the car.

E.Z. was a few steps behind her, and when he caught up to her, he got in and pulled her against him, rocking her with his body, as if she were the child who needed comfort. "She's gonna be fine, babe," he whispered. "You have to believe that."

"It's just so *loud* in there," Jo sobbed. "How can a baby sleep in all that noise? Children running and fighting, parents shouting at them, people arguing. . . . It isn't right, E.Z."

The tightness of his arms told her lies . . . lies about security and love and living happily ever after. But those lies contradicted his words. "That's the way it is," he said dismally. "You knew that before. That's her life."

Jo released herself from his embrace and looked up at him. "What's the use of caring? Of loving someone? What point is there in that when you turn around one day and they're gone? Why bother, E.Z.?"

E.Z. pulled her back into his arms, making her absorb his strength, his warmth, his faith. "We bother because we have no choice," he said.

Jo looked up at him, her eyes blurred with tears, and touched his face with a hand that memorized the texture of each feature. "That's the problem with letting your heart make your choices," she said. "It always leads you wrong."

She wept into his shirt for a short piece of eternity, and finally, he tipped her chin up so that her shimmering eyes locked with his. "You're safe with me," he whispered. "You know that, don't you?"

Jo shook her head, all her old skepticism, her old anger, returning like a flame that had never quite died. "No, E.Z. I don't know that at all. You're as temporary a fixture in my life as Carmen is, and I'd be a fool to think anything else."

The bitterness of her words stunned him, and he released her, allowing her to move to the other side of the car. "Jo, I'm not going anywhere," he said.

Jo's wet, swollen eyes were expressionless when she looked at him. "Take me home, E.Z.," she said. "I want to go home."

Swallowing with great effort, E.Z. started the engine. It coughed and grunted. "If that's what you want," he whispered.

He took her home, but in her frenzied, depressed state, he couldn't make himself leave her. Instead, he followed Jo into the house, watched her dig urgently in the living room drawers for her bank book and saw her fill out a withdrawal slip for several thousand dollars.

"What are you doing?" he asked, when it was clear she wasn't going to volunteer her intentions.

The fire in her eyes seemed out of control, a bit too hot to contain, as Jo dashed around the house. "I'm making a withdrawal today," she said. "Closing my Shreveport account. I keep all my savings here."

"Why?" E.Z. asked, confused.

"Because I'm going shopping," she said, her expression daring him to object. "*We're* going shopping."

He rode with her in her own car as Jo went to the bank and withdrew all her savings. Then, still in the dark, E.Z. donned his tinted glasses and baseball cap and followed her into the mall, almost running to keep up. Jo made a beeline to the children's department, and began grabbing clothes and throwing them into a basket as fast as her hands could grasp them.

"Who...who are those for?" he asked when he reached her.

Jo's hands trembled as she pulled the clothes from the hangers. "For Carmen and her cousins and all those other children there. I don't have enough money for everyone, but it's a start, E.Z. It's a start."

He saw the frantic energy in her eyes, the fever flush to her skin, and he grabbed her arm to stop her. In a harsh whisper, he said, "You can't do this, Jo. That's your savings!"

"I have to!" she replied. "That's all I have. I don't know what else to do!"

"But Jo, this is crazy!"

Jo spun around, letting her hair graze her face. Her eyes were wild with fury. "What's crazy is that here, in this city, children don't have homes! *That's* what's crazy!"

"Then do something to help them," he whispered. "They need your time, not your money!"

"I can only give them what I have!" Jo cried. She took the armload of clothes to the cash register and threw them down on the counter. Smearing her tears across her face, she tried to stop crying. The cashier pretended not to notice.

"Jo, let me pay. I'll take care of it," E.Z. said.

"No!" She pushed his hands away from her, waving a threatening finger in his face. "I have to do this. I have to do *something*!"

E.Z. closed his eyes and turned away, knowing that her mind was made up. Somehow she believed that these clothes would make her feel better about the problem...would make the children feel better about their plight.

He kept his opinion to himself as Jo spent every last penny she had, then wept because she didn't have more. Silently he carried the bags out to the car for her and remained quiet as she drove back home. "Will...will you deliver these to them tonight?" she asked, her voice trembling as she spoke.

He looked over at her, deep lines of concern etched on his forehead. "Why can't you? It was your money. Your idea."

"Because it should be anonymous, otherwise they'd treat me differently. Besides, I have a meeting tonight."

E.Z. nodded, the lack of emotion on his face revealing. "I see. But you think spending your life savings on some clothes that somebody else delivers to them will make you feel better about the children sleeping in that warehouse?"

His tone was judgmental, and she felt the old argument coming between them again.

"Will you deliver them or not?" she asked coldly.

"I'll deliver them," he said. "If you're sure you don't want to."

Tears streamed down her face as she drove, and finally she managed to speak again. "If Carmen's crying, E.Z., hold her until she goes to sleep. Don't let her cry, okay?"

E.Z. set his chin on his fist and stared out the window, wishing to heaven life didn't have to be so hard. "I won't let her cry," he whispered. After a while he turned back to Jo, seeing that her tears hadn't subsided at all since they'd left the mall. Gently he reached across the seat and wiped a tear from her cheek. ''But who's going to keep you from crying?''

Jo didn't have an answer for that, but it didn't seem important, anyway. Jo Calloway had always dried her own tears. It was too late to change now.

JO COULDN'T KEEP her mind on the meeting that night. The fight to censor rock lyrics seemed insignificant now, and despite a Herculean effort, she couldn't muster any more anger. She listened absently while the newly elected president discussed the fact that as many members as possible were needed to go with Jo to Washington to support her while she testified. Somehow, the whole discussion seemed to concern someone else. Jo wasn't the same person who had first rallied their support. Now she was keenly aware that there were children in the United States condemned to sleep in warehouses, runaways without direction and families without food. Didn't these people know there were more pressing needs in the world, her heart asked its hollowest chambers? Didn't *she* know?

The doors to the auditorium burst open as the president took a show of hands, and Jo looked up to see one of the activists bolting in, panting as if he'd just discovered gold in a coal mine. ''E.Z. Ellis is in town!'' the man shouted, disregarding the protocol of the meeting.

Jo came to her feet and gaped at him, suddenly feeling as though she had been exposed as a traitor... but the man didn't seem to know of her connection to the star. ''What did you say?'' she managed to ask.

''It's true,'' he said. ''He's been here for a couple of months, at least. A friend of mine works at the airport, and he said that E.Z. Ellis has been flying in and out, and that he drives some beat up old Volkswagen. He heard a rumor that he's staying in a cabin out on Lake Bisteneau.''

The crowd roared, and some people came to their feet, ready to take action. Pandemonium broke out in the room, threatening to lead them out and guide them blindly. Pulling herself together, Jo rushed to the podium and grabbed the microphone. "Wait a minute!" she yelled. "This has got to be a rumor. What would E.Z. Ellis be doing in this town? And driving a beat up Volkswagen? Give me a break."

"He's here, I tell you!" the man shouted. "I say we go find him!"

The crowd roared in agreement, and Jo struggled for control. "We aren't some kind of lynch mob!" she shouted. "We are private citizens trying to get a law changed. Nothing more!"

"If we want results," someone hollered, "we have to go to the source!"

"Like we did the other night at the concert?" she asked, her voice blaring over the others. "That wasn't a peaceful demonstration! It was a catastrophe! If you go out there like that, the Commerce Committee will laugh us out of Washington!"

"We just want to talk to him," someone at the back of the room called out. "Are you with us or not?"

Jo looked around at the animated faces, full of excitement and anticipation. She felt like a hypocrite, and she hated herself for it. Still, she couldn't betray E.Z. "No," she said. "I don't think it'll accomplish anything. If you go looking for him, you'll do it without me."

The crowd booed and jeered at her words, and Jo knew, then, that she was outnumbered. There was determination on their faces—the same kind of determination that had driven her for years...about the wrong things. Defeated, she stepped down from the podium, gathered her things and went out the door. Only a handful of people followed her.

Behind her, as she left, she heard them plotting to drive in a convoy out to the lake and search around until they found the man who, as they said, had "some tough lessons to learn." The words sounded hauntingly familiar, and as she got in her car to drive away, Jo realized she'd said the same thing once, herself. Only she was the one who had learned.

CHAPTER SIXTEEN

JO DIDN'T WASTE any time going home after she left the meeting place. Instead, she drove with breakneck speed to the lake, trying to reach E.Z. before the others did. Desperately, she hoped he was at Sullivan's. But what if he wasn't? What if he was at home, working on his album, and those people showed up and surprised him?

She pulled into his driveway, saw that his lights were on and the VW was parked in its usual place. She put the car in park, cut off the engine and dashed to the door.

E.Z. opened it before she'd knocked, and she tried to catch her breath. "You have to come with me," she panted. "They know you're here. They want to come see you tonight."

His expression distorted in confusion. "What? What are you talking about?"

"They *know* you're in town, and they know the car you drive and that you're living at the lake. E.Z. you have to leave here before they come. If they can't find you, maybe they'll have the night to think this out rationally. Then I can convince them to leave you alone."

E.Z. muttered a curse and left her at the door. She stepped inside and watched him go to his piano stool, drop down on it, and bang his elbows on the keyboard. The sound rang out ominously. "How the hell did they find out?" he asked.

"Someone at the airport," she said. "I don't know how they knew where you're staying. Just come on. We've got to hurry."

"I was working!" E.Z. said. "My album is almost finished . . . it was almost ready . . ."

"Bring your guitar," she said, gesturing to the new instrument leaning against the wall. "You can work at my house. You can spend the night there."

"I can't work there," he shouted. "I've got all my equipment here. What am I supposed to do?"

"E.Z., please," she said. "If you aren't here, they'll go home. One night won't make that much difference."

E.Z. breathed a curse again, and, with harsh, angry movements, turned off his keyboard, unplugged his recorder, carefully removed the tape of the song he'd been working on, and set it in a box with the others. "I should stay here and confront those fools."

He went into his bedroom and began stuffing some things into a duffel bag. "But if I do, I'll be exposed and I'll have to leave town before I'm ready. I don't want to leave town yet, Jo. I'm still needed here."

"I know you are," she said. "If you come with me, tomorrow I'll try to convince them that your being here was a stupid rumor. I'll concoct some story that you're on tour in Russia or something. Max could help. He could issue a press release."

"I might as well be in Russia," he muttered, "if your friends succeed in screwing up democracy the way they're trying to do."

It was no time to fight with him now. "Just come on," she said, flicking off the lights. "We'll take my car. If they pass yours on the way out here, they'll know it's you and follow you."

"And if they see my car parked here," he said, "they'll know this is my house."

"And they'll turn around and go home when you aren't here," she said with absolute certainty.

E.Z. slammed the locked door behind him and flung his duffel bag into her car. With anger etched on every line of his face, he got in.

E.Z. was quiet all the way to Calloway Corners, and Jo knew that he blamed her for the whole ordeal. Groping for some common ground, she asked, "Did you take the clothes to Sullivan's?"

"Yeah," he said grudgingly. "It was like Christmas. Most of those kids have never had anything new. I told them Ford's church donated them."

"Did everyone get something?" she asked. "Was there enough?"

He looked over at her, his eyes harsh against the night. "There's never enough, Jo. You know that."

She forced the lump out of her throat and told herself not to cry. It wouldn't help now. "What about Carmen?" she asked. "Was she all right?"

E.Z. looked out the window, his face catching both the lights and shadows they passed.

"Was she?" Jo asked, her voice rising with alarm.

"She was just like any other two-year-old girl who'd been given a basis for comparison," he said. "She prefers you over her uncle who's spread so thin you can see through him. And she prefers your bed over that godforsaken cot."

No longer able to keep her tears at bay, Jo threw her hand over her distorted mouth. "Oh, Lord. She was crying, wasn't she?"

The hard lines on E.Z.'s face softened by degrees, removing the bite from his voice. "I held her," he whispered, "until she was asleep."

Jo looked at him through her tears and saw in the moonlight that there were tears in his eyes, as well.

"We're getting deeper and deeper," he said without inflection. "And heaven knows how we'll ever get out of this unscathed."

Jo swallowed the tears obstructing her throat. "Do you mean with Carmen?" she asked. "Or us?"

His gaze settled on her as she drove, but he seemed distant, detached. E.Z. considered the question and finally released a broken sigh. "Both," he said.

The rest of the drive to Calloway Corners was silent. There was nothing more to say.

With Eden there, Jo and E.Z. refrained from further argument that night. In fact they hardly exchanged words at all, and it was clear there was tension as thick as Pacific fog floating about the room. When Eden finally retired for the night, Jo made up the sofa for E.Z. to sleep on, wishing she could stroke the anger from his face and kiss away the disgust.

"I know it's silly for you to sleep here, after the nights we've spent together," she began awkwardly. "But since Eden's here ..."

E.Z. took a pillow from her and tossed it onto the couch. "Don't worry about it. This isn't my idea of an amorous evening, anyway."

The cutting remark hit its target, and she stood up straight. "What do you mean?"

"I mean that if I'm going to spend the night with you in your house, I'd rather it wasn't to avoid some rabid pack of dogs that you pointed in my direction."

"I didn't point them in your direction," Jo said. "I never told them you were here."

He grabbed the blankets from her hands and laid them over the couch. "I'm talking about all that rhetoric about what a threat I was to America's youth," he said, yanking them around the cushions. "If it weren't for all your persuasion, they'd just see me as some bozo out there who likes to sing songs. And the worst they'd want from me is my autograph.''

Jo locked her eyes on the couch, not seeing it, and told herself there was no use talking to him. E.Z. was angry, and now, so was she. Until things calmed down, she couldn't reason with him. "If you need anything," she whispered through pursed lips, "just call."

Jo left him downstairs, in the darkness of the living room, and went up to her room. It seemed cold and barren tonight, she thought. Not at all the sanctuary it had once been. She dressed for bed in a long white gown, brushed out her hair, and crawled into bed.

It wasn't E.Z.'s anger that upset her the most, Jo thought. It was his disappointment in her, as if she'd let him down, fulfilling some prophecy she'd battled all along. Her alienation from him kept her awake, gnawing at her like a disease. Did he see her in a different light? Had tonight destroyed whatever fragile relationship they'd built? Did he still think they should join forces?

It was long after midnight when Jo finally decided she had to see him, restore the peace on his face and know that he didn't hate her. She got out of bed, leaving her hair tousled and tangled, her feet bare, and tiptoed down the stairs.

By touch, she made her way through the darkness, found the couch and stooped down next to him. E.Z. lay on his back, his face an empty canvas devoid of either emotion or judgment. He breathed with a deep, unhampered rhythm.

For a long while Jo only watched him, knowing with every sense she possessed that life would prove to be worthless when the time came for him to leave her. What would she do? Who would she be?

The sudden urge to touch him overcame her, and instead of fighting it, she reached out a trembling hand and pushed the hair back from his forehead. He stirred slightly. Then, knowing that it would wake him, she leaned over and kissed the corner of his mouth.

E.Z.'s eyes opened, and he saw her kneeling beside him. His eyes were soft, sleepy, but even so she could see that he still clung to the remnants of his anger. "What is it?" he asked.

The cold question startled her, for it was a world away from the sensitive embrace she'd needed. Self-conscious and not certain why, Jo searched for an excuse for being here. But it was no time for games. Tonight, in the darkness of his scrutiny, only the truth would count. "I was just thinking how much I love you," she whispered.

The glaciers in his eyes melted away, leaving the deepest well of sadness she'd ever seen. "Sometimes love just isn't enough," he said.

Jo dropped her head, as hurt as if he'd physically shoved her away. She knew what he meant, that what he needed besides love was her commitment . . . but not to him. To the people he cared passionately about, to causes other than censorship. Even now, though it was the one thing that could bridge the gap between them, Jo knew she couldn't abandon her fight.

"Sometimes love is all there is," she whispered. And before his words could cut her deeper, she got up and left him lying there alone.

JO SPENT TOO MUCH TIME in the bathroom the next morning, trying to cover the dark circles and red, swollen patches under her eyes. Finally she had to admit that no makeup yet invented could cover them. She would have to face E.Z. as she was.

E.Z. sat pensively on the couch when she went downstairs, the blankets he'd slept on folded neatly beside him. She heard Eden in the kitchen, smelled the eggs and bacon she fried and the freshly ground coffee she always brewed for company. E.Z. turned to the staircase when he heard Jo's footsteps, and she could see that their brief encounter in the night had kept him awake, as well.

"Hi," she said.

He looked distant. "Hi," he responded.

"You look like hell," she said.

"So do you."

Disheartened by the ironically meaningful small talk Jo went to the coffee pot Eden had left on the table and poured herself a cup, racking her brain for some magic words that would make everything all right. Finally when the tension became too much to bear, she turned to him.

"E.Z.—"

"Jo—"

The words were uttered simultaneously, and they both stopped, waited, then spoke together again.

"Go ahead."

Before either of them could take more initiative, the telephone trilled out an interruption, startling Jo. Still looking at E.Z. and wishing to heaven for thirty seconds in which to make things right, she picked it up.

"Hello?"

"Miss Calloway?" a man's voice asked. "Jo Calloway?"

"Speaking." She kept her eyes locked on E.Z. He had propped his elbow on the sofa back, and was rubbing his eyes.

"I understand you're trying to find jobs for some of the unemployed in your area," the caller said. "I think I have something that might interest you."

Jo's eyes widened instantly, and she tore her gaze from E.Z. and began pulling out drawers as she looked for something to write on. "Yes," she said. "Go ahead."

"Well, I'm in charge of hiring for a large tobacco farm out on Avery Island, and we're searching for experienced farm workers. We're offering to house the ones we hire."

"Jobs?" she exclaimed.

The beginnings of a smile came to Jo's eyes, and she turned back to E.Z. He was looking up at her now, anticipation easing the weariness on his face. He stood up and stepped toward her.

"I know of at least a dozen people," she went on. "When do you need them?"

"Next week," the man said. "Have them contact me. I can probably hire them by phone."

Jo took down the information and the name of the person hiring and thanked him from the bottom of her heart. Then, hanging up, she looked at E.Z., trying to contain the joy she felt. "It's some jobs," she said. "And free housing. Juarez is qualified, and so are a lot of the others."

E.Z. frowned and took a grudging step closer. "Jobs?" he asked, not yet convinced. "You got them *jobs*?"

"Yes!" she sang out, punching the air victoriously. "One of the people I called the other day put some feelers out and told this guy to call me. Oh, E.Z. Juarez will have a job, and a home! And Carmen..."

Her joy shattered like dropped crystal as reality dawned on her. "And Carmen will have to go all the way to south Louisiana with him...and we won't see her any more...."

Tears stung Jo's eyes again, burning the already swollen rims, and she turned away. A moment passed and she clenched her fists, telling herself to be strong, to think of Carmen...of Juarez. But she didn't feel strong. "I hate myself when I'm so selfish."

E.Z. came behind her, putting his hands on her shoulders. The depth of feeling he had once had for her was trapped somewhere between his anger and his awe. Finally, as if the mere contact purged him of all the ill feelings he'd harbored, his touch became more gentle. "Selfish?" E.Z. asked. "How can you say that?"

"It's true," she said. "Here I am with the best news Juarez has heard all year, and all I can think about is myself, and how I'm losing someone who was never mine to begin with."

Answering her deepest unuttered prayer, E.Z. spun her around and pressed her head against his chest. "She'll be better off there," he whispered. "She'll have a home, and her uncle will be able to support her. She'll have quiet at night, and the lights won't be blaring, and she'll have her own bed...."

Jo nodded and squeezed her eyes shut, knowing intellectually that things were looking up for Carmen. But in her heart things didn't feel better. "I guess we should tell him and the others right away," she managed to say. "They'll need to make plans to go."

E.Z. kept his arms around her shoulder and ushered her toward the door, forgetting the breakfast Eden had cooked. And as they walked out to her car, Jo had the miserable feeling that E.Z. was taking her to kiss one of the sweetest parts of herself goodbye.

WHEN CARMEN SAW JO that morning, she ran to her as if she were her dead mother come back to life. The force with which Carmen embraced her broke Jo's heart, and she picked the child up, holding her as if she never intended to let her go. But she knew better. Carmen had been crying, she could tell, and her little face was drawn and pale.

Juarez looked as if he'd been dragged through the worst hours of his life. "She cried all night," he said. "I had to walk with her outside, to keep her from waking the others."

Juarez's look was so condemning, that Jo knew she should put the baby down. The man blamed her for mak-

ing Carmen hate where she was, she knew, but it was too late
to erase the past few days. All she could do was concentrate
on the present. And now Carmen needed her. "I'm sorry,"
she said, meaning the apology from her heart. "I didn't
mean to spoil her. I just thought she needed some attention. She's just a baby."

But Jo knew that her observation wouldn't help Juarez
sleep at night or sustain his family during the day. Only a
job would. Only a home. She stroked Carmen's hair, trying
not to burst into tears as she spoke. "I found you a job,
Juarez. On Avery Island. The farm offers free housing for
its workers."

It was as if the lights in Juarez's eyes flicked miraculously on, and in that moment, Jo guessed that he had once
been a handsome man...before life played its dirty game on
him.

She told him about the job, while E.Z. went to other men
he knew were qualified and told them the news. The ones
who weren't able to do farm work sat on their cots, staring
dully at the joy on the others' faces. And Jo felt as helpless
as she had last night after E.Z. had delivered the clothes. It
wasn't enough. There was never enough.

She held Carmen as Juarez made the crucial phone call,
and then he was back with his family, telling them the good
news and listening as they sent whoops bouncing off the
metal walls. Juarez had a job, and they would all have a
home!

But Jo didn't feel that little Carmen was destined to live
happily ever after.

"We'll leave today," Juarez told the family as he frantically began to pack the few belongings they'd brought with
them.

Jo caught her breath and gaped at him. "No!"

The children turned to look at her. Juarez stopped what
he was doing.

Jo forced herself to temper her voice. "Please," she said. "He doesn't need you until next week. You could wait a few more days."

Juarez's face displayed a mixture of disgust and amusement. "And sleep with my family in a shelter with three hundred others? On cots lined up with no privacy? With noise that never stops and lights that shine all night? Why would I want to stay one more day?"

Because I don't want you to take Carmen! Jo wanted to cry. But she couldn't say that. Instead, she grasped at straws. "I just meant that . . . the house may not be ready for you . . . you wouldn't have a place. . . ."

"The man told me I could come now," he said. "And that's what I'm gonna do."

Jo began to tremble, and she knew that Carmen sensed it. Distraught, she looked around the room, searching for E.Z. as if he might stop Juarez. E.Z. saw her expression from across the room, and came toward her.

"What is it?" he asked.

Jo struggled to contain her tears. "He wants to go today," she said.

E.Z. swallowed and touched Carmen's little head. The child stared up at him with innocent, adoring eyes. He wrenched his eyes from her and turned to Juarez. He could see that the man was adamant. Opportunities so rare could not be put off. E.Z. touched Jo's hair, then pressed his face against it. "Put her down," he said gently. "You have to let her go. She belongs with her family."

"She doesn't *have* a family!" Jo bit out on a sob.

"She does," E.Z. said. "Her uncle loves her, and he'll take care of her. You have to let her go."

Jo squeezed her eyes shut, fighting the pain of losing yet one more love in her life. It was a nightmare she was destined to live over and over. But determined not to make it harder on the child, she forced herself to stay calm. Jo bent over and set Carmen down.

Carmen clung to her neck, sensing that she was leaving her. "No-o-o-o!" she screamed.

Jo didn't remember anything in her life being so hard to do, as when she pried Carmen's arms from her neck. She told the child that she loved her and then ran from the building, listening to the little girl's anguished cries ring out like an alarm that would never be silenced again.

E.Z. followed her outside, and pulled her into his arms, holding her once again, letting her weep like the little girl who'd been abandoned.

When she was in control again, E.Z. took her back to her car, got in the driver's side and drove out toward the lake. Neither of them said a word.

Finally, E.Z. broke the silence. "It's my fault. I should never have taken you there the first time. I should have known you'd wind up hurt."

Jo stared out the window, her eyes swollen. "You were trying to teach me something," she said. "And it worked. I learned some of the toughest lessons of my life."

E.Z.'s tone was self-deprecating. "But it didn't change anything. You're still who you were when I met you, and I'm still who I am."

"And Carmen's still who she is," she said. "It's funny that we can have so much of an effect on each other and still not really affect each other at all. Not when everything's said and done."

The truth of her words left them both pensive and lonely. They didn't speak again until they neared the turnoff to E.Z.'s cabin.

"I wonder if those lunatic friends of yours found my house last night," E.Z. mumbled.

"Probably," Jo said.

His voice hardened again. "Hell, they're probably camped out on my doorstep, waiting to stone me to death when I get there."

Jo peered out the window, knowing the issue would never disappear from between them. "They just wanted to talk to you. Just like I did the first time I came out there."

"There's a difference. These people operate in numbers. That's where mob scenes come from."

"They're reasonable people," she said.

"Yeah. That's why they almost started a riot at the Byzantine concert the other night. Real reasonable."

Jo pursed her lips, in no mood to feed this fight any longer. When he pulled into his driveway, E.Z. would see that no one was there, that everything was fine, that . . .

Her thoughts trailed off as he turned into the driveway, and she saw a garbage drum that hadn't been there before, smoldering as if something had been burned in it. She glanced at E.Z., saw the alarm in his eyes and held her breath as the car inched closer.

From the window, she could see that the door had been beaten in and hung open on one hinge, its glass broken out. A piece of equipment she couldn't identify lay on the lawn, and a string of recording tape was draped from somewhere inside the house to the smoking garbage drum.

"Oh . . . hell," E.Z. muttered.

No, she thought, her mind seeking an explanation. *It couldn't be . . . they wouldn't . . .*

The car jerked to a stop, and Jo scrambled out. E.Z. was behind her, turning over the pieces of equipment he found as he went toward the house, shouting expletives and cursing the people who'd done this.

Feeling betrayed by the very cause she'd created, Jo stumbled inside the doorway, stopped and beheld the damage they had done. The keyboard had been broken in half, his guitar was bashed in, and all of the pages with his songs and lyrics had been torn out of their notebooks, presumably burned in the drum. Strung all over the house, like crepe paper at a birthday party, were the tapes with E.Z.'s new songs...the songs no one had ever heard before...the songs that were going to help the homeless...the songs that no longer existed, for everything was gone... Suddenly, profoundly, Jo knew why he'd named the album "E.Z. to be Hard."

She spun around to E.Z., denial dancing like wildfire in her eyes. "They wouldn't do this," she cried.

"The hell they wouldn't!" E.Z. turned on her, like a man who'd been betrayed. "You started this! You're the one who lit their fire! You're the one who told them how rotten my music was!"

"But I didn't tell them to do *this*!" she shouted. "I didn't know—"

"*Why* didn't you know?" he yelled. "They were only finishing what you started."

"I didn't start this," she protested. "I wasn't even here!"

"You didn't have to be here!" he said, ripping up a tangled handful of tape that he'd worked on for months. "All you had to do was give them your banner to carry. They know what to do with it. I warned you it would get out of hand! You can't award this kind of power to a handful of people. It makes them dangerous, Jo! *This* is why censorship can't work!"

Jo shook her head, frantically trying to make him understand that she was as appalled as he. "I didn't know they were capable of this, E.Z." She rushed forward, started trying to untangle some of the tape. "Look, if we work together, maybe we can salvage some—"

E.Z. grabbed the tape out of her hand and flung it across the room. "It's ruined, Jo!" he yelled through his teeth, his eyes two blue-hot flames that scorched her heart. "Everything I've been working for. All the notes, the music... That money would have helped people like Carmen, but those self-righteous bastards you created have ruined that now. *You've* ruined it! Are you happy? Is this your demented brand of censorship?''

''No!'' Jo screamed, her face crimson with the effort to make him see her innocence. The problem was, she didn't feel blameless. ''No, it isn't what I wanted. You know it wasn't!''

''Well, it sure as hell wasn't what I wanted when I got involved with you,'' he said. ''I thought you were somebody with substance! I thought you had some depth. You can't see that by succeeding at this, you're failing miserably. And you're making *me* fail. And you're making all my efforts fail!''

''That isn't fair,'' she cried.

''Hell, no, it isn't fair,'' E.Z. said. ''Damn right.''

She caught her breath on a broken sob. ''You could...you could call the police,'' she choked out. ''I'd tell them what I know...''

He kicked the broken keyboard out of his way, lifted the empty notebooks like war casualties he couldn't save. ''If I call the police, the press will be on me like bloodhounds. Everyone at Sullivan's will find out who I am, and I can never go back. Hell, I have to leave now, anyway. You and your friends saw to that!''

E.Z. went to the broken door, motioning for her to walk through it. ''I'm sick to death of your empty idealism, Jo. Why don't you just get out of my life before anybody else gets hurt?''

Jo stifled a sob and gaped at him, pain shooting rockets through her heart. ''E.Z., please. You can't blame me for this.''

"I do, though," he said, his eyes two open wounds. "I blame you and everyone like you. I was a fool to ever think I could have a life with you."

Jo's hands came up to cover her face, as if she could ward off the hateful words. She had been a fool, as well, she thought. She had loved him, knowing what it would ultimately do to her. And now, she too, was a casualty of this senseless war.

Lifting her chin and gathering the tattered remnants of her pride, Jo walked through that door. And even though it was broken, E.Z. managed to slam it behind her.

CHAPTER SEVENTEEN

I WAS A FOOL to ever think I could have a life with you.

The words ate at Jo like a plague for the next three weeks, keeping her awake nights, making it impossible for her to eat, destroying her concentration. The cause she had once so passionately espoused had betrayed her, and now she found it impossible to go to the meetings and face the people who had destroyed E.Z.'s album, and her along with it.

After a few days, she had taken Eden's advice and gone back to his house, prepared to plead with him to forgive her for what he saw as her failure. But E.Z. had left town. The door of his cabin still hung open, broken and half-hinged. All his things were gone. All that was left was that little hibachi on the back patio, the couch in the living room and the stripped bed where he'd sung the song he'd written for her. But like E.Z., it was gone now, too. She doubted he'd have the spirit or desire to rewrite it.

Too drained to cry, she had left the cabin and driven for hours, sorting out the fragments of her life. She was supposed to be back in Baton Rouge, then go to Dallas, then Houston, campaigning for censorship. She was supposed to be working like a fiend on her speech to the Senate Commerce Committee. She was supposed to be pulling together all her resources, so that she'd have a case when the time came.

But now her heart wasn't in it.

For a week she had lived for this afternoon, when the year's Farm Aid concert would be telecast nationally on MTV. E.Z. Ellis was one of the featured performers, and she'd sat before the television with fevered eyes, desperate for a glimpse of him, a tiny morsel for a dying soul.

But after six hours of praying he'd be the next in line, it was announced that he had canceled. E.Z. wouldn't be performing that day.

Something inside her had snapped after that, and Jo felt herself flailing, functionless, as she wept out her heart. And neither Eden nor Mariah nor anyone had been able to loosen the cloak of misery she had wrapped tightly about herself. Only E.Z. could do that, and heaven only knew where he was.

Jo sat back in her bedroom at Calloway Corners now, staring at nothing as thoughts fluttered like debris in her mind. What was he doing now? Was he trying to rewrite the tunes he'd lost? Was he arranging ammunition against her group to use before the committee? Was he feeding the hate and disgust he had for her? Had his decision not to perform been meant as punishment to her, since he must know how badly she needed to see him, to hear his voice....

Distantly Jo heard the doorbell ring, heard Eden letting Mariah in downstairs, then recognized one of the voices as Tess's. Eden had, no doubt, called her sister in Dallas, told her of the sinking spirits that had paralyzed Jo completely, and Tess had come home for a mercy mission to shake Jo out of her depression. That was nice, Jo thought, but it was a wasted trip. All she really wanted was to be left alone.

In moments, when the sisters finished their whispered consultation in the living room, they filed up the stairs into Jo's room, and stood over her, each as lost as the other about how to approach the one sister who rarely needed comfort. Jo regarded each of them with dull eyes, dreading what was to come. Eden would shower her with sympathy... which she neither wanted nor deserved; Tess would want her to talk... but Jo had nothing to say; and Mariah would try badgering her with a pep talk... but none of it would matter.

Mariah sat down on the bed facing her and forced her to meet her eyes. "Jo," she said, "you've got to snap out of this. You have work to do. I've never known you to shirk your responsibilities before."

Jo looked up at Mariah, then shifted her gaze to Eden, then Tess. "I thought you all thought the censorship thing was frivolous. I thought you were all against it."

"But *you* believed in it," Tess said, as if that was all that mattered. Eden dropped to a chair, leaned toward Jo. "Whether I agreed or not, I've always admired the courage you had to believe in things the way you do. Don't let it go, Jo. Don't stop believing in things, just because a few people got out of hand."

Jo shook her head and pushed her hair back from her face. She knew she looked worse than she ever had in her life, but she didn't care. She couldn't remember ever *feeling* worse. "I don't know why I bother," she said. "Whatever I touch is destroyed. I rallied all those people to help me in the fight, and they wound up destroying something that could have brought so much good to people's lives."

Tess climbed onto the bed next to her, put her arm around her. "I loved a little girl," Jo went on, "and showered her with so much attention that now she thinks one more person in her life has abandoned her. And I fell in love with E.Z. only to make him hate me profoundly, by indirectly ruining everything he stood for."

Her eyes ached with unshed tears, and she looked dully at her sisters. "I can't stand the thought that he despises me. I can't stand the thought of walking into that Senate hearing and lambasting E.Z. the way I'd been doing before I met him."

Tess's own soft eyes filled with unshed tears. "Jo, you've got to stop dwelling on what can't be changed. Look at what you still stand for, what you've accomplished. Do you still believe in censorship or not?"

Jo wadded her hair and tossed one hand up in the air. "I honestly don't know." She studied the ecru lace on the bed-spread, the uniformity of its pattern, and wondered why life couldn't be that way. "There are still stars glamorizing Satan worship, suicide, sadistic behavior, perversions.... They need to be stopped. But not like that. Not through violence and destruction. That wasn't what I wanted."

"Then tell the committee that," Mariah said. "Go in there and tell them what you've learned. Tell them how you feel. Be yourself."

"Be myself," Jo said, realizing that her tears weren't spent, after all. "Who is that, I wonder? The angry little girl who spent her life righting wrongs? The one whose goal in life was to win whatever argument she was engaged in? The one who thought only *her* injustices mattered, and that those of everyone else could be damned?"

Eden left her chair and joined the others on the bed. There was something comforting, nostalgic, about the way they crowded around Jo. "Sounds to me like that little girl has grown up," Eden whispered.

Jo looked at her older sister, breathed a profound sigh and wiped the tears stinging her raw eyes. "Oh, Eden. I don't think I've grown up. I feel just like I did when I was five, and I was so angry that Mama didn't come home, and I hated Mariah for coming instead, and you for not being old enough or mature enough to step into Mama's role, and you, Tess, for withdrawing into yourself when I needed someone, and Dad for never being able to reach out..." Tess embraced her, and Jo's voice broke. She fell against Tess's chest, weeping her heart out.

The floodgates had been released, and now she was powerless to stop the words from pouring out. "E.Z. left me because I was such an angry person, so ready to lash out, so ready to lead a fight my way, because, of course, it was the *only* way. Just like the way I was with Carmen. Doing things *my* way, and not listening to anyone's warnings about what it would mean to her when I was gone. I'm such a failure ... such a failure."

Mariah leaned across the bed and stroked Jo's hair. "You're not a failure," she said. "You're there for *me* when I need you. And you were there to touch Carmen's life and open her uncle's eyes. And whether you think so or not, E.Z. Ellis was in love with you. In all my eternal wisdom, I think he'll still love you when the smoke blows away. But when it does, Jo, you've got to be there, too."

Jo let go of Tess and sat up straight and wiped her face with trembling hands. Mariah was right. It was too late to run away now. Taking a deep breath, she regarded each of her sisters, absorbing the encouragement they offered her. "I'll go to Washington," she said, her words delivered in a high-pitched rasp. "Because I think I have something important to say to that committee. I just pray I don't break down in front of them when I see the hate in E.Z.'s eyes."

"I'll go with you," Eden said, and everyone turned surprised eyes on the sister who'd never been out of the state. "You'll need a friend. Besides, I'm about ready to see a little of the world."

Jo smiled through her tears and held Eden's hand in both her own. Though she still felt like a falling rock in an eternal abyss, things weren't quite so grim as long as she had her sisters to cushion the fall.

NEITHER JO NOR EDEN spoke much on the flight to Washington. Eden, who had never flown before, was as wide-eyed and awestruck as a child. Jo only stared off into space, sorting out the things she would say to the committee. But when they finally landed and reached their hotel room, she realized she was no closer to knowing what to say than she'd been when they'd set out. What did she stand for? What did she believe? It all seemed so muddled to her now.

The morning of the hearing, she dressed as meticulously and as quietly as if she was marching to a death chamber. Still, she hadn't a clue what she would say when she got her turn to speak.

The steps of the capitol building were overrun with press members and photographers when she arrived, but they weren't there for her. They were surrounding E.Z. Ellis, and security guards were holding back his fans. Jo paused on the steps, trying to see him, but the press had closed in too tightly around the reclusive star. She saw Max standing off to one side, hands shoved deeply into his baggy trouser pockets. He gazed at her with condemnation in his eyes and she knew he'd been told the whole story.

Drearily she moved past them, up the steps, hesitated at the door and took one last look back at the crowd. Beside two cameramen she saw E.Z., dressed in a black business suit, and wearing reflective glasses that completely concealed his eyes. Even so, she knew the moment his eyes met hers. E.Z. stopped talking and stared at her, the lack of expression on his face reminding her just how banished from him her soul felt today.

Eden took her arm. "Come on," she whispered. "Don't do this to yourself."

Forcing herself to move, Jo stepped inside, saw a group of the citizens she had rallied there to support her and their cause. She greeted some of them, nodding absently when they told her to "kick butt." And then she went in and found her seat at the witness table. There was no place near her for Eden, so her sister walked to a seat farther back. Jo felt that her only support system was gone—she was left to flounder on her own.

It took a while to get all the rock stars who were testifying away from the press and settled in their seats. Jo felt the lights of the news cameras boring into her, waiting. She felt the anticipation of all those whose consciousness she had raised, waiting for her to represent them. She felt E.Z.'s eyes from a few seats behind her, burning into her with steely condemnation.

And she knew that coming here just might turn out to be the biggest mistake of her life.

SHE'S STILL GOING TO DO IT, E.Z. thought as he watched Jo sitting rigidly in her seat, on every news network in the country. *She didn't learn a damn thing.*

The realization that her determination had not wavered, even after all that had happened, made his blood boil. But more than that, his heart twisted painfully inside his chest. She'd professed to love him, and yet she would tell the country, in just a few minutes, that his music was evil and offensive. *You're still who you were when I met you, and I'm still who I am,* she had said. Nothing had changed. Nothing at all.

Propping his elbows on the arms of his chair, E.Z. crossed his hands and held them in front of his mouth, hoping that the cameras couldn't reveal his nerves or the pain in his expression. Damn that committee, for making him speak right after her. He'd have to address whatever she said about him. To defend himself, he'd have to make her look stupid. He honestly didn't know if he could do it. The dread made his stomach burn.

It was his imagination, E.Z. knew, but as he watched Jo, he could swear he smelled her fresh scent. His fingers itched for the touch of her hair, and his lips felt rough, in dire need of hers. He saw Eden sitting nearby, watching her sister with deep concern, as if there were something to worry about. But Jo didn't seem too ruffled, he thought. She seemed as cool and collected as she had been the first time he'd seen her. And he was certain she would be just as persuasive.

The tie he wore was too tight, he thought, and this god-forsaken suit was hot as hell. But he needed every advantage he could use. He listened, his facial expression hard and unrevealing as she began to read the notes she'd written, no doubt, before she'd even met him. She told the committee about her neighbor's daughter, the cult group that took E.Z.'s song as its anthem, the subliminal messages in other artists' songs, the satanic lyrics and the glamorization of drugs, violence, suicide, sex. She quoted specifics, none of them involving his lyrics, but damaging to him, nonetheless. And she read quotes from teenagers she had interviewed, quotes about what came to their minds when they thought of certain songs. The quotes didn't paint a pretty picture.

E.Z. dropped his hands, and they bunched into fists, his fingernails cutting into his palms. His mouth trembled with restraint, and he wanted to forget the fact that millions of people would see this on the news tonight, or that hundreds were crowded into this incinerator of a room. He wanted to disregard everything and stand up, and ask her how she could condemn him when she knew him better than anyone else in his life ever had?

Jo reached the end of her speech, but instead of the "thank you," that would signal she was finished, she looked down at her papers, then cleared her throat. All eyes watched her, waiting. This time when she continued, Jo didn't refer to her notes, and from where he sat, E.Z. could see her hands trembling. Her voice wobbled as she spoke.

"Mr. Chairman," she said, her voice rasping, "I wrote this speech weeks ago, when I truly believed every word. I still do. But at the time, there were things I didn't know, and I guess you could say that I was seeing things through tunnel vision. Naively, I believed that censorship would solve all of these problems."

E.Z.'s hard, expressionless façade melted away, and he leaned forward, hanging on her words. Like everyone else, he waited for her to go on.

She cleared her throat again. "What I didn't know, and what I know now, is that some of the songs that offend me and my group have an opposite effect on others. Recently, I had the opportunity to hear a song—one that I would previously have considered offensive—but this song had a positive effect on a teen runaway. If I'd had my way and banned the song, that child would not have been influenced to return home. I've also had the opportunity to see the far-reaching potential of rock music. We've all heard of the efforts of Live Aid, Band Aid, Farm Aid, USA For Africa... What I didn't know weeks ago is that E.Z. Ellis's next album has been dedicated to the homeless, and all of the proceeds from it will go to set up a foundation that will aid millions of Americans."

E.Z. didn't notice when several of the cameras switched to him, or when Max nudged him, or when the senators whispered among themselves. All he saw was Jo, struggling not to cry in front of the entire country. "And yet, a couple of weeks ago," she went on, "the members of my censorship group in Louisiana broke into the cabin where E.Z. Ellis was staying and destroyed the tapes and notes for that album, along with all of his equipment and instruments."

Jo's voice broke, and he saw that she had lost the battle with her tears. "I have to take blame for that, because I once believed, and taught others, that I had the right to make choices for the masses. But I was wrong."

The pro-censorship supporters standing in the rear and near the doors gasped, and a low roar of dissension passed over the crowd. E.Z. felt his anger melting, along with his heart, and when she had to stop until her voice was stable enough to go on, he fought the urge to go to her and help her find her way through this hellish maze in which they'd both lost themselves.

"What we need to do is better educate the teenagers about the tricks used by some cheap musicians, so that they can make their own choices. Because what's offensive to me may be a life-saving factor to someone else. I now have to say, in all honesty, that I don't believe censorship is the answer. It's just another problem. Thank you very much."

The committee members seemed to grow flustered, and covered their mikes to confer among themselves. The press corps darted from the room to call in Jo's statements before the noon news, and censorship advocates began heckling and protesting loudly. The chairman banged his gavel and ordered a short recess before they would hear other testimony.

E.Z. got to his feet, and without regard for the cameras focused on him, went toward Jo. But before he could reach her, reporters descended on her. He saw that she was still crying, refusing to speak, and he watched helplessly as she fought her way through the crowd and out into the hall, too far out of his reach.

JO MANAGED TO GET PAST the crowd of reporters without speaking, but it wasn't as easy to avoid the censorship people who'd come from Bossier City to support her. She looked at them as she passed, wishing desperately that she wasn't crying.

"How could you do that?" one of them asked. It was someone she was certain had played a part in trashing E.Z.'s house. "How could you come here and betray us and our cause?"

The accusation cut through Jo's despair, and sparked her fire again. "I didn't betray you *or* the cause," she told him. "You betrayed me when you appointed yourself judge and juror and ruined something beautiful that you didn't have the capacity to understand!"

And then she shoved her way through the crowd and broke free, running for the first cab she saw, without a destination in mind. All Jo wanted was to get as far away from there as she could.

The cab let her out near the Washington Monument, several blocks away from her hotel. She wanted to walk and think and avoid facing Eden and the people who would probably be waiting to lynch her when she got there. But most of all, Jo wanted to avoid facing herself, now that everything she had believed about herself was shattered.

She strolled down Madison Drive, peering in windows of restaurants at lovers who dined without complication, at children whose mothers wiped their mouths, at families who bickered among themselves. None of that was in her future, she thought miserably. No child, no lover, no family. She had lost Carmen as she had lost E.Z. She should never have let herself love either of them.

And now she had jeopardized her future. No one in his right mind would hire her as a lobbyist or consultant now. As soon as she got home, she'd tender her resignation as director of AFCRL, unless they managed to fire her first.

Sooner than she was ready to, Jo reached the block where her hotel stood and immediately saw the reporters gathering on the front walk. Like vultures waiting to attack their prey, they watched the cabs approaching, looking for her with their cameras poised. The number of reporters surprised her. Had what she said been such a shock that they were determined to get a statement?

Jo kept her head low and tried to hurry past them without being noticed, but one of them spotted her.

"There she is!" he shouted, and suddenly the whole pack swallowed her into their midst, yelling questions constructed to implicate her. "Miss Calloway? How long have you know E.Z. Ellis?"

"What is your relationship to him?"

"Did he convince you to change your position on censorship?"

The nature of the questions shook her, for they had nothing to do with the hearings. It was only E.Z. who interested them—not her broken heart, or her crushed confidence, or her cold, hollow loneliness. She wondered why they didn't just ask him. She hesitated a moment, struggling to find the answers that in the past had always come so easily to her. But nothing came to her now.... Finally, on the verge of hysteria, she shoved through them and headed for the hotel entrance.

"Miss Calloway, please—"

Two reporters pushed through the revolving door after her, but Jo broke into a trot and reached an elevator just about to close. Miraculously, the doors snapped shut behind her, blocking off the reporters.

Jo collapsed back against the wall, and taking a deep breath, tried to collect herself. What if more reporters waited on her floor, a panicked voice inside her asked. What if she broke down before their cameras, making a bigger fool of herself than she already had?

She would run, she decided as the floor numbers flashed over her head. She would get off the elevator and make a mad dash for her door and evade their questions if she could. Trembling, she dug in her purse for her room key. It wasn't there, she realized with a sick feeling. She had given it to Eden that morning, never expecting to be separated from her.

As the elevator reached her floor, Jo dropped her face in her hand, letting her curtain of hair hide her, and prayed that Eden had come back to the hotel before her.

The elevator doors opened, and she peered out cautiously. The hall was empty. Still not trusting her luck, Jo rushed to her room and banged urgently on the door. "Eden? I forgot my key. Are you there?"

It was a direct answer to a prayer when the door opened, but it wasn't Eden who greeted her. Instead, E.Z. Ellis stood before her, leaning against the casing, gazing at her like a man who hadn't seen color in days, but now confronted the most vivid hues his eyes could bear. "Eden gave me her key," he whispered.

Jo caught her breath and stood gaping at him, too numb to feel, too stunned to move. They stared at each other for a long moment, their eyes eloquently expressing what words could not. What was there to say, after all?

Nothing, except what Jo had longed to hear since the first night she'd spent with E.Z. at Sullivan's...the night love had hit her like a tidal wave, sweeping her into its arc, then drowning her with its power. "I love you," he whispered, pulling her into his embrace and burying his face in her hair. "Oh, Jo, I love you so much."

"I love you," she whispered. Tears tumbled down her face, tears of joy, tears of the new fire burning inside her, tears that the heartache was over.... "Oh, E.Z...."

His mouth found hers, and in his kiss were volumes of undeclared promises—that he'd line up the stars and corral the comets for one glimpse of her sunshine smile; that he'd swap his talent for her embrace; that he'd exchange his guitar-calloused fingers for one touch of her face. He kissed her with the strength of the misery she'd felt for days, surpassing it and filling the void within her that had yawned wider and wider each day she'd spent without him.

In his kiss, Jo was both weightless and bound to him, as though she floated in a dimension where sadness had no place. Undressing was a slow dance, underlined with impatient urgency that made the deed pass without conscious thought.

E.Z. carried her to the bed, anchoring her with his weight, and at once he was inside her. There was no time for titillating games, for teasing or taunting. For it had been too long already. Jo gasped with the force and depth of his passion, and clung to him with all her might as he moved with the rhythm of his most sensuous song.

"I love you," he said again as their ardor sparked into a raging fire that seared through her, consuming every fiber. "I love you . . . I love you. . . ."

Jo exploded and imploded and gripped him covetously as she did, heard his fierce exhalation of breath, felt his heart scampering in a vicious cadence. As if she experienced a drunken dream, she heard the words he whispered over and over . . . the words she would never hear enough if she lived three lifetimes. "I love you . . . I love you . . . I love you . . ."

Afterward, they lay in the bed, clinging to that love as if it would escape them should they turn their heads. "I missed you so much I thought I'd die," she whispered. "I thought you'd never forgive me. All those wonderful songs ruined, all that money that could have helped the homeless. . . ."

He finger-brushed her hair back from her face and ca-
ressed the ivory skin that was more precious to him than all
the tans in the South of France. "Hey, I'm a creative guy. I
can remember the basics of most of the songs, and the lyrics will probably come out better the second time around,
anyway. The album will still get made." He ran his finger
down the slope of her nose. "You can reconstruct a song,
but a relationship is harder to salvage. I thought I'd lost you
forever. I picked up the phone a hundred times to call you.
But my pride got in the way...my pride and my anger...."

"You're back," she whispered, basking in the phenome-
nal fact that he loved her—*her*, the spitfire, the steam-
roller, the angry little girl who had only now grown up.
"That's all that matters. Everything's good now."

"Almost everything," he said.

Jo sat up to see him better, her weary eyes brighter, but
not bright enough for him. "What do you mean?" she
asked.

He ran a finger over the shell of her ear, down her neck,
and across her breasts that had come to delight him so. But
his delight faded, and a remnant of sadness revealed itself
in his eyes. "Carmen," he said. "You never really got to say
goodbye," he whispered.

"I think I could come to terms with her being gone. But
in my dreams, I hear her crying—" Jo's voice cracked, and
she forced down the emotion in her throat. "I need to know
she's happy. That she's eating. That she's being cared for."

E.Z. tipped her chin up and smiled. "Then we'll go to
Avery Island," he said. "We'll go tonight."

A flicker of joy lit her face, but faded just as quickly. Jo
sat up, searched his face. "We can't," she said. "If she sees
us, it'll just be worse. It'll hurt her all over again."

"Not if we can show her that we aren't out of her lives forever," E.Z. said. "If she understands that we'll come to visit her, it won't be so hard for her."

Jo's eyes brightened tentatively, and that brightness spread to his. "Do you think so, E.Z.?"

He pulled her against him, tucked her head under his chin. "I know so. And I'll do anything it takes to get that sadness out of your eyes, and see the fire back in them again."

Suddenly, Jo had the feeling that he *could* make everything right. All he had to be was E.Z.

E.Z. AND JO slipped away that night after diverting the press, and Eden agreed that she would stay in Washington one more night and would fly home the next day as planned. Max was showing her the town, she said, and while he wasn't exactly her type, she was having a wonderful time with him.

It took a few hours for them to reach Avery Island, in the southern part of Louisiana, and another hour to rent a car and find the farm where Juarez had gone to work. The employee houses were lined in a row down a dirt road, all the same size and shape, their paint peeling and roofs patched. But they were homes, nonetheless. Still, dread stung Jo as she imagined the conditions the families suffered. How could Juarez fit eight children into one matchbox structure? Where did Carmen sleep? Was she any better off than she had been at Sullivan's?

Jo's heart sank as they went to the porch, stepped over the rotten hole gaping in the center and knocked on the door. One of the older kids answered, took one look at them, and shouted back inside, "Daddy, it's them!"

Jo and E.Z.'s eyes met in silent question, and they heard Juarez running to the door, his steps shaking the little house.

A wry grin lit his eyes as he beheld them. "I saw you both on television!" he said. "On the news tonight. You're famous!"

That familiar guarded look came over E.Z.'s face, and he stepped back, adjusting his tinted glasses as if he'd been exposed as a criminal hiding from the law and could save himself by altering his appearance a half degree. "I...I had on shades. How did you—?"

"I wouldn't have recognized you," Juarez said, laughing aloud. "Except that I recognized her." He nodded to Jo, his eyes as big as silver dollars. "It all came together after that. You're E.Z. Ellis, aren't you?"

E.Z. sighed, then glanced from side to side, expecting fans to leap out of the woodwork. But no one was there except Juarez and his family. He nodded reluctantly. "Yeah. Guess I am."

Juarez clapped his rugged hands and laughed again, turned back to his daughter and ruffled her hair. "Come in, you two," he said. "Please."

They stepped into the old structure, saw that the children were at the dinner table, eating their own meal in their own kitchen. Jo had no doubt that even in the poverty they still endured they were better off in their own home. It gave each of them a new look of dignity that they hadn't had before. A look of belonging that was the birthright of every child.

But, as if she didn't share that birthright, Carmen was nowhere to be seen.

"We came to see Carmen," E.Z. said. "And to make sure you were all settled in."

"Carmen's asleep," Juarez said, but motioned for them to follow him to one of the two bedrooms in the back of the house. He led them down a dark hall, then into a room where five mattresses were lined up on the floor. Little Carmen lay on one, uncovered, sleeping restlessly with her thumb in her mouth in a room of pitch-black darkness. Jo turned on a lamp without a shade, and at the sight of the dirt and scratches on the walls, wondered if Carmen had been better off without light. She went to her side and stooped down, her heart breaking.

At least she's clean, Jo thought, trying, at least, to console herself with that. Her hair had been styled into a crude pair of ponytails. But her eyes were swollen, as if she'd cried herself to sleep, and she looked as thin and pale as a ghost trapped in a dimension she didn't understand.

"She'll be glad to see you," Juarez whispered. "She hasn't gotten over you yet."

His voice stirred Carmen to wakefulness. Her heart aching, Jo pushed Carmen's bangs back from her face. Carmen opened her eyes irritably, shoved the hand away...but then, as she beheld Jo with her distinct red locks and her olive eyes, she bolted up and threw her arms around her neck. "Jo!"

Jo gathered the tiny girl into her arms and stood up and turned to E.Z. with unquenchable misery in her eyes. Coming here was a mistake, she told him silently. It would be even harder to leave her this time.

"Has she been eating?" Jo asked Juarez, who watched the child sadly. It was as if he knew she would be hurt, but couldn't bear to deprive her of a moment's joy.

"Not very well," he said. "She sleeps a lot, though. She's withdrawn. She doesn't talk like a child her age should. And she doesn't play."

Jo closed her eyes and squeezed Carmen tightly against her. A prayer she didn't mean to utter rose up in her heart. A prayer that some joy would erase the anguish from Carmen's heart.

They followed Juarez back into the kitchen and sat at the table coaxing Carmen to eat. She ate heartily for Jo and

E.Z. and laughed at the games they played with her. And the way she kept touching their faces, memorizing their textures, shaping their jaws, made them despair even more profoundly.

Maybe he'll let us take her for a week, Jo thought as she played with Carmen and her cousins after the table had been cleared. *Maybe if I promise to bring her back in a few days . . .*

But Jo knew that each time she brought Carmen back, the abandonment would be more pronounced. Occasional visits would do the child no good. And it would break her own heart each time she did.

They stayed late into the night, until Carmen had fallen asleep from utter exhaustion, and continued to hold her after the other children had been sent to bed. And then Jo gathered all her courage together and prepared to say goodbye once and for all.

Tears began to stream down her face even before the moment came, and E.Z. sat beside her and held her as she held Carmen. Juarez watched them silently, not uttering a word to break the final moments between them. Finally, E.Z. whispered, "We've got to put her down, babe. It's time for us to go."

Juarez stood up, and Jo saw the tears in the man's eyes. He started to speak, swallowed back the words, then tried again. Jo and E.Z. watched him, waiting for something that might make the moment easier, some morsel of wisdom to ease the pain.

"I want you to take her," he said finally.

A deep fissure of uncertainty cut into Jo's forehead. E.Z. rose slowly to his feet. "What?"

"I want you to take her," Juarez repeated. His voice shattered into broken shards of sound, but he went on. "She's happier with you than with me. My sister didn't want her to grow up like this. She wanted her to be loved and cared for.''

E.Z.'s face was a study in poignancy. "But your children *are* loved and cared for," he said. "We don't question your ability to give her that."

Juarez gave a despondent shrug. "But she's so young. And she's lost so much. The only parent she ever knew, her home and—" he gestured toward both of them "—her friends. She needs you. I do what I can for her, but I have to leave her in the care of the older children while I work. They try, but they can't give her what she needs. She has no future here. But you . . . you can give her everything."

Jo felt a sob rising to her throat, and she looked at E.Z., confused hope in her eyes. In her heart she wanted to take Juarez's offer more than anything she'd ever wanted in her life, but reality intruded like a blaring siren. It couldn't work, and yet . . .

"You two talk it over," Juarez whispered. "I'll be in the kitchen."

Jo watched Juarez leave the room, his shoulders drooping with the weariness of a man who'd just made a dear sacrifice for someone he loved. She turned to E.Z., saw that he was as stunned as she, but a soft smile tugged at his lips. "You heard the man," he said.

Jo stood up, still holding Carmen, who's little head rolled against her shoulder in deep relaxation. "E.Z., I want to more than anything," she whispered. "But I'm scared. I'm single . . . and I don't know the first thing about being a mother. . . ."

E.Z. pulled Jo to him, pressed his forehead against hers, kissed her nose. "You know all you need to know," he said. He took Carmen from Jo's arms, cradling her in his own. His eyes misted over as he gazed down at the sleeping child, a bundle of innocence who deserved a second chance. When he looked at Jo again, there was a tentative smile in his eyes. "Besides. Carmen won't just be getting a mom. She'll be getting a dad, too."

Jo stared at him, desperately trying to separate what he meant from what she wanted him to mean. Her eyes were sparkling with hope, but her heart didn't dare let her feel it. "What are you saying, E.Z.?"

"I want you to marry me," he whispered. "We'll make a hell of a family...."

Jo breathed in a sob and threw her arms around him, waking the child in the process. Carmen opened her sleepy eyes and gave a grumpy look up at them. A moment of fear passed over her fragile face, but turned to a slight smile when she saw them.

It was right—Jo thought suddenly—so right for them to be a family. Destiny had a plan for them, and who were they to fight it? "I love you, E.Z.," she cried. "I can't promise never to make you angry, but I swear I'll make you happy."

E.Z.'s smile faded, and a profound look of sincerity colored his azure eyes. "You do make me happy," he said. "You make me whole."

She wiped the tears from her face and reached out for Carmen. The child put one arm around E.Z.'s neck and the other around Jo's.

"You ready to go home, Carmen?" he asked, his voice hoarse.

Carmen only gazed at them both.

"Where *is* home?" Jo asked quietly. "Yours isn't really a home, and neither is mine..."

E.Z. shook his head and set Carmen down. She stood looking up at them, as if she knew instinctively that she witnessed something that would change her life forever. E.Z. pulled Jo into his arms and held her as if he never intended to let her go again. "Don't you know yet that home isn't a building?" he whispered.

Jo framed his face with grateful hands and wondered when she had gotten so lucky.

Their lips met like the final verse of a song that lingered in the mind long after the last note was played. And before it was finished, Jo felt Carmen tugging on her skirt. Together, they looked down at the child who would become their own . . . the child who had taught them both to love.

Home followed them, that night, to the little all-night chapel where they were married by a star-struck minister. It followed them back to the jet that took them over to New Orleans. And it followed them to the house that was unfurnished and unlived-in.

And as the scattered fires of Jo Calloway merged into one single, invincible flame, Jo learned that justice was more than a concept . . . it was the happiness in a little child's smile. And home was more than a place . . . it was the absolute love in E.Z. Ellis's arms.

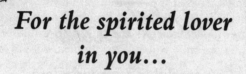

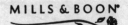

MILLS & BOON

Christmas Treats

A sparkling new anthology
—the perfect Christmas gift!

Celebrate the season with a taste of love in this
delightful collection of brand-new short stories
combining the pleasures of food and love.

Figgy Pudding
by PENNY JORDAN
All the Trimmings
by LINDSAY ARMSTRONG
A Man For All Seasonings
by DAY LECLAIRE

And, as an extra treat, we've included the
authors' own recipe ideas in this
collection—because no yuletide would be
complete without...Christmas Dinner!

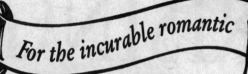

RISING
Tides

EMILIE RICHARDS

The reading of a woman's will threatens to destroy her family

As a hurricane gathers strength, the reading of Aurore Gerritsen's will threatens to expose dark secrets and destroy her family. Emilie Richards continues the saga of a troubled family with *Rising Tides*, the explosive sequel to the critically acclaimed *Iron Lace*.

1-55166-273-6
AVAILABLE NOW IN PAPERBACK

DEBBIE MACOMBER

THIS MATTER OF MARRIAGE

Hallie McCarthy gives herself a year to find Mr Right. Meanwhile, her handsome neighbour is busy trying to win his ex-wife back. As the two compare notes on their disastrous campaigns, each finds the perfect partner lives right next door!

"In the vein of When Harry Met Sally, Ms Macomber will delight."

—Romantic Times

JAYNE ANN KRENTZ

Joy

When a couple win a mysterious emerald bracelet in a poker game, their peaceful Caribbean holiday becomes a rollercoaster of adventure, desire...and deadly peril.

"Jayne Ann Krentz is one of the hottest writers in romance today."—USA Today

1-55166-062-8
AVAILABLE NOW IN PAPERBACK

MIRA